In the Lord's Library

P.J. Marsden

AmErica House
Baltimore

First printing

ISBN: 1-58851-570-2
PUBLISHED BY AMERICA HOUSE BOOK PUBLISHERS
www.publishamerica.com
Baltimore

Printed in the United States of America

Dedication

*To my ex-wife Brenda . . . for tolerating and loving me all those years.
And for Bill and Lynn Scotland, for believing in me . . . when others
wouldn't.*

Part One
"The Journey"

Chapter One

The creature coiled and struggled on the surface of the cool dirt, and if it had any eyes it would have seen that it was in grave danger. Regardless, it could certainly feel it, for nerves along the front of the segmented, red brick color of its body sensed the danger, tingling as they sent signals to the receptors of its tiny cerebrum, located near the tip of its body.

The signals pulsed a definite warning, indicating that it might be in some kind of trouble, and blind instincts told it that deep below the moist earth would be its only salvation. A child sat on a yellow lunch box in the dirt next to the earthworm, and although you would have guessed him a seven-year-old by height and body mass, he held the reasoning and thought capabilities of a three-year-old. They called him Brodie, and as he sat there in the sunshine wearing his gray cotton shorts, a baggy tee shirt and blocked, orthopedic shoes, a message was being sent to his brain as well. Brodie reacted with more fervor than the earthworm, and half closed his eyes in ecstasy as he relieved his bladder, feeling the wet warmth as it pooled around his bum and ran down the bottom of his bare legs, wetting the tops of his socks. Brodie giggled with delight, then poked a fat finger at the squirming earthworm, blocking off all avenues of retreat, now diminishing a hopeless situation to an outright dismal one. Brodie looked up from his cornered prey, twisting his head around to look for Miss Noble, who stood in the sand by the large metal swing set, alternately pushing his three classmates as they squealed gleefully with the pendulum motion of their simple ride. They were only thirty feet away as he sat near the edge of the thick coniferous forest, so Brodie had to be careful.

He liked Miss Noble, especially when she wore shorts to school, like she did today. Whenever Brodie felt lost and hurt, which happened a lot these days, he could run to Miss Noble and hug her warm, reassuring legs while she hushed and calmed him. The three girls who comprised the rest of his small class he could have done without. They were loud, bossy, and they always had something to say about anything he did, whether it was finger painting, counting beads, drawing on the chalkboard or eating worms.

5

Although easily mistaken for some kind of isolating, behavioral pattern that coincided with his mentally challenged mind, Brodie put some space between himself and the girls during recess so he could simply get a reprieve from their constant pestering. The girls weren't being mean though, they were just being girls, and when you outnumber the boys in your class three to one, or four to one if you counted Miss Noble, then it would be a natural course to consider the school term open season for teasing boys.

Brodie checked out the swing set one more time. None of the girls were paying him any heed and Miss Noble momentarily had her back to him, watching the girls as they pumped their legs back and forth to keep up their increasing momentum. The earthworm squirmed and wiggled valiantly as Brodie picked it up and pushed it into his mouth, swallowing the creature whole. It felt cold as it went down, and he quickly looked once again at the girls on the swing set, but they still weren't looking, and neither was Miss Noble.

The child had a habit of eating things he shouldn't, a problem compounded by his uncaring father and his constantly struggling mother. Brodie had become well known to the medical staff at the Island's small hospital, and on no fewer than six occasions they had treated him for ingesting things his small body could have done without. Miss Noble glanced over at him, giving him one of her huge smiles that told him everything would be okay, at least for a while. Until he went home.

Judith Noble kept an eye on the child as he sat on his yellow lunch box, which he took everywhere he went, but she didn't know he'd just eaten an earthworm. There existed nothing hazardous to put in his mouth within the bounds of the schoolyard, and certainly the forest harbored no dangers, unless the child scurried off into its cool dark shadows. Fortunately, or unfortunately, depending on who you were and how you looked at it, Brodie Bandie wouldn't be going anywhere fast wearing those ungainly, orthopedic shoes. The boy may as well have had large blocks of wood strapped to his feet, but it made him easier to supervise, even if the sight of him always tweaked you somewhere deep within. Judith watched as the child got off his lunch box, and then started routing through the soil on his hands and knees, pushing the moist dirt to one side with his fingers.

The wet urine stain on his backside became obvious against the light gray color of his shorts, and the spreading mark suggested he'd piddled a fair amount. Oh great, Judith sighed, now she'd have to change him, using the clean clothes from the small knapsack that accompanied him every day to school. It wouldn't be the best way to end what had so far been a perfectly fine Friday afternoon, but it had to be done, so she chased the sigh away, and replaced it with a smile of quiet concession. While not in her job description, Judith had agreed to change the lad whenever he had these occasional accidents, rather than disrupt the school day and send him home to be castigated by his shiftless father. It didn't happen very often, although a few months back he'd really soiled himself, and Judith figured Brodie had held his breath and grunted everything into that stewing mess. Some of the other teachers criticized Judith for cleaning the child up, saying it set a dangerous precedence for the next contract negotiations, fearing the wiping of children's backsides would eventually be on the bargaining table. They were wasting their breath whenever they brought the issue up and they knew it, for Judith had a steadfast reputation for her strong independence and unshakable will to do things her own way. However, she could also be a godsend, for teachers with her skills and training in educating the mentally disabled were hard to find, and her willingness to take on the "special" class had alleviated a lot of burdens. So if Judith changed the odd set of soiled clothing, and the teachers union didn't seem to want to make a stink about it, then the hell with it. The world would undoubtedly proceed to rotate on its axis, the sun would probably continue to rise every morning, and Judith Noble would persist in changing their clothing, regardless of what anyone thought or said about it.

As she leaned against the cool metal tube of the swing set, Judith watched as Brodie mooched around in the soil. He'd sat down on his backside so now he had a layer of dirt stuck to his wet shorts, which made laundering them all the more worthwhile. The child appeared to be having fun, and Judith knew there was little of that in the boy's life, so she let him be. Brodie's head suddenly came up, momentarily dropping his excavating project while he turned to look at Judith. She quickly looked the other way, watching the girls on the swings for a moment, before glancing back to the young boy as he returned his attention to the soil. It had become a bit of a game the pair played, although Judith at all times stuck steadfastly to the rules of school yard supervision, and the boy never knew that his teacher noticed his every move. Except for the earthworm.

She had failed to see him eat the earthworm, and she couldn't have stopped him in time if she had and it was doubtful that the creature would do him harm anyway. Brodie probably got more vitamins from the squirmy annelid than from any meal he would have received at home.

Judith watched the little boy as he plucked another worm from the dirt, holding it close to his face for an examination. Yes, this would do, nice and plump and full of squirming energy, not too much dirt stuck to its body. Brodie opened his treasured lunch box with one hand, and then dropped his prisoner inside, quickly closing the lid and removing all hope of a speedy escape. The child's motor skills were exceptional despite his challenged brain, and at times he could be a mindful surprise. Judith already knew the worm would be a gift for her, for Brodie was continually dragging species from every corner of the animal world into the classroom. Just for her, dead or alive, beautiful or repulsive, winking or screeching. Brodie would track them down and capture them, so he could proudly present them to the teacher he so loved.

Judith didn't mind though, for it brought great delight to the child's face, and just seeing his smile made the whole effort a worthy cause. She had a desk drawer full of dried out, chitinous exoskeletons, birds' beaks and a varied collection of insect appendages that would have made an entomologist envious. They didn't stink too much and of course she didn't have the heart to throw them out. Judith looked down at her watch, and then clapped her hands together; a signal to the children that recess had ended. Brodie stood up from his digging site clutching his lunch box, then started running across the gravel toward Judith and the girls. She called out to him in warning, but it didn't reach him in time. The child couldn't run, not with those bricks tied to his feet, and had only enough time to build up some speed before he tripped and fell, skidding into the gravel. One of his cheeks rubbed viciously into the coarse pebbles, and his lunch box popped open, spilling the captive worm onto the ground. Judith walked over to him as he started crying, and it was a piteous wail that had become all too familiar to her ears. Gently, she picked the child up and stood him back on his feet, holding him as he cried, the tears rolling freely down the cheeks of his pink face. Brodie had an angelic, child's face, but it was one that had been cruelly distorted with downs syndrome. His eyes were spaced wide apart, with skin folds on his upper eyelids, and his skull had been molded at birth to grow broad and short and would attract attention wherever he went. Judith thought about the twins, she always did whenever she comforted Brodie, and she thanked God she had them, and that they had been born with no abnormalities.

She continued to hold Brodie until he quieted down, and as she knelt beside him, the three girls had gotten off the swings and had gathered around to help console their classmate. It was the only time they cut him any slack, when he got upset or hurt himself. The youngster soon cried himself out, and Judith wiped the dirt from his face, examining him with her soft, caring eyes. He looked at her and smiled, and Judith gave it back to him in return, then all four of the children stood around, looking at each other reassuringly, smiling broadly, like they'd achieved some sort of a small victory. At times Judith would swear that the four of them, although all mentally challenged and from unrelated families, could talk to each other with just their eyes and their silent thoughts. She had seen it before as she watched from a distance, when they worked alone on some special project in the classroom. They seemed to know what the other was thinking, because they would accomplish their assigned task with very few words ever being spoken. Kneeling down as best he could in the restrictive shoes, Brodie picked up his lunch box and the worm that had been working its way to freedom. He held his hand open, triumphantly offering Judith the wiggling gift, a proud smile reaching across his face.

"For you, Miss No-bull," he beamed.

The hand that held the gift was broad with short stubby fingers, and when Brodie spoke, the words fell with uncertainty from his thick tongue.

Judith accepted the gift, thanking him while he placed it into her open hand.

Good she thought, everything would be all right now, another crisis successfully dealt with. A small, caring hug could go along way with these children, something Judith had learned a long time ago, but hadn't been taught in any practical courses as far as she knew.

The four children all held hands as Judith led her charges back through the double doors of the small school, and down the hallway to her classroom. She had her class take recess at different times than the other kids, at least until they got older, and could better understand the world around them. Children at times could be relentless with their teasing, and some of the kids in the school were brutal with their mean comments while in the open yard. The principal, an ignorant, old-fashioned relic who should have retired decades ago, and preferred to be called *Mister* Quigley, thought differently though. He'd called Judith into his office one day after school; having decided to tell the young schoolmistress just what was what, and just exactly where the bear would be pooping in the buckwheat. Within scant seconds he had Judith so pissed that she leaned over his desk, her knuckles white with anger, and the whole faculty had heard about the dressing down she had given him.

9

The old bastard hadn't been that scared since the elderly and somewhat loopy Miss Calkins had invited him over for dinner one evening. It had been a fairly acceptable night out, involving a pork roast with a honey-mustard sauce. Then after the meal old Miss Calkins had stood up from the table and disrobed right in front of him, boldly announcing, "she was to be the dessert." Rumor had it that Mister Quigley had broken the ten-minute mile the night he'd raced home from Miss Calkin's house. One would have thought that he'd realized from that episode that the female creature could be a dangerous folly indeed, especially when cornered. Mister Quigley strayed once again into unchartered territory the afternoon he took Judith on, for when it came to the kids, and what would be best for them; she gave no ground nor took any prisoners.Twice bitten, Mister Quigley retreated to a corner to lick his wounds, fully appreciating that Miss Noble's bark was probably as bad a her bite. There were only three elementary schools on the island, and Judith had become the only teacher with the special training required to educate the four mentally challenged pupils, so it would be her way, or no way at all. Old Mister Quigley had sucked back so fast his face nearly imploded as he readily agreed with the feisty, blond haired teacher's conditions. This also included cleaning up any unfortunate accidents the children might have while in her immediate care, as opposed to sending them home in disgrace.

Judith had also included the principal as part of her assertive deal, and although Quigley taught one of the five classes that made up the small school, she would call upon him to keep an eye on her pupils whenever she took one of them to the washroom, like today. After the three girls had been seated at their desks, Judith took Brodie's knapsack from the cloakroom and led him into the hallway, knocking on the door across from her own. The door opened and Quigley stuck his rooster like neck out, craning it as he looked around the hallway. He wore an old three-piece suit with a loud, colorful bow tie, and the half-moon glasses he peered over completed the outdated ensemble. He wasn't only just obsolete Judith thought. He was all together on the wrong planet.

"Yes, Miss Noble," he quietly asked. He had a shrill, neurotic voice, and it made you wonder if something bad hadn't happened to him during his own childhood. For an educator of young people, Quigley had become relatively intolerant of their energetic ways, and some of the ideas he presented at the faculty meetings were more suggestive of a salt mine, than an elementary school.

"I have to change Brodie, Mister Quigley, would you please keep an eye on my class?" Judith asked.

Quigley craned his neck further out, peering around the edge of his door, and when his eyes fell upon young Brodie, he did nothing to hide the disdainful look on his wrinkled old face.

"Now Miss Nobel, you know I don't approve . . ."

"Button it Quigley," Judith murmured, "I don't have time for your crap this afternoon. Will you watch my class or not?" Quigley got all flustered with the curt dressing down, his eyes darting up and down the hallway, hoping for an alliance with one of the other teachers, but the corridor remained empty. He never did like Judith, and he was wont to label her behavior as cowardly bullying, holding her in absolute scorn for her loose scruples and quick, peppery tongue. Unfortunately, the world had changed greatly since Quigley had been a young man, but he still disapproved of a lot of the things that happened around him, such as Judith Noble being an unwed, single mother of eight-year-old twin girls. All he could do though was cluck his tongue in quiet condemnation, and shake his head slowly whenever the spunky teacher had a run at him. Heathens he thought, the whole world was turning into fornicating, godless heathens.

"Well?" Judith invited, "Will you?"

"Oh . . . I see . . . why, uh, certainly Miss Noble, I will uh, look after your class."

Judith nodded him a thank-you, then led Brodie down the hallway to the staff washroom. She couldn't use the student's washroom, as it would be devastating for Brodie if another pupil walked in while she was cleaning him up. Even though using the staff washroom for these clean up jobs had become another contentious point with Quigley, he knew better than to chirp his displeasure, so he kept his beak closed regarding that particular issue.

Judith entered the small washroom then locked the door, filling the sink with warm water after adding some liquid soap from the wall dispenser. She placed the nylon knapsack on the counter, and then unzipped the top, taking out a face cloth, a bath towel, and a clean pair of underwear, socks and a pair of clean pants. She laid the clean clothes out on the counter next to the sink as the child watched. Brodie knew the routine, but still wondered why his teacher never got mad at him whenever he had these small accidents. Of all the adults within the bounds of his disconcerted world, Miss Noble had the most patience, and gave him the most smiles.

"Sorry, Miss No-bull," he quietly said.

11

Judith stopped what she was doing, and looked down at the child, smiling.

"Its okay Brodie, these things happen. We all peed our pants when we were very young, and weren't very sure of ourselves. Some of us will even pee our pants when we get really old and gray."

"Will I ever stop peeing n' pants, Miss No-bull?"

"Yes, Brodie, you will. I promise you that."

"Will I be smart like you, Miss No-bull?"

"You're already a smart little boy, Brodie."

Twice as smart as your goddamned father, Judith thought.

She knelt down and undid the child's shorts, sliding them and the wet underwear onto the tiled floor. Then she undid the buckles on his boxy, cumbersome orthopedic shoes, and then pulled his feet free from their little prisons. Judith pulled his socks from around his ankles, peeling them off one at a time while Brodie steadied himself with a hand on her shoulder. She gathered up all the wet clothing, and then stuffed it all into a white garbage bag that she'd found tucked into one of the side pockets of the knapsack.

Gently, she picked Brodie up under the arms, and then turned to sit him down on the counter top. As she placed him next to the sink, she noticed in the large mirror the angry red welts that criss-crossed the fleshy skin of the child's buttocks. Judith stood him on the counter, and then quietly turned him around, to examine the wicked marks. Brodie had been beaten, or whipped with a belt or something just as innocuous, until it was turned against a child.

"Who did this to you Brodie?" She calmly asked.

"Daddy," he said. The child had twisted his head around so he could inspect the damage himself. Judith felt the bile rising in her throat at the child's sudden and violent disclosure. The son-of-a-bitch that Brodie had for a father was the very dirt beneath her feet she thought.

She said nothing else about the assault, taking the warm, wet face cloth and lightly washing Brodie from the waist down, carefully rinsing all the urine from his skin. Judith then patted him dry with the clean bath towel, and then quietly dressed him with the fresh clothes. Good as new she thought, zipping up the knapsack then took the boy by the hand and walked him back down to the classroom. She found Mister Quigley scooting back and forth in the hallway between the classrooms like a cornered ferret, and she quickly collared him, glibly announcing she had a phone call to make. Judith knew better than to apprise the skittish principal of the latest developments. If it didn't happen at the school then it's none of our business, had been one of his favorite, archaic sayings at the staff meetings.

The office stood only two doors down from her classroom, and Judith had already gotten there before Quigley could spout any protestations. She walked into Quigley's simple office, shut the door, and then dialed the number of the Regional Police office, gladdened when she heard Cheryl Montague's voice at the other end. Officer Montague wouldn't waffle on a sensitive issue like child abuse, and she had a reputation for not troubling easily with any of the local turds. Especially when it came to dealing with the miscreant, hairy assed apes who were endemic to the sleazy bar at the southern end of the island. Brodie's father was one such loser who infested the tavern at Skinny's Reach, and Judith's temper now flared every time she thought about that cowardly, drunken twerp. The police officer wasn't a big woman by any means, but once you got a snoot full of pepper spray, or felt the crack of her extended, metal baton against your femur, it was suddenly "yes ma'am . . . no ma'am . . . three bags full ma'am."

Judith told Cheryl just what she had seen, and how she had come about seeing it. Office Montague advised that she would be attending the school within a half hour with a social worker, and would have to secure a written statement to start the investigation. Judith advised that would be fine with her, and told the police officer which classroom she could be found, and if she ran into a grumpy old fossil in a three-piece suit wearing a bow tie to just ignore him. Judith said goodbye, returned the phone to its cradle then let out a long sigh, the kind that comes from deep within, although it wasn't for her, it was for Brodie. She stood for a moment, mulling over the misery of the last half hour, and thought if she could wave a magic wand and make Brodie's father disappear, she would quite cheerfully have done so.

Within two hours though, Judith herself would be a victim of Martin Bandie and his criminal, besotted ways, and had she known this, she might not have chased the thought entirely from her mind.

* * *

Chapter Two

It was one of the biggest Islands within the clear waters of the southern gulf, in an area known as the Pacific Northwest. Some called the place a bit of heaven on earth, an as of yet to be urbanized, uncut, and unpolished rough diamond, one that conveniently bordered on the bustling mainstream of humanity. Others claimed it had the most fertile soil in the country, and combined with the sunshine and moderate amount of annual rainfall, produced the best marijuana crop this side of the Mexican border. Many others, like Judith Noble and her small family, just called the place home. The island was approximately sixteen miles long, and seven miles across at the widest point, which lay in its southern portion. The north part of the island, through millions of years of shaping and forming, eventually brought both the western and the eastern shores together at the tip of a long spit. Deep forests of fir trees and meadows of tall grasses drew nourishment from the rich soil, inhabiting nearly three quarters of the free land that formed the valleys and the hills to the north, as well as the stubby mountain range to the south east, where a lone peak vaulted high above the surging waters of the narrows. Arbutus trees, with their rust-colored limbs and peeling bark, could be spotted growing amongst the fir, dappled as well with hearty stands of deciduous trees, coming into their own when the chill of autumn would suck the sugars from their leaves, leaving them the burnt, crisp colors of the fall.

The farming of small livestock would be one of the principal industries on the island, but if you looked hard enough, you could find some people who'd tell you that just "living" was in fact the main industry. Life on the island offered a style that few people were even aware of, far from the street gangs, drug pushers, home invasions, pimps and prostitutes that occupied the nightly news casts of the urban realities. Most of the Island's population was farmers, with the artisans a close second or third. These artist folk would carve, pot, paint, and weave a living from their houses and shops that dotted the country lanes and the store front shops of the islands two main towns. The tourists flocked to the island to espouse the quiet life style and behold the artisan's wares. They came with their traveler's cheques, their plastic money and their truckloads of disposable cash. Many would purchase a great deal of the funky artifacts, which they'd drag home to their condominiums perched high above the sleepless streets of the metropolitan centers.

Once the artisans had drawn the visiting tourists from their urban nests, they all needed places to sleep, and restaurants to eat in, and well as clean beaches to loaf on with their howling offspring. For the large part seasonal, a lot of the younger people nonetheless worked in the tourist industry, which could easily lay claim to be the islands second, or third largest employer.

If you had a stomach for it, and a temperament that wasn't easily bent, then you'd have no problems working for one of the many country motels, bed and breakfasts, or restaurants and pubs that could be found in virtually every corner of the island. In any one of these establishments you could be served hand and foot by an overworked staff, toiling hard to appease the "yups" who flocked to the island every summer. The population would swell during the summer months from five thousand reasonable souls to about seven thousand, the latter part comprising of the yups, who would encroach upon the land like it was some form of baptismal rite. Easily spotted driving their sport utility vehicles at twice the legal speed limit, they would toss their empty beer cans out the window, looking cavalier in their designer sun glasses and hand stitched dock shoes. They either came by vehicle ferry, or piloted their own vessels into the two large marinas that had been dredged into the bays that fronted the two main towns. As far as the locals were concerned, there were only two types of people who inhabited the face of mother earth, those who lived on the island, and those who didn't. It was the inhabitants themselves who hung the term "yups"on the non-residents, because of their droll attempts to mimic the indigenous, laid back vernacular. Whenever you asked them if they had come from the mainland, they would provide you with a thoughtful pause then reply with an all too casual . . . "yup."

The service industry, such as schools, medical clinics, hospitals, police and fire protection made up the smallest, but probably the most important part of the Islands diverse population. A tiny portion of the inhabitants were fishermen, who were a starving species given the dismal state of the salmon stocks. Others turned their hands to oyster farming and there was still a handful of loggers, their chain saws for the most part rusting, another unpopular and rapidly fading occupation. There also inhabited among the islands populace a sprinkling of retirees, or blue hairs, as they are called. The lack of a full time hospital, along with a lack of the finely tuned equipment that at times kept people alive (if in body only) was enough to encourage the elderly to spend their golden years elsewhere. The rest of the residents mainly consisted of the highly secretive, conniving little band of marijuana growers, their names conspicuous by their absence from any official polling list. If you weren't registered to vote for the Socialist pigs that ran the country, then you obviously didn't exist, and if you had become a non-entity then you certainly couldn't break any of their repressive laws. This enigmatic crowd even had the balls to form a local co-operative, much to the chagrin of the Regional Police Office. If one took into account the amount of high grade dope that was produced on the island, then brazenly exported to all points of the globe, then the annual marijuana harvest turnover would put the farmers with their grade 'A' lamb chops to absolute shame, to say nothing of the artists. Even though some water-front acres with their monolithic homes were rumored to be owned by some Hollywood actors, the pot farmers were without doubt the richest people on the island, both in spirit, and in monetary assets.

All that aside though, one of the biggest attractions of the island had nothing to do with small animals, off the wall artwork, or the high grade smoke the surreptitious co-operative exported by navigable channel after the cops had gone to bed. Peace and quiet, as well as all the privacy you could endure was there for the asking by any one of the island's inhabitants. The choice was yours, especially if you lived away from the main road that led you to the two towns and their "busy" streets. Judith, as well as one other person, had come here for that very reason, to lose themselves among the quiet hills, still forests, and expansive beaches that this large island could give them. Judith had arrived over ten years ago, far from the prying eyes, and inquisitive lips that formed unwanted questions. She had come here because of the job offer, and to give birth to her twins. Most important though, Judith had come here to grieve, to be alone with her misery while she struggled through morning sickness, and then the lonely, tearing pain of multiple childbirth. After their births, she had quickly come to recognize the twins as a blessing, and loved them more than anything she could ever love again. Giving love was one thing, but the recipe couldn't be complete without receiving love in return, a gaping void the twins had managed to fill with their eager innocence. They both had bright red hair like their father, and both were genetically identical, like two shiny brass buttons on a uniform. Yet both had become as different in personality as a thimble and a wine glass.

17

Jenny had become the demure, studious type, who enjoyed reading and taking in as much knowledge as her waking hours would allow. Jody, although intelligent, turned her fancies more to play, rather than things that required a lot of thinking, at least when she wasn't sitting in Mister Quigley's classroom. Jenny sat in the front seat of the mini van, as this week was her turn, and Jody sat in the back, strapped into the middle of the bench seat so she could see both Jenny and her mother, who of course was driving. They both wore glasses, which they hated as it enhanced their replication all the more, but they both offset their physical similarities by dressing differently. Jenny wore a blue denim dress with embroidered white ankle socks, while Jody chose a sleeveless red checker patterned shirt, and a pair of blue jeans with the legs rolled and cuffed up over her cowboy boots. Jody would be astride one of the two ponies moments after they got home, and having to change clothes to go riding meant less time in the saddle. Judith reflected on all these things as she drove the mini van home from school, taking the high road as the twins chatted excitedly about the approaching weekend. Officer Cheryl Montague had shown up at the school as planned with one of the local social workers. They'd both verbally interviewed Brodie, and then had a quick look at his backside in the staff washroom so Cheryl could establish reasonable grounds for an arrest, and the social worker could seize the child and remove him to a safe house. The social worker had left moments later, taking Brodie with her to visit the medical clinic, while Cheryl took a witness statement from Judith in the principal's office, leaving that brooding old goat Quigley to watch over her class.

By the time Judith had read her statement and signed it, the afternoon bell had sounded, ending the school day and announcing the start of the weekend. When she left Quigley's office, the twins were sitting on a bench in the hallway, anxious to start their Friday evening.

Together they filed out the main door of the school, past the flagpole and down to the staff parking lot. As the three climbed into their blue mini van, they were discussing what videos they would rent for the weekend, a little something for everyone's viewing pleasure, including Uncle Walt. But only after all the homework had been done. Their plan would consist of the usual Friday afternoon routine, with a stop at the Country Junction market to get their movies, and any other supplies that would sustain them in comfort over a forecasted rainy weekend. Already, distended clouds the color of prune dust pushed eastwards over the lone mountain peak to the south, chasing away the blue skies and the sunshine. It would be a good weekend to light the fire and read a good book or drink coffee with Uncle Walt. Jenny and Jody would ride the ponies regardless of the rain, they always did, and when they'd had enough, they would quarter the animals then come in for hot soup and watch their movies. The road that Judith drove along was the main, paved road that formed the backbone of the island, connecting both towns and all the side roads together in a functional grid system. At the north end of the island lay the town of Balford, which had a gas station, marina, store and a pub that catered exclusively to the yups, who'd tie up their gleaming vessels in the privately owned harbor. Balford was viewed by the locals as nothing more than a "hitching post" for the visiting, floating gin palaces, whose crews would gather in the trendy water front pub and hoist a few. Or a few dozen, if they were so inclined. The place offered employment to a lot of the younger folk, especially during the summer months, so the community viewed the town as more of a contributor, than a loud, flashy annoyance.

In the South lay the main commercial center of the community, Skinny's Reach, which also had a large harbor, although most of the vessels there belonged to the locals, with limited transient moorage available. Almost two thousand souls lived within the municipal boundaries of the Reach, where most of the shops, bakeries, art stores and suppliers could be found. Pubs and cottage type motels lined the roadway that followed the waterfront as it curved long and wide near the top of the elongated bay. Judith would make a monthly pilgrimage into the Reach to get her main supplies and groceries, but for the most part, she shopped at the Country Junction, where the staff was friendly and unobtrusive. The store wasn't far from home, and it carried virtually everything the family needed from fresh bread to oats and feed for the ponies. The twins however, liked the store for all together different reasons, and his name was Ben, the ex-policeman.

Ben had a gentle demeanor about him, which the twins liked, and when he addressed young people, he didn't speak down to them like they were some kind of a family pet. He wasn't very tall, although he towered above the twins, but he was built husky and strong, like a pallet of bricks, with no fat hanging anywhere from his solid frame. Ben had a smile that could even soften the hearts of the two man hating lesbians that lived up the road from Judith's place, and when he spoke his voice came across as both soft and deep. His curly blond hair receded around his tanned temples, and touched his shirt collar at the back of his neck, and although many wouldn't have called him handsome, he certainly wasn't ugly. When he talked to you, his eyes, and the color of light blue ink, danced and twinkled, openly displaying an honest sincerity not often seen in human beings. From where the twins stood though, the best part about Ben would be the way his eyes would light up whenever their mother entered the store. He'd asked her out a couple of times, and even though they were both in their early thirties and single, Judith kept turning him down with an apologetic smile and a simple no.

All anybody knew about Ben Trilby was that he had belonged to a large city police department, where he'd been shot one night while on duty. They'd given him a cane to walk around with as well as a discharge and a monthly medical pension, and then he'd moved to the island about a year ago after buying the Country Junction store. Nobody could really be sure, but Ben seemed to be running away from *something*, or maybe even just running to *something*, but just like Judith, there were some things he was certainly trying to forget. If there were something in your past that you wanted to leave behind you, then the island would be the perfect place to flee to, and start all over. The Country Junction store stood at the intersection of the main high road, and the islands secondary road, tucked well back into a forest of alders. A long building, it had been covered with unstained cedar planks and all the wooden trim on the windows and doors were painted a bright green. The structure also had an adjoining feed shop and a green house, which stood away from the cool shade cast by the canopy of leaves from the alder trees. Ben lived alone in a matching cedar sided cottage directly behind the store, but he spent most of his time running the business, which employed a handful of young people on a full or part time basis. A large gravel parking lot lay in front of the worn, wooden steps that led into the main store, and Ben had been by the potato chip stand, looking out the window when Judith's blue mini van pulled into the lot.

An ex-veteran police officer and man-about-the-big-city, Ben puzzled over why he would feel a surging jolt every time he saw Judith's soft face.

Turning, Ben leaned against his aluminum cane and limped ungracefully over to the cash register that stood beside the main counter. On station behind the till would be his best chance to talk to Judith, for all the grocery purchases went through that one till, and she always bought something on Friday afternoons, even if it was only a box of low fat, microwave popcorn. He wished he could have dressed a little better, especially on Fridays, but the denim farmer's overalls and dark shirt best suited his dressing needs with his damaged hip. In the mornings after a shower, he would step right into a clean pair, then pull them gently over the throbbing joint, buckling them up over his shoulders. Judith entered the store through the main doors with her twin girls, and he was in for a bit of a treat because she wore dark-blue cotton shorts and a white summer top, which did nothing to hide the lines of her femininity and exquisite tush. Ben really liked Judith, and not in a horny ram cat kind of way. He *truly* liked her.

She always smiled, despite all the grief he had heard she'd suffered, and her face was clean and free of any make-up, and the way she wore her blond hair, cut short and straight gave her face a mischievous look. Ben himself still hurt, physically, where the bullet had smashed his pelvis, and emotionally, where someone had plucked his love-stricken heart and flushed it down the toilet along with his police career. But the time had come to move on, to put the pain behind him, to climb back up on the horse and learn to ride again. Not only was Judith single, intelligent, and nice looking, but also she had a sense of humor and stood for absolutely no crap, positively admirable attributes from Ben's point of view. Another reason, albeit a big reason that he liked her was because she didn't conduct herself like some of the other island women, who smoked pot and walked around with hairy legs and only bathed every other full moon, or on Labor Day, whichever came first.

Ben smiled and nodded at Judith and the girls as they entered the store then walked across the wooden planked floor. He was genuinely happy to see them, and appreciative that no one else was in the store.
"Hello girls, and how are we doing today?" Ben asked.
"Ducky Ben, just ducky, and you?" Judith replied. The twins smiled at him, then giggled and peeled of toward the video shelves.
"I'm fine thanks, Judith. Rough day?"
"Oh, just a little bit, Ben . . . but life goes on."
"That's what they keep telling me. Would you like to talk about it, Judith?"
"Thanks, I appreciate the offer, but I can't. It's one of those confidential things."
Judith walked over to the counter, and leaned against the glass top, looking directly at Ben.
"Uncle Walt needs some more snuff though, if you happen to know his brand."
Ben turned and limped over to the tobacco shelf, taking a small, round cardboard box of menthol snuff from a stack below the cigarettes. He

placed it on the counter, watching Judith as she looked for her wallet, routing through the nylon fanny pack she had strapped to her front.

Perfect, Ben thought, no one else in the store with big ears, just you and her, alone at the counter.

Being an ex cop, Ben didn't fart around too much, especially when it came to asking ladies out, so he promptly threw all the small talk to the wind and got down to the important stuff.

"I have a couple of tickets for a concert at the playhouse in Balford two Saturday's coming, would you be interested in going?" Ben tried to make the proposal as innocent as possible, knowing Judith shied away from going out with men, and he supposed he really couldn't blame her from what he'd heard. But still, he had to try.

She looked him in the eyes when she replied, a regretful look, except this time Judith hesitated before she answered him, almost as if she had considered the answer first.

"Thank-you anyway Ben, but no, I really can't. Who knows . . . maybe someday?"

"That's okay. I'll only just ask you again next Friday. You don't mind if I keep asking do you?"

"No Ben, I don't, and I'm sorry I have to keep saying no. But like I said, maybe one day."

"Sure Judith, I understand. I'll be right here."

She turned and walked over to the video shelves to ensure the twins didn't slip anything racy into their choices. Judith liked Ben, she saw him as a warm and kindly man, who wasn't all that bad to look at either, and the fact that he limped around on a cane mattered to her not one bit. He had been a police officer though, and Judith knew all about public safety workers and some of the grief their work brought them. There would be no more public safety workers in her life, she had promised herself that a long time ago. It just wasn't worth it. She would have supposed by now that she might have been ready, but even after all these years the painful feelings still clouded her wants, and she still found herself saying no to the man's offer of a night out. Even though a part of her wanted to say yes.

As she approached the twins, they eagerly displayed the colorful jackets of the four movies they had picked out, and Judith read the narratives on the backs. Her main concern would be the violence they might contain, not so much the swear words or revealing love scene that seemed to appear in most movie these days. It was the violence that Judith wished to censor from the twins, as well as from herself. Judith hated the graphic brutality that was usually depicted within the fictional confines of modern movies. People didn't need to see that kind of crap, even if it did only involve some blasé acting with fake blood and copious amounts of pig's guts. But the girl's choices were fine, and they had even picked out an old black and white John Wayne western for Uncle Walt. He'd probably seen it years ago when it first came out in the theaters, but he'd watch it again nevertheless, and hoot and holler when the good guys finally won. After returning the cardboard jackets to the shelves, Judith followed the twins up to the main counter, where Ben and his patient smile awaited them.

They paid for the movies and the snuff, then wished Ben a good weekend and walked out of the store. He waited until they had reached the bottom of the wooden steps before hobbling out from behind the counter and back over to the potato chip stand, to gaze out once again through the window. Ben watched as they climbed into the mini van, and just before they backed out of the parking lot, Judith looked up to the window and waved to him. He gave her a gentle wave back, not the least bit concerned that she had caught him looking at her. Human beings did that sort of thing after all - looked at each other, and given the way Ben felt about Judith, there was nothing rude about his open admiration for her and her small family. Ben kept watching as the van pulled onto the main road, and then turned east onto the island's secondary gravel road that led down to the rocky cliffs that lined the eastern shores. Eventually the van disappeared from view, and Ben let out a long sigh as the dust from the gravel floated up to powder the alder trees. One day he thought, and with a modicum of luck, you're going to say yes Judith, then I can finally move on and start living again, the way a young man was meant to.

*   *   *

Chapter Three

"You rotten bastards," Judith exclaimed loudly. She stood at the aluminum mailbox near the entrance of her long driveway, holding a formal looking piece of paper in her hand, seething at its contents. "Mom, you're not supposed to swear," Jenny called from the front seat of the van. "Sorry honey," Judith replied. She returned her attention to the letter, getting even angrier as she read it through a second time. It had come from the regional district, warning her that if the long weeds that fronted her property on her side of the drainage ditch weren't cut down by Monday night, they would do the chore for her, then send her the bill. The weeds were unsightly the letter said, making an eye-sore as the tourists drove the secondary road to the chalets and bed and breakfasts that had been established along the southeast shore of the island. Obviously a neighbor had complained, Judith thought, but she was damned if she would pay those union turds forty bucks an hour to fell some weeds. She looked to the west, noting the rain clouds and their steady progress as they marched across the late spring sky. They looked fairly ugly, and the forecasted rainfall would be steady for the entire weekend. She then sized up the weeds that fronted the open land of her property line, just this side of the white railing fence. An onerous job to be sure, Judith calculated a couple of hours using the weed whacker would quell the griping hordes, and she might just as well start now, before the rain began falling.

Uncle Walt could be seen in the distance, cutting the lawn up near the house using the tractor.

At least, she could see the tatty red baseball hat that she figured he'd been born with, moving slowly back and forth across the grassy horizon. Judith could hear the tractor's engine from where she stood, and she was glad that chore had been tackled. She climbed back into the van and started motoring slowly up the gravel driveway, trying to keep the dust to a minimum. She already knew that Uncle Walt would insist on cutting the weeds, but he did enough around the place as it was. Just his steady presence was comforting enough for Judith and her family, never mind the work he did, and the fact that they had come to dearly love the old man. Walt Brem had come with the place, quite literally, when Judith had purchased the property over a decade ago. It had become part of the official transaction, and had even been written in the offer to purchase. Walt and his wife Grace had owned the huge log house and the matching log stables that stood on a looped road at the end of the driveway. Judith had purchased the acreage with cash, and the deal allowed for the Brems to rent the two-bedroom suite above the stables.

Grace had terminal cancer and wanted to spend her last days on the property where she had spent so much of her life. A nurse had come out to see her daily, to care for her, administering the painkillers and scarcely two months after Judith had moved in, she passed away in the middle of the night. It had broken Walt's heart when his wife died, she had been all he had left in the world, and he ended up hanging around the place like a stray pet, then Judith started feeding him and the rest just sort of fell into place. Judith quickly bonded with the lonely old man, endeared to his caustic tongue and warm heart. He really came into his own when the twins were born, washing up, getting groceries and helping her around the house when there weren't enough hours in the day. Judith knew that some of the more uncharitable neighbors talked about them, like they had become some sort of a perverted couple, but she couldn't have cared less. Uncle Walt continued to live above the stables, and although he paid Judith rent, he insisted on doing a lot of the yard work. She had soon learned not to argue with him, particularly when you considered the size of the property and her full time job as a schoolteacher.

On one side of the driveway stood a forest of stout fir trees, and the other side was all grassed, a quarter of a mile as it spanned from the main road up to the log house. Judith watched Uncle Walt as he turned the orange tractor around in the distance, and started driving toward them, pulling the sets of mechanical mowing blades behind him across the lawn. He waved when he saw the van, and Judith stopped and waited for him on the driveway as the tractor ambled over the grass. She could smell the fresh cut crass through the open window, and watched on; smiling as the tractor steadily approached her. Uncle Walt was a small man, who favored dark colored work pants, wide construction suspenders, logging boots and plain old wash and wear work shirts. His gray hair cropped short, he always wore the same old red sweat stained baseball cap with the peak turned to one side, the way a small kid would wear it. His most notable feature would be his face, which had been badly deformed from a bullet. It had happened during the last Great War when he'd stormed a cement bunker in France as an eighteen-year-old soldier.

"A real piss whipper of a scrap," Uncle Walt had called it.

His left eye now stood in a fold of skin where his cheekbone used to be, and most of the skin on his face was now smooth and hairless from the skin grafts they had taken from his buttocks.

A small, circular indentation at his temple above the "droopy eye" was crossed with scars where the surgeons had put a metal plate before stitching him back up. Judith had determined long ago that there was more to Uncle Walt than she could ever discern in the nine short years that she had known him. Still, she knew very little about his past, and felt there was more to his fractured face than he would ever let on. If she had learned anything during her thirty-odd years walking this planet, it had been that everybody had closets, and virtually everybody had something they wanted kept inside, locked away and out of sight. Uncle Walt had suffered somewhere, of that much Judith had been certain, but it failed to show in his disfigured face for he would laugh almost every five minutes, and at simple, everyday life things. Whenever he really got rolling on a giggle, his left eye would water uncontrollably, a physical characteristic the twins were quick to notice. Now they constantly pecked at his easy humor, drawing the laughter from him to the point that he now carried a red handkerchief in his back pocket to staunch the tears. He took most of his meals with Judith's family, and usually wandered over for coffee first thing in the morning, once he noticed a light on. On the weekends, he would come over early Saturday and make them all a big breakfast that would fill them up so much it would last them until suppertime. There was only one Uncle Walt in the world, and the three Noble girls were certainly glad he belonged to them.

As the tractor turned on the grass and came alongside the van, Uncle Walt stopped it and turned the engine off. He smiled as usual, and you couldn't help but let him pull the happiness from deep within you, even if you were having a bad day. Looking every bit like a playful kid with his smooth skin, misshapen face, and baseball cap sitting on his head all askew, you could do nothing else but smile.

"Why, hello there ladies, everything okay today?" He asked

"Fine Uncle Walt." The girls all answered at once, and this set him to chuckling, shaking his head with glee. He spoke with a noticeable drawl, forming his words slowly, like he mulled each one over before he let it out. The absence of any formal education other than grade school could also be detected in the manner in which he spoke, but what Uncle Walt lacked in literacy he more than made up for with his kind consideration.

"What's that you got in your hand, little lady?" He nodded at the piece of paper Judith had just picked up from the mailbox, still grasped in her hand.

"Oh, this. I'm supposed to cut all the weeds out front on our side of the ditch, or they'll send some workers out from the district to do it for me."

"My, my, how very nice of them." Walt replied.

"Yes sir, then they'll send me the bill for it."

"Jee- zus . . . " Walt said slowly, "that's why them son-of-bitches were sniffing around here. They even drove up to the house."

"You're not supposed to swear Uncle Walt," Jenny scolded from the front seat.

"Sorry honey," Uncle Walt said, "Yeah, anyway, I was wondering what them guys wanted. That fat son-of-a-bitch Cody from the district work's yard came on the property looking for you Judith. I told him if he didn't get his fat ass out of here, I'd pepper it with rock salt. Jee- zus . . . I should have shot that lard assed son-of-bitch anyway's."

Judith looked up into the sky, partly to hide her smile from the girls, and partly to gauge how much time she would have before the rain started.

"But don't you worry none, Honey," Uncle Walt continued, "I'll take care of them weeds for you."

"Thanks, you're a darling Uncle Walt," Judith said, "but I'll do it, I need the fresh air and some exercise."

"All right then, I'll start supper when I'm done with the grass. Did you get my snuff?"

"Sure did," Judith replied.

"Oh you're such a sweetheart. Hee hee hee."

Uncle Walt laughed as he started up the tractor, muttering loudly.

"Jee- zus . . . them jerk-off son-of-bitches."

He put the machine in gear and rattled off over the lawn, shaking his head and cursing to himself, saving the rich stuff for when the girls were out of earshot. The twins laughed openly as Judith took her foot off the brake and continued the slow drive up to the house.

She followed the long driveway until it curved around to the front of their log home, and she stopped the van in front of the large gabled roof that vaulted high above the front doors.

The gable reached well out from the main structure of the house, held up by log rafters it provided the front entryway with ample cover from the weather. If you continued along the driveway, the large circular route took you over to the stables, before doubling back onto itself, eventually taking you back out to the main road. In the middle of the grassed circle, Judith had removed all the sod and had dug a large vegetable garden, whose crops she willfully shared with Uncle Walt and the local deer. Planted only a month ago, shoots and leaves were already reaching above the soil, seeking out the nourishing rays of the sunshine. The log house was huge, far too big for Judith and the girls, but she had fallen in love with it when she had first seen it, complete with its sprawling lawns and natural forested acres.

Built from eighteen-inch diameter logs of winter cut, air dried, hand-peeled Douglas fir, the focal point of the house was the great room. An expansive opening, it encompassed the kitchen, dining room, a big bathroom and the family room into one big hall. A large fireplace built from mortar and smooth river rocks stood in the middle of the great room, and during the winter there would be wood burning in the brick fire box at all times. Uncle Walt would feed the fire and keep it stoked while Judith and the girls were away at school. It produced enough radiant heat to keep the living areas cozy, as well as the four bedrooms and main bathroom that opened onto the handcrafted balcony that overlooked the great hall. Steps made from half logs led up to the upper living area from the dining room, and each girl had the luxury of their own bedroom. Although when the winter winds would howl through the log joists under the cedar soffits, the twins would scamper along the balcony to Judith's room, where they would warm their feet as well as their fears, snuggled in her massive bed. Judith had the largest bedroom, with an en suite and a gabled ceiling that extended out from the gentle slope of the main shingled roof, covering a set of sliding doors, leading to a small wooden balcony. The balcony had become a private sanctuary for Judith, especially throughout the warmer months. Then she would sit on her lounger at night and watch the stars in the icy blackness of space, or smile contentedly in the predawn light as the robins hopped about in the wet dew on the grass, searching out worms.

Most of the furniture had come with the house, a comfortable assortment of hardwoods and durable cloths of workmanship that withstood both time, and the stamina of growing children. The dining room had a huge unit of Mennonite tables and chairs, with two matching dish cupboards, all of it built many decades ago within the flourishing Pennsylvania-German communities. Only the bedroom furniture had been purchased separately, and Judith had ordered the pine beds with their round, varnished posts, matching vanities and chest of drawers from a furniture maker on the Eastern Seaboard. All the flooring throughout the home had been constructed using four inch wide planks of hemlock, the warm beige color contrasting with the darker, hardwood furnishings. Only the main entrance, where a double set of frosted French doors welcomed you into the house, had the floor been built using a more durable material. As you sat near the front doors on one of the two oak Deacons' Benches to remove your footwear, you would find your feet on the smooth surface of square, terra cotta tiles that flowed from the foyer out to the great room, where the hemlock took over. Opposite the front doors, on the far side of the great room stood expansive wall-to-wall windows that overlooked the straits, with the mainland and its mountains ranging far to the east.

The house stood on a rock bluff overlooking a beach that rambled far in either direction, and access could be gained by walking out the kitchen door and following the wooden steps that led down to the rocky shores. Uncle Walt had built the solid steps with their sturdy banisters many years ago, when he and his wife Grace had first bought the property. Exactly ninety-two risers and steps (Jenny had counted them) took you down to a small sandy beach that dried on a low tide. If you didn't feel like swimming in the cool salt water, you could always pry oysters from the rocks, or comb the low water mark for whatever treasures the waves would cast upon the shores. The whole house and the surrounding landscape looked very much like some form of a utopian delight, and it had most certainly become just that. A number of people on the island who had nothing better to do, thought Judith's purchase of the property a bit stand-offish, and wondered out loud where the hell a school teacher got the money for such a spread.

None however, dared to ask, and had they bothered they would have received a very curt, Judith Noble type answer for their troubles. Unfortunately, a lot of these impertinent people failed to recognize that the heartbeat and spirit of a home came from the people who lived there.

It didn't come from the size and style of the house, the beauty of the land, or the equipment used to trim and care for it. Nor could it be found in the two ponies that were quartered in the stables, or the deer that nibbled at the immense gardens at night. The inside of Judith's home was filled with the peal of open laughter, and as much love as the weathered walls could tolerate. That was one of the standing rules of the household, strictly enforced by both Judith and Uncle Walt.

All frowns were to be checked at the front door, that's if you were lucky enough to be invited inside. Yes, there had been sad times, like any household that contained a family, but these were generally treated as growing pains, something to learn from and make you stronger in character.

The extreme sadness of years past Judith had put behind her where it belonged, and she had as yet to explain it all to the twins, but that day would come soon enough, when they got older and had a right to know. For now though, the log house contained laughter and delight for a large portion of the time, which suited everybody who lived there just fine.

Every time Judith entered her home, much the way she did this afternoon, she could feel its secure embrace fall upon her, smell the oils from the vast assortment of wood, and practically hear the joy echoing from days past. She walked through the front doors and took her shoes off, then put her fanny pack away in the closet, the events of the day soon forgotten. She had already dismissed the wretched circumstances surrounding young Brodie and the beating he'd suffered from his father. Judith had left that incident behind the minute she had left the school, without so much as a fleeting thought, and the second she stepped into her house it would no longer even be a memory. Strictly a defense mechanism, Judith had learned long ago to leave the burdens of her working world behind her. Far too many times it had crept in to ruin a perfectly good evening, or linger over a long weekend, tainting the precious time she had with her family. Judith followed Jenny up the stairs to their bedrooms, as Jody, already dressed for a ride, had scampered off to the stables to saddle her pony. Entering her bedroom, she went straight over to the walk-in closest, where she quickly shucked her shorts and shirt, throwing them onto the laundry pile. After peeling her white ankle socks off, she pulled a pair of heavy work socks from the built in drawers against the far wall. Next to the set of drawers stood a silver-coated cremation urn with a tarnished brass plaque tacked near its base. A section of the closet had been dedicated to hold all her grubbies, and as she hopped across the throw rug to that end of the enclosed room, she deftly pulled the thick gray socks onto her feet.

Judith selected from her collection of grubbies an old pair of blue jeans that were splashed with white paint, and a light-blue sweatshirt that had wood stain splattered across the front. She wasn't the most careful person in the world when she had a brush in her hand, so whenever Uncle Walt spied her hauling a can of paint or wood stain into the house, he would invariably come over to watch television, soon offering some carefully worded advice to prevent any slopping or spillage. Judith left her bedroom just as Jenny peeled away from the bottom of the steps, heading for the front door to go riding with her sister. They'd had the ponies for a few months, but only after Judith had insisted on lessons at the riding stables located at the north end of the island. She had purchased the ponies there as well, and planned to buy horses when the twins had outgrown the smaller animals, but that was still a few years away.

Both animals were mares, which the twins had called Jack and Jill, thinking the white one with the brown spots was a boy, and neither Judith nor Uncle Walt saw any purpose in dispelling the harmless ruse. When she got downstairs to the kitchen, Judith followed the hallway down to the back door, entering the utility room that held the deep freeze, washer and dryer, and an assortment of hand tools that were stored on some shelving. She went over to the freezer and pulled out a bag of salmon steaks, then returned to the kitchen, placing the frozen bag on a dinner plate. A microwave oven stood on a walnut stand against a tiled wall, and she put the salmon inside, setting the timer and the power level for defrosting. Uncle Walt had been a meat and potatoes kind of guy most of his life, but he had learned to like Judith's low fat meals, although once a month she would take the time to build him a pot roast with all the trimmings. Satisfied that everything was perking away nicely inside the microwave oven, Judith went to the front door and pulled on a pair of black gum boots that she kept in the closest. Looking every bit like one of the islanders she had become, she went out the front door to find Uncle Walt waiting for her in the driveway on the tractor. He'd folded the grass cutting blades up into the travel position, and had already picked up the weed whacker, the gasoline can, and the required safety equipment from the tool shed behind the stables.

All the equipment lay on the transmission near his feet, and Judith appreciated his thoughtfulness, as it would be a long haul from the tool shed down to the road. Uncle Walt watched as she approached the tractor, dressed in her grubbies and gumboots.

"Jee-zus, girl. Ain't no wonder you never get asked out, dressed like them two queer gals up the road."

"Up yours, Uncle Walt," Judith chided, "or that's where you'll be living, in a stew pot with those two man-eaters."

"Yes ma'am. Hee hee hee." Uncle Walt chuckled at the good-hearted haranguing, shaking his head while wiping a big tear from his smooth cheek.

Judith hopped up onto one of the fenders that curved above the tractors large rear wheels.

Uncle Walt nodded at her, then put the machine in gear, letting out the clutch and they started moving down the driveway. The rain clouds had taken over much of the sky, spanning away into the far distance toward the mainland, and they had already started to shed rain, as Judith could feel the drops flecking her hair. She sat silently as the tractor rambled down the driveway, enjoying the fresh scent that always preceded a rain shower.

Already the moist air had dampened the dust on the road, and the wet weather would save her the job of having to water the vegetable garden, offering up one less chore for the weekend. When the tractor got down to the bottom of the drive, Uncle Walt drove onto the main road and turned the machine around, facing it back toward the house. Judith hopped from the tractor, reaching up for her equipment as Uncle Walt passed it down to her, placing it all on the ground at her feet.

"The weed whizzer's all ready to go for you, it's fueled and warmed up," he advised.

"Thanks Uncle Walt, you're a sweetheart. Oh, and before I forget, there's salmon steaks thawing in the microwave, please don't overcook them this time."

"Jee-zus," Walt replied, "goddamned fish again?"

Judith nodded at him, "yes sir, and if I keep feeding you that stuff you'll probably live until you're at least seventy."

"Jee-zus girl. I'm already past seventy."

"See? There you go Uncle Walt. This healthy food is already working for you. Any time you have left is just gravy."

The old man laughed again at her easy smile, shaking his head as he started to motor the tractor back up the road. Judith turned and bent down to the gear, picking up a pair of clear plastic goggles, which she pulled over her head, adjusting the elastic band so it didn't pinch her short hair. Next she put on some hearing protection, carefully positioned the plastic, earmuff type defenders over her ears, playing with them until they sat comfortably. If Uncle Walt caught her using power tools without the proper safety equipment, he'd have at least two conniptions, then bless her with a couple of swear words that Judith herself had never even heard. Picking up the weed whacker by its slender aluminum body, Judith started walking the two hundred or so feet along the ditch to the edge of her land. An orange surveyor's peg marked the property line, placed in the loose dirt near the edge of another dense forest. At this point the main gravel road curved sharply down through a thick set of trees that grew on both sides of the roadway. This road eventually took you back to the intersection and the Country Junction Store, a pleasant, ten-minute drive through the forested country. On the second pull the weed whacker started, as well as the steady rain, but Judith struck out regardless, squeezing the throttle and starting with the weeds around the wooden power pole, slowly working her way back to the driveway.

Nearly fifteen minutes later she took a short break, surprised that she was nearly half finished, and even considered cutting the weeds in the ditch. But screw that noise she thought, those lackeys from the district can do the ditch themselves. They started this little war; she would at the very least ensure that they'd bloody well finish it. By this time, the rain had soaked Judith to the skin, and the water had even dribbled into her gumboots, pooling around her feet. The rain had also slowed the weed cutting progress as the thin stalks stuck together, clumping up, no longer scattering as easily as when they'd been dry. Judith pulled back the sopping sleeve of her sweatshirt, looking at her wristwatch. Exactly four-thirty it read. I'll give it another five minutes, then pack it in for the day, she thought, no point in being stupid about all this. She took a moment to undo the nylon strap that looped over her shoulder. It supported the heavy tool at the point of balance, but her wet clothing now created friction, causing it to dig into the soft skin of her neck. Judith throttled the machine up, and with slow, sweeping motions started once again at the edge of the sticky weeds where they grew just above the wet ground. At that point in time, the Marine Corps Band could have been standing beside her playing a stirring rendition of John Philip Sousa's Semper Fidelis, but the young schoolteacher wouldn't have heard a single note. Not with the ear-defenders on and the two-stroke engine of the weed whacker howling away at full speed.

Judith most certainly didn't hear the siren from the police car piping away in the distance, nor did she hear the old red pick-up truck that came careening through the forest and into the sharp corner on the gravel road, not one hundred feet behind her. She did however, feel the ground tremble as the pick-up truck failed to take the corner, going straight for the deep ditch at an unhealthy sixty-five miles an hour. Even though the driver of the truck had managed to take his foot off the gas pedal, the inertia formed by the vehicle's forward motion, as well as a small rise at the edge of the ditch, was apparently just enough to send the truck hurtling into space. Judith felt the ground shake violently beneath her feet as the pick-up truck wrapped its front bumper, engine compartment, cab and driver around the wooden power pole, transferring all its kinetic energy into a powerful force that snapped the ancient pillar in half. The wires came down, and a bare, high tension, sub transmission line snapped, coiling out onto the wet grass, appearing to spit smoke as it touched the weeds, sparking and wreathing as if it had a life of its own.

The end of the live wire crackled as it fell across the aluminum handle of the weed whacker.

It offered scant resistance to the very high amperage and the seven thousand six hundred and eighty volts that coursed through Judith's hands, leaping directly into her mid section. In an instant her lithe body was flung fifteen feet across the tops of the weeds, where she collapsed into a heap in the tall, wet grass. The current's violent shock had paralyzed her diaphragm, interrupting the nerve impulses that regulated her breathing, as well as breaking the normal rhythm of her heart, causing ventricular fibrillation. Judith had stopped breathing, and her heart muscle went into an irregular fluttering, failing to beat normally and pump her life-giving blood. As she lay in the grass with the rain falling onto her still face, Judith Noble had clinically died. Uncle Walt had heard the bang and had watched the pole topple as he climbed the stairs to his suite above the stables. He'd been on his way up to wash up and change before starting supper in Judith's kitchen.

"Holy shit." He muttered.

He bounded up the remaining stairs to his suite, grabbing the telephone on the coffee table in the living room. Quickly and efficiently he dialed 911, but he needn't have bothered, for a marked police car had already arrived at the accident scene.

*   *   *

Chapter Four

Some of the people put on this earth were meant to suffer. No matter what they do or how hard they try, everything they turn their hands to falls apart before their very eyes. Martin Bandie was one such person. Just ask him, and he would most assuredly tell you. Although many drunks did their best whining when parked on a bar stool with a face full of liquor, now might not have been a particularly good time to inquire about Martin's rotten misfortunes. As he sucked back one beer after another in Riley's Marine Pub in downtown Balford, he kept one eye on the front door, and one eye on the backside of the waitress.

Martin normally did his imbibing with the rest of the subhuman types who infested the urine-smelling dive that sat atop the pilings down at Skinny's Reach. Different urges however, had compelled him to seek out a different venue, so he'd driven up to Balford. Here, it was hoped, he could conduct some new business, and sniff out the tidy new waitress named Nancy. Martin had learned a long time ago that beer was beer, and drunk was drunk, no matter where you went, but the low-paid gash that served it would change on a constant basis. He had planned to talk the waitress into accompanying him down to Skinny's Reach where his fishing boat was tied up in the municipal harbor. Once he got her into the fo'c'sle, he would show her a thing or two about lustful intercourse, and even imagined her screaming out for more. He'd best do it before his speech got too slurred though, or she might catch on that he was just a tad drunk, and think him somewhat ungentlemanly and vulgar.

The philosopher, or common folk, or whoever the hell it was who penned the phrase "once you've hit bottom, the only way to go is up," had never considered the Martin Bandie's of this planet. Martin had become an incredibly gifted human being when it came to doing three-dimensional feats, such as digging himself deeper into an already festering quagmire of trampled misery. Most folk could stand by and watch this kind of self-destructive behavior with a casual interest, maybe even use the intoxicated antics as a bad example. Sadly enough though, Martin's blotto, feral ways deeply impacted the lives of two others, which unfortunately happened to be the members of his immediate family. Nora would be one, his petite and long-suffering wife of six years to whom he openly referred to as the slut, and his son Brodie would be the other.

He called his son the "tard," which was short for *retard,* and had resented the child since the day he had been born. The child had become a living monument. Proof of Martin's hopeless luck, and that nothing he ever did amount to an awful lot.

Martin had taken a bamboo stick to Brodie's bare butt the other day after he spilled his macaroni and cheese all over the kitchen floor. It was one of those thin, swishy sticks, that you used to tie up perennials in your garden, and it even hummed as it cut through the air, snapping when it curved over Brodie's bare skin. Goddamned, did that little bastard ever howl, and Nora got a fat lip when she tried to intervene. She always stood up for the kid, still more proof that the child had been seeded from some other guy's loins. But it was time to forget about those two, Martin had to concentrate at the tasks at hand, which would get progressively harder the more he drank. Nora and the "tard" would get theirs once Martin got home, especially if his attempt to pick up the tasty waitress Nancy failed, which in all likelihood it would. Not a lot of girls in the northern hemisphere would have willingly screwed Martin Bandie, even when he was sober and all cleaned up. Indubitably, he would have to leave the continent to find anyone who would eagerly crawl under him when he was drunk. This would include his poor wife, and the somewhat refined Nancy the waitress.

Martin's other course of business was to talk to Harvey, who according to gossip down in Skinny's Reach, was the CEO of the local marijuana cooperative. Martin had no idea what a CEO could be, but he assumed he would have to be somewhere near the top. Harvey didn't have a second name, at least none that Martin had heard about, but he frequented Riley's on Friday nights, where he'd drink draft beer and play snooker. Martin hoped to collar him and eagerly point out to him that he owned a thirty-six foot fishing boat that could easily accommodate a few tons of the cooperative's illicit product. Being he was a local boy, Martin felt he should be cut in on the lucrative, exporting venture that had made a fair number of the other residents not lacking for anything. The plan of action, and only if the succulent Nancy had already snubbed him, would be to buy Harvey a pitcher of cold beer and a game at the pool table. With the offer of another boat on the table to carry Harvey's product far and away, Martin figured he couldn't go wrong, even though most of the island's salty types viewed his boat as a floating latrine.

Like all cowardly, slothful drunks, Martin viewed the world through glassy eyes that tended to distort things, especially when he was driving his vehicle around the island, or admiring himself in the mirror on his boat. He fancied himself as a rather *cool dude*. Yes indeed, if Martin were to use two words to sum up his bearing and character, those would be the two words he would have to use. He'd already used them in court to an unappreciative Judge who gave him three months in jail for driving while under the influence, and a two hundred dollar fine for contempt of court.

Nevertheless, if a person would only stop long enough to take a good look at Martin Bandie, they would undoubtedly find an item or two about the way he dressed, and the way he looked, somewhat cool. Even if he wasn't attuned to the styles of the present decade, and the clothes he wore were best suited to the late fifties, cool was cool. You see, Martin had become a bit of a movie buff, at least during the few times he'd spent in prison, where they showed those crappy old black and white flicks on Saturday nights in the gymnasium. From these films alone, he had gleaned his method and style of dress as well the manner in which he conducted himself whilst in the public eye.

Cool would be the way his tight blue jeans clung to his skinny ass, and the way he wore his white tee shirt, tucked in and dappled with sweat stains, a pack of cigarettes folded up into the short sleeve. Cool was the way he wore his long, dark, greasy hair that hung down to soil the collar of his tee shirt, and the square toed black biker boots he wore on his feet could definitely be construed as somewhat poised. Even the pimples that still marked Martin's face at twenty-four years old did nothing to inhibit him, and in fact left him feeling somewhat integrated, especially when he sold drugs to some of the local high school students. He was also one of maybe eighteen people on the face of the earth who could walk around with a toothpick in his mouth, and look trendy while doing it. Never one to play second fiddle, Martin Bandie could also smoke a cigarette and drink his beer while the toothpick danced on his lips, which made him one of seven such talented people on the planet. The only thing missing from Martin Bandie's physical attributes would have been a tattoo. A large "L" for loser, emblazoned across his forehead would have been an appropriate marking. An indicative symbol of a way of life that had amounted to the square root of dick, but had been entirely of his own making. On the human dignity scale, this miserable piece of flesh wouldn't have even made it on the yardstick of humanity, and sitting as he did in Riley's Marine Pub, he looked as out of place as a condom machine in a kindergarten class.

Riley, a huge man who owned the pub and happened to be tending the bar because it was quiet, normally didn't allow this kind of trash into his establishment. But Martin was his only customer, so he would take his cash until someone else wandered in, at which time he'd toss him out into the parking lot. Riley figured the rain clouds and the fact that it was still early Friday afternoon had kept the place quiet, but that would soon change. It always did. Riley was justifiably proud of his swanky digs, for it attracted yachties from both sides of the border, as well as their seemingly endless amounts of expendable cash. From the moment they stepped from their gleaming vessels and took a wrap with a line on one of the cleats in the marina, until their stern wake left the harbor, the meter would always be running. The only thing that was free in Riley's place would be the fresh air, the weather, and the fluctuating tides. The cruising public got what they paid for though, which amounted to a clean, secure marina with spotless docks, and a very nautical pub in which to mingle with their boating brethren. Riley's supreme achievement had been the pub, purchased with sweat, hard work, and the money that floated into his well-kept docks.

Built on a rock bluff that overlooked the harbor, it was an open, post and beam affair with polished cherry wood paneling lining the walls and the booths as well as the front of the wet bar.

Ships lanterns, of antique brass and wired to the main lights were mounted to the walls throughout the place, as well as framed and glass-covered charts of the local areas. Colorful prints hung from every wall, including the washrooms. Each told a story of eighteenth century man-of-wars and copper-bottomed frigates, all on the high seas, engaged in naval battles long since interned to the history books. In the center of the pub, hanging from the angled wooden beams was a varnished, red mahogany lapstrake rowboat, hoisted upside down to expose its yellow spruce ribs and burnished thwarts. If it wasn't nautical, big Riley didn't want it in his pub, and the seedy squirrel that occupied one of his leather-topped bar seats was about as nautical as a chuck wagon, and probably just as intelligent. Riley looked upon Martin with a fair bit of scorn affixed to his fleshy face, and who the hell could blame him. Compounding the situation was the fact that Martin had rolled into the place with a healthy jig on, and the way he leered at his new waitress would eventually lead to some grief. He could just tell. Riley had done nothing as of yet to jeopardize his treasured annual liquor license, nor was he about too. Still, he didn't need one of the local police officers conducting a bar walk, only to discover one of the island's finest citizens swaying atop a bar stool.

The local police used his place as *their* watering hole, so he wanted to keep the place respectable, but at the same time he had to be careful when he threw Martin out on his ear. It could be bad for business if he tossed him without a really good reason, and word got around the island very quickly. When someone broke wind in the northern part, they soon got a whiff of it down in the southern section. If Martin got his disposition too warped, he might just muster his pals and start showing up with the rest of the lowlife dregs, which could very quickly sewer Riley's classy livelihood. The last thing he needed would be a herd of shit rats hanging from the pub's cedar balcony, swilling beer and pissing into the ocean while one of the megalithic yachts entered the harbor, looking for a berth and bringing with it a few dozen referrals. Just a few more minutes Riley figured, then I'll have him, especially the way Martin followed Nancy with his eyes full of unbridled lust. In a few minutes more Martin Bandie would cross over that line of nautical pub protocol, and Riley could get out the fly swatter, squash him like an insect, then flick him outside. Riley polished wine glasses with a soft cloth, then slid them into the wooden rack above his head, all the time watching Martin, conveniently seated within striking distance near the end of the bar. Martin had a toothpick sticking out of his mouth, as well as a lit cigarette, and he slowly nodded his head as he scanned the room, as if he were keeping in tune with some music that only he could hear.

Nancy stood near the bay windows that looked out onto the harbor, wiping down the tables and chairs, more to put some distance between herself and Martin than for cleanliness. She didn't like the drunken twerp, not since he first walked into the pub, exuding his cool attitude and brainless wit. He was the sort of fellow her parents had street proofed her against when she had been a child just starting grade school. Nancy kept her back to him as much as possible, allowing Riley to deal with him, but then she heard a car drive into the parking lot and turned to look up, which had been a mistake. The goon Martin was looking right at her, wagging a finger and beckoning her. She rolled her eyes melodramatically and did nothing to hide it, then walked slowly over to him. Riley watched on with interest, for Nancy had only been working for him a few days and he wondered how she would handle herself around riffraff like Martin Bandie. It was most unfortunate that Nancy's mettle had to be tested so soon after being hired, but Riley wasn't one of those proprietors who steadfastly abided by the golden rule that the customer is always right.

The customer *is* always right, until Riley said otherwise. Martin had a lecherous smirk on his face as Nancy crossed the floor, and he did nothing to avert his gaze as he stared at her breasts. Here we go Riley thought, show time. Hopefully Martin will say something inappropriate or altogether rude, then Riley can shuck him before the Friday afternoon crowds start to arrive.

Nancy walked up to Martin and leaned on the bar, looking him straight in the eyes. Good, thought Riley, this is good, stare the bastard down, don't take any crap, and remember, never swear at the customer. Nancy had a smile on her face, although you could tell she was straining to keep it there.

"Yes sir?" She asked Martin.

Martin took a puff on his cigarette, and then pulled the smoke from his mouth, obviously incapable of talking with both a cigarette *and* a toothpick hanging from his lips. He got right down to the business of rutting, dispensing with all the usual small talk. His opening line was one of absolute buffoonery, and for a second Riley couldn't believe his ears.

"Listen Toots," Martin slurred, "I've got this beautiful boat down in Skinny's Reach . . . "

Nancy cut him off before he even got his proposition on the table, and Riley soon realized he'd hired a true artist. Here was a waitress who could rebuff and insult a person like Martin Bandie long before they got the chance to make complete fools of themselves.

"If I was stranded on a small desert island," Nancy began, "and you were the last man on earth, driving the last boat on earth, I'd still slit my wrists." She turned and walked away from Martin, who looked absolutely stunned and crestfallen.

Another customer had walked into the pub during the verbal jousting, and had taken a chair near the pool table. Riley recognized him as Harvey Bentley, a Friday afternoon regular who quietly drank his beer while he played a few rounds of snooker. Harvey always came to the pub dressed in blue jean overalls and brown sandals, with a red bandana tied around his forehead, securing his shoulder length blonde hair close to the nape of his neck. His long beard would also be tapered into a ponytail, held in a tight tuft with elastic bands. Riley figured the man must work a lot around moving machinery, and the bandana and elastic bands kept his hair away from the running pulleys and spinning parts. In his late thirties and nearly as big as Riley, nobody was really sure what Harvey did for a living, for he never said and nobody cared much either, and that had become one of the unique reasons some people had moved to the island. Nancy walked over to Harvey to take his order and he smiled up at her from his chair. She nodded and spoke briefly to him, then returned to the bar, and this was when Riley noticed the scornful look on Martin's face, the sudden hurt caused by Nancy's rebuffing comments had now vanished. Martin Bandie looked like he might break into a sudden rage, and Riley thought there would still be a good chance to

thump the young man, and then legitimately fling him into the parking lot. That kind of advertising could be acceptable and beneficial, a clear message to the slugs at Skinny's Reach to steer clear of Riley's Pub. Martin suddenly slid from his stool and started to lurch across the floor in Harvey's direction, slopping his beer as he carried his drink along with him. Not only was Riley a big man, but also he could be incredibly quick on his feet when the need arose, like right about now.

He came from behind the bar silently and menacingly, shadowing Martin as he steered a crooked course toward Harvey, who looked on without so much as a notion showing on his tanned face.

Martin stopped unsteadily when he got to where Harvey was seated, swaying badly, then took a pull on his beer, dribbling the amber liquid down his chin, soaking the cigarette he'd forgotten to take from his mouth.

" 'Lo Harv," Martin slurred.

Harvey looked at Martin and politely nodded to him.

"Buy y' a beer, Harv?" Martin asked.

"Nope," was Harvey's curt reply.

Martin looked down at him, so drunk that his head jerked around on his neck, and his eyes appeared all out of focus. Riley stood behind him, ready for the coup d' gras, then realized that Martin must have had a jag on long before he got to his pub, because he'd only drunk three draft beers since arriving. Two and a half if Riley cut him off right now. No one could be that drunk on two and one-half beer, so Martin obviously had something else coursing through his system.

"Can I si' down?" Martin continued.

"Nope, but you can certainly piss off," Harvey said quietly.

This was terrible. Things weren't going quite the way Martin had planned. He had been hopeful that at this particular place in time Nancy would have been sitting on his lap, licking his ear while anticipating a wild sexual encounter on his boat. Meanwhile, he and Harvey would be cutting a lucrative deal that would bring him lots of money and broads, as well as many uplifting changes to his woebegone life style. Things were now unfolding the way they normally did in his wretched life, and Martin was becoming a trifle agitated with the responses he'd been receiving. Why, he thought, he might even have to kick a little ass to get what he wanted. But first he would get angry, move things along in an escalating manner, offering them a chance to renege before things got too ugly. Martin had to remember that he was a little drunker than he had meant to be.

He'd badly miscalculated the impact of two lines of cocaine he'd snorted about an hour ago, and the pint of whisky he'd drank on the drive up from Skinny's Reach. Martin wasn't at home either, where Nora and Brodie would have been cowering in the corner as he quickly built himself into a terrifying fury.

Riley watched on, smiling as the veins in the back of Martin's thin neck became engorged with a liquor and drug induced apoplectic rage.

"Why you fat *prick*," Martin sputtered at Harvey.

Ah, at last, time to sweep the floor. There will be no ballyhooing in this establishment, at least not today. Riley reached around and deftly plucked the glass of beer from Martin's hand, placing it on a nearby table. He then grabbed Martin by the shoulders and herded him toward the double doors of the pub. Martin decided to try a little passive resistance, which might have worked for the Mahatma Gandhi, but turned out to be a big mistake given Riley's size and present temperament. The burly pub owner felt Martin apply the brakes, and then quickly seized his prey by his ultra fashionable, thick, black leather biker belt. The one with the big, gaudy chrome buckle and the Harley on the front. Riley chased away the last of Martin's feeble credibility, carrying him by the back of his belt as his arms and legs flayed disgracefully, moving him like a sack of manure over to the door, which he opened with one hand. Riley walked across the front steps and dropped Martin into a shameful heap on the gravel parking lot, there he lay motionless, the rain spotting the back of his white tee shirt.

"Bandie, if you ever come back into my establishment any time while I'm still alive, I'll rip your face off and stuff it in your back pocket." Riley turned and walked back into his pub, with yet another name to chalk onto his permanently barred list.

Once he heard the door close, Martin picked himself up with as much dignity as his predicament would allow. He was licked this time and he knew it, but there would be another time to get back at Riley and that selfish lump Harvey. He was utterly angered, for he really thought he had a chance at getting a little piece from that scrumptious tart Nancy. Now he'd have to settle for his wife Nora, which would be the same as dry humping a log.

44

And if that "tard" kid opens his mouth when I get home, he'll be kissing the back of my hand, Martin thought miserably as he staggered down to his pick-up truck. He'd parked the truck in the lower lot behind the pub because previously the bartenders had called the police on him after he'd left and driven off into the night. The rotten bastards, they take your money and ply you with liquor, and then they call the cops on you after you've finished doing your business with them. The whole goddamned world was nuts, Martin thought, as he opened the driver's door and prepared to hoist himself in. Then he saw a rock about the size of a baseball lying in a corner on the gravel, and he tottered over to it, bending down to retrieve it. It felt cold in his hand, the perfect size and shape for what he had in mind. Might just as well start exacting the vengeance while he was still here. There was no time like the present, someone had once told him.

Martin climbed into the truck, placing the rock beside him on the seat, and then started the engine.

He backed out of the parking lot just as the sprinkling rain turned to a substantial downpour, and only then did he appreciate just how drunk he was, because he had to squint his eyes to stop seeing double. He may not even bother taking a piece from Nora after all, especially when he was this loaded and it went all soft on him right in the middle of his grunting. It was probably a good thing that Nancy had spurned him, saving him a very embarrassing situation. Martin could always try her again when he wasn't so drunk, and she wasn't so snotty. He drove the truck a short distance up the main road then stopped, backing it into the upper parking lot of the pub, stopping only feet away from the front doors. Martin rolled the window down in the cab, then picked up the smooth rock and flung it out the vehicle. The rock smashed the paneled windows on one side of the double doors, spreading shards of glass inside and outside of the building.

"That'll learn ya . . . . yaaa pricks." Martin yelled.

He then punched the accelerator down, spitting wet gravel over the front of the pub, pelting the windows and the bright paintwork as he spun from the parking lot, fish tailing dangerously down the road. Martin, with his drunken, cowardly act of revenge and senseless sabotage, had just set into motion a series of events that would eventually put an end to his years of rotten luck.

*   *   *

Chapter Five

Sergeant Cheryl Montague of the Regional Police was having one of those days that seem to plague every police officer at least three times a month. It would be one of those shifts that would put her behind in her paperwork, and increase her already expanding investigative file loads. These shifts always occurred when the office would be short handed, and lunacy seemed to pervade almost every corner of the community. With twenty years as a police officer, Cheryl had come to expect days like today, and had become seasoned enough to know they would eventually end, and she could go home. Then someone else could carry the shift while she relaxed and listened to classical music while drinking chilled Perrier. Cheryl had a Bachelor of Arts degree in Sociology, and at one time considered herself a modern, aspiring, and optimistic young woman. Now she considered herself an overeducated cop, somewhat older, and somewhat more cynical than the idealistic young woman who had first joined the Regional Police Service. Even though the fallacy that police work was best served by men had been shattered decades ago, Cheryl still had an uphill climb, and she soon found that being a woman with a university degree sticking out of her back pocket intimidated *some* of her male counterparts. Her knowledge of the study of human social relations did little to help her in her job of street level policing. Although she might fully understand why a small part of the island's inhabitants behaved the way they did, the end result would always be the same. She would arrest them, and then lodge them in the cells, and all the educational degrees in the world weren't going to change that sad fact.

When Cheryl finally made Sergeant and was posted to the island as the Unit Commander of the local Police Detachment, there had been some indiscreet whining as to the promotion being predicated by the color of Cheryl's skin, and just what she *didn't* carry between her legs.

Cheryl knew better though, for hard work and dedication had got her to where she presently stood, and being a female African-American had diddlie-squat to do with it. Having said that, the view she got from her commander's desk in the office wasn't as peachy or as fulfilling as she had hoped it would be. She had a good crew in the seven police officers she supervised, and she'd found a haven in the cottage she'd bought on the north end of the island, only a block from a secluded, sandy beach. The endless stream of paperwork that entered her office at times had her wondering just where it was that upper management had parked their heads. Today Cheryl should have been doing her month end returns, which were nothing more than recording on a tally sheet how many speeding tickets, federal offences, and misdemeanor cases her detachment had investigated in the previous month. These were dutifully forwarded to some drone Inspector at headquarters who no doubt picked his nose for three days of the workweek. If your stats were down, then he'd send you a rude warning letter advising you to pick up the pace, and if your stats were up, then you'd receive another rude letter advising that you were losing control in your area, as crime was obviously rampant.

While going through the morning mail, Cheryl had found a letter from headquarters announcing that the policing of senior citizens would be the banner of the month, held high and waved for all to see. Along with this proclamation came a questionnaire that Cheryl was to take around to twelve randomly selected seniors who lived in her policing area. Two of the seniors on her list had died months ago, leaving Cheryl to wonder just how headquarters had obtained their magical list. She was to sit with the seniors and drink herbal tea while asking them the important questions that were contained within the questionnaire. Once she had dutifully recorded all of their answers, the forms were to be forwarded to headquarters where an appropriate decision could be made. Sergeant Montague took her favorite red felt pen from her desk drawer and wrote across the bottom of the seniors request, "sorry, no time for this sort of crap, have a nice day, I know I will." She then signed her name using the felt pen, employing large, graceful loops as the thick red ink spiraled across the entire width of the page. Taking the form with the scrawled, unyielding message, she threw it into the out basket for the clerk to put in the mail. Cheryl had a hand on the pulse of the community she policed, and she knew there were no problems with the small collection of seniors. The questionnaire from headquarters was nothing more than a make work project that would lead someone to a promotion, and she would have nothing to do with these unnecessary tasks.

Cheryl had been regarded as a problem child for some time now by the old guard who squatted and clucked like old hens at the headquarters building on the mainland. Their suspicions were confirmed when a staffing officer had called her one day to offer some direction. Cheryl had succinctly told him that if they had a problem with the way she ran her detachment, then it would be just that, *their* problem, not hers. She pointed out that in the year that she had been in charge of the detachment there had yet to be a complaint made about the manner in which she and her officers policed the community. Cheryl left them with an open invitation to come and visit her whenever they preferred, at which time she would be more than happy to open her books, and even offered them a bed in one of the jail cells if they felt the audit might take a couple of days. They'd left her alone ever since, until this senior's questionnaire arrived this morning. But that had been dealt with in the usual, efficient manner that had endeared Cheryl to her subordinates and the general public alike. The senior's letter unfortunately had heralded the start of what had promised to be a reasonably quiet Friday morning, although it soon took Cheryl very close to what police called the lunatic fringe. It would be one of those days when the complaints came in one after another, and seemed to just get more weird as the day grew on. Cheryl's day man had phoned in sick, and the other one had taken leave, so she was left holding the key to the fort.

Not a problem however, the day would eventually end, they always did. Then the weekend would start, and she could go home and play in her garden while listening to her classical music, effectively tuning the rest of the world out. Unfortunately though, the social assistance cheques had been mailed out this week to those unsavory individuals who relied a little too heavily on the state for their existence. Subsequently, the shenanigans started a little earlier than usual, and they started where they normally started, down at the sleazy hovel some called a bar, atop the pilings down in Skinny's Reach. An hour after the place had opened, at eleven o'clock, the calls started coming in about the fighting and the noise that spilled out from the balcony and across the quiet bay. Cheryl hoped to one day win the weekly lottery, and when that happened, she would buy that squalid bar on the pilings and promptly torch it, allowing it to burn to ashes then fall onto the stinking sand that lay below. In the meantime, like right now, she would have to go down there and hopefully be given the opportunity to throw somebody in jail for the day, which ordinarily put the rest of the reveling crowd back on the straight and true. After the first complaint, she drove slowly down to the bar from the office, leaving behind the pounds of paperwork that were scattered across her desk. Cheryl, like all veteran police officers never rushed to a bar fight, she
always took her time. That way the combatants would be either beaten up or out of breath when she got there. Those who were bloodied

were taken to the hospital in the back of an ambulance, and the rest who were stupid enough to hang around went to jail. No matter the outcome, it always became a terrible waste of the community's emergency resources. Five minutes later, Cheryl parked her white patrol car with the blue "Police" decals just in front of the tavern, and radioed her location to the telecom center on the mainland. They would check on her every few minutes and if she failed to answer them, they'd call out the cavalry, whomever the cavalry might be. Cheryl got out and insured one of the back doors of the police car was left ajar so she wouldn't have to play with it when she came back out with one in custody. The face of the bar had clapboard style construction, using thin strips of cedar that had been painted a moss green color. Although most of the paint had chipped off and fallen into the long grass, exposing the soft, brown wood beneath. It had no official name, which struck many as unusual, although the local townspeople called it the pigsty whenever they petitioned the municipal government for its permanent closure. How they came up with this label would be anyone's guess, but all that aside, the lowlife who frequented the bar thought it an apt name, and fairly soon the designation had stuck. The bar stood atop old wooden pilings that reached out across the sulphuric smelling sand at low tide, and hovered just above the oily looking water on a full flood. All the windows that fronted onto the narrow street had been painted black, possibly so unwary pedestrians couldn't gaze in and get sick at what they saw.

When Cheryl entered the dimly lit bar, two loons were fighting on the pool table, and the acrid, dank smell of urine rankled her nose, making her skin crawl. She had a pair of disposable rubber gloves on her hands, so the more astute among the drunken crowd already knew that somebody would be going to jail. The two fools on the pool table stopped fighting the moment they saw her, and jumped down, scurrying back to their tables before they got throttled. Cheryl hadn't been in the place for more than thirty seconds, still sizing up the crowd, looking for the weak links, when the unthinkable happened. That's when a skinny rack they called Frog, because he looked so ugly, sidled on up to her with his sour breath and a yearning of romance in his bleary eyes. Frog kind of liked the police officer, even though she was a little older, and he thought she looked great in her light blue uniform, which accented the tight muscles in her backside. He even liked the way she wore her dark hair, short and tightly curled, and she had neat things like handcuffs, that would take sexual encounters to new heights. Frog came from Cheryl's blind side and slopped a clammy hand over her shoulder near her bare neck, and her reaction became impulsive and instantaneous. She swung her fist like a pendulum, right into the lad's crotch, driving his testicles up into his mouth. At least, that's how it felt to poor Frog. He collapsed against the pool table, gasping for breath, his eyes round and terrified. His plums felt like a very large horse had just stepped on them, and the cruel pain stabbed through the very core of his internal organs. While Frog fought to get some air, Cheryl flipped him onto his stomach on the edge of the pool table and cranked his arms behind his back, expertly flipping her stainless steel handcuffs onto his wrists, tightening them down to the bone. She pulled him to his feet, and then marched him out the door while she read him his rights, advising him he'd been arrested for being drunk in a public house.

After leaning him face down on the trunk, Cheryl searched him, and then opened the back door to her patrol car, helping Frog climb in the caged rear compartment, where he slumped over, moaning loudly. She walked back into the bar after locking the doors of the car and advised the bar manager that she'd be pulling his license as allowed by law for over serving his patrons if she was called back any time today. The rest of the bar watched on in silence, knowing that Frog's imbibing had just been drastically curtailed for at least twelve hours. They had no wish to join him in the drunk tank, not with so many fine drinking hours left in the day. Cheryl left the bar to find Frog beating his head against the plexiglass screen that separated the front compartment from the prisoners' cage. A lot of them tried that, hoping to cut themselves. Cheryl would then have to take them to the hospital, where they could play martyr for a while as they got a few stitches put into their noodles. After leaving the pigsty she advised telecom via the radio that she had one in custody, and then drove her patrol car down the long lane that led back to the center of town, halting rather abruptly at the stop sign at the bottom of the road. Frog did a sudden face plant against the hard surface of the plexiglass, and it must have hurt because he cried out. Cheryl got her message across though, and like a trained lab rat that'd just received a corrective jolt of electricity, Frog kept his face clear of the screen.

Cheryl drove straight back to the office, and was busy in the back cell area booking Frog in when a call came in about a disturbance aboard the inbound ferry. This complaint held a bit of urgency to it as the vessel would be filled with families, and weekend traffic heading for the island. Once she got Frog (who refused to give his real name, and would rot there all weekend until he did) lodged into the featureless walls of the drunk tank, she telephoned for a civilian guard to come and baby-sit him. Cheryl jogged back out to her patrol car and by then had already decided that it was going be one of those days. She drove straight down to the ferry landing located at the north end of the island, wasting no time as a "freak in a trench coat," had been reported dancing in the restricted area on the flat, open bow of the ferry. This kind of call could easily turn into a sudden death, or a missing person file if the subject decided to take a dive.

Those kinds of investigations could follow you around for a long time, and your only hope to a timely conclusion was if the remains were washed up on some distant shore. After parking the patrol car on the elevated end of the loading ramp, Cheryl again radioed her location. She got out and opened the back door of the car, readying it to receive another prisoner, then watched as the ferry came in for a docking, pushing slowly through the cold water, not two hundred feet from the ramp.

Sure enough, a longed haired young man of about twenty stood precariously on the edge of the ship's bow, yodeling loudly with his head tilted back, his yellow teeth exposed like a braying donkey. He wore an old, olive drab great coat that he'd found in some military surplus store, and a couple of the crew members were doing their best to talk him back inboard. Nonetheless, you could tell they had no intention of going anywhere near him. They were paid twenty-five bucks an hour to direct traffic and scratch themselves, not to hold fruitless conversations while attempting to rescue longhaired morons. There had been no mention of this type of stuff in their union contract, and if they, or the screeching young man were to fall overboard, the bodies would be spit out the stern end as regular ground meat. The double set of bronze propellers would reduce a human body to nothing more than fresh hors d'oeuvres for the crabs who dwelled on the sandy bottom.

When the lone yodeler spied the police officer standing on the ramp, he cranked up his pagan shrieking an octave or two, enjoying the presence of a challenging audience. Cheryl could tell from where she stood that the choir boy had swallowed, snorted, or shot-up some sort of mind altering drug, and that the crack of her metal baton might be the only thing that would catch his attention and quell this offensive serenading. As the large, rounded bow of the ferry nudged its way into the reinforced pilings and stopped, Cheryl leapt from the ramp, dropping the four feet or so to the single car deck where the young man stood, still vigorously chortling away.

He wore an old pair of army boots on his feet and didn't seem to be wearing any socks. As Cheryl approached him he clutched the front of his great coat, and unfurled it like a small sail, holding the coat open in his outstretched arms, defiantly exposing his nakedness. His foreskin hung like a piece of gristle from an old chicken skin, and the whole apparatus reminded Cheryl of the wrinkled, long necked, pacific geoduck clams she'd seen at the fish market in Skinny's Reach. The young man appeared proud of this bold display, but the pride quickly fell from his face when Cheryl gave him a goodly burst of Oleoresin Capsicum solution from the pepper spray canister that fit into the palm of her hand.

The lone crooner grasped his dirty hands to his burning eyes, rubbing the chemical into the soft, membrane of his exposed peepers, sucking back great amounts of fresh air as the irritant filled his lungs, making them feel as if they were turning inside out. He started screaming in agony, but he wouldn't be finding any sympathy from the stalwart police officer who wasted few seconds in placing her handcuffs onto his bony wrists. Cheryl watched on as he did a painful little jig on the fore deck, his penis flopping like a pathetic puppet through the opening of his great coat. She kept an eye on her prisoner while he continued with his distressing dance, reading him his rights while she pulled on a pair of disposable rubber gloves from a pouch on her leather gun belt. At that point in time the young man couldn't have cared less about his rights, free phone calls, or bottom feeding lawyers who would do their best to discredit hard-working police officers. In fact, he hadn't even heard a single word that Cheryl had said, so intense had the stinging pain become. Cheryl couldn't have cared less either, she read him his rights and that was all she was required to do under the law, and if her detainee failed to hear or understand her, well, that was life in the sticks. She searched her prisoner, finding an old brown wallet in one of his deep pockets, then led him away still howling, over to her patrol car.

She placed him into the back seat, and then returned directly to the office, parking the car in the vehicle bay that lay adjacent to the cellblock. Cheryl helped the prisoner from the back seat and guided him over to an eye wash station that stood against one of the walls. Placing her hand on the back of his head, she gently guided his face over the ceramic bowl where two directional spigots pointed up to his face. She reassured him by speaking quietly, then pushed the large, flat handled lever forward and the cool water started flushing the young man's face, rinsing the concentrated, but entirely natural pepper solution from his eyes. Once the whining had stopped, and his eyes appeared a healthier shade of red, Cheryl took him to the cell area and booked him in, lodging him into the drunk tank where Frog had already urinated all over the floor. Most of the urine had gone down the drain, but the reconstituted draft beer had the cellblock smelling like a back alley on skid row. That's just the way it would stay for now, and both prisoners could enjoy the stink until long after midnight, which would be about the time of their release, sober, and *after* the bars had closed. Cheryl asked Frog once again for his name, and received a barrage of foul language for her efforts. Most of the verbs, nouns and adjectives he used pertained to her African-American heritage, and the delicate folds of skin that formed her sex organ. Frog, or whatever the hell his name was, just wasted his breath, for Cheryl was a professional, and it would take a wee bit more than a few coarse words to provoke a response. By this time the longhaired minstrel had removed his great coat, and stood naked with his manhood swollen for all who cared to look, crowing loudly, which quickly captured Frog's attention. Maybe the freak preferred skinny young men, and calling the nice police officer vulgar names suddenly didn't seem like a very smart idea. Frog had no place to go in a cell that had no partition, no bed, no nothing, just a weirdo with a hard on. The small, smooth walled enclosure offered no place to hide, and it suddenly left Frog feeling vulnerable and very exposed. He'd heard stories about men and jail cells, and he realized his present situation would warrant some careful negotiations, but he would first have to retract all the cruel names he'd just called officer Montague. In fact, Frog was just preparing his apology when Cheryl smiled at him and bid him a good day, leaving the cell area to write up the mandatory files that went along with these two most recent arrests. She slammed closed the metal fire door to the cellblock area, but could still hear Frog's pitiful bleating as she walked down the hallway to her office.

After filling her coffee cup from the glass pot in the detachment's small kitchen, Cheryl returned to the desk in her office and continued sifting through the paperwork. She managed to get in a couple of hours of uninterrupted reading, and even jammed up the paper shredder a couple of times. Although, some of the bureaucratic requests she did manage to answer. About a dozen or so curt responses she typed out on her computer, then sent them out via the e-mail. The white pile of paper actually appeared to be diminishing, and Cheryl thought she might end up owning the day when Judith Noble called from the small elementary school just outside of Balford.

She took notes as Judith talked, and she soon realized the rest of her day had just become an assault causing bodily harm investigation. This was the worst kind, a child abuse case, and a sensitive, spineless crime that would likely keep her busy until long after the afternoon shift had shown up. Cheryl immediately called Social Services who had an office in Skinny's Reach, arranging for a meet at the school with a caseworker. From what Judith Noble had said - and people didn't get anymore credible than the spirited school teacher - Cheryl had already decided the child would have to be seized for his own protection. She'd had enough of the child's father, Martin Bandie, who always seemed to be one step ahead of the law when it came to drunk driving, selling drugs, and assaulting his small, defenseless family. This time however, it would finally be different.

An independent witness who wouldn't be bullied had discovered physical evidence that would allow for his immediate arrest. This would lead to a bail hearing, and at a bail hearing Cheryl could request conditions of release be imposed, if in fact Martin was even released this time.

Getting a judge to slap an abstention order on Martin Bandie as a condition of his release would be a routine procedure, given the alleged violence and his past criminal record. Best of all, the outcome of such an order would be highly predictable. A recognizance ordering Martin to abstain from alcohol and drugs until the case went to trial would be like telling a bevy of starving crows to stay away from an open garbage dump. Cheryl could use a stopwatch to measure the time it would take Martin to enter a bar or a liquor vendor after his release. Once Martin breached his recognizance, he would go directly to jail where he could shake with the delirium tremens to his hearts content. Cheryl got up from her desk and picked up the aluminum briefcase that sat under the coat rack, placing it down on top of the paperwork that still covered her desk. She unsnapped the latches, and then opened the case to inspect its contents, checking that it contained rolls of film for the 35mm camera, and that the flash equipment had fresh batteries. Everything looked fine, so she carefully stuffed the equipment back into the molded foam that protected it, then flicked the latches shut. Cheryl walked from her office telling the clerk, Susie, to have a nice weekend if she didn't see her again, which was highly probable, then taking the camera left the red-bricked building for the drive up to Balford.

Twenty minutes later, Cheryl stopped in front of the elementary school, parking the patrol car by the cement steps that led up to the front doors. She entered the building; promptly running onto Mister Quigley, that primordial life form they had for a principal. Cheryl found him in the hallway, scurrying around like a cockroach in a dither, his eyes fluttering like antennae, tuning, searching and puzzling for a reason why the police would be in his school. Cheryl Montague knew all about Mister Quigley, and how he'd been lost in some kind of a time warp, still thinking he lived in the early sixties, when some people considered wife beating and racial discrimination a national pastime. Cheryl of course would eventually have to appraise the aged goat of the incident, but not until she had gathered the facts, had a good look at them, and had Brodie in the safe custody of the social services. In the meantime, Mister Quigley's thin lips trembled as he objected strongly to the intrusion imposed by Sergeant Montague entering his school in such an abrupt manner. The old man nearly choked when he said the word "sergeant," a positive mouthful for his kind, especially when addressing a woman. Why, the old bastard even suggested to Cheryl that next time she write a letter, or maybe even call him first. Cheryl reminded him in a firm voice that if he wasn't party to the solution, then he had to be treated as a contributor to the problem. The principal took great offence to this dressing down, especially from a black woman, so he took his wrinkled old frown then scuttled back into his classroom and shut the door, which suited Cheryl just fine.

Moments later, Judith Noble brought the young retarded boy Brodie out into the hallway, and Cheryl and the social worker led him down to the unoccupied principal's office. The social worker was a young woman whom Cheryl had never met before, but the staff was forever changing due to the low pay and stressful situations they were constantly exposed to. They placed Brodie in a chair and knelt down beside him, so they didn't appear intimidating, and explained to him in simple terms why they were there, and what would be happening to him. After confirming that the child fully understood, they asked if he would mind if they had a look at his backside. Cheryl needed to see first hand the welts that marked the child's buttocks, to establish a prima facie case, providing her with the evidence of reasonable and probable grounds to believe that Martin Bandie had committed a brutal assault. She also had no doubt that Martin was capable of re-offending, which supplied her with the authority to seize Brodie and put him in the custody of an undisclosed safe house.

Cheryl took the camera out of its case at the front counter of the general office so as not to startle the child, then while the flash warmed up explained to him about taking the pictures. They walked Brodie down to the staff washroom, locked the door and stood him on the counter, where he obligingly pulled his pants and underwear down just enough to expose his buttocks. Brodie shook with fear, and it pained both Cheryl and the social worker to look at the red marks that laced his soft flesh. To see an innocent child treated this way tore deep within them, but no emotions passed over their faces, nor did they look at each other. They had seen this sort of thing before, and they would see it again. They both knew if they opened their hearts to any of these victims, they would end up buried in emotions, and soon become victims themselves. Cheryl efficiently took a dozen calculated photographs of Brodie's buttocks from different angles and distances. The photos, combined with a medical report, would be sufficient grounds to take the offence to a criminal trial, although where it went from there would be anyone's guess. Criminal law never has been, nor ever will be an exact science. If somewhere along the course of an investigation something isn't done, appears to stray from the norm, doesn't seem appropriate enough, or the proper asses aren't kissed, then stand by as the appeal gates are flung wide open. Cheryl, like all police officers, became acutely aware of this process many years ago as a rookie. Case law constantly changed the interpretation of an individual's constitutional rights, and what appeared to be an undisputed given on the surface, could easily end up being dissected by the highest court in the land. Then tossed out, just in time for cocktails.

Writing comprehensive reports, seizing and scrutinizing *all* the evidence, and taking detailed notes would be all the investigators could do in the field, and as long as they did their best, they stood to receive a lot less criticism than the law courts. Cheryl treated this investigation as she treated all her files, whether it was simple shoplifting or an attempted murder. She always tried to think ahead, to second guess the defense lawyers, stay one step ahead of their foolish, desperate questions and slick adjournments. Like the majority of all police officers who had sworn an oath, Cheryl felt she owed it to herself, and to the victim's to do her utmost as they were the true beating hearts of every criminal investigation. Once she'd taken the photographs of young Brodie's damaged backside, she asked him what happened, to determine who had done this to him and when. She waited patiently for his reply, then recorded every detail of the disclosure in her issue notebook, including the time and place, as well as who was present. These precise notes would hopefully frustrate any upcoming courtroom insinuations regarding any possibility of coercion.

The interview in the staff washroom had concluded in a matter of minutes. The social worker then carefully explained to Brodie what would happen next, and just why it was going to happen.

When the social worker took the child out to her car for the trip to the medical clinic, Cheryl secured a quick witness statement from Judith. She would obtain a more detailed one later on, but for now, this, and the physical evidence on Brodie's backside would allow her to search the island and arrest Martin Bandie on sight. Cheryl thanked Judith for her timely actions then left the building, returning to her patrol car.

The most obvious haunt to bag a drunken coward would be at the pigsty down at Skinny's Reach, and that's just the direction Cheryl steered her patrol car in. She wasted no time in getting there, for the investigation had only just begun, and the hours left in the day wouldn't be getting any longer. Once she had affected the arrest of Martin Bandie, the work would only just be starting. Cheryl had hours of paperwork ahead of her, all pertaining to Brodie's assault, and whether she could get Martin into custody or not. There were District Attorney reports to be written; a criminal record synopsis to be checked and confirmed; violent crime reporting forms to be completed; victim impact reports to be filled out; more witness statements taken; then the roll of film had to be sent to the lab at headquarters for developing, the request forms obligingly filled out in triplicate. Cheryl would have to interview Martin's struggling wife Nora, who would be considered an accessory to the offence until otherwise cleared. The sooner Cheryl had Martin in custody, the sooner she could start wading into the paperwork, so she took the quicker, lesser known back routes to Skinny's Reach. As she drove up to the front of the pigsty, Sergeant Montague realized that this wouldn't just be an in and out job, not with the slob lying stagnant on his back in the long grass next to the steps. Whoever it was had his fly undone, and his shirt lay open at the sides, his bloated white belly, heavy with beer, flopped to one side like a water balloon. Cheryl could hear the loud snoring from inside the patrol car, and could feel her temper rising as she radioed her location to the telecom center.

Now she was pissed. And pissed could sometimes be a dangerous emotion for a police officer. Cheryl however, had learned to direct her temper, to give it purpose, which brought her moments of focused and controlled energy. God help the first prick that opened his mouth and started with the witless yammering. Virtually everybody in the bar would be blitzed, except maybe for Louie the bartender and the harried waitress, and there could only be one way to handle this situation. Cheryl entered the bar, standing with her back to the door, quickly taking everything in, checking her exits and all possible items that could be used as weapons. The room had a pungent layer of marijuana smoke hanging in the stale air, but Cheryl didn't have the time nor the inclination to start shaking everybody down. Within seconds she had analyzed who might be a problem, and who would roll over and play dead. Martin Bandie wasn't among the crowd, but the bearded wonder in the far corner with the biker's leathers had an attitude fixed to his face and would require close watching. A few of the boys were having a bit of a drunken scrum in the small hallway that led to the filthy washrooms. Louie the bartender, a fat, sweaty individual who preferred loud Hawaiian style shirts was pulling pints as if he were in a race. Just as fast as he could fill the glasses, the pasty-faced waitress put them on a tray and relayed them over to the tables for some serious swilling. At two of the small round tables, the patrons had passed out, their heads flat against the red, gaudy terry cloth that covered the tops. Cheryl watched as the waitress put drinks in front of them, removing the half empty glasses and then taking money from the pile of bills that lay near their heads.

Some of the boys who had been enjoying the thumping in the hallway scrimmage had stopped, taking full note of officer Montague, and her none too pleased facial expressions. The more intelligent ones, and those who could still walk fairly straight, were already heading for the exits, having full regard for what it was like to be stacked like cord wood in the police detachment's drunk tank. Now would be a marvelous time to go have a party at a private house, and give officer Montague all the room she would require to swing that evil baton of hers. Cheryl walked straight over to the bar, and Louie became visibly nervous when she walked behind the counter and glared at him. The pigsty fell into silence as Cheryl pulled the manila colored liquor license from the wall behind the bar, folding it up before placing it in her notebook.

"This shit hole is now closed until further notice," Cheryl announced, her dark eyes scanning the crowd as she spoke. "I'm revoking the liquor license as required under law for the over serving of alcoholic beverages. Each and every one of you is intoxicated, and if you are still here two minutes from now, you will be arrested for being drunk in a public place, and you will spend the next eighteen hours in jail. Questions?"

There was nary a peep as the whole herd, including the bearded wonder with the biker's leathers all rose to their feet and shuffled for the main door. Every one of them was fully aware that officer Montague was capable of carrying out these very real, and perfectly legal threats, and fighting her would only postpone the inevitable they might suffer.

Many already knew they stood to lose more than just their freedom if they failed to comply with Cheryl's ultimatum. Even though the police officer was dreadfully outnumbered, she had some very neat and compact equipment strapped to her black weave leather gun belt. Things that could appear as if by magic, within her steady hands, and with a quick flick, or a short squirt, you would be left gasping, embarking down new avenues of exquisite pain. Officer Montague's instructions weren't up for quibbling, and a few thoughtful ones even helped the two fellows who had passed out at their tables, pocketing their money before whisking them out the door.

Cheryl looked up into Louie's sweating face, and she could smell his acrid body odor from two paces. "You seen Martin Bandie?" She asked.

"Yeah," Louie replied, "he went up Balford way a little while ago, said something about the new waitress up at Riley's."

"Uh, uh," Cheryl nodded. "You come see me on Monday Louie, and we'll talk about your liquor license."

"Do you have to file a report, Cheryl?" Louie asked hopefully.

"Yes, you know I do. And if the owners have a problem with that, they can see me on Monday as well." Cheryl already knew she wouldn't hear so much as a squeak from the bar's owners, who lived far and away on the mainland. After Cheryl had forwarded the applicable paperwork, they would probably be assessed a fine by the licensing board, and ordered closed for a few days.

It would be pocket change for them to pay, and the closure would easily be recouped in beer sales the first hot afternoon. Cheryl had more paperwork to do now with the bar closure, but at least the pigsty would be quiet for the rest of the weekend.

She walked back out onto the street, watching the malcontents as they slithered away to their secret holes to continuing drinking, snorting, and whatever else it was they put into their systems. Even the fat goon who'd been snoring in the grass by the steps had managed to disappear. Cheryl looked to the sky, noticing the rain clouds moving steadily in from the west, and she welcomed their appearance, as the wet weather would keep the crowd from the pigsty off the streets.

Playing in the garden after work had become a wishful dream now that her afternoon had evolved into a series of investigations entailing several different statutes. It had undeniably turned into one of those days, and Cheryl was profoundly aware that her watch was far from over. Not until Martin Bandie was in custody, and the afternoon shift had shown up could she effectively pass the torch. Until then, everything that happened on the island that was of a police nature and got reported, would be her bailiwick. She could only hope that the foolishness had ceased for the time being, and she could once again concentrate on Martin's capture. After climbing back into her patrol car, she advised telecom that all was well, then followed the narrow road out from the bay, taking a different route through the town. She now had to drive out to Balford, so she might just as well drop in at the Bandie residence as it would be on her way, and if she was really lucky, she might find Martin there at the same time. Regardless, as part of Brodie's assault investigation Cheryl had to speak with Brodie's mother Nora, and past experience told her that Nora never strayed far from the hovel she called home.

Once Cheryl left town, the two-lane asphalt road followed the long base of the island's lone mountain peak. It curved back and forth through persistent stands of fir and pine trees, their roots clinging to the craggy, rhino gray bedrock that broke the surface of the dark soil in numerous places. Where the rock hurdled high above the landscape, the road simply skirted around the obstacle, causing sharp corners and numerous dips in the roadway. Although a secondary road, it was a bad place for accidents if you didn't heed the traffic control signs, and Cheryl herself had attended several fatal collisions during the winter months. Like all her associates in law enforcement, she had learned to loathe fatal motor vehicle accidents, and could literally taste the dread on her tongue when the call would come in over the radio. Assisting the volunteer fire department with the extraction of the mauled victims from the tangled wreckage would mark the beginning of what most police officers referred to as "haunters." The investigation into the actual impact, and who was doing what just before the crash could take months, especially if there weren't any survivors to offer any explanation as to what wasn't always obvious. Every gouge, skid, and yaw mark left on the road could speak a great deal about what had happened prior, during, and just after the moment of impact. But they could never tell you the complete story. Someone once said that truth could be stranger than fiction, and that expression would aptly describe a fair amount of fatal collisions.

Most of these investigations would be open for years, with pending lawsuits and letters of request from insurance adjusters, more paper to thicken up the file. Many times the investigator would be subpoenaed to the High Courts to give testimony, reconstructing the terrible collision for a Judge and Jury, using photographs of the contorted wrecks and whatever evidence they had found at the accident scene. On countless occasions, the investigator would try to demonstrate, or reconstruct an accident scene that really couldn't be explained. At their disposal were the scant scrapings they'd taken from the road as evidence, the autopsy reports, and the proven theories on motor vehicle characteristics using the same terrain and weather conditions. These were the ones they called the "haunters," for it was doubtful that divine intervention could even explain them. As Cheryl swung her patrol car through a rise in the road that veered sharply to the left around a large, rocky outcrop, she slowed her vehicle to the recommended speed of twenty miles an hour. The road had been banked with the high point on the outside shoulder of the road, where it formed a relatively steep, man-made gradient. If you chose to ignore the posted cautionary speed limit and the yellow sign warning of a sharp curve ahead, the grade could easily send you flying out into a flat, over grown field of lush ferns.

Cheryl glanced over to the shoulder of the road, and could still see the fluorescent paint marks on the asphalt that she'd made with a spray bomb on a cold, moonless night not two months past.

The fluorescent arrows indicated the start of a set of tire tracks as they gouged the loose gravel where a pick-up truck had vaulted from the road at high speed. Cheryl thought back to that terrible night, as that one had turned into one of those unexplainable haunters and Cheryl couldn't help but think about it every time she drove past the scene. She reflected upon it now as she gazed briefly out onto the open field. She'd been the lone police officer on night shift, catching up on paperwork in the office when the anonymous call had come in. Cheryl had arrived at the accident within five minutes to find that a pick-up truck had left the road and flipped end over end, finally resting a good two-hundred feet from the curve. It landed on its roof in the field of waist high ferns, where it burst into flames.

So violent were the forces of impact that the roof of the cab had been flattened level with the chrome door handles. When Cheryl arrived on the scene the vehicle was fully engulfed, fueled by the ruptured gas tank, lighting up the trees and the horizon like a small sun. Watching helplessly, Cheryl exhausted the two small fire extinguishers that every patrol car carried in its trunk. Like peeing on a volcano, she thought as the second red bottle sputtered the last of its chemical onto the flaming pyre. The fire department had been called, but the volunteers had to drive to the fire hall first, get into their turn out gear, and then respond with a truck to the scene. Two pumper trucks responded from Fire Hall number three, located in Skinny's Reach, but by the time they arrived and got the two-and-a-half inch hoses across the field and charged, they were cooling down the wreck more than they were putting any fires out.

Now they had to open up the smoldering, metal can and extricate whoever had been trapped within the cab. The fire fighters got a portable generator going, then set up square, halogen lights that were mounted on extendable poles, perched high above the field on sturdy tripods. Once they could see what they were doing, they started up the gasoline motor that ran the compressor, and then set to work on the crushed cab, using their hydraulic chisels and Jaws of Life. After fifteen minutes of hammering and expanding the heat-tempered metal, the fire fighters peeled back the driver's door to the find the blackened cab still hot but empty. Just what Cheryl needed right about then, a little mystery. Where the hell was the driver? Moments ago this appeared to be a straightforward fatal accident, complete with incinerated, human remains. She already knew who owned the vehicle; that information she had obtained after the telecom center had checked the license plate she'd found next to the burning heap. Although one should never assume anything in police work, Cheryl thought she had already figured this one out, and had become fairly confident with the conclusions. The owner of the truck was another known troublemaker, and odds were good he'd been returning home from a night of drinking at the pigsty. Emboldened with a belly full of liquor, the driver no doubt took the sharp corner at a speed just slightly slower than the sound barrier.

This had propelled the truck out into the field, giving the occupant one last wild ride of his life.

Cheryl helped the fire fighters turn the floodlights around to face out into the field, and they began a physical sweep through the deep ferns. Walking in a wide, straight line, they encompassed the far reaches of the field where a body could have been thrown from the moving wreck. They found nothing but a brand-new chainsaw that had been flung from the open bed of the truck, and Cheryl recognized it as one of several stolen from a recent break and enter in Skinny's Reach. Cheryl was about to call the telecom center requesting a dog man from the mainland, when the tow truck arrived at the scene. It was now thought that the driver was badly injured, and had wandered off into the dark forest. A police service dog would be the most efficient method to track such a person down before he died of his injuries, if he wasn't already dead. Before she made the call though, Cheryl had the tow truck driver pay his cable out across the field and take a wrap on one of the truck's axles. Returning to his truck, the operator worked the long levers near the back deck, winching the thick cable back onto its greasy drum. As the vehicle was slowly lifted up, Cheryl peered under the hood with her flashlight but saw nothing at first. Then her nose repulsed as the sweet, sickly odor of burned human flesh cloyed within her nostrils.

The vehicle was brought up onto its side, then heaved on until gravity caused it to tip right side up, resting on its metal rims. Two bodies lay in the squashed, scorched ferns, and Cheryl was at least thankful she could still recognize their faces. There would be no delay in notifying their next of kin, a thankless chore that would have to be carried out as soon as she had cleared the scene. Both men lay flat on their stomachs in the field, their hands and feet burned to charred nubs from the intense heat, and just how the hell they got underneath the truck would be the topic of much subsequent debate. When the coroner arrived, he conducted his all-important sniff around the entire situation, nodding his head and smiling wanly at everything Cheryl told him. He eventually ordered the bodies bagged and removed from the scene by an ambulance crew, where they could cool down in the sliding, steel drawers of the hospital's small morgue. Not even the police traffic analyst from headquarters, who came to the scene the following morning could determine how the victims ended up beneath the burning truck. Shaking his head, he carefully stowed his surveyor's clinometer and measuring tapes back in his van, and quietly declared to Cheryl that the whole thing was another haunter. Part of the victims livers that didn't get cooked were taken during the autopsy the next morning, and the lab report Cheryl received days later confirmed that both young men had a blood alcohol level three times the legal limit. The autopsy also revealed that the trapped men had asphyxiated while inhaling super heated gases that seared their lungs, and snuffed the life from their still beating hearts.

Once Cheryl had cleared the accident scene she went to the homes of the deceased, knocking on the front doors, full of immeasurable dread as she waited for the lights to come on. When each door opened, she was greeted by a young wife, half asleep, standing in a housecoat. Cheryl entered each home, and as gently as she could, she delivered the news that would destroy their lives, telling them that their husbands had died in a terrible traffic accident. She held them as they cried uncontrollably, their tears soaking the shoulders of her patrol jacket. One of them had two small children, who peered out from their bedrooms down the hall, running to their mother when the sobbing started. After leaving the small, decimated families behind, Cheryl walked quietly back to her patrol car, thinking how much she hated her goddamned job. She thought this every time she did a next of kin notification, but at least these two didn't get violent like they sometimes do.

Shoot the messenger, it was called. That evening became one of the longest nights of Cheryl's police career, and the sun had just streaked the eastern sky when she finally sat in front of the computer in her office, to start the myriad of forms and reports that always followed these incidents.

Because the vehicle had burned, she would also be required to complete one of those extremely detailed, and extremely asinine fire reports that kept someone employed at the Fire Commissioner's office at the capitol. She already knew that no one read them because as a rookie she had submitted one describing a structure fire in a dollhouse. She had listed the two victims as Ken and Barbie, found in the act of copulation, melted together on the kitchen table. In the brief narrative, Cheryl had described how a jealous Mister Potato-Head, who lusted after Barbie, had torched the place after peeking through the kitchen window. No one at the Fire Commissioner's office ever twigged onto that report, but policy was policy, and redundant, idiotic forms were just that. By midmorning Cheryl had finished most of the initial reports, then had the day shift member drive her home, as she was too tired to continue. She let the cool morning air play on her face through the open window of the patrol car, saying little to the driver. Watching the forests of pine trees rolling by were like a tonic, for she felt both drained, but relieved that the worst of the incident was now behind her. She wouldn't have to attend any of the autopsies as no charges were going to be laid, unless you considered stupidity unlawful. Unfortunately though, the macabre results of the accident hadn't ended with the removal of the bodies and the charred truck. There would be one more episode to follow this misadventure, something that would only add to the puzzle, further confusing the circumstances that already surrounded the whole, unfortunate event.

In the days that followed, Cheryl had come to call the investigation the weenie roast (within the sacred confines of the office) and the 'foot' incident she described on a continuation report. That particular incident became page one-hundred-and-seven, volume two of a rapidly thickening file. Referring to a double fatal accident as a weenie roast was nothing more than a standard, gallows humor response, and an invisible coat of armor that every police officer used to keep any horrific memories at bay. Nonetheless, Cheryl viewed the 'foot' affair as somewhat humorous, and had even gone on to call it the "guess what the dog brought home for supper," adventure.

An old man lived in a cabin about a mile up the road from the accident scene, and four days after that terrible evening, his golden Labrador retriever, whom he called Fred, had brought something home to play with. The old man noticed a rather ripe stench when he went out to fetch some firewood from the porch, and took a closer look at just what it was that Fred was lolling his tongue over. It was a human foot and Fred had found it during his daily travels, which happened to include peeing on a certain fern that stood only feet from where the truck had crashed and burned. Fred was a well cared for animal, given all the kibbles and bits he could scoff back, and kept warm at night on a thick blanket by a hot stove. Dogs however, will be dogs, and bringing things home was to be their instinctual nature.

Just which accident victim the foot belonged to didn't matter much as they were both dead, and returning it to the rightful owner wouldn't change a thing. Cheryl drove down to the old man's cabin and obligingly put the foot into a clear, plastic exhibit bag, then thanked the old man for his concern, giving Fred an encouraging scratch behind his ears before leaving with her little package. The foot she disposed of in the incinerator at the local hospital and nothing more was said about it. Like all fatal motor vehicle accidents, not a lot of good comes out of them, nothing ever does. Except with this one there were now two less undesirables on the island for the police to deal with. A slightly encouraging ratio, it never stood for very long though, and Cheryl had learned years ago to view modern policing as a mystical vacuum of sorts. Your community would no sooner rid itself of two reprobates, and four more would be sucked into the previously occupied time and space.

Ah well, at least Cheryl wouldn't be laying any charges in this case, an exercise that would have involved filling out endless pages of court briefs. Nevertheless, the file would drag on for some time and would be considered "still under investigation" months from now. Almost eight weeks had passed since the night of the accident, and Cheryl still awaited written accounts from various agencies. The mechanical reports had yet to be received, the traffic analyst forms were apparently in the mail, and until the coroner got off his ample backside and forwarded his completed revelations, the file would remain open. A haunter. Cheryl smiled wryly as she drove her patrol car through the abrupt corner where the accident had taken place. The ferns had already grown back in with the warm weather of late spring, and there was nothing left to indicate the spot in the field where the truck had burned.

The road widened just after the dangerous curve, straightening out and opening up to green fields of tall quack grass that rolled out to the base of the solitary mountain. No sooner was the curve in her rear view mirror, and Cheryl had forgotten all about the fatal accident. She had to remain focused on the investigation at hand, and the impending arrest of Martin Bandie. This would require her to be fully alert, an absolute state of mind anytime a uniformed police officer walked onto the Bandie property. Martin Bandie had inherited the acreage from his father Wally, who had died from cirrhosis of the liver a few years ago. Martin had also inherited from his old man the drinking habits, volatile temper, as well as the high-powered rifles. Ideally, the best place to arrest Martin Bandie would be at a routine vehicle check, where Cheryl could use her patrol car as a protective block, and have some control over the situation. She thought of her options as she drove past the small cabin where the old man who'd found the foot lived. Cheryl glanced over and could see him raking a small patch of dirt he had for a garden. He waved to her as he spotted the marked patrol car, and she returned the wave, noting that his dog Fred slept peacefully on the front porch. The bottoms of the rain clouds had finally opened up, and a light drizzle fell, misting over the countryside, forcing Cheryl to put the wipers on, smearing the pus-colored guts of the dead bugs across her windshield.

A couple of miles further up the road, Cheryl pulled her patrol car over and stopped on the gravel shoulder, gazing up at the Bandie spread, a good four-hundred meters in the distance. A ratty old single-wide trailer stood atop a gentle sloping knoll, with a unpainted, plywood Joey shack built along the side, forming a mud room and a front porch. The trailer stood in the middle of an expansive orchard that hadn't been pruned or cared for since Moses was a lad. All the branches on the rows of apple trees grew wild, their spindly shoots and blossoms mingling with each other, the roots below the soil competing for whatever moisture fell from the skies. Cheryl studied the faded aluminum sides of the kiwi-colored trailer, searching for signs of life, noting with some relief that Martin's pick-up truck was absent from the yard. Good she thought, for whatever else came out of this day, she wouldn't have to take Martin down on his own turf, something she'd rather avoid if at all possible. Cheryl pulled back onto the road and drove her patrol car at a healthy clip toward the open metal gates of the Bandie property. She slowed the car only slightly as she came even with the gate, then cut sharply to her left, accelerating up the two dirt ruts that formed a road through the orchard. The orderly rows of trees offered little cover as Cheryl approached the trailer, and she knew her only ally at this point would be some speed. If Martin *was* home, and was watching from the greasy panes of his front window, the less time he had to react to Cheryl's approach, the better. As she flew over the sharp dips and swung through the abrupt curves of the trail, Cheryl held the microphone to her mouth, advising the telecom section of her location, requesting they check on her in five minutes.

Within seconds the patrol car crested the top of the small hill where a clearing opened up in the orchard for the singlewide trailer. Refuse lay scattered around outside of the house, and clouds of large blue bottle flies hovered over some of the more succulent pieces of rotting food, jockeying to lay their eggs. White garbage bags lay in every corner of the yard, shredded open to expose their treasures to the scavenging animals and insects. An old fridge and stove lay beside the open, slatted walls of a wood shed, their sides punctured with bullet holes, the little craters rusting where the enameled paint had chipped off. Cheryl wondered briefly if the target practice had taken place inside the home, or outside in the yard, as either location was dangerous should a stray bullet find a distant, unsuspecting mark. After stopping the car next to the Joey shack, Cheryl quickly got out of her patrol car, turned on the portable radio mounted to her gun belt, then climbed the short flight of two by ten steps to the wooden door. She knocked several times, then stepped to one side of the door frame, giving her self some clearance should anything antagonistic come flying at her from the other side. Cardboard boxes full of empty beer bottles lay stacked on the steps, and some of the sides had rotted away, spilling dozens of the brown, tall-necked bottles onto the ground. The smell of decaying garbage, dog dirt and animal urine permeated the air around the house, and it became even more intense when the door to the Joey shack opened, allowing an invisible wave of tepid stink to waft over Cheryl's face.

Martin's wife Nora stood in the open doorway, looking down at Cheryl, and a more wretched human being you'd not find anywhere else on the island. Nora stood dressed in dirty, light blue shorts and a white tank top that displayed blotches of crusted blood and other stains whose origin Cheryl didn't even want to think about. Her pale legs were dirty, covered with little red sores just below her knees, where the fleas that invested the damp carpeting inside had bitten her.

Cheryl knew they had a couple of big dogs, and she could see one of them, lying torpid on the floor against one wall of the Joey shack, next to the cold wood stove. The dog's brown hair was all matted together in tight knots that hung like large tumors from its panting belly, and dried mud patched the fur along it's back. Inside the Joey shack a thick rug had been laid over the plywood sub-floor, except where the wood stove sat, and Cheryl could almost see the teeming fleas jumping gleefully from their soiled jungle. On a far corner of the rug lay a freshly coiled dog stool; at least Cheryl *hoped* it was a dog stool. The whole place had become an unimaginative statement on self-imposed poverty, a tribute to what one could truly achieve if one really didn't try. Any wee doubts that Cheryl might have had about seizing young Brodie Bandie at school and turning him over to social services had been chased completely from her mind. Unfortunately, the young retarded lad hadn't been Martin's only victim, and like a lot of domestic violence, it usually didn't end with just one. If there were two or three defenseless people living under one roof, the aggressor was quite likely to share his physical fury. Cheryl could plainly see that as she stood on the front steps, looking into Nora's battered face.

She was a slim woman, with short brown hair that was as matted as the dogs, and Cheryl could see a pretty face hidden under all the years of abusive pummeling and enduring anguish. Nora's shoulders were badly bruised around the loops of her tank top, and Cheryl could nearly make out the slender finger marks where Martin had grabbed her and probably shaken her senseless.

Her right eye was swollen shut, that whole side of her face was puffy and tender; the color of purple mulberries, and her bottom lip had been split open. Dark spots of fresh blood blotted the fabric of her shorts around her crotch and Cheryl's experienced eyes told her that she'd been assaulted there too. Everything about the Bandie place, including the beaten young woman who stood at the door, had become drenched in human despair, and nothing short of a large fire could ever cleanse it.

"Hello Nora, is Martin home?" Cheryl asked.

Nora shook her head slowly, her one, undamaged eye flickering with fear.

"Did Martin do this to you, Nora, did he assault you again?"

Again Nora shook her head, her lips starting to tremble. The last thing she needed was a police officer showing up at the front door, especially if Martin were to return home about now.

Justifiably, she was near the point of despair.

"Why don't you come with *me*, Nora, I'll drive you down to the hospital, then I'll get you into a safe house," Cheryl offered. She already knew the answer, she'd heard it countless times before, but she had a duty as a peace officer, and more importantly as a human being, to present the options. Once again Nora shook her head . . . no.

This had become a typical response that Cheryl had come to expect from her. Nora rarely said more than five words at once, and when she did, her voice came out quiet and hollow sounding, its tone indicative of abject surrender.

Nora Bandie had become a woman who had given up on life after years of beatings and endless intimidation. She didn't live anymore, she merely existed in a painful isolation, and Cheryl suspected that her son Brodie was the only reason Nora hadn't put one of Martin's rifles to her head. Despite all the social safety nets, Martin held some sort of a vicious spell over Nora, and she had resigned herself and young Brodie to tread within the dreadful rut that had become their lot in life. Until now.

Until Sergeant Cheryl Montague had arrived on Nora's front porch with the authority and the evidence to arrest Martin Bandie. Even the most liberal minded Judges took a dim view of child abuse, and a couple of years in the pokey would be an achievable prediction for Martin's near future. Things were about to drastically change, whether Nora liked it or not, and Cheryl quietly pointed these facts out to her.

"Nora, Martin has assaulted Brodie, it was discovered at school today by his teacher."

Nora nodded this time, covering her mouth with a hand, her whole body starting to shake.

"I've seized Brodie under the Child Welfare Act, and I've turned him over to social services." This bit of bad news reduced Nora to open tears. Brodie was all she had left in this rotten world, the only bright spot within that terrible, black cloak that had become her entity. Without Brodie, she had nothing to warm her soul, nothing to exist for, no reason to even carry on. Cheryl recognized the woman's mounting grief, and had already discounted her as having any part of the assault on the child. Nora probably received her own beating when she tried to intervene when Martin whipped the boy. The situation was still salvageable, and Cheryl knew she had to give Nora some hope, something to cling to else Brodie be left without a mother as well.

"Listen to me Nora," Cheryl continued gently, "you now stand to lose your child, but you can probably keep him if you make some changes. You and Brodie can't keep living here, not under these conditions. If you want to keep Brodie I'm going to need your cooperation, as well as some assurances from you. Once I find Martin I'll be arresting him, and I'll be requesting he be kept in custody for you and Brodie's safety. With any luck, he'll be put away for some time. But you're going to have to move from here, probably even leave the island altogether, and I'll do anything I can to help you. Do you understand what I'm telling you, Nora?"

Nora nodded as the tears rolled down her face, dropping from the end of her chin, falling to her dirty feet and the carpet below. Her body shook as the sobs overwhelmed her, replacing all her physical pain with the distress that she might lose her child.

"This abuse has gone on long enough Nora. It's time it was stopped. . You're going to have to be very strong now, as well as brave, if only for Brodie's sake. Are you sure you don't want to go to the hospital?"

"No," Nora said softly.

"If Martin returns home before I find him, I want you to call 911, and I'll come right over. I have to arrest him, and charges will be laid this time . . . all right Nora?"

"Yes, I understand."

"Does Martin have any of his guns with him?" Cheryl asked.

"No," Nora replied.

"Good, I'll let you know once I have Martin in custody, then we'll talk about your next move."

Nora nodded, then turned from the door, slowly closing it.

Cheryl walked down the steps, just as the light drizzle turned to steady rain, forming dark spots the size of quarters on the light blue of her uniform shirt. She climbed back into her patrol car just as the telecom center called on the radio to check up on her. She answered them using the small microphone that was attached to her portable radio. It hung from a leather strap at one of her epaulettes, and she could speak into it with just a slight turn of her head. Cheryl advised them she was back in service, and would be patrolling the island for an assault suspect. After starting the car she maneuvered it back and forth a few times over the piles of strewn garbage to get it turned around. Life didn't get any sadder than this she thought as she drove slowly from the trailer, threading her way back through the orchard. Cheryl dearly hoped she would find Martin Bandie, and find him quickly. She also hoped that when she did, he would resist arrest, so she could kiss the side of his skull with the round tip of her expandable, metal baton. Cheryl turned left when she got to the main road, and drove north through the rain, heading in the direction of Balford, and Riley's Pub. Night would fall early today, now that the clouds had effectively filtered out the sunlight,

71

and as she drove, Cheryl thought once again what a frenzied kind of a day it had been.

It wasn't over yet though, and she cautiously reminded herself of that as she followed the wet gravel road up the center of the island. Had Sergeant Montague a crystal ball she would have realized that her day was only just starting, despite her regular shift having ended nearly a half hour ago. Regardless, it wouldn't have made any difference. It wasn't like she could take her toys, go home, and forget about everything until Monday morning. The policing of small, semi-isolated communities never seemed to work in conjunction with whatever you had carefully planned as a shift schedule. They never have . . . and undoubtedly they never will.

*   *   *

Chapter Six

Martin Bandie felt really good after throwing the rock through the front door of Riley's pub, a just and fitting culmination to an unsuccessful afternoon. Martin wasn't a quitter though, not by any scope of the definition. He'd already planned to hit up Harvey the hippie type some other time for a position with his lucrative marijuana exporting business. As far as the delectable waitress Nancy was concerned, he knew where she lived, above the five and dime store in an apartment down in Skinny's Reach. Martin had all summer to get her, whether she wanted him or not, and he might even take her one night when she drove home from the pub. He thought and schemed about all this as he drove his decrepit old pick-up truck south through the rain, taking the secondary gravel road that the cops rarely frequented.

Martin was really shit-faced this time, and he knew it.

Drinking that pint of whisky on the drive up from the pigsty at Skinny's Reach probably wasn't such a good idea. Martin had become quit talented at pacing himself when it came to ingesting liquor and narcotics. Although now he figured he'd taken one snort too many of the cocaine that Louie the bartender had sold him down at the sty. Even the dopey, ceramic dog with the brown velvet fur and the bobbing head that sat on his dashboard became all blurry when he tried to squint at it. He shouldn't have been driving, but he was in no condition to walk. Martin chuckled to himself when he mulled over this bit of brainless reasoning. He could be a sharp thinker when he applied himself, and he'd have to remember that one for the boys at the bar.

The windshield wipers on the truck didn't work, and this made driving in the rain all the more precarious, but he'd had the truck in the pumpkin patch before and just as sure as he was that he'd been born with two livers, he'd have it there again. He'd never even bruised himself on the occasions when he had left the road, but this afternoon it wouldn't be such a good idea, as he'd be left with a long, wet, walk home. Martin had meant to fix the windshield wipers during several inspiring moments, but it required a new thing-a-ma-bob, and he preferred to spend his money on more important things, like liquor, cocaine, and cigarettes. He slowed the weaving truck right down and was forced to drive with his head out of the open window so he could see where he was going. It pissed him off because his face was soon soaked and he couldn't smoke. The cramps that jabbed deep within his guts did nothing for his dark moods either, and if they didn't stop soon enough, he'd have to find a piece of bush to get behind and drop his drawers. Martin had a bad case of the "rum trots." It was an affliction of the lower intestine that most chronic alcoholics suffered in their attempts to get more liquor into their stomachs than food. A veteran drunk like Martin knew that food only delayed the absorption of alcohol and drugs into his blood system, which would invariably stall the sought after, intoxicating effects. Consequently, he ate very little, and anything he might have eaten when he wasn't quaffing liquor, or inhaling stuff through his nose, eventually turned into sharp pains, followed by loose, watery bowels. Not until after Martin had a good brew on, and was coasting along nicely on a euphoric high would he even start thinking about something to eat, like about now. Although by now, whatever he'd eaten for breakfast had stewed into a brown, acidic river that was screaming to get out.

Martin squeezed together the muscles of his buttocks as he drove, attempting to clamp down on his sphincter, holding everything in, feeling the liquid gurgling and pressing as it searched for an exit. The bowel dilemma and ensuing pain had used up the last of Martin's drunken concentration, so he failed to notice the white, marked police car to his right-hand side when he blew through the stop sign at one of the more remote intersections. Sergeant Cheryl Montague watched on as the old red truck sped over the crown of the intersection, proceeding southeast in the direction of the country junction store.

"Oh joyous bode . . . you Gomer." Cheryl said aloud to herself. She immediately recognized the vehicle, she'd pulled it over enough times in the past, and she had already presumed that Martin would be drunk. Cheryl accelerated from the intersection, quickly catching up to the truck, following a few car lengths behind it. She started taking mental notes of Martin's driving patterns for corroborating evidence, aiming for an airtight impaired driving charge. The fool didn't even know that Cheryl was behind him. She could see him driving along with his head hanging out the window, like some elated dog being taken to a park. Martin's vehicle had become what a lot of police officers referred to as a highway patrolman's dream, because just checking the vehicle would bring you some pleasure. If it had been a slow shift, stopping the Bandie truck guaranteed you at least a half dozen motor vehicle act charges, and a handful of fix-it slips. Cheryl could see numerous infractions by just following the rolling wreck. The back license plate was improperly attached, swinging from the frame by a single bolt; the rear tires were bald; the bumper was missing; there was no rear view mirror on the driver's side; the front windshield was cracked; and there was crap rolling around the bed of the truck with no tailgate to keep it all in there. Yes indeed, officer Montague would be exhausting a ballpoint pen or two once she'd finished writing Martin up. But only after she'd arrested him, lodged him into cells, and had impounded his vehicle as a public safety hazard.

As they neared the country junction store, Cheryl had seen enough swaying and wandering to form the opinion that the driver of the red truck in front of her might just possibly be impaired. Reaching down to just above the radio, she flicked a toggle switch, activating the aerodynamic light bar on the roof of her patrol car. The red, blue, and white flashing strobe lights were so bright and intense that Cheryl could see their beacons reflecting off the steady wall of rain, extending well past the front of Martin's pick-up truck. She would give him a moment to pull over, and if he didn't, she would activate the piercing wail of the siren, which would leave no doubt to anybody of her true meaning. Martin had noticed the lights, just as soon as Cheryl had turned them on, and he had nearly driven his vehicle into the ditch as he craned his head around to see who the cop was.

Bad news he thought, it was that nigger-bitch-cop, Aunt Jemima. She'd run him up the flagpole of the nearest penitentiary and leave him there. No amount of ass kissing or pleading would sway her toward pitying a poor, unemployed white boy on social assistance, who had a wife and a retarded child to feed. Martin had a better chance of becoming a field operator for the CIA than of harvesting any sympathy from Officer Montague. Regardless, Martin promptly pulled his truck over to the side of the road and came to a stop.

He would have to play this one as it unfolded, maybe leg it across the open field or drop the cop with a hearty kick to the crotch. It always silenced his wife Nora. The one thing that Martin could be certain of at this particular time was the fact that he wouldn't be going into custody. Being arrested this time would be non-negotiable, and fighting Officer Montague, or simply fleeing from her were the only two options available to him. Last time he had appeared in front of that hard-nosed prick the island had for a Circuit Court Judge, he had gone to jail for a few months for driving while under the influence. As well, the judge had given him a ribald dressing down in front of a packed docket. He'd called Martin everything but a human being, and had made it quite clear that if Martin ever graced his courtroom again as an accused, he'd be heading for the drain, and for at least eighteen months. Jail most certainly wasn't on any of Martin's agendas, not after the last tour. There he had suffered incarceration on the mainland without so much as a sniff of liquor. Then a few of the big boys had entered his cell, bending him over the bottom bunk and holding him down, so their leader could drop his pants and roger him from behind. Nope, Martin wouldn't be going back, not this time, although he had a problem or two to contend with first.

For one thing he was really loaded, and Officer Montague could smell an impaired driver from her backyard while on her days off. This would make it his fifth impaired driving charge in as many years. Martin could almost hear the judge's admonishing voice in his head, with its deep, Scottish brogue haranguing him in packed courtroom before sending him back to jail. The boiling diarrhea in his guts further reminded him of the calamities that prison could impose upon his tender ass.

Cheryl stopped her patrol car directly behind Martin's truck, positioning herself so she could still see the rear wheels of his vehicle, and the center of her hood was in line with his driver's door.

This gave her an optimum view of the suspect vehicle, as well as placing the three hundred and fifty cubic inch engine between herself and any firearms that might hastily appear. Complacency killed a lot of police officers, and if the worst were to happen to Cheryl, then at least the investigators could conclude that despite all precautions - fate, and not a simple error, had taken her life. She had already radioed her location and Martin's vehicle description to the telecom center, and had advised the operator that the suspect was known for violence, which told them that Cheryl could reasonably expect trouble. The telecom operator would already be running the license plate on her computer, obtaining within seconds everything one would ever wish to know about Martin Bandie. Cheryl climbed out of her patrol car, maintaining observation on Martin while she reached behind to her gun belt to turn her portable radio on. She had left her uniform hat behind on the passenger seat, even though it would have shielded the rain from her eyes.

You never wear your hat into bars, and you never wear it to a street fight. Too many souvenir hunters picking at your gear when it fell off during a tussle, and too many reports to fill out once you'd lost it. Cheryl walked steadily over to the pick-up truck, maintaining vigilance on Martin and his hand movements. Although she carried an assortment of weapons on her gun belt, Cheryl kept all these weapons secured and snapped in their black, basket weave holsters. If a fight started, Cheryl would decide at that time the applicable weapon, and the amount of force she would use to dissuade any further resistance. She also carried a practiced knowledge of ground fighting, which entailed using everything at her disposal, including her finger nails, at any area she could reach including a suspect's soft eyes or undefended genitals.

As an upholder of justice, and a fighter of crime and/or evil, Cheryl treated all offenders and suspects with the same courtesy and respect, even if she knew she would be arresting them. Drunk or sober, Martin Bandie *would* be arrested for the assault of his young son Brodie, and if he was found to be intoxicated (which would be a sure thing) then a driving while under the influence charge would make the effort really worthwhile. Whenever Cheryl approached a driver in a vehicle stop, she always started the officer/violator contact using polite and casual conversation. She never tipped them off to what she knew, and if she had to make an arrest, she waited until the moment was right, usually after they'd been lulled into thinking she stopped them for a simple traffic violation. Pulling a driver you've just arrested from behind the wheel of a motor vehicle while they fought you was never a good exercise for healthy back maintenance. Progressive force however, whenever viable, was always employed, which meant the first steps would be verbal commands. Quite often they would go to the back of your patrol car willingly, obeying your instructions to the very vowel as you handcuffed and searched them. And sometimes you would be in the dirt, on your hands and knees, fighting for your dignity and possibly even your life. This roadside check would be no different from any other, and Cheryl would start out by being verbally professional, as well as polite with young Martin. If perchance, he started to get rowdy, then the formalities would be dropped, and she would get down to the business at hand. As she got to the cab of Martin's truck, Cheryl stopped with the door handle just to her front. This forced him to turn around to look at her, and foiled any plans he may have had of forcing the door open in an attempt to knock her down.

"Good afternoon, Martin," Cheryl began, "Do you know why you've been pulled over?"
Martin cranked his head around to look at her, and the way it wobbled on his dirty neck, as well as the vacant look he beheld in his glassy brown eyes told Cheryl he wouldn't be doing much fighting.

"No," Martin said, "why'd ya pooh me o'er?" Even his lips were jerking, almost spasmodically as he tripped over his words, and the rank odor of stagnant liquor rolled over Cheryl's face despite the rain. This was good she thought, I won't have to bother with those goddamned sobriety tests the Supreme Court ruled as mandatory if the level of intoxication was questionable.

There were no questions here. Martin was definitely drunk.

"I've stopped you," she continued, "because I have reasonable and probable grounds to believe that you have . . . "

Cheryl was about to dispense with the idle chitchat and arrest Martin while he could still walk, but then the telecom operator called her on the portable radio. She tilted her head over to the small microphone that hung from her shoulder epaulette, answering the call while maintaining eye contact with Martin.

"Sixteen-bravo-four go ahead." Cheryl pushed the small microphone button as she spoke, phonetically pronouncing the permanent call sign appointed to her patrol car. She released the button as soon as she'd transmitted the message, and the telecom operator answered right away. The operator's voice was suddenly full of static and badly garbled.

"Sixteen-bravo-four, say again," Cheryl, repeated.

The distorted voice came back once again, the static overriding and scratching the transmission.

Cheryl glanced around, noticing that she had stopped Martin in a small dip in the road, and the small, stubby antenna mounted to her portable radio didn't have the range to transmit or to receive. She could either walk to a higher location or use the more powerful radio in her patrol car. Either way, she had to answer them as something more urgent than Martin Bandie could be taking place somewhere else. Cheryl glanced down at Martin, whose head had started to bob against his chest, and she exploited his lagging consciousness by jogging back the twenty feet or so to her patrol car.

Opening the door, she reached in and keyed the repeater on the radio, throwing open the channel. Cheryl pulled the microphone from the metal clip on the dashboard, standing by the open door as she spoke to the telecom operator. Martin's head continued to bow up and down on his chest, like he was some sort of a puppet. The telecom girl advised Cheryl that another operator in the center had received a complaint about five minutes ago from Riley's Pub in Balford. Apparently an intoxicated Martin Bandie had flung a rock through the glass door of the establishment after being thrown out for becoming belligerent. Cheryl acknowledged the complaint, and then reached back into the car, returning the microphone to the dashboard clip. She glanced at her sport watch. Four-thirty-seven was the exact, numerical time reading under the crystal face. Things couldn't get any better than this she thought. On top of the assault causing bodily harm file, there would now be a drunk driving charge, as well as a willful damage complaint against Martin. All of which should suitably impress the Circuit Court Judge to no end.

Without any warning, Cheryl saw Martin moving against the outer edge of her field of vision, and she instinctively knew what he was doing and why. The rear wheels of the pick-up abruptly spun onto motion, spewing pea gravel and wet sand onto the windshield and hood of the patrol car as it careened off down the road. This put a terrifying slant onto what seconds ago had still been a peaceful, rainy, Friday afternoon on the island. Instantly, the adrenalin started dumping into Cheryl's charged system, causing a sharp pain in her lower back as she scrambled back into her patrol car. Within seconds she had taken up the chase, engaging her siren to complement her overhead lights, giving the motoring public all the warning she could, hoping to Christ she could stop Martin Bandie before something dreadful happened. Cheryl's patrol car immediately snagged onto the rear of Martin's truck, aggressively pacing the fleeing vehicle. They blew through the four-way stop sign at the country junction store, flying down the gravel road in a southeasterly direction. Ben Trilby, the ex-policeman and current owner of the store stood on the covered wooden porch, ceasing his sweeping motions and leaning momentarily on his corn broom as he watched the high speed chase unfold. Both vehicles cleared the intersection and quickly disappeared behind the stand of alder trees, speeding down the island's secondary road. The penetrating sound of the siren bounced off Ben's skull, the repetitive screaming quickly fading in the distance within the defined scope of the Doppler effect. I don't miss that shit one bit, Ben thought, shaking his head before he continued with his peaceful chore.

Cheryl could feel her vehicle's center of gravity shift as the car bounded over the intersection, and she was glad her view was clear for hundreds of meters before her and Martin had throttled through it. She had already advised the telecom center of the high-speed chase, holding the microphone in her hand as she steered the patrol car through its progressive strides. Her clipped announcement had cleared the air of other radio traffic and got the back-up recording machines rolling, taping all conversation and marking the times as the tense event unfolded. As the gravel road dropped through sloping corners, Cheryl took her car to the inside lane, hugging the bottom of the road, and accelerating rapidly as the vehicle climbed out of the dip. All police patrol cars come from the factory with heavy-duty sway bars and significantly fortified shock absorbers and coil suspensions. Combined with the proper training, the average criminal didn't have any chance of losing a police officer in a high-speed chase. That wasn't the concern though. Speed, as well as Martin's advanced state of intoxication had become Cheryl's biggest problem, both for Martin and anyone else who might be using the road. The fact that Martin's vehicle was a mechanical nightmare, and the present manner in which he bombed across the island did nothing for Cheryl's precarious cause. On several of the curves he nearly lost control, the truck lurching dangerously toward the top end of each corner. If one of his wheels caught in the soft dirt, the vehicle would cartwheel into the brambles, and there wouldn't be a lot that would save Martin from certain death.

Cheryl was alarmed when they rounded another corner onto a straight section and she glanced at the flat, compact radar unit that sat on the dashboard above the steering wheel. The red, digital figures that constantly and accurately displayed her patrol speed showed the pursuit at eighty-two miles per hour. Martin constantly craned his head out the window of his truck, looking to see where he was going, and each attempt brought him closer to disaster. Cheryl had become painfully cognizant that if another vehicle appeared from the other direction, this assertive chase would instantly turn to anguished mayhem. As the pursuit progressed, Cheryl called out the speeds and her location into the microphone, transmitting to the computers as they recorded her calm voice and careful account. Knowledge of the area, as well as the increasing speed convinced Cheryl to call the chase off. About a mile ahead lay a sharp corner; down near the Noble residence, and with a posted speed of twenty-miles per hour, it suddenly became imperative that Cheryl persuade Martin to slow his vehicle down. Promptly, she pulled her patrol car over to the side of the road and turned off all her emergency equipment, leaving no doubt to the escaping felon, and anyone else, that she had terminated the pursuit. She watched as the red pick-up truck raced away in the distance, barreling in the direction of the sharp corner.

"Telecom, sixteen-bravo-four, high pursuit terminated. Time check?" Cheryl asked.

"Telecom, ten-four. Pursuit terminated sixty-two seconds after initiation."

"Ten-four," Cheryl replied, "thank-you."

She leaned over the passenger seat to make a couple of notations on some foolscap when she heard a loud bang, and a powerful shock wave caused the windshield of her patrol car to vibrate within its frame. Ah fuck, Cheryl thought. She had been a police officer long enough to know the forbidding significance behind that bang, and that her day had just gone from manageable to borderline impossible. "Expect the unexpected," an instructor at the police academy had told her graduating class so many years ago.

"And when that happens," he added, "you can then expect the situation to get worse."

Cheryl accelerated the patrol car back onto the road, re engaging her lights and siren, making good all possible speed down to the accident scene, hoping against all odds she didn't have another fatal accident to contend with. She advised telecom of the possible accident, and requested they get a paramedic unit rolling from the ambulance hall located at the north end of the island.

Cheryl covered the mile of open road that led into the extreme corner within moments, and she could once again feel the adrenalin flooding her system, causing the stabbing pain to return to the small of her back. She took her patrol car through the corner at twice the posted speed limit, but the finely tuned vehicle stuck to the road as if it were affixed to a set of rails. Both sides of the curving roadway were dense with forests of tall pine trees, but Cheryl noticed a red smear through a gap in the woods on her left-hand side, next to the Noble property. Gently she applied the anti- lock brakes as she swung through the corner, controlling her drift while at the same time slowing her patrol car down.

Cheryl stopped her vehicle when she came to the demolished truck, advising telecom she would be out on foot with her portable radio. Martin's truck had wrapped its front end around a power pole, snapping it in half, toppling the thick, creosote-dipped pillar down onto the cab, caving in the middle of the roof as well as flailing out some live wires. Steam hissed from the open top of the engine compartment as coolant sprayed from the cracked block onto the hot exhaust.

Country and western music spilled out over the scene as a cassette tape continued to play from somewhere within the smashed vehicle, and the music playing was one of those guitars that howled sadly as it twanged along in four-four time. The soprano singer sounded as if he'd just been castrated while he chanted piteously his simple lyrics, relating a sad story about how his "gal had just done left him." Cheryl was soon reminded of long fingernails scraping down the flat surface of a blackboard and she remembered why she disliked the screeching, artless music, and anyone who played or listened to it. From where she stood surveying the scene, she already knew there wouldn't be much life left inside the vehicle, although she could see Martin's head through the back of the truck even though the cab had it folded itself around the pole. The rear window had burst out on impact and had shattered when it flopped onto the road.

Live wires were popping and sizzling in the tall grass about twenty meters down from the truck, so Cheryl carefully picked her way through the ditch and out to the vehicle.

Calling telecom back on her portable radio, she requested the power company attend, and by this time she had walked up to the wrecked truck, and then requested they call the coroner as well. Martin was dead, and of that fact Cheryl was absolutely certain. She also asked that the volunteer fire department attend to the scene, as it would take everything they had, and then some, to extricate Martin's squashed body. Large amounts of energy, and vehicle accidents worked in mysterious ways, and Cheryl took a moment to view the devastation, taking it all in while allowing her pulse to slow down. The steering wheel on the old truck had been driven into Martin's mid section as the column was driven through the firewall by the force of the collision. He had been effectively pinned by the wheel against the rear wall of the cab where it enveloped his inert form. The driver's door had been peeled off the vehicle, and where it presently lay would be any body's guess, but it would make extrication easier and Cheryl had an unobstructed view of Martin's compressed body. Three of his ribs had cracked almost in half, sticking out rudely through the ruptured skin where his white tee shirt had been torn free. They were held together where they had snapped with just splintered bone and stringy muscles. His face looked like a mash of dark, ripe berries, and his whole upper lip had been ripped away, including most of his nose. Martin's left leg was missing about a foot below his kneecap, the whole stub exposed as the blue jeans that covered that portion had gone with the appendage. On top of everything else that was going on, Cheryl would have to go looking for the missing limb, that's if one of the local dogs hadn't already dragged it home. Of all Martin's injuries, the missing limb told Cheryl that the destruction was definite, and most indeed fatal.

Martin Bandie's twenty-four years of horrible luck had just come to an abrupt end.

The corky, scarlet pulp of the bone marrow hung below the dismembered leg, it's cloven, bluish blood veins and the reddish arteries lay like lifeless worms against the beef colored muscle, which appeared swollen where it stuck to the bone. It was the lack of blood spurting from the ruined arteries that indicated to Cheryl that Martin's heart had stopped beating, no longer pumping his life giving blood. The steering wheel had crushed his chest cavity, undoubtedly exploding most of the internal organs, melding them into a clotted mass, arresting them of their critical functions.

Cheryl could also smell feces, the odor warm and heavy in the wet air, and when she glanced down at the vinyl covering on the driver's seat, the pant leg of Martin's thigh was stained brown from a watery, fecal river that had blown from his bowels upon his death. The noxious liquid flowed down the bottom of his pant leg, dripping off the end of his severed leg like a slow tap, forming a brown pool on the rubber floor mat. If Martin had put on clean underwear this morning Cheryl thought, it was now a complete waste of time. There was never much dignity in a violent death, and Cheryl wasn't sure which bothered her more about this one - the glutting smell of the feces, or the insufferable, nasal sounding plucking of the country and western music that pervaded the air around the accident scene. The smell of shit she could do nothing about, but the music was something she could certainly work on. She walked around to the side of the crumpled engine compartment and peered into the mutilated metal, the hood also long gone and laying somewhere within close proximity.

Cheryl smiled as she spied the twelve-volt battery still clamped into its box, mounted to the firewall. One whole side of the plastic battery case had cracked, and she could see the clear electrolyte seeping down the side, the rotten egg smell of the sulphuric acid filled her nostrils.

Reaching in, Cheryl guided her hand across the long, sharp edge of a twisted section of the front fender. Cautiously, she grabbed the nearest battery cable, twisting the lead clamp until it worked its way free from the post, and the music finally ended with a satisfying moan.

Silence, especially at a fatal accident scene, could indeed be golden.

Cheryl looked around her, mulling over the irony that the Brodie Bandie assault file could now be concluded as the father and perpetrator was now dead. She took some time to mentally line up her investigative procedures, giving thought as to just what would be required to sift through this tangled carnage. That's when Cheryl saw the weed whacker lying in the freshly cut grass. It lay on the ground only twenty-five feet from the severed power pole and she could clearly hear the spitting sound as the raindrops fell onto the hot muffler. Sergeant Montague let go a long, fateful sigh, for she had ruefully expected the unexpected, and now she realized she could expect the situation to only get worse.

Cheryl walked cautiously over to the edge of the tall grass, mindful of the wires that still snapped and sparked near the bottom of the ditch. Within seconds she spotted an indentation in the deep weeds, about fifteen feet from the edge, and she ran over to find Judith Noble, supine and lifeless among the long, wet stalks.

"Dear Lord," Cheryl mumbled, "please . . . not her."

She squatted down, using her knees for leverage, and grasped the schoolteacher under the armpits, dragging her from the long grass out into the open, quickly putting some distance from the downed electrical wires. Judith was dressed in a light-blue sweatshirt, with an old pair of paint-flecked denims and a pair of black gumboots. Gently, Cheryl lowered Judith to the ground, and noticed a scorch mark on her blue jeans near the top of one of the black gum boots. This was her second clue that the young teacher had been electrocuted, and that all hope wasn't lost.

Cheryl had already noticed that Judith wasn't breathing, and administered two breaths, then placed her index and middle finger along the side of her neck, feeling for the telltale carotid pulse.

Judith's body lay void of any pulse, in a state of full arrest, and Cheryl knew in an instant what needed to be done, and without further haste. She leaned over the teacher's face, tilting her head back, pinching her nose with her fingers, making a seal with her lips before filling Judith's lungs twice with her own breath. Cheryl moved over Judith's chest area, placing her fingers at the bottom of her rib cage.

She started along the side, just above her waist, tracing her fingers along the inverted "V" of the cage, right up to the bottom of the sternum. Where the top of the rib cage joined the sternum, Cheryl placed one finger directly over the junction, land marking for the exact location to place the heels of her hands for the chest compressions. She heard some huffing and puffing, and looked up to see the old guy they called Uncle Walt jogging up to the little drama. Cheryl had heard that the elderly fellow had come to the

84

island aboard the ark, and the stories that circulated about his ruined face were just as absurd. It mattered not though, Uncle Walt had arrived, and Cheryl planned to put him to work.

"Jee-zus, no." Uncle Walt gasped.

"Jesus, yes," Cheryl replied, starting the chest compressions. "Start pumping or blowing Uncle Walt. As troubling as it appears, there's an admission charge to this miserable tragedy."

"Jee-zus . . . girl, I don't know sweet dick about cardiopulmonary what-ever-you-call-it."

"Do you know how to do mouth-to-mouth?" Cheryl asked.

"I suppose I do," Uncle Walt replied.

"Good, then get down here Sunshine, and get ready to blow. If we can't save this girl, then there's no point in us having climbed out of our beds this morning . . . I'll tell you when."

Cheryl nodded encouragement to the old man, and he got down on his knees, cradling Judith's head against his thighs. Tears ran down Uncle Walt's shiny, deformed face, but he had to keep his emotions checked. Cheryl started the chest compressions on Judith's lifeless form, counting out the time as she pushed against the breastbone. This wasn't going to turn into another double fatal accident. Not if Sergeant Cheryl Montague had any kind of a hand in it.

*　　*　　*

Chapter Seven

Judith Noble knew that she had departed on a fascinating journey, embarking down an extraordinary, yet wondrous path, drifting toward a place very different from the world she had known these past thirty-two years. She already knew it to be a place that held the promise of ethereal qualities, a place unsubstantiated by any of the sciences, yet very real, if only in the hearts and souls of mankind. Even those who didn't believe in such a place, and had a right to discuss freely their opinions, secretly hoped that such a place existed, especially when they had to lay a loved one to rest. Judith knew she was crossing over to such a place as she floated high above her dormant body, looking down upon the terrible accident scene. Now a vignette, the whole sight appeared hazy, and undefined around the edges. A feeling of significant sadness fell upon her, and it wasn't borne from the tragedy of what moments ago had been a peaceful, yet dull chore of cutting down some weeds. Judith agonized because she had to leave her precious twin girls behind, the adorable Uncle Walt, and she never even had a chance to say goodbye.

She felt a cutting sorrow, because had she known there was going to be such a dreadful incident, she would have hugged all three of them, speaking quietly to their soothing faces. Judith would have told them how much she dearly loved them, how much they seasoned her routine days, and how much joy each put into her life, in their own special way. Now it was too late. She'd only needed a minute with them, but the time was gone, in a cruel flash of fate. In a flickering of lights, almost like a moving, colorful canvas, Judith watched on, fascinated, a seraphic spectator, looking down as Uncle Walt and the police officer Cheryl Montague knelt over her still form, attempting to revive her. She then realized that there was probably a lot she should have done before this grievous blow, and regretted having put them aside for so long, for not taking the opportunity to reach out, to make them real, and then follow them through. Taking the twins on a long holiday had been one such postponed activity.

Within moments, although acutely aware that time would be drastically altered on this journey, Judith also realized there were a couple of people she should have made her peace with, including herself. She grieved for these losses as well, for allowing the chances to slip by her, choosing to surround her life and her children with a self imposed incommunicado. One such loss was her mother, for Judith had relinquished those invisible bonds years ago, refusing to ever go home again. But in this sad process, she had unthinkingly denied her twin daughters a fallible, yet loving grandmother. Within a brief thought, Judith acknowledged that she had been wrong, and affirmed to herself that things should have been different, and if given a second chance, they would be. Suddenly enveloped by darkness, Judith looked down, and the accident scene was gone, replaced with an infinite, inky blackness like deep space, void of any stars, void of any fear. As she floated through the impenetrable oblivion, Judith realized she couldn't see the rest of her body, except for her hands, which appeared white as if dusted in talcum powder.

She wondered why she would need her hands up here, and the answer soon became apparent, as she found herself sitting in a large, high backed, burgundy colored chair. The chair had neat lines of brass tacks holding the material to the frame, and it was both comfortable as well as soothing. To her front stood countless rows of polished hardwood bookshelves, towering high above her comfortable chair, so long that they faded into tiny brown dots in the undefined, black distance. Each shelf contained orderly stacks of white leather bound books, with flowing gold script that decorated the length of their thick spines. Judith's chair suddenly moved forward in an immeasurable flicker of time, between the long rows of bookshelves directly to her front. She felt no pressing hand of gravity as she sped along, nor any kinetic, forward motion as the chair abruptly stopped. A soft light cast its white glow over Judith and the chair, and when she looked up, she couldn't tell where it was coming from, so indirect, and so undefined was the illumination.

She looked to the nearest shelf, which stood level with her eyes and within easy reach on her left-hand side. She recognized most of the names that were penned in gold, meticulously handwritten over the white, pebbly surfaces of each book.

This is when Judith heard the voice, and although she recognized it, it puzzled her, tweaking her memory as to where in her past it belonged. The voice seemed to be inside her head, although at the same time strangely distant, and she wasn't even sure if it was a man or a woman talking. Judith instinctively knew she hadn't been brought here to ask questions, so she sat quietly, embraced, feeling at ease and warm within the soft boundaries of the over sized chair.

"You may be here for a while Judith," the voice said. "Why don't you read?"

Judith reached across to the bookshelf and retrieved the first volume from the single row. The book felt light in her hands, and when she placed it on her lap, she could now see the rest of her body, her bare feet sticking out from beneath a white, gossamer gown, just reaching the edge of the chair. Carefully, she opened the book to the first page. The white rectangular parchments were clean and crisp around the edges, their centers filled with a bold, gothic font where the paragraphs were formed, offering Judith their story. She started reading the sentences, and immediately became lost in the detailed, and accurate accounting that someone had written about her beloved sister Meryl.

*   *   *

Chapter Eight

Ben Trilby stopped sweeping the front porch of his store the second he heard Cheryl Montague's siren cease its detached wailing. His experienced ears told him that Martin Bandie, the driver of the fleeing red pick-up truck, had both pulled over and stopped for the police officer, or else Cheryl had called the high-speed chase off. Having spent a couple of years as a traffic cop, Ben had estimated their speed at approximately eighty miles-per-hour when they blew through the intersection in front of his store. Martin's truck even had some fresh air showing between the rubber and the earth as he bounced across the crown of the road, vanishing in a red blur behind the alder grove. Ben knew Martin as well as the old truck, for he had twice caught him trying to pilfer liquor from the beer fridge located near the produce section.

The second time, even with a reconstructed hip and a walking cane, Ben had managed to toss him out on his beak, forbidding him from ever entering the store again. Ben looked into the wet, gray distance and truly hoped the young man had enough sense to stop for the pursuing police officer.

There had been an unfortunate succession of high-speed police chases from one end of the country to the other, which had caught some of the media's attention, as well as their predisposed opinions. There had been much outcry in the newspapers as of late, even though most of the public were in support of their local police and their actions. Some of the tabloid papers regarded the compulsion to chase armed bandits through the well-maintained, peaceful streets of upscale suburbia somewhat distasteful, if not outright Hollywood. Unfortunately there had been a crash or two, and some regrettable loss of innocent lives, which did nothing to sway the media's opinion to the side of law enforcement. Others of course, just couldn't help themselves, and had to stick their noses into the fray. Never being a herd to sit on their backsides when controversy was afoot, this fueled the unconventional Jim Dandie nay sayer politicians to the point that you could see them flapping their lips on the nightly news. They would be standing on some hastily erected podium downtown, wearing their eighteen-hundred dollar suits and waving their law degrees while they spouted off, publicly demanding that these renegade police officers be hung by the pointed end of their badges. A few weeks back, one cretinous individual who was running for public office on the mainland based his platform on vague, but long overdue sweeping police reforms. The fool even went on record as saying "if the police stopped chasing the criminals, then the criminals would probably stop fleeing from the police." He never got elected, and even managed to throw one last, vehement snit before vanishing into a brooding obscurity.

Communists, Ben thought as he resumed his sweeping, they were all a bunch of goddamned Communists. That was when he heard the loud bang coming from the direction of the high-speed chase. An unhealthy thump, it was dulled as the sound waves shot through the pouring rain, but still managed to vibrate the boards beneath Ben's feet. He sighed heavily, because he'd already realized there had been a violent crash, and he hoped it wasn't Cheryl's patrol car although that was doubtful. Cheryl Montague was a pip of a police officer and Ben figured she had more balls than most of her male counterparts. She constantly reminded him of his last patrol partner, Lisa. Both Lisa and Cheryl had about them a consistent, no nonsense professional manner in which they conducted police business. He missed Lisa to this very day, and her loss brought him a guilt that pained him as much as his game hip. Ben limped over to the front door of the store and traded the corn broom for the cane he had left leaning near the front door. He reached inside and flipped the "closed" sign so it faced out, then locked the door of his store and shuffled down the steps to his vehicle. Ben grimaced with pain as he eased himself into the low slung, hunter green colored sports car he'd owned for the past four years. The time had come for him to trade it in for something more practical, something that wouldn't twist his afflicted hip every time he crawled into it. Something more domestic, like a mini van.

Ben cringed every time he thought about getting a more sensible car, but he needed a vehicle that wouldn't slowly erode his ruined hip joint every time he got in and out of it. Something that would be good for the body, but hell to play on his young soul. He would be the first to admit that the sports car was a bit of a testosterone thing, a high-powered phallic symbol that was nothing more than an extension of his once lusting crotch. Although he'd bought it four years ago, at that time he had two good legs, a healthy untainted perspective, and a promising police career lay before him. All of it there for the offering, and all Ben had to do was reach out and take it, but it was lost within seconds of an incomprehensible act of flashing violence. At least he had lived, which at times seemed like an unjustified compensation for his burdening remorse. A remorse that pervaded his dreams, calling him when sleep finally came each night. Ben started the engine of his sports car, and backed out onto the road, shifting through the gears as he brought the vehicle up to speed, driving down to what he was now sure had become a terrible accident. He wasn't going there because he wanted to have a gander at the bloody mayhem; he was going there to offer Cheryl Montague a hand. Ben knew how the shifts worked in small town policing, already guessing that Cheryl was alone on shift, and she could probably use some assistance, even if it meant just holding the "dummy" end of the tape as she took her accident scene measurements. The island was a small community, and such things were done at times of misfortune, and the fact that Ben happened to be ex-police officer had little to do with it. He was going there because despite everything else he'd lived through, Ben was still a caring, sympathetic human being.

*   *   *

Chapter Nine

Sergeant Cheryl Montague felt her heart gladden just a smidgen when Ben Trilby pulled up to the accident scene. He parked his sports car well away from the destroyed truck, so as not to drive over any evidence or fresh gouge marks that may be lying on the gravel road. The pathetic rescue effort wasn't going well at all, and it reminded Cheryl of the children's tale about the three little pigs and the old wolf who huffed and puffed, and became so breathless he couldn't even blow a kiss. Uncle Walt was doing his best to get air into Judith's lungs, but the wheezing and panting was producing barely enough air for himself, and he was soon gasping for breath. It wasn't his fault though; the poor old guy was traumatized, as well as winded from his quarter-mile sprint down from the house. Cheryl kept up the chest compressions and was further elated when she could hear the siren from the paramedic unit as it sprinted down from its hall at the north end of the island. Ben quickly climbed from his car, limping as fast as his aluminum cane would allow, through the ditch and past the mangled truck. He took a second to examine Martin's ravaged body, something he couldn't help, the part of him that was still a police officer. They'll be no bagpipes lamenting a somber dirge at that lad's funeral he thought. Blowing taps for people like Martin Bandie would be a complete waste of time, not to mention the undue wear and tear on a perfectly good set of lungs.

Ben hobbled over to where Cheryl and Uncle Walt were giving their all to save a young woman's life, and he stood stunned when he recognized Judith's still form. Within seconds he'd already determined what had happened to the energetic young teacher. His experienced eyes had already taken in and analyzed the abandoned weed whacker, the downed power lines, and the apparent electric burn on Judith's body helped to complete the story.

"You know CPR?" Cheryl looked up at him while she continued with the chest compressions.

"Yes," Ben nodded.

"Take over from Uncle Walt. I'll nod when I want you to start . . . one breath every fifth compression, okay?"

"Okay," Ben said. He then eased himself down to his knees in the wet grass, feeling his hip grinding as he crawled over to relieve Uncle Walt. Gently, he snagged the side of Judith's head into his hands. Upon Cheryl's anticipated nods, he used both hands to pull gently on Judith's jaw, thrusting it out to align the windpipe, then sealed her mouth with his own, forcing the life-giving air into her lungs. Ben watched as her chest rose with the resuscitating breaths, noticing Judith's lips were still warm against his own, a very encouraging sign. Ben had done this numerous times before on perfect strangers, when they were cold and dirty, and very much beyond hope. Although he should have been, Ben never concerned himself with AIDS, or Hepatitis C, or any of the other host of microscopic viruses that could have caused him some distress with his insides. If an injured human being needed help while he had been a police officer, well, Ben got down and gave them a hand, and if the rest preferred to watch, squirm, or harp on about the sanitary conditions, then there wasn't a lot he could do about it.

Cheryl kept up with the chest compressions, counting out loud and Ben would give Judith one breath right after the fifth compression. Poor old Uncle Walt had become a real mess, the emotions finally overtaking him, the misery of the accident finally sinking in, and he stood leaning against the fence sobbing quietly. He'd lost his wife Grace just a decade ago, and Judith had put some warmth into that part of his soul that had gone numb, becoming both a daughter and a compass for his lost emotions. Uncle Walt was getting old, and he didn't think he could survive the loss of another loved one. The only blessing on the whole situation was that Judith's twin girls were still out riding their ponies somewhere on the property, or had returned to the house because of the rain. Minutes later, the paramedic unit arrived, a white, one-ton cube van that parked as close to the rescue scene as was possible. The white strobe lights and red flickering beacons cast both color and furtive shadows over the kneeling rescuers. Two paramedics climbed from the cab of the vehicle and jogged around to the double back doors, and Cheryl warned them about the downed power lines. One of them gave her a friendly nod as they pulled a wheeled gurney from the rear of the vehicle. They had plastic toolboxes as well as metal air bottles strapped to the top with neatly folded gray blankets, and they walked the whole affair through the ditch with practiced precision. One of the paramedics was short and dumpy looking with blond curly hair, and the other was big and dumpy looking with dark curly hair. They both wore blue uniform pants and rumpled white shirts that had never been within three feet of a hot iron, but Fred and Barney (and yes, those were their real names) were the best paramedics to ever crack an oxygen bottle. They quickly got up to where Judith lay, efficiently unstrapping their plastic toolboxes and oh-two bottles, placing them on the ground beside their patient.

"Electrocution?" Fred asked.

"Yes," Cheryl replied, "it appears that way. I started CPR almost immediately."

Barney relieved Ben, and after taking a clear, plastic oral airway from one of the toolboxes, he quickly and skillfully inserted it into Judith's mouth, sliding the tube down her throat. Fred checked Judith's pulse, his two fingers lying across her carotid artery, but he shook his head seconds later. With Cheryl and Ben's help, they loaded Judith onto the gurney, and the two paramedics continued with the resuscitation, Fred applying chest compressions while Barney squeezed the rubber ambu bag that fed air directly into Judith's lungs.

By now a lime colored pumper truck with six volunteer firefighters had arrived from Skinny's Reach, and they jumped into action while the truck was still moving, pulling lengths of two-and-a-half-inch snake skin hose from the ready bins at the side. They were all attired from head to foot in the modern, canvas type turn out gear with the reflective tape, rubber boots, and yellow helmets with face shields. It was an ironic twist when you considered the pouring rain.

The firefighters playing with the water would be the only ones staying dry today. Everyone else was already soaked through. Two of the firefighters were already geared up with self contained breathing apparatus, the clear oval masks protecting their faces, the yellow bottles that supplied them air, strapped to their backs. The firefighter who drove the rig stood next to the chromed panel at the side of the truck, engaging the main pump by throwing levers and twisting knobs. He watched attentively as the needles on the gauges moved beneath the round glass, providing him with the main pumps revolutions per minute, as well as the amount of water being fed to the hoses. The pair with the breathing apparatus dragged a two-and-a-half-inch with an adjustable nozzle out to the wrecked truck, and stood by once the pump had charged the full length of their hose. You could hear the diaphragms on their breathing masks purging noisily as they sucked air from the bottles, their breaths becoming short and quick as they gazed upon the ghastly sight of Martin's squashed body.

Although there was no fire, the charged hoses were a precaution should an ignition source or spark from the rescue tools ignite any gasoline that may have leaked from the gas tank the pick-up truck. There were no water hydrants out in the rural areas so the firefighters depended on the eleven hundred gallons they carried in a reservoir on the truck. One of them walked over to where the paramedics worked on Judith, while the other two prepared the rescue equipment, starting the portable air compressor, then carefully laying out the thin, red air lines that fed their pneumatic tools.

Cheryl addressed the firefighter, a Lieutenant, as he stood watching the paramedics.

"We need to get the body out of the truck, but not until the Coroner shows up."

"Sounds good Cheryl," he said, then turned and walked back to supervise his crew.

Fred and Barney had decided to get Judith to the hospital, where the on-call doctor and some highly trained nurses would be waiting with the proper medication and a defibrillation machine. As there were only two paramedics on shift at any given time on the island (budget cuts you know) they were forced to make an unusual request, and asked Ben if he would drive the ambulance. This would free the paramedics to continue their resuscitation efforts on Judith while en route to the hospital. Ben looked expectantly at Cheryl, and she quickly told him to go. She knew why he'd come to the scene, and she certainly appreciated his help, but she wouldn't require him as a helicopter was flying over from the mainland with a traffic analyst onboard.

The telecom center had already advised her of his impending arrival when they had radioed for the exact location. Cheryl wouldn't be investigating this one as it had resulted from a high-speed chase in which she had been directly involved. There had been no assumption of guilt with this decision. Headquarters dictated the policy in an attempt to remove all perceptions of a conflict of interest from the public's mind. Members of the Regional Police weren't allowed to investigate motor vehicle accidents that they were directly or indirectly involved in.

Cheryl and a couple of the firefighters helped carry the gurney down through the ditch and up to the ambulance as Fred and Barney continued with the resuscitation. They gently loaded Judith into the back of the ambulance as Ben climbed into the cab behind the wheel, then drove off in the direction of the hospital, the emergency lights still flashing and blinking clearing their way. With Judith Noble and her critical dilemma now in very capable hands, Cheryl could concentrate on her other duties. She walked over to her patrol car and retrieved a stack of bright orange traffic pylons from the trunk, then jogged up the road in the direction that the chase had come from. Cheryl set the cones out across the road, just at the beginning of the sharp corner, a measure to prevent motorists from driving over any evidence that Martin's truck might have left on the road. She returned to the scene then took a minute to comfort Uncle Walt, who stood shaking with grief, standing in the rain as he leaned against the white railing fence. Cheryl put a consoling arm around his shoulder and gently suggested he return to the house to take care of Judith's young daughters. Someone had to inform them as to what had happened, and although it looked grim, not all had been lost just yet. Uncle Walt nodded his head, looking tired as he walked slowly along the fence line, a desolate figure treading through the deep, uncut grass. Cheryl felt a sorrow for him, and wished she had the time to give him some support, to be with him when he spoke to the twins, but she couldn't. She had to maintain continuity on the accident scene until the traffic analyst arrived from the mainland. It was of little comfort, she thought, but someone else would be up to his or her lips in paperwork for a change. Albeit, Cheryl would soon be swimming herself, mired in the controversy that would surely follow this unhappy event. Once the preliminary facts had been gathered and examined by the traffic analyst, headquarters would issue a press release advising of the unfortunate accident and the circumstances surrounding it. Cheryl would be well advised to stand back as the media show and the editorials started.

The island would soon be amok with news reporters, all flocking to the scene of the devastating carnage. Then the cameras would roll tape as the newscasters spoke their predisposed assumptions on how they felt the incident should have unfolded had only cooler heads prevailed. Whether the late Martin Bandie liked it or not, he was about to become a martyr. Another fine young citizen killed because of an unrestrained police officer who couldn't hold her exuberance in check.

Although the chase had lasted for only sixty-two seconds, "those facts do not a good story make." Cheryl already knew that tidbit of information would receive scant coverage in the media reports. It wasn't accurate journalism that appeared on some of the television stations anymore. Even the reporters had been reduced to acting, displaying shocked and dismayed faces during their opinionated sequels. Some of the nightly news had become nothing more than a theater in the park with film at eleven. Cheryl walked over to Martin's vehicle, just as the power company truck lumbered up the road from the direction of Skinny's Reach. It was a big service truck with a boom and a basket extended over the back, a hydraulic rig that could place their personnel well above the tallest power pole. The Coroner's black van skirted around the slow moving power company vehicle and stopped next to the ditch across from Cheryl. She looked into the van and could see the pudgy red face of the Coroner as he beamed her a smile from where he sat behind the wheel. His name was Millar and he always seemed to be smiling at these events, although Cheryl could never be sure why. It was either the princely sum they paid him for his official attendance, or it was because he was a horny bastard who liked to ogle Cheryl while trying to chat her up. Night or day; rain or shine; one dead body or a dozen; nicely decomposed or freshly killed; Millar always seemed to be smiling whenever he arrived at these dismal occasions.

He still smiled as he lowered himself from the van and trundled over to where Cheryl stood beside the wreck. Dressed in black coveralls with green gumboots he had an olive-drab body bag rolled up under his arm, and he clutched a clipboard in his plump, sausage like fingers. On his thinning dome he wore a white, sweat stained baseball cap with an officious looking crest sewn above the peak. The word "coroner" was embroidered in blocked, silver letters across his chest, just in case you forget who the hell he was and just why he was there. However, just what Millar did at these incidents in Cheryl's opinion was debatable, for it usually didn't amount to an awful lot.

Outside of a bit of routing around, taking some notes and making small sketches, the coroner did little else except make grunting sounds as he bent over to peer under something, or crawl over some rubble to look at some unfortunate person's remains. In all fairness though, Millar was only a deputized coroner, ordinarily turning his hand to the meat cleaver he used in his butcher's shop down in Skinny's Reach. Appointed by the Government, he received a cash payment for each sudden death he attended, and although the police did the majority of the paperwork for him, he was a Government Agent nonetheless.

That aside, Cheryl thought he looked more like a large black medicine ball, dressed as he was in his coveralls with little green feet sticking out of the bottom. She giggled in spite of the circumstances, and Millar mistook this for a happy greeting or a friendly salutation. He offered Cheryl a fleshy smile, gibbering away, attempting to turn a soaking wet fatality into some kind of a social event. Married about a dozen times, Millar was in his early fifties, and boasted of a kid on every continent. He presently shared his apartment above the butcher shop with one of the local hairdressers, but that would change just as surely as the sun would go down. Cheryl knew he was a lecherous toad, and was well aware that his 'little head' longed for some intimate exploring, so she kept their relationship at a distant and professional level. Already puffing once he'd climbed from the ditch, Millar chirped away at how glad he was to see Cheryl again, using an overworked joke about how they had to stop meeting like this, and how he was about to throw his girlfriend out making him again one of the island's most eligible bachelor types. During this entire long-winded dribble the firefighters looked on, bored now that all the excitement had ended and they had no fires to put out. They simply wished only to pull Martin's body from the wreck so they could bag him, and then go for a beer. Cheryl politely cut of Millar's romantic solicitations when he got to the part about still owning a waterbed, as well as having his "love palace" apartment to himself for the weekend.

"I won't be investigating this fatal accident Millar," Cheryl interjected, "there was a high speed chase which I called off sixty-two seconds after it began. The driver of this truck however, one Martin Bandie, decided to continue on. A traffic analyst is inbound from the mainland to take over the investigation. If you like though, I'll take some photographs of the deceased so the firefighters can at least remove his body and return to the fire hall."

"Oh, certainly Cheryl. By all means. Please, lets us get some snaps," Millar intoned.

Cheryl nodded at the Coroner then turned and walked over to her patrol car. She popped open the trunk and bent over the aluminum camera box, retrieving the camera and shielding it from the rain with her body. She cranked the little handle on the top, rewinding the thirty-five-millimeter film that held the exposures of young Brodie's savaged backside. Taking a fresh roll of film, she loaded it into the camera, then made the applicable notation in the small log book that accompanied the camera case. Cheryl started walking back to the truck when a Bell Jet Ranger helicopter broke the horizon on the seaward side of the road. It flew in low from the steep bluffs that overlooked the ocean, just feet above the coniferous trees that bordered the Noble property. The thumping of the machines main rotor blades seemed to reach out like an invisible hand, tapping on Cheryl's skull, and as it flew over the small gathering the wash from the blades plucked at their wet clothing, driving the rain like little needles into their exposed faces.

Cheryl could even read the Regional Police decals along the slender boom of the aircraft, it had flown in so low, and the pilot skillfully kicked the tail over so he faced them then flared the aircraft just feet above the roadway.

Gently, the pilot put both skids down onto the gravel road, just on the other side of the power company truck. A uniformed police officer dressed in a long, dark blue nylon rain coat climbed from the passenger side and opened one of the back doors. Within seconds he'd unloaded the thick, plastic cases that held all his investigative equipment. He left them on the road beside the aircraft's skid, and then keeping low to the ground, ran out to the front of the helicopter where the pilot could see him. The pilot gave him thumbs up, and the police officer acknowledged it with a wave. Seconds later the pilot pulled up on the collective stick beside his seat and the helicopter leapt into the air, quickly gaining both speed and altitude as it raced away, soon becoming a dot against the gray sky. Cheryl recognized the traffic analyst as a fellow officer named Dave Tuck, a corporal from the headquarters traffic section, someone she'd known since her training days. She walked down to give him a hand with his equipment, and to brief him of the events thus far, but well out of the earshot of the firefighters and the Coroner. Tuck had just lit a cigarette, cupping it in his hand, inhaling contentedly on the blue smoke, watching quietly as Cheryl moved down to greet him.

"Hello Cheryl," he said with a smile, "you've been playing bumper cars again I see."
She returned his smile, knowing it was genuine.
"Kind of looks like it," she said.
Cheryl liked Dave Tuck, an experienced police officer as well as an absolute magician when it came to reconstructing baffling traffic accidents. They were both about the same age, except Tuck was much taller, and thin boned. He had sandy colored hair and a waxed handle bar mustache that curled into tight circles above his cheeks, a brazen flaunting of his disregard of the service dress regulations. A fellow renegade as well as a noncommissioned officer, his humorous attitude and dancing, boyish eyes the color of spring ice made him hard not to like. Cheryl could talk to Dave Tuck in a manner that she couldn't with her seven subordinate officers. Whoever said it could be lonely at the top, must have been a Detachment Commander at some semi-isolated police posting. At these places you were expected to be perfect, even though no such human beings existed, so

Cheryl welcomed the casual, unguarded conversations she could have with Tuck. She could bitch about anything that plucked her fancy, and without fear of it being repeated, for Dave Tuck's presence provided such an avenue with his impartial ears and relaxed attitude. A dedicated professional, if Tuck had any faults, it would be his addiction to cigarettes, and the haggard looks that lay just behind his smiling eyes. Dave Tuck had gone to one fatal accident too many, and it had started to grate on his resolve, a sure sign of burn out, exuded by his chain smoking and off-duty drinking. He had become one of those police officers they had warned Cheryl about in training. The one's who didn't eat properly, didn't exercise and smoked and drank too much. Tuck's heart would probably explode about eighteen months or so after he had retired, while he sat in a lawn chair in his backyard, bored and sipping on a double high ball. Cheryl helped him with his gear, and they walked slowly through the rain up to Martin's truck.

Tuck puffed on his cigarette, the white tube spotted with raindrops, wagging between his lips as he spoke, his hands full of gear.

"Much of a loss?" he asked.

"No," Cheryl replied, "one of the locals . . . a drunken, wife beating shit rat."

"Huh uh, that doesn't happen too often. Usually they stagger away unscathed after killing somebody else."

"Well, he's probably done that as well, Tuck. Right now they're trying to jump start a young mother who got electrocuted when he brought down some power lines."

"Ouch," Tuck said.

"Yes . . . ouch. And as always the case, she's one of the good ones. I'm really starting to hate this goddamned job Tuck. I really am."

"Time for a transfer?" Tuck asked.

"Nah." Cheryl said, "it's the same crap no matter where you go, only the faces change."

They walked the rest of the way in silence, placing Tuck's gear on the grass near the smashed pick-up truck. Tuck borrowed Cheryl's camera as it was all ready to go and was just as good as his own. He lit another cigarette then began taking a dozen or so close-ups of Martin's body. Once he'd taken the photographs, he slowly circled the truck, inspecting it from every angle, jotting down notes and figures in his issue notebook.

When he'd finished, Tuck looked at Millar the Coroner.

"Okay to remove the body?" He asked.

"Yes, go ahead," Millar replied. "You can stick him in the back of my van."

The firefighters started the air compressor and bent to their extrication task like a well-rehearsed drill team. First they wrapped a short length of chain around the steering column, feeding it through the bent frame of the windshield, then looped another one around the base of the severed power pole. One firefighter held the bulky Jaws of Life just above the engine compartment, it's arms fully extended. Two others secured both ends of the chains to the tips of the jaws, snagging them up and attaching them back onto themselves with metal hooks. Everybody stood well away as the operator of the jaws applied the throttle, and the arms slowly moved, coming together while pulling the steering column away from Martin's crushed body. The arms eventually came together, and the operator nodded to the other firefighters, who moved in close to the cab.

They all wore industrial style rubber gloves, and within seconds they had freed Martin's body, gently laying him down in the wet grass. The movement however, and gravity itself caused a large amount of thick, coagulated blood to spew from what remained of Martin's mouth, spattering the feet and the legs of two of the firefighters. They had hastily backed up when Martin's corpse made a gurgling sound, but they weren't quick enough. One of them, his turn out pants covered with thick blood, ran over to the ditch where he threw up his lunch in loud, violent heaves.

He stood gasping for air while he leaned over with one hand on his knee, the other wiping the caustic bile from his mouth.

"Are you okay?" The Lieutenant called.

The firefighter nodded and walked back to where the body lay, helping his companions unroll the stiff material of the body bag. It had a heavy-duty zipper down the middle, with six reinforced loops sewn to the edges for handholds. After laying the open bag next to Martin's body, they gingerly lifted him up and placed him in the middle of the bag, holding their breath to keep away the overpowering smell of feces. They were about to zip the bag closed when Tuck interrupted.

"Over there . . . about sixty feet," he said casually.

He pointed out to the middle of slender strip of field that bordered against the Noble property.

"Over there what?" Cheryl asked.

"Over there is where you'll find the rest of this young man's leg."

104

"Oh . . . " Cheryl nodded then turned to walk through the tall grass, pacing off the distance while she pulled a pair of rubber gloves from a small leather pouch on her gun belt.

"About there," Tuck called out to her a half minute later.

Cheryl stopped and pushed the weeds aside with her hands as she leaned over, immediately finding Martin's bloodied, lower left leg and foot. The skin was pale and waxy looking, the black biker boot was missing as well as the sock, and Cheryl could see the years of impacted dirt that had gathered under the long yellow toenails. She snapped the gloves over her hands and picked the appendage up by the ankle, returning to the awaiting muster. One of the firefighters held the bag open as Cheryl placed Martin's leg beside his body. He then grabbed the large tab of the zipper, and pulled it up over Martin's face, enclosing his remains within the watertight bag. Millar nodded his supreme approval, then waddled after the firefighters as they hoisted the body bag to waist level, carrying it out to the roadway and the Coroner's awaiting van.

Cheryl looked at Tuck, who stood beside her lighting another cigarette.

"So what do you think so far?" She asked.

Tuck drew deeply on the cigarette, holding the smoke in for a few seconds before exhaling loudly. Cheryl wasn't sure if it was a bid to get more nicotine into his system, or just a plain old weary sigh.

"Well . . . Cheryl," he pondered slowly, "so far it doesn't look like this accident is going to make a lot of sense."

"Oh?" Cheryl turned to face him, crossing her arms as the rain had started to chill her body.

"And why is that?" She inquired.

"Look at the elevation of the road," Tuck offered, "as compared to the elevation at the point of impact against the power pole."

Cheryl looked and could see it right away. The point where the truck had left the road was at least three feet lower than the base of the power pole. She could plainly see the gouge marks left by the tires of the vehicle where the pebbles had been disturbed, piled into two, distinct curving mounds of pea sized gravel. If anything, Martin's truck, even at a high rate of speed should have plowed into the other side of the deep ditch and then flipped end over end, eventually coming to a rest after striking the power pole. But there were no furrows or marks of any kind cut in the soft surface of the grass topped soil. It was almost as if something had picked Martin's truck up and flung it head long into the power pole.

"So how do you figure this accident happened?" Cheryl asked quietly.

"Right now Cheryl, I haven't got an inkling. And it takes about a thousand inklings to make just one clue."

"What would you suggest then Tuck . . . divine intervention?"

"Nope, that kind of reasoning doesn't exist within the confines of a traffic analyst's vocabulary," he said slowly. "But the word haunter certainly does, and that's just what we have here Cheryl, another haunter."

*　　*　　*

Part Two
"Meryl"

Chapter Ten

Nearly twenty-two months separated Judith from her older sister Meryl, and her earliest memories had been when she was about ten years old and Meryl was nearing the awakening, teenage years. They had been the only children to inhabit the strict confines of the Noble household. One doctor later suggested that was a contributing factor to Judith blocking everything out, good or bad that had happened during those impressionable, early years. It had become some kind of a defense mechanism, triggered within her brain by the trauma, causing Judith to effectively isolate and forget her first ten years, which ironically enough had been the happiest times of her young life. Judith thought about this as she sat in the celestial library, strangely pacified with the warm, burgundy chair embracing her and the white book resting lightly on her lap. Quietly, she read about the sister she had loved more than any other human being.

She soon realized that she wasn't reliving the past, but had become more of an observer, watching on from the boundless periphery as she read the story, even being allowed to feel her sister's emotions, and those of the people who had surrounded their young lives. Much of what she was about to read would be all new to her, but combined with her own memories of the past, a complete picture would eventually emerge and many things would finally make sense. Above all, these surprising disclosures would finally allow Judith to forgive those who needed it the most.

The formative years of Judith's life evolved on the northern coast in a small mill town that had been built by the company on the outer most brink of a wide, and very long peninsula. Approximately twenty-five hundred souls inhabited the town, located at the end of a desolate asphalt two lane that had you winding for miles through a massive region of untouched rain forest. That was all you would see while driving the curving, mountainous road that led you from the nearest town of any consequence. Four hours of watching the snaking, wet road, and four hours of staring at the thick girthed, rust-colored cedar trunks and the rough, nutmeg bark of the tall Douglas firs. As you followed the road a constant low misty cloud swirled around the tree limbs, obscuring the mountain peaks and the sunshine, making you feel tiny and insignificant.

There would be the odd, white boulder that had rolled onto the road, giving a driver something to skirt around, keeping his mind sharp and alert, breaking the hypnotic repetition of a road that featured one sharp curve after another. After long hours on the zigzagging drive, when you were starting to feel lost and with your gas tank nearing empty, the road finally broke from the dark forest, leading you into the town. The company had built the town decades ago, which meant they spared the creativity; so the end result was a bleak looking village with matching, stucco sided buildings and houses.

In this particular part of the world, the annual rainfall amounted to almost fifteen feet, which did absolutely nothing to enhance the pedestrian looking structures and the social problems that plagued some of the families that lived inside of them. The isolation, as well as the constant rain made the occupants feel like prisoners at times, and indeed a portion of the town folk did behave as if they belonged in a jail. But that came with every community. A large percentage of the town's occupants were employed at the mill, which had been built on the other side of the peninsula above a well-protected, deep-water harbor. A half hour drive brought you down to the massive work's buildings with the continuous clouds of steam and effluent vapors that were pumped by the ton into the moist, sticky atmosphere. Acres of flat, cured cement stood stretching into the distance near the water where countless orderly piles of wood awaited the forklift or the dock cranes. Millions of board feet of graded lumber were exported annually out from the mill in the big container ships that would drop anchor in the harbor. There they would swing on the hook, waiting their turn to dock at the cement pier where the longshoremen would fill their holds with the kiln dry lumber. If it weren't for the deep-water bay, the town and the mill would never have existed. Only a suicide jockey would have driven a lumber laden, flat-decked eighteen-wheeler through the switchback hazards that formed the only road into town. That lonely, unforgiving road held more over the town than any other inanimate object within three hundred miles. Although depending on which side of the environmental consciousness you chose to stand, both the isolation and the dilapidated state of the road would prove to be a beneficial feature to the community's existence.

The long haul kept the freaks, granolas, and the earthy types well away from the settlement, a precarious trip when made in mechanically neglected old school buses and Volkswagen vans with balding tires. This tiresome drive also kept the media huddled in their warm offices in the cities well to the south, venturing out only to report on the armed robberies, drive by shootings, and gangs that roamed the streets like mindless sheep. These high tech journalists weren't the least bit interested in traveling to such a desolate corner of the world, just to visit a stinking mill town that held nary a hint of a Holiday Inn or a trendy restaurant. No sir, a journey that far up an abandoned goat's trail, in a wet forest where they had never even heard of a frequent flyer plans was just not to be. Especially when the only action the media would find for their efforts were the self-proclaimed, unemployed guardians of mother earth. Filming their melodramatic shows as they chained their lips to the steering wheel of a front end loader, or laid across a logging road like a bunch of soft skinned speed bumps wasn't even worth a passing consideration. It was the lack of a good road, the media, good accommodations, and some other untamed calamities that would keep the town "an environmentalist free zone." Nevertheless, one had to give due course to these earthy types, for at least one dedicated group did make an honest effort to protest the "raping of the forests." Even though it turned into a near disaster.

A couple of decades ago, when Judith was about ten and a half years old, a group of novice, misinformed radicals made the trek into the thick woods of the peninsula. Dressed in shabby military cast-offs with leather sandals on their feet and wearing wire-rimmed granny glasses, they drove a van single-mindedly across the rough logging road to enter a section of the forest that was being actively harvested. News of their presence spread fast, for it was viewed as a direct threat to the town's livelihood as jobs in other industries had become nothing more than a socialistic dream. In addition, the protesters had brought some long overdue excitement to the dull streets and the crowded taverns inside the township. Even the children with their acutely tuned ears, talked about the "goddamned hippies" and their occupation of the life-giving forest. Regular reports were sent back to the eagerly awaiting towns people on the crusaders progress, supplied by the bush crew who felled, bucked, and skidded the logs from the forest. Shortly after their arrival, the protesters set about building a couple of platforms using hand tools and wood that had ironically come from the very forest they were standing in. The on site bush crew stood back and watched with mild interest as they sawed, hammered, nailed and then hoisted their platforms a good distance up some magnificent looking Douglas Firs. It was quite a show to behold. It truly was. The protesters' fumbling efforts even made the local government look organized but in the end, they achieved their short-term goals. Their long term plans however, well, they just sort of fell apart.

A few of the earth people confidently ensconced themselves onto the platforms atop the trees and settled in for the long wait. They were going to win this one just as surely as the neighbor's large dog, the one with the healthy bowels, would crap habitually on your beautifully manicured carpet of Kentucky bluegrass. The protesters had it all figured out and were already planning the victory party, writing up their international press statements, slamming "Larry the Logger and the Evil, Forestry Empire." Unfortunately, it was the bears that turned out to be the protesters absolute undoing. A woebegone scene, to say the least. No sooner had the protesters taken up residence in their penthouse suites when the bush boss, a skookum, clean cut young man named Jeremy Salter, ordered his entire crew out of the area. No problem here, they would go cut down some healthy trees elsewhere on the large peninsula. There was room for everybody, including the large, coastal grizzly bears that also made the vast forest their home. Alone and in the forest, the protest moved along nicely, and at an acceptable pace that one would even call sedate.

Thus far, the only glitch was the human feces and toilet paper that were starting to pile up around the base of the trees. A day or two later, Salter returned in his three-quarter-ton pick up truck to check on the unprogressive yet somewhat lofty demonstration. He'd brought a couple of the union boys with him, and together they peeled the lids off a couple of large barrels they had lashed upright in the back of the truck. Using metal buckets, they formed a line, and set about unloading many pounds of fresh salmon heads and tasty fish entrails, dumping it all around the base of the trees.

The protesters, although somewhat earthy in their demeanor, hadn't spent much time in a real forest and assumed this tactic was the initial strike by the corporate puppets to see who could stink whom out of the woods first. After spreading the malodorous goo about the ground beneath the trees, Salter bid the tree huggers a friendly adieu then promptly drove from the area. Ever the sturdy types, the gangs of earth people were still celebrating the drawing of the first blood when one day later three cinnamon colored grizzly bears, each about the size of a single car garage, wandered sniffing from the forest. It would appear that the inviting smell of rotting salmon heads had beckoned, calling the bears from the distant valley's, having them abandon the dried pithy berries that at present provided their daily sustenance. Now the time had come for a picnic, just like in the nursery rhyme, except the grunting, salivating barks that came from the feeding bears at the base of the trees didn't sound anything like the cute mewling bears you could see in your imagination. The tree huggers watched on, at first enchanted that they were finally as one with nature, and until they realized the only convictions they held about wild bears were total misconceptions. One of the first things they discovered, despite anything they might have seen at the local zoo, was that bears aren't stupid. In fact, this particular crowd of bears, having scoffed back all the salmon castings, had quickly correlated the fishy smell at the bottom of the tree, with the repulsive pong that floated down from the longhaired, unwashed bodies that were perched near the top. Indeed, dessert was but a short climb and a scream away. Right about then, the three bears blew another fallacy clear out of the post secondary biology books. Grizzly bears can, and will climb trees, especially if you smell ripe and are willingly attainable, like so much plump fruit hanging from a tree branch.

The protesters were beside themselves. Mother nature appeared to have turned against them, and now these ill-mannered bears were raising wanton havoc with the only people considerate enough to fight for their rights. One of the bears had clambered up one of the thick trunks, sending large pieces of bark cascading to the ground below, causing the platform near the slender top to shake and sway back and forth in a dizzying motion. There was much caterwauling and undignified shrieking as the bear rapidly ascended, eagerly raking the bottom of the platform with claws as long as pencils. In no time the bear had made some notable progress, splintering through the wooden platform, eyeballing the tasty morsels squirming and yelling on the other side. This was about the time that Salter returned in his truck, driving agonizingly slow and watching the fracas as he moved down the logging road. It was a company vehicle, so he had to drive slowly, carefully coaxing the high slung four by four-vehicle through the numerous potholes. Among other attributes, Jeremy Salter had become a vigilant fanatic when it came to using other people's equipment, especially the company's. So who could criticize him if he didn't come flying over the rocky hill, clamoring pell-mell like a cavalry troop to the rescue. Treat other people's stuff like it was your own, his old man had once said.

Salter stopped the vehicle about three hundred feet from the base of the trees, then got out with a high-powered rifle that had an evil looking scope affixed along the barrel. Despite all the screaming, some very succinct communication was achieved between the bush boss and the protesters, all the while the huge bruin working industriously away at the platform with his massive claws. Within short order, a truce had been brokered between Salter and the protesters, and their word was given to assure the deal. The bush boss laid his rifle across the hood of the truck, then produced one of those hand held, canned air horns. He held it above his head and pushed the button, producing a long piercing shriek that split the low cloud and rain, echoing like a volley off the shrouded mountains for many seconds afterward. The two bears on the ground immediately took their appetites and beetled back into the hills without so much as leaving a gratuity or tossing grateful glance back. It took a bit more encouragement to convince the third bear to forgo his dessert, but he finally slid down the tree and ran off into the mist once Salter fired a round into the air from his rifle.

Moments later the protesters shinnied down from their exalted perches, hyperventilating, wide eyed and terrified from the bear experience. Some had even wet themselves, which disgusted the bush boss to no end. Nevertheless, the protesters were good and licked, and they knew it.

Salter patiently reminded them of the unconditional truce, and they needed little prodding as they packed up their crap and their trampled ideals, and left the area, never to return.

And so Salter the bush boss instantly became a local hero, his picture appearing on the front page of the weekly newspaper, his accomplishments touted the full breadth of the village on the local a.m. radio station. He was a modern, thinking kind of man who reasoned his way through the faddish problems that infused a decade and beyond. A young Judith Noble couldn't have known it at the time, but Jeremy Salter had already engaged in an affair with her mother, and in the end he would become more to her than a local hero. It would be the remoteness of the town, and her father's overly pious ways that would urge Judith's mother into these sexual trysts as well as giving her a fondness for orange juice, liberally spliced with vodka.

The remoteness of the village played differently on each of the town's inhabitants, although as a whole, it had made the community hearty, self reliant, and somewhat spirited. This same isolation would also help develop Judith's strong resolve, as well as indirectly place immense grief upon her young shoulders. When Judith and Meryl were young, the solitude was a good place to come of age, drawing the sisters unusually close, forming a loving and seemingly unbreakable bond. Even from a distance one could quickly tell they were sisters, with alike mannerisms and a devout familiarity, almost like each others shadows, something rarely seen or explained in siblings. The home these two had been raised in was a company house, a boxy, three bedroom stuccoed accommodation that sat unremarkable from the rest of the town's dwellings. They had been fortunate though for they lived across the road from an expansive, white sandy beach. If you walked the beach at low tide, it followed the gradual curve of the peninsula, bringing you around to the bay where the mill had been built. The beach offered the children a source of great joy in the summer time, its cool face changing and yielding different treasures with each turn of the tides. During the long winter seasons, which lasted for nearly nine months, the beach would become a thundering ogre. Waves would roll in all the way from the mid pacific ocean, gathering speed, volume, and height as they rolled across the shallowing bottom, making a noticeable transition, turning themselves into deadly ground swells. These massive waves would break the shoreline to the front of the Noble household, where the incessant Gail force winds would rip the tops off the foaming waves, soaking the front windows and stuccoed walls of the house, leaving them crusted with white sea salt. At times, when the sisters were allowed to watch television, they had to turn the volume right up to get above the howling wind that vibrated the front door only feet from where they lay on the living room rug.

This kind of weather kept Judith and the rest of the town's wee folk indoors a great deal of the time. They say that fresh air and sunshine are healthy contributors to a growing child, but in this case Judith would have to be the exception. The isolation, and the unrelenting weather only encouraged her to nurture her young mind, to yearn for the wonders of a world that beckoned to her well beyond the coastal mountain ranges. Sensations and goals she could only explore while reading in her room at night from the colorful books she'd borrowed from the library.

These books were written about far off places and cities, and they brought Judith great joy, fueling her young dreams as she drifted off to sleep each night. The books she read, and playing school with Meryl in her bedroom brought her the most delight, as Meryl was always considerate enough to let Judith play the teacher. As far back as she could remember Judith had wanted to be teacher, and the hours spent playing this game while outdoors the wind blew the rain sideways came to her as naturally as walking. Her father had painted one side of a piece of three-quarter inch plywood a flat black, then had built a sturdy easel using two by two's for the wood to sit on. The chalkboard and the miniature wooden play chairs

113

immediately qualified Judith's small bedroom at the back of the house as the town's third school. Classes would commence once Meryl and the five or six rag dolls had been seated in their chairs, quietly waiting for Judith to begin her classes. Meryl would always be the smart one, always the first to put her hand up to answer a question while the rag dolls sat with vacant smiles stitched to their coarsely woven, muslin faces. Meryl would also be the first to become unruly, attempting to disrupt the class, eventually receiving a scolding and a detention for her efforts.

The rag dolls made up Judith's special class, the pupils who needed the extra time and understanding required to guide them through an education. When Meryl grew bored with the game, which would be a likely occurrence after a couple of hours, she would be dismissed and then Judith could focus her time on her special kids. Here she would engage her natural patience while she demonstrated something on the blackboard, or read aloud to them a fine story she herself had enjoyed. Many hours of Judith's free time were spent in this manner, reading and playing school, a harmless pastime that allowed her to absorb endless knowledge, while at the same time playing and growing. Some mothers checked their children's hands for cleanliness before a meal. Judith's mother Molly always checked hers for the chalk dust. Molly was a pretty woman, with long blond hair and a genuine laugh and a genuine love for her two growing daughters. When all three were together, Molly's genes could easily be seen spread throughout the willowy figures of her daughters. From the curly blonde hair and mischievous smiles that were always but a wink away from crossing their lips, right down to their slender feet and blue eyes. The girls appeared to have pure Molly, with very little of their father coursing through their blood. Some in the township were wont to say that the girls couldn't possibly have sprouted from their father's loins, so unlike him they had both become. Judith and Meryl both inherited their mother's good humor, as well as her stubborn attitude, but unlike their mother, they also carried a spirited will to adapt to their surroundings and use what they had to keep themselves happy and occupied.

Molly had never really liked the town, the isolation, the weather, and above all, she'd probably never really loved her husband. She thought she had, back when they were younger and free spirited and sex was treated with all the casualness of eating a sandwich. The girls had known something was wrong for a couple of years, or rather, had *felt* that something *wasn't* quite right.

They were too young to know that their parent's marriage was falling apart, yet old enough to feel the cold that pervaded their conversations, incessantly, like the sound of the cold surf that pounded the sand right across the street. In retrospect, if someone were to levy some blame, it would probably fall upon the shoulders of Judith's father Elwood. He had always been what many would call a dedicated Christian, the kind of person who went about his business in a quiet, friendly manner, and attended one of the town's two church's every Sunday, bringing his delightful family. Elwood and Molly had been married in a church, before they had moved to the company village where Elwood took a job in the mill's accounting office. A tall man, he was soft spoken, with a face that was fairly plain but unblemished. His urbane manner, the way in which he wore his dark hair short with a clean tie and a sweater, creased dress pants, and smooth black oxfords made him appear every inch a children's television show host. Like most everybody else who lived in the town, the seclusion began to affect Elwood's psyche in a way considered neither bad, but not altogether really good. His devout attitude had been there for years, though now it gathered momentum, indiscernible at first, but slowly building as the remote way of life niggled away at his insides. Regardless, there was more growing inside of Elwood Noble than just an evangelical zest, something apparently fueled by the bothersome, mundane existence found in a small town at the end of a remote peninsula. No one knew, nor could they, until it was too late.

Judith was almost eight months into her twelfth year when she and her sister really noticed the disturbing change within their father. Almost overnight, he had proclaimed himself a born again something or other, but born again would be an inappropriate term to affix to Elwood's affliction. Pontificating, loudmouthed, religious zealot would have been a bit closer to his present calling. For if it was secular and ungodly in any way, then Elwood wanted nothing to do with it.

Period, end of discussion. His malady rapidly gained velocity, sending his mind orbiting past the point of no return while his young daughters watched helpless and afraid. Elwood took to carrying a leather bound bible wherever he went, constantly caressing it in his hands until the rough grain of the leather became smooth. Once again, a harmless, relatively normal trait to most people living in the free world. Until he started hauling it out every time he felt an urge, like in the crowded grocery store, or the town's only movie theater during a weekend matinee. Or worse, while attending the company board meetings.

On Friday mornings while seated at the big oblong table in the boardroom above the first-aid station one could view his stirring performances, if one could only get a seat. There Elwood would noisily clear his throat during question period, and once he had their rapt attention, he would raise his voice an octave or two then expound the verses from the scriptures that seemed to apply to that particular predicament. The secretary, Miss Pibbles, a grand old dame with a hairy mole on her chin would meticulously record the minutes of every board meeting but wasn't sure if she should be writing all of Elwood's babble down. In the end though, she followed the lead set by the others, and watched on slack-jawed as the fool from accounting only entrenched himself deeper into a deranged quagmire. One of the baffling components of his slide from normality was his ability to still do his job, and do it well. So rather than reach out to the man as they should have, management let him be. They soon came to enjoy these expected outbursts, which enhanced their dull Friday morning meetings, contributing more than enough topics of discussion while lined up with their quarters at the coffee machine.

Elwood's sudden outbursts however, were starting to get embarrassing for the family, and were the cause of much argument inside the drab walls of the Noble household. Elwood would start flipping through his bible the minute Molly attempted to discuss family matters and the impending, marital break down. Seated at the kitchen table he would instantly set into Molly with his righteous spouting and it appeared to Judith as if her father had a magical on/off switch for his turbo-charged, religious intensity. A blank look would fall over his face whenever Molly sat with him at the table, trying to reason with him. But just as sure as the winter rains would fall from the skies, Elwood would produce his bible, berating Molly, attempting to persuade her to follow its reverent ways and hardy salvation. Like everything else in the world good or bad, a person could get too much of a certain thing, and Judith and Meryl were starting to realize this sad fact as they sat miserably in their bedrooms, listening to the bickering and their father's perpetual droning.

This unwholesome preaching caused the three Noble girls a great deal of stress, especially the young ones, who dearly loved their father but were too young to understand his plunge into a deepening abyss of his mental illness. If he wasn't chanting a prayer, then he was certainly thinking about saying one, and god help all young girls who chose the path of the promiscuous, philistine sluts. The marriage had rapidly deteriorated having already passed the point of being salvaged, and Molly would be the first to fall from the loyalty wagon, entering into a silent, but covert revolt. Elwood had been denied honey pot privileges for over a year now, and there wasn't a lot he could do that would reinstate his sexual liberties, nor did he seem to care. Molly had already found refuge in the bed of Jeremy Salter, the muscular young bush boss who lived alone in the company apartments, a short walk from the Noble home. She had met him one weekday afternoon in one of the bars, seeking to quench her growing thirst for the numbing embrace of liquor, as well to find some diversion. Salter was ten years junior to Molly, and the romping she did with him in his bed brought her a new found ecstasy of unimaginable proportions. She had never had an orgasm before. Every time they were together in his bedroom, Salter would bring Molly to that emotional tier of discovery, with his caressing mouth and knowing fingers. Thrilled with his own treasured find, Salter was to become an eager host to the good looking and willing Molly, an altogether alluring rarity in a tiny mill town. She was a find not to be scoffed at, or ignored.

This kind of lavish attention caused Molly an immediate addiction to the highly charged, physical climax whose voltage shot to every nerve ending within her body, leaving her tingling with glorious spasms as she gasped for breath. Something that had been missing from her marriage all these years, and she felt cheated for having lived so long without savoring these sensual, satisfyingly draining pleasures. These sexual liaisons intensified and Molly didn't have to work hard to cover her tracks. Salter worked twelve-hour shifts in the bush; four days on, four days off. Elwood worked Monday to Friday at the accounting office while Judith and Meryl attended school. By now however, Molly had become totally fed up with Elwood's god-fearing meanderings and she couldn't have cared less if he found out or not. The encounters were kept clandestine because Molly loved her girls, and wanted to protect them from the town's vicious circle of gossip.

Judith didn't realize how deep the damage had gone in her parents' marriage until she got up one night for a pee and found her mother sleeping on the couch under a comforter. She crawled in for a snuggle and could smell the liquor on Molly's breath, her voice dreamy and distant as she explained to her youngest daughter that all was not well inside the household, that one day she would be eventually leaving Judith's father. Judith fully understood what her mother had told her, and even understood the need to keep it a secret. A very tender age for a young girl to have to swear an allegiance, holding close to her the disturbing knowledge that the emotional bonds of her family were about to be torn apart. She fell asleep in her mother's arms on the couch, crying softly into her warm shoulder. In the morning, the little girl who still played school with her rag dolls in her bedroom had grown up in more ways than one, and not entirely out of choice. In many ways she had grown up out of necessity, and because of the secret she now shared with her mother.

Judith's family unit was slowly dissolving around her, and all she could do was watch, wait, and hope that when her mother did leave, she would take her and her sister with her. Judith had subconsciously picked sides in the peaking dispute, but once again, it was something done out of necessity. That, along with a failing confidence in her father. Shortly after waking up the next morning, Judith got her turn in the family's single bathroom and was horrified when she found blood spotting her cotton panties. She broke into tears once again, and her mother rushed to her side, closing the bathroom door behind her. With all the emotional turmoil taking place under the roof, Molly had forgotten to talk to Judith about her maturing body, and imminent biological seasons. Now it was too late. Judith's young body had come of age and the process had utterly terrified her. Molly sat on the toilet seat and held her youngest daughter, cursing her selfish stupidity while she calmed Judith down. Once the crisis had passed, Molly gently explained to her daughter about her monthly flow, and how some girls started earlier than others. Meryl's had begun just a half a year back, so Judith, two years younger, had come as a bit of a surprise. Molly then showed Judith where the feminine hygiene supplies were kept, demonstrating their use then patiently answered the dozen or so questions that her daughter had. On top of everything else going on in her disconcerting world, Judith Noble had started the natural, challenging progression into womanhood. Although it was something she wasn't entirely sure she was ready for.

*   *   *

Chapter Eleven

Already precocious, Meryl became the second Noble to revolt against her father's rapid slide into a secluded, sanctimonious oblivion. Meryl's unthinking, spontaneous actions however carried far more consequences than her mother's indiscretions ever would. Approximately four weeks had gone by since Judith had found her mother sleeping on the couch and not a lot had changed around the dispirited household. Elwood continued with his righteous ravings and if anything, they seemed to get worse for now there was much mention of the devil, and the skulking shadows he had for disciples. "The bastards were everywhere," he would holler. But like the crashing surf and the relentless rain the three girls became accustomed to the sound and could tune him out without so much as a shameful thought. Very soon though, even the rhythmic tone of the heavy rain and the breaking waves subsided as the town was treated to an early, cloudless spring. Molly's fling with Jeremy Salter continued unabated and the pair was starting to develop strong feelings for each other, discussing the future while they lay spent in each other's arms. The fact that Molly had two growing girls seemed only to delight Jeremy rather than to deter him, making him even more of a rare find. Molly had gone to his bed strictly for the promise of lustful sex, but as the relationship matured she soon became sedate and blissful with the direction it was heading and did nothing to stem her blossoming feelings. If anything, the sex had developed into something more intimate and passionate, brought to new levels by the natural course of their affections.

Judith had stopped playing school with her rag dolls and couldn't be sure why she had cast aside something that brought her so much joy. She was growing up, and that thought never entered her mind as she dusted off a space on her pine book case then lined the dolls up on a shelf and left them there smiling. Meryl had grown tired of playing school a long time ago, so Judith concentrated her efforts on her second love, feeding her strong desire for as much knowledge as her head could hold. Summer wasn't too far away and as the days grew longer the children of the town, their faces blanch from the sunless winter appeared on the streets of the village, running and laughing through the wet grass of the parks. The isolation and the common denominator of their parents work at the mill brought the children and the

119

teenagers together in close groups, segregated by age only. Judith became conspicuous in her refusal to join any of these groups, choosing instead to put her nose into a descriptive book about the Roman Empire, or the far journeying Crusades of the Middle Ages. Reading necessarily didn't mean staying indoors, for part of the attraction to these books was their portability. Judith could usually be found near the fringes of these groups, sitting on a park bench, or even walking down the main street obliviously reading as a story danced off the quickly turned pages.

Meryl chummed around with a mixed group who had built a clubhouse of sorts in the dense woods above the town site. Nothing had been planned regarding the construction of the small dwelling until a truckload of cedar planks fell scattered from a flatbed on a sharp corner near the edge of town. The wood had been destined for the community hall where it would cover the tired facade of the old building. Meryl's gang was unofficially led by a pubescent, pimply-faced, conniving son-of-bitch whom constantly picked his nose and always wanted to show the girls his penis. His name was Kyle Mortimer and he must have had nearly a yard of metal fused to his teeth to help tame his comical over bite. The braces and the installation alone must have cost close to four thousand dollars, never mind the free helicopter rides in the company chopper to the big city where the orthodontist would make his monthly adjustments. Once Kyle and his followers stumbled upon the abandoned load of cedar planks they carted a good portion of it into the woods where construction commenced on the clubhouse as soon as school had been let out for the weekend. Kyle's father was the mill manager, something that led him to believe that he could have free run of the town, something that would eventually prove itself a sad truism. Mister Mortimer and his family lived in the largest house in the community, a two-story affair with a double car garage set well back from the rest of the village in a secluded clump of fir trees. If you worked at the mill, and you probably did, and if there was ever an ass you might want to think about kissing, then big John Mortimer's buttocks would be the set that would do you the most good.

It would be the power that John Mortimer wielded over the town, the building of the secluded clubhouse and the rapid, mental decline of Elwood Noble that would all contribute to Meryl's unpredictable fall from good poise and innocent virtue. Once a proper survey had been conducted in the woods, Kyle's merry band found four sturdy trees growing close together, their bases surrounded by a thick bed of soft green moss. These growing posts nearly formed a perfect square, so it became a small matter and some concentrated effort to nail the planks up the sides of the trees to form the walls. Using tools borrowed from their fathers' workbenches and nails stolen from the local hardware store, Kyle and his intrepid crew had built their official clubhouse during the span of a warm Saturday afternoon. Kyle Mortimer of course supervised the whole construction, and any lip or arguing from his young serfs quickly found the violator banished from the project. By the end of the day they had a roof over their heads, and the rough-hewn planks and living trees had been transformed into a functional abode. Word of this monumental achievement quickly made its rounds, passed among the young people of the village and fairly soon groups of kids made the pilgrimage into the forest to view the highly secretive fort. Days later Kyle had a loyal following of thirteen and fourteen year old young people who stole away with him to the clubhouse to smoke pilfered cigarettes and listen to music on a battery operated radio. Judith wasn't the least bit amused that her older sister had taken up with this somewhat dysfunctional crowd. True, she may have had her face buried within the informative pages of a good book, but even Judith could see that this shack in the woods would eventually come to no good.

Two days later however, Judith herself had surrendered to all the hoopla, her curiosity tainting her better judgment. She walked up alone into the forest, clutching a large book, finally deciding to have a look at the much talked about clubhouse. As she approached the shanty she thought herself to be alone but when she peeked inside she found Kyle sitting inside the sturdy four walls, mindlessly picking away at one of his nostrils. He jumped to his feet and smiled openly, displaying the metal tracks that lined his teeth, graciously welcoming her inside.

Judith stepped through the narrow opening that formed the doorway and looked around while Kyle rummaged through a canvas rucksack that hung from a nail on one of the walls. In short order he produced a large, red rubber dildo that was fashioned after a man's penis. Kyle held up the disgusting cylindrical device as if it were a trophy, then flipped a switch causing it to buzz in his hand like a set of barber's clippers. He then reached for his fly, tugging on the zipper, inviting Judith to have a look at what was causing the bulge in his trousers. Judith would have nothing to do with Kyle's vulgar exhibitions and told him so, calling him a filthy little ne'er-do-well before promptly leaving the premises. Kyle quickly followed though, begging her not to tell anyone about the dildo because he'd stolen it from his mother's underwear drawer. Judith ignored Kyle's whining as she walked quickly along the worn footpath, leaving him behind in the forest while she returned to the late afternoon sunshine of the town's only park. Sitting alone on one of the hardwood swings she eagerly returned to her picturesque book, flipping through the pages as she read as much as she could take in about the French Revolution and the subsequent beheading of Marie Antoinette and King Louis XVI.

As the sun descended into the western sky the air became chilled, cooled by the immediate proximity of the cold pacific ocean, raising goose bumps on Judith's bare arms as a slight wind wafted through her blonde hair. Marking her place by making a fold in the corner of the page, Judith tucked the book under her arm and followed the back alley that led her home. She entered through the back door of the plain house to find the windows all steamed up, an open pot of water boiling on the stovetop. Her mother sat at the kitchen table drinking a large glass of orange juice with square ice cubes floating on the top, tinkling against the clear walls of the tumbler whenever she took a sip. Molly's mood was cheerful but spurious, brought about by the half pint of vodka she'd already consumed since coming home, having spent another glorious afternoon in Jeremy Salter's bed. At the time Judith knew nothing about Mister Salter, nor did she know about her mothers slide toward alcoholism, preferring to blame her giddy behavior on her father's increasing weirdness.

Her mother beckoned to her and she walked over to receive a reassuring hug, enjoying the warm embrace as well as the kiss her mother left on her forehead. Judith placed her book on the sideboard then wandered over to the stovetop to peek at the pot of boiling water and the two boxes of macaroni and cheese that sat on the counter top. A cookie sheet with those disgusting, gooey pieces of pastry you wrap wieners in stood near the boxes of macaroni, ready for the hot oven. As of late the meals in the Noble household had been turning into a pathetic experience, a fact one couldn't help but notice. Although Judith's father didn't seem to recognize the declining quality of the meals. He would sit down at the table and invoke quiet spells, condemning the world's sacrilegious to a fiery hell, then give hearty thanks for the hot bounty that lay limp and colorless on his plate. Life inside the house was in dire need of some change. Something to give the pace a bit of a lift, something to put the smiles back on the occupants faces, and if that meant Molly leaving Elwood, then maybe that wouldn't be such a bad thing after all. Judith still kept her mother's secret about leaving home close to her heart, and she hadn't even told Meryl about it. Changes were on the way however. Drastic, painful changes that would be set in motion by a very unexpected quarter of the family. Judith let out a long sigh as she started for her bedroom door, leaving her mother to sip quietly on her orange juice. Halfway down the dimly lit hallway she heard her mother call out to her, requesting she go out to fetch her sister for dinner. Judith let out another quiet sigh. Her homework would now have to wait until after supper, when all the dishes were washed, dried, and put away in the cupboards.

Judith returned to the kitchen, giving her mother a weak smile as she took a red knit sweater from the coat rack near the back door then walked down the wooden stairs and out into the falling twilight. The western sky had turned a deep bluish hue, almost the color of lavender and it stretched out until it appeared to meld with the dark ocean on the curving, distant horizon. In the east above the treetops, some of the brighter stars were already winking down from the black canopy of deep space. Judith paused for a moment to put her sweater on and button it up, gazing up into the heavens, taking in and savoring the wonder of it all, appreciating the rare peacefulness of the moment. She then retraced her earlier steps back to the park, hoping one of the kids still playing there might know the immediate whereabouts of her sister. She approached a girl from her own class, a tiny, shy oriental child named Susie who sat alone on the swings. Susie shook her head no. She hadn't seen Meryl anywhere. Judith walked over to the remaining two or three kids who were playing tag by the sand box but they shook their heads at her polite inquiries as well. Meryl might have gone up the hill to the high school to smoke cigarettes with a couple of her friends, but for some reason Judith felt drawn to the clubhouse in the forest. Might as well check the clubhouse first she thought, as it was on the way to the high school. She would take a sturdy stick with her this time in case that twerp Kyle was still there and decided to get cheeky again.

Judith left the park, talking the sidewalk that paralleled the road , trudging in the direction of the forest above the town, the twilight rapidly slipping into the inkiness of another night. When she entered the forest she stood on the edge for a minute, allowing her eyes to adjust to the darkness. She found a long broken piece of fir branch lying next to the trail and she picked it up, finding it to be fairly swishy with a diameter that fit neatly into her small hands. Buoyed with the courage the simple weapon brought her, Judith set off into the dark woods, following the narrow trail that led to the clubhouse. Minutes later she arrived at her destination, the wooden shack easily spotted with a faint, white light shining out from the slits in the planked walls. She approached quietly, hearing muted voices, preferring not to alert Kyle to her presence if at all possible. Judith could quickly peek between the cracks in the walls and if Meryl weren't there, she would quietly be on her way. Carefully, she walked across the bed of springy moss, putting one foot down before shifting her weight to the other. As she got up to the walls of the clubhouse a large knothole was positioned in one of the planks, conveniently located at eye level for Judith's viewing pleasure. She put her eye up to the hole, then let go an involuntary gasp, for she didn't much like what she saw. In fact . . . it outright sickened her.

A round plastic flashlight lay on the green mossy ground, it's light illuminating the inside of the clubhouse, casting long shadows against the opposing wall. Meryl lay on her back on an old gray blanket, naked from the waist down, her slender legs spread, exposing the delicate creases of her sex, the soft, blonde downy hairs tufting above the skin of her pubic area. Kyle knelt above her, his pants and underwear down around his ankles, his penis hard, a sorry looking thing that wavered obscenely bellow his white belly. Kyle lowered himself on top of Meryl, prodding away with his whang, searching blindly for the opening that would let him enter her young body. Meryl suddenly cried out in pain as Kyle found his mark and thrust himself into her. The young man's bare ass pumped up and down about three times before he stopped and shuddered, gasping out with what appeared to be raptured pleasure. Judith had seen enough of this wicked act and made for the opening of the shack, drawing back on the fir branch so it stood poised above her shoulders. She hesitated only long enough to make out the pus-colored pimples that dotted Kyle's backside, then swung the limb with everything she had, bringing the stick down, swishing the air as it broke across the young man's buttocks. Kyle screamed out as a thick rising welt spanned both his soft cheeks like an instant tattoo, ample evidence to Judith's sudden anger. He rolled away from Meryl, rubbing the stinging flesh of his ass and looked threateningly at Judith. She held what was left of the tree limb in her hands, the jagged tip inches from Kyle's sneering face and there could be no mistaking her meaning.

Judith would have loved to have beaten the life from the tiny wet appendage hanging between his legs but it soon became a tricky target, shriveling up to the size of a sun-dried tomato.

She held Kyle at arms length as Meryl quickly pulled her clothes on, shivering involuntarily from the cold now that the moment of heated passion had passed. Once Meryl was dressed, Judith gave Kyle one last piece of sage advice before leaving him alone in his clubhouse.

"You ever take a run at my sister again Kyle I'll knock your teeth out, so help me god."

Her voice was quiet and controlled, uttering the words in a manner most suggestive of the reality of such a violent act. A sure signpost from Judith that the warning wasn't a hotheaded, off the tongue threat. At that moment in time Kyle Mortimer, son of big John the Mill Manager, feared for his well-being and that of the little worm he carried around in his pants. He would have to think twice before ever suggesting again to Meryl Noble that he bring his dilly out so that she could play with it. Kyle glanced away from the ominous look that Judith had fixed to her face, reaching down to his ankles for his underwear, quickly preparing a rebuttal and suggesting a possible peace plan. By the time he'd pulled his underwear up though the sisters were gone, having vanished into the chilling night. Nevertheless, there would be one more occasion in the coming months when Kyle and Judith would tangle once again, and when that happened the outcome would not be a pretty sight at all.

Judith pulled her sister by the hand through the woods, hurt and angered by what she had done and whom she had done it with it. She had learned all about sexual intercourse from her mother and the books she had read from the library, so there were no misconceptions as to what had taken place inside that vile wooden clubhouse. Meryl pleaded as Judith pulled her along, trying to down play the physical coupling as if it were some kind of a harmless experiment, but Judith would have no part of her explanation. They exited the woods to find the roadway almost as dark as the forest behind them and as they followed the short road down to the town, Meryl continued with her pleading, begging Judith to hold her tongue about what she'd seen. But all she received for her entreating bleats was an icy silence, and Meryl allowed herself to be pulled in the direction of town by her sensible sister. Judith could see the ebony flicker of bat's wings against the stars above her head as they fluttered through the night sky in search of flying insects. The night had turned strangely quiet, with most of the village at home having dinner, or at the distant mill starting the afternoon shift. Meryl realized then that she had a sister who was wise and intelligent and had matured years beyond her own age.

By the time they got to the edge of the deserted park Meryl had been reduced to sobbing tears, crying out for Judith's forgiveness, beseeching her not to tell anybody about what she had done.

The tears broke through the last of Judith's formidable determination, and she turned to face the sister she loved so very much, reaching up to put her arms around her. They stood alone in the park, under the stars, both crying and holding onto what seemed to be the last solid splinter of their fractured lives. Judith promised Meryl she wouldn't tell anybody of what she had seen in the clubhouse. It now became a secret, something bound by the close affections of two sisters lost in the fragile and unsettling complexity of everyday life. Now Judith had two secrets to hold close inside of her; her mother's revelation of leaving her father, and now Meryl's misconduct in a wooden clubhouse in a dark forest. It was a hell of a burden for any twelve-year-old to carry on their shoulders.

But then . . . Judith Noble wasn't just any twelve-year-old.

*   *   *

Chapter Twelve

The days at the village gradually grew longer with the onset of the summer months, the temperature steadily rising with each passing day and week. It was shaping up to be one of those rare seasons when the rain clouds would disappear for weeks at a time, bringing the small animals out for their daily foraging, while putting smiles on everybody's faces as they shucked the listless confines of a wet spring. Squirrels darted among the deep grasses of the park, one beady eye sweeping skyward where the bald eagles circled on the rising thermals that were created when the cold air from the ocean rolled over the warm, sun soaked land.

The children of the village had taken to running through the streets in sleeveless shirts and wearing shorts, their pale skin slowly turning a nut brown as they toned up with the sun's unobstructed rays. As the days grew with the promise of a bright, energetic summer, so did the disorder that afflicted Elwood Noble, taking him deeper into a self-righteous obscurity. Judith's father had slipped to the point where he now let his meticulous grooming fall to the wayside, preferring to bathe and shave every second of third day, choosing to use the toilet with the door wide open, sitting there tooting and blowing while he mumbled outlandish spells to himself.

There were however, long hours of apparent stability, times when he seemed quite normal, times when he would reach out to his daughter's and hug them lightly, but even these moments of limited affection were rapidly diminishing. Elwood somehow managed to continue balancing his tally sheets at the accounting department at the mill while still receiving the attention of a modest sized audience at the weekly board meetings. Every seven days without fail, he would deliver onto them his rousing, sermonizing performances.

Molly still lived at home and this appeared to the girls as a hopeful reconciliation of sorts, a possible salvation to their parent's deteriorating marriage, even though she still slept on the couch. The union however was breathing it's last gasping breath, wallowing on in a loveless existence, held together by the piece of paper that made their bond legal if only in the eyes of the law. Molly had fallen in love with Jeremy Salter, and the feelings were returned in kind.

Their surreptitious affair continued at a furious pace, and word of the liaison had started to drift through the coffee shops and park benches that dotted the village. One can be as careful as one likes, but affairs in small towns can't be concealed forever, for sooner than later someone eventually spies something not all together ordinary and the scandal lines start to heat up.

Isolated communities thrive on juicy, sexual gossip, and talk of Molly's fling would be what was needed to put some vigor into the middling days.

During this period of early summer and grown-up scandal mongering Meryl celebrated her fourteenth birthday. Her family had a bit of a party, but it would go the way of everything else in the household, ultimately spinning into a dismal affair. Molly and Elwood, during one of the rare times they could agree on anything had bought Meryl a cassette player with headphones so she could listen to music without vibrating the walls of the house. The device had a folding handle on the top and could be operated with batteries, so Meryl could take it with her wherever she went.

Molly had purchased a specially decorated triple layered chocolate cake for the gala event, having called ahead to the old German couple who ran the local bakery. It had a plastic cheerleader with long yellow hair and a pleated skirt doing the splits in the thick brown icing and even though she wasn't a cheerleader, Meryl reckoned it was the thought that really counted. Supper would comprise of Meryl's favorite pizza, which had been ordered from an old grease stained menu found in the doohickey drawer in the kitchen. The three girls were gathered at the kitchen table and the merrymaking moved along at a reasonably happy pace.

Then Elwood came home, the buttons on the front of his shirt undone, his fly wide open and his dark hair sticking up all over the place. He went straight into the bathroom down the hall without so much as a happy birthday or a howdy do. There he "hung a rat," standing with the door wide open while he urinated into the toilet bowl with the seat still down. Judith looked at Meryl with a sad expression, feeling woeful for her sister, knowing that her father's inconsiderate behavior was symbolic of where her sister's special day was now headed. Elwood then came to the kitchen to join the festivities, having forgotten to wash his hands, his sloppiness further enhanced by the urine stains spotting the front of his pants. Elwood was having another one of those agonizing days where he had an invisible devil perched on one shoulder and an angel hovering above the other, both shouting into his ears at the same time. When their father had one of those days, the Noble girls were systematically drawn into it for nobody likes to suffer alone.

Regardless of their father, the two girls gathered their plucky courage and sang happy birthday for Meryl. Judith was still singing the verses using her own words when the front door bell rang and the joy fizzled out as the evening came crashing down. Elwood, being the man of the house got up to answer the door, finding the pizza delivery boy standing on the cement steps with two large, flat, steaming boxes. Of course, the boy was in Meryl's homeroom class at the high school and of course he was regarded as the town crier. Elwood instantly ripped into him because his baseball cap had a caricature of a dancing devil on the peak, the pagan mascot of some faraway hockey team. The young lad's eyes rounded into two very large brown marbles as the fear fell upon his face and it became a wonder he didn't wet himself. Seconds later the boy had run off into the night without even waiting to get paid, back to the sanctity of his parents take-out restaurant located up the street. Molly opened up on Elwood the moment he returned to the kitchen with the food, calling him a son-of-a-bitch and a bastard and a whole host of other rude names she deemed appropriate for the situation. Elwood quickly returned fire, safe in the knowledge that the lord was wholly on his side, then the hissing and spitting started, soon escalating to the wonderful heights of an outright shouting match.

Molly and Elwood were on their feet, standing toe to toe on the tacky yellow linoleum and during a slight lull Meryl took some of the pizza and went to her bedroom to plug herself into her birthday present. The other daughter was hastily given some money by her mother then sent up the road to pay the food bill. As she walked through the calm evening Judith fought hard to hold back the tears, trying to make sense of what was happening to her father and why. No one seemed to care too much about what happened to Elwood any more except his two daughters, and they could only watch on as he drifted deeper into a psychological hole.

When Judith got to the restaurant she paid the food bill, quietly apologizing to the delivery boy's parents. They couldn't understand English anyway so she returned home straightaway to find her parents still arguing, their cheerless voices reaching out to the street as she approached the house. Silently she went inside the house, got herself a plate from the cupboard, and took some food from the pizza boxes while world war three erupted around her. Judith went to her room then shut the door, collapsing on her bed, leaving the pizza to go cold on her desk.

Too much . . . too fast, she thought. The Noble sisters were starting to get overwhelmed with the emotional bedlam, which at best was all that remained of their once stable family life. Things were going to get worse though, for the family's problems had crept into the only refuge the girl's had left, the only neutral ground they knew of, which would be their schools.

In the days following the wretched birthday party, Judith and Meryl would become the victims of some vicious teasing while attending classes or on the school grounds at recess. Some of the mean spirited younger folk had heard about Elwood's ranting's from their parents, or had seen first hand a verbose exhibition at one of the local stores. Now word of Molly's affair had started to make the rounds and the stories fell easily from the mouths of the adults, spurred along by the juicy gossip, quickly picked up by the ignorant ears of their children to be repeated in the supposedly innocent hallways of the schools. But kids will be kids, and they were too naive to have known about the grief they were causing the Noble sisters. Much to their credit, Judith and Meryl continued to put up a strong, brave front, shouldering the ruthless taunting while saving their anguish for their pillows at night. It was this idle talk and the relentless teasing that brought the sisters closer together, at the same time driving them to seek some seclusion, which they had found about a mile down the road from their house. A natural upheaval of rocks cut through the width of a lonely beach forming a long jagged wall that eventually plunged below the breaking waves of the low tide. Found quite by accident during a lengthy, idyllic walk, Judith and Meryl took to retreating to this remote spot and would sit for hours in the warm sunshine during the weekends and after school. They would talk and console each other, venting their feelings while far away from prying eyes and rude lips. Their only company would be the barking seals and the squawking seagulls that would foolishly swoop upon the eagles for whatever tidbit they held in their beaks. Judith organized a hopscotch game in the firm part of the sand using carefully chosen, slender pieces of driftwood. After placing the wood to form the borders of the large squares, Judith would play alone, tossing a clamshell from the starting line to begin her one legged hopping. Meryl watched while they talked, thinking herself a bit old for hopscotch, but nonetheless joining her sister in the odd game. That's what sisters did. They became closer then than they had ever been in their entire lives, an intimacy shared by two siblings whose world was being mercilessly dismantled around them. The pair felt safe on this piece of sand, and they felt fortunate to have found it.

On the weekends they would take a lunch and a thermos of juice that Molly had packed for them, and they would steal away to they private beach, under strict orders not to go near the water.

But they did anyway. An early afternoon swim was always on the agenda, but they didn't venture too far into the cold surf, retreating after their brief dips to loll around on a wide log, blonde head touching blonde head, talking girl stuff while their incriminating wet clothes dried in the hot sun. Nearly six weeks before school had recessed for the summer, Molly had to take Meryl to the Doctor one Tuesday morning after she woke with what appeared to be a stewing fever.

The Doctor had her go to the lab at the hospital where they took some blood and had her pee in one of those absurdly small dixie cups. Meryl was kept home sick for the rest of the week, which put the brakes on Molly's extra curricular romping with Mister Salter. Come Friday, Meryl had managed to make a remarkable recovery, just in time to join her sister for the trek down to their beach. Getting in a couple of hours of sunning and innocent laughter before suppertime was just what doctor Judith had ordered. It turned into an unusually hot afternoon, and Judith even talked Meryl into playing hopscotch with her, after first hunting down two dissimilar looking clamshells.

Within minutes the sand became marked with the imprints of their slender feet, and you could readily tell Meryl's as her feet were slightly longer than Judith's. The sister's hopped up and down on the beach for about an hour playing hopscotch, tossing their clam shells while the warm sun fell toward the ocean. They had sat down in the sand to drink their sodas when Molly's head appeared above the tall boundary of broad leaf sedge. The grass grew wild along the side of the road; its long slender leaves the color of bok choy, forming a thick border that stopped the sand from blowing onto the roadway when the westerlies blew in from the ocean. Molly called out to them, and then followed the trail down to the white sand, standing in front of them as they drank their pop. Her expression told the girl's that something serious was afoot, and they quietly shielded the sun from their eyes with their hands as they gazed up into their mother's face.

Meryl had to return to the doctor's office, something had shown up in one of her tests and the results needed to be discussed. Molly would take her there in the family car, meeting their father at the clinic after dropping

Judith off at home. Wordlessly, Judith and Meryl gathered up their belongings and hurried after their mother to the brown station wagon that sat idling at the side of the road.

After climbing into the front seat of the car with their mother, Molly turned the vehicle around and drove back into town. Judith could almost taste the trepidation inside the car and neither girl said a word, taking their cue from their normally effervescent mother. Molly stopped the car in front of the house and Judith quietly got out, standing for a minute on the worn, cracked cement of the front path. She watched as the station wagon drove off, threading its way among the old clapboard buildings of the downtown area, heading across the village to the medical clinic located on a rock bluff behind the public library. For some reason, Judith felt helpless and alone as the family car vanished on the other side of a steep hill that marked the geographical center of the town. The family Doctor was a kindly old codger with warm gentle hands, rheumy eyes, and a soft laugh that told a sick child that everything would be all right as long as he had his fingers on your pulse. Except this time it would be different, for the gloomy bit of medical news and the consequences that was about to be imparted on young Meryl, not even the kindhearted Doctor could reverse. Inside of a meager twenty-four hours, the already agitated world that Judith had come to know would abruptly change and to such an indeterminate degree that it would forever chase away the innocence of the young girl that dwelled inside her.

*   *   *

Chapter Thirteen

During the course of the evening low clouds had blown in some three hundred miles from across the Pacific Ocean. Floating motionless after the wind had spent itself, they obscured the ragged peaks of the coastal range and smudged the entire sky the tint of wet shale. The base of these clouds started near the elevation of the tree line where fir and spruce gave way to the solid bare rock, a place so cold and barren that not even a thought could grow there. This would be the altitude the company helicopter would be flying at. Below the clouds, so the pilot could utilize visual flight rules, which employed contour maps, ground feature orientation, both a digital and magnetic compass, and then radio signals once the aircraft cleared the static confines of the mountains. The pilot, a short stocky balding man they called "Digger," was busy doing his pre flight checks, having already removed the tie downs that secured the two main rotor blades on the Bell Jet Ranger helicopter. He moved over the machine using both his hands and practiced eyes to check for any obvious irregularities that could spoil an otherwise typical flight to the open, smoky skies of the big city. Even though his mechanic had carefully gone over the aircraft the previous evening, Digger was exclusively responsible for anything that occurred after take off and during the flight. Not only was Digger concerned about his own safety and that of his passengers, but he was also a company man who enjoyed all the benefits of a good pay package and endless hours of flying without having to pay a dime for the fuel and the maintenance costs. He took great pride in taking care of and flying this very expensive piece of high tech machinery.

The helicopter's exterior had been detailed in the company's colors of yellow and green, with a decal of the distinct corporate logo centered over the machinery and freight doors located aft of the windowed crew compartment. They had even taken the time and money to paint the slender boom that housed the tail rotor a bright fluorescent orange. It looked a bit gaudy and it played pure hell on your eyes if you looked at it long enough in the bright sunshine, eventually giving you sneezing fits. However, gaudy or not, the brash color allowed you to be quickly spotted by the search and rescue folks should you have the kind of a day that ended with a crash. Digger had never crashed an aircraft and had no intention of ever thundering in, but he would take all the insurance they could give him, including the loud colored tail boom. Army-trained and well-experienced, he had been with the company for well over a decade, and although the Jet Ranger was smaller than the wide bodied Huey's he'd flown in South East Asia, it had become the perfect job for a veteran pilot in his late forties. These milk runs were easy on the soul, good for the heart, and with a couple of years left to a full pension there could be no better way to float the days away until retirement.

The helicopter had its own landing pad behind the mill and close to the tidal waters of the bay, where all the approaches had been cleared of standing fir trees. One of the shop painter's had put down a large "H" in bright yellow paint on the asphalt a few hundred feet from the last of the stacks of drying lumber. A hangar with an office had been built and devoted to the pilot and his mechanic. On a tall aluminum pole above the hangar stood a red and white-stripped nylon windsock, presently dangling lifelessly from its swivels in the still air. Digger hummed to himself as he pulled the logbook from his thick leather briefcase, which sat upright on the pilot's seat.

Holding the wide ledger across his arm, he stood by the aircraft as he entered the date and time on a fresh page, ensuring he adhered to company rules by using black ink. Sorting through his brief case, he organized the contour maps that he would need for the flight down, and then slid them into a flat pocket at the side of his bucket seat, all within easy reach. Digger knew most of the roads, rivers, forests, and outcropping of rocks that led you safely through the valley's and deep gorges of the coastal range. Ever the diligent pilot, a quick scan at a map while moving over the land at one-hundred-miles per hour would go a long way at reconfirming your position, as well as further eliminating the chances of any pilot error.

This trip would be one of those swan jobs that tended to come Digger's way every few months or so. Excursions like these helped make up for all those goddamned nut crushers he'd flown overseas while fighting that miserable scuffle some called a war. Digger's instructions for today's flight couldn't be any clearer, or any simpler.

Or any sweeter for that matter.

He was to fly one of the office employee's and his daughter to the city for some urgent medical attention, and he was to languish there in a four star hotel until they were finished, which might take a day or two. The mill manager had called him at home last night to authorize the mercy flight and the expenses involved. Digger, alone in the big city and with a quarter inch of cash in his wallet could truly be something to behold, especially after many weeks of geographically enforced celibacy. There weren't a lot of single girls in the village and those who were willing and eager, well, the less said the better. While living in the one-bedroom beach cabin the company rented him in the village, Digger stuck to his self-imposed rule of not pissing in his own backyard. A discipline that required him to keep his frankfurter zipped up in his pants, a mammoth effort for someone as virile as Digger. His sacrifice returned huge dividends in keeping the horny strays from sniffing around his front doorstep. That was one of the things that always irritated him about women. They always wanted to hang around after doing the dirty deed, snuggling and purring in your ear when you were trying to eat left-over pizza and channel surf. The rules for rutting in the big city were different, and were the only set of rules that Digger liked to play by. Once he had purged himself he would toss his partner from his hotel room then sit on the bed in his underwear and call room service to send up a clubhouse and a frosted beer.

"Sweet, unobliging intercourse be mine . . . yes!" Digger thought this to himself as he checked his briefcase one more time for his box of ultra latex, thin ribbed condoms. His game plan would be simple and his goals could be construed by many as somewhat Neanderthal. Digger's method of attack would be crude at best, readily summed up in two diverse stages of execution; drink lots of draft beer, then engage in lewd, sexual intercourse with some lucky "broad." This uninhibited pilot wasn't too particular either, as long as the women he picked up in the bars on the hotel strip weren't overtly ugly, looked acceptably clean and had at least taken the time to shave their armpits.

No dogs, no weirdness, no hairy armpits. No sir, not on this trip.

Happy with his condom stash and entirely confident he would exhaust his supply, he strapped his briefcase into one of the back seats just as a crew cab truck drove slowly from behind the towering piles of stacked lumber. Perfect, Digger thought. His passengers had arrived. The truck was driven by one of the company security guard's, and it stopped well away from the stationary helicopter. A man and a young girl climbed from the truck and Digger recognized the tall man with the disheveled dark hair as the born-again loon from the accounting department. The blonde haired, teenaged girl he'd never seen before. She carried a portable cassette player with her, holding it by the handle, letting it swing loosely at her side, the headphones snugged down over her ears. She had been crying so much that each startling blue eye looked like the puckered red dot of a pig's ass and Digger hoped that it wasn't cancer that had caused her all this grief.

Her father carried two overnight bags in his hands and had a black leather bible tucked away under one of his arms. Digger walked out to greet them, taking the bags from the man and quickly and efficiently stowing them behind a thin door along the fuselage.

He helped the girl into the rear passenger compartment, then showed her how to buckle and unbuckle the harness that fell over her slender shoulders. Her father, the religious fanatic named Elwood was the subject of numerous stories making the rounds throughout the company lines, so Digger decided to keep the conversation light. Elwood climbed into the left front seat of the helicopter, and Digger secured the door for him. They always liked to slam the doors on his aircraft like it was some kind of an old dump truck, and nothing pissed Digger off more, so he secured the delicate latches for them. He walked around the clear bubble nose of the helicopter, giving the machine one final once over with his eyes before climbing into the right-hand side.

Elwood managed to get himself buckled in without any direction so he couldn't have been an out right simpleton, but Digger decided to forgo showing him the headsets and boom microphone that hung on a hook the bulkhead above his head. This was going to be too good a trip to be spoiled by some lunatic quoting bible verses into his headsets. Not while he concentrated on his flying, and his beer drinking, and of course his much anticipated coitus.

Digger pulled his own headsets on, adjusting the boom mike while flipping toggle switches above him and on the instrument panel mounted in the center of the cockpit. He then started the main turbine engine, listening carefully to the smooth whirring as it spun to life, gaining momentum as the main rotor blades starting to turn above the plexiglass canopy. Reaching for the radio dial below the main instrument panel, Digger flicked the frequency to one-twenty-six-point-seven, and then spoke clearly into his boom mike. Adopting his deep, professional pilot's voice he broadcast his call sign, location, and direction of travel to any conflicting pilots who might be airborne in the area. Greeted with a satisfactory radio silence, he could now assume there would be no other aircraft plying the friendly skies in his immediate vicinity.

At this early stage of the flight, Digger had no radio contact with any air traffic controllers, nor would he until he cleared the mountain ranges. Once free of the solid rock that impeded his radio transmissions to the airport, he would identify himself to flight control by pushing a button on his radio, "squawking" them a signal that would identify his position on their sweeping radar. They would then direct his flight into the busy international airport, adjusting his bearings and altitude as he flowed into the crowded flight paths. A flight plan had been filed and phoned in first thing this morning so his route and estimated time of arrival were already known to the flight controllers at his destination. Digger liked to think himself a careful pilot as well as lucky, a combination that had thus far played big in his fast paced lifestyle. He had witnessed many fine young men die when he'd served in Asia, very nearly having his own ass shot off a goodly number of times while flying those endless combat missions. Digger hadn't survived that lopsided, unpopular, futile charade they called a war to ignore routine flying procedures at this stage of his career. During the war he had become a firm believer that when your time had come there wasn't a lot you could do about it, and when it happened you'd know because you'd hear either the devil or the Lord knocking on your door. Digger had no idea who would be knocking when his time came, but with a box of condoms stowed in his briefcase he did have his suspicions. Luck, playing safe, and fornication were three of Digger's closest companions.

Watching the main temperature gauge on the instrument panel move into the operating parameters, he turned in his seat to give the young girl behind him an encouraging nod, but she was listening to her music while staring vacantly out the window. Her father appeared lost in a trance as he sat like a ballasted lump in the seat beside Digger, looking straight ahead, mouthing some sort of a prayer as his lips moved every few seconds. There couldn't be a lot of joy in this family Digger thought, not with the father so messed up and he couldn't help but feel sorry for the young girl seated behind him. Gradually, he pulled up on the collective stick that was positioned beside his seat, causing the aircraft to wobble lightly on its skids. With his feet placed lightly on the aluminum pedals, he controlled the synchronized tail rotor, which kept the aircraft in a straight line, as well as allowing it to turn as his feet applied the required pressure. Abruptly, the aircraft's pair of tubular skids became unstuck, hovering tentatively above the asphalt. Digger applied more collective then gently pushed on the cyclic stick that was located between his legs, dropping the nose slightly as the helicopter swooped forward, rapidly gaining altitude. Erection time was the phrase Digger liked to affix to this particular time of a flight. Right after take off, when your seat vibrated and the earth fell away rapidly, the powerful whooping of the rotors crawling into every one of your joints, reminding you of the power you held in hands, defying all that was natural and known to mankind. As a pilot, Digger fully understood the physics behind how these machines flew, but he still held the whole process in awe, amazed at how easily and how constantly they could defy the invisible, gravitational borders of mother earth.

Using the foot pedals and the main rotor for banking, he steered the aircraft over the town site as it gained altitude, approaching the base of the clouds that would define his ceiling. Meryl sat quietly behind the pilot, a bulkhead separating the front and back compartments, the top few inches open so she could peek over. She still had her headphones plugged into her stereo but there was no music playing, a deceptive ploy to shut out her father's evangelical droning. It had started first thing this morning right after she had opened her bedroom door, her first sight being Elwood sitting in the kitchen in his underwear eating some toast. Molly sat next to him in her housecoat, appearing disgusted and drinking black coffee. Elwood laid into Meryl with a god-fearing chastising the second she sat at the table with her bowl of cereal, so she wordlessly left the kitchen to retrieve her cassette player, returning to her soggy breakfast with the headphones over her ears. She hadn't put a tape in at that time because she still wanted to hear what her mother was saying, but it turned out Molly didn't have too much to say at all.

They had left the house early to make the flight and the medical appointment, and Molly had decided to let Judith sleep, saving her from any further emotional strife. This denied Meryl the opportunity to say goodbye to Judith, to tell her how scared she was and how much Judith truly meant to her. Now, as she looked at the gray dawn through the side plexiglass of the helicopter, Meryl spotted her house near the beach below, and took the opportunity to whisper a silent good-bye to her sister. She felt nauseated and wasn't sure if it was the motion of the aircraft or her present affliction, and a mild tweaking filled her chest like a dull sadness. The aircraft followed the road out of town and within seconds Meryl could see the secluded beach that she and Judith had recently been escaping to. Even at the helicopters present elevation Meryl could make out the thin brown outline of the hopscotch game, their own scattered footprints like tiny dots in the sand.

Soon the beach vanished from her view, disappearing behind the trees and fading on the horizon.

Raindrops streaked swiftly across the side of Meryl's window, the rotor wash and the air speed driving them over the clear surface, leaving barely discernable trails like little snails crossing a flat plain. The aircraft crossed over the main road that led out of town, climbing to its maximum ceiling below the clouds. Shortly, the winding blacktop became a dark line carved into the mountainside, vanishing from sight every few seconds as it threaded its way through a dense forest of tall firs. On both sides of the helicopter the mountain peaks were obscured by extensive clouds, their granite slopes forming sheer walls in places, plunging twelve-hundred feet to the tumbling white water that coursed a path at the bottom of the canyon. Moving at over one-hundred-miles per hour the aircraft took a bearing right down the center of the deep gorge, appearing to fly almost eye level with the prominent tree line.

Every few miles Meryl could see sharp curving ridges that had won the geological test of time when the last ice age had cut through the rock walls of the mountainsides. Here they formed saddles, and the land spread out behind them, emerging into wide valleys. These flattened out beyond the natural rock gates of the saddles, forming fertile lands that spanned as far as you cared to look, almost obscured by the low clouds. Here you would find lush meadows of both deciduous and coniferous trees, a place where wildlife could flourish without mankind interfering with their evolving seasons. The valleys were far and away from any of the company's active logging shows located up the peninsula, and would remain as they were for eons to come.

These nutrient rich ecologies supported a diverse variation of life forms, from the single-celled microscopic amoeba, to the large deer flies that sought the salty moisture from the unprotected eyes of the lurching grizzly bears. Every tranquil pond and square inch of the woodsy plateaus held life forms, allowing the long valleys to remain as wild, nurturing shrines that required no artificial nudging to move them along.

Some things on this earth weren't meant to be messed with, and the sights that filled the aircraft's window opposite Meryl were such places, but like a typical teenager she quickly tired of the magnificent vistas. She had her cassette player perched on her lap and she fished a tape from the side pocket of her jacket. Carefully choosing the correct side, she slid the tape home then closed the smoky-colored cover, pushing the play button at the

139

top of the stereo. In short order the music flowed across Meryl's eardrums, and she adjusted the volume, giving the rolling tunes a little more bass, which allowed the music to sound as if it were playing inside her head. The music helped to cheer her up, lifting her spirits slightly higher than the ailment that presently chased away her usually good humor. Soon she thought, soon this would all be over. Although she knew she was only kidding herself, for with her father's rapidly deteriorating mental condition, things were just beginning to heat up inside the depressing walls of the Noble household. Meryl held the cassette player close to her body, hugging it tightly while she tried to lose herself inside the consoling music, even tapping her foot, silently mouthing the lyrics she had memorized through long hours of repetition. Once again she glanced out the side window of the aircraft, hoping to chase away the nausea that kept flooding and receding on her senses like an invisible but irritating wave. Meryl hoped that looking at a distant forest or a running stream might help keep her senses balanced, but the aircraft had been suddenly swallowed up, completely engulfed by the pallid, wispy clouds. She returned her attention to the cassette player, wiping some dust off the top with her fingers, permitting herself to relax to the soothing music.

To Meryl's front, Digger the pilot had become anything *but* relaxed. At times it was impossible to tell where some of the undefined edges of the cloudbanks began, especially when the clouds were virtually the same color as the sky around them. Digger had reached for one of his contour maps from the side pocket on his seat, glancing up seconds later to find the aircraft enveloped in white, the two dimensional sheet instantly ruining his depth perception. A pilot navigating while using visual flight rules in the middle of a mountain range without the use of forward scanning radar needs to be able to see. And not now . . . but right now. Digger could feel his sphincter muscle strumming as a dose of low voltage fear shot through his system, but he reacted instinctively to the situation. He immediately pulled back on the middle, cyclic stick while simultaneously pushing down on the side, collective stick. This dropped the aircraft's speed from one hundred miles per hour to about seventy-miles per hour. The helicopter reacted instantly to the control changes, raising the nose into a high attitude while the tail rotor dropped below the machines center of gravity. Digger pushed the left pedal over and banked with the cyclic stick, turning the helicopter so he could head back out of the low clouds, regaining his bearings once he re-sighted a land mass. But the vertigo fell upon him in seconds. A pilot's worst enemy, the sickening vertigo rapidly destroyed Digger's orientation capabilities to the point that he couldn't tell if he was right side up, or upside down. Unfortunately, in the high-speed technical life of an aviator, that's all it takes for a tragedy.

With confusion and nausea jostling all of his senses, Digger had unintentionally slacked off the pressure on the left pedal, allowing the tail to straighten up, momentarily baffling him as to which direction the aircraft was now headed. Once again he intuitively pushed down on the collective stick while pulling back on the cyclic control between his knees. Once more the helicopters' tail rotor dropped below the center of gravity as the nose adopted a high attitude, its forward speed sinking to just above fifty-miles per hour. Digger saw a flash of green through the dense clouds, a simple flicker through the plexiglass at his feet. Before he could apply more collective in an attempt to gain altitude, the tail rotor struck the trees. Both red and white blades were torn away from the spinning shaft at the end of the boom, and without the tail rotor, Digger lost all control of the helicopter. The machine promptly started to spin cruelly below the mast that turned the main rotors, and the force instantly drove Digger's head into the aluminum doorframe at his side.

His skull fractured, he sat stunned in the pilot's seat but there was absolutely nothing he could do to save the doomed aircraft anyway.

Not even God himself could stop the terrible accident, and that was one reason they called them accidents. The wildly spinning helicopter dropped through an open space between the tall growths of trees, slamming into the ground with enough force to bend the support struts on the skids beneath the fuselage. All three of the aircraft's occupants were thrown forward on impact, their torsos lurching forward over their knees until their shoulder harness's locked, their bodies held in the seats by their waist belts. The two men in the front seats were but a whisper away from death, and didn't have to suffer any gruesome spectacles like poor Meryl. When the unconscious Digger flopped forward he leaned on the cyclic, which caused the main rotor disc above the cabin to tilt down, forcing the already flexing blades to drop even lower. Low enough that they tore through the forward section of the canopy in one heartless swoop, taking the top portion of the cabin completely off. At the same time the blades decapitated Elwood Noble and Digger the company man, their heads rolling from their necks to the floor of the aircraft. Meryl's head slouched back on her shoulders when she recovered momentarily from the crash. Badly stunned and with both her legs shattered she watched on in mute horror for a millisecond as fountains of blood gushed from the neck stumps of the two dead men. Some of the blood turned into a sticky mist, wafting throughout the entire cabin as a reddish blue cloud, caused by the draft of cold mountain air, which was blown inside by the spinning, shattering rotors.

As the blood coated Meryl's face she screamed, but she couldn't hear herself over the noise of the disintegrating rotor blades, the mast still a revolving blur above her head. When the tips of the blades broke up and flew from the wreck, all centrifugal balance left the body of the helicopter and it rolled onto it's right side, pulled over by the inertia of the moving machinery. What remained of the rotor blades flailed madly against the hard surface of the ground, ripping the entire drive train that was mounted directly behind the passenger cabin from its internal mounts. All that tremendous energy was transferred directly to that metallic box of spinning gears and it needed a place to go. The whole component tore through the thin walls of the rear bulkhead, braining Meryl and crushing her skull, killing her instantly. A tiny heartbeat later, the life of the fifteen-week-old fetus that grew inside her womb was extinguished as well. From the time that the helicopter had entered the clouds until the time it had impacted with the ground, a total of twelve seconds had elapsed. So fast had the accident unfolded that the machine's moving parts hadn't even slowed down, still grinding, hot and lubricated, merely a twinkling after the devastation had finally ended.

*   *   *

Chapter Fourteen

Once all the helicopters gears, shafts, bearings and the high speed turbine had ceased their high velocity momentum, the metal began cooling as the cold air touched the hot coverings of the engine and transmission case. The slowly contracting metal sent pinging sounds across the area of the crash site, although no human ear stood within ten miles to listen to the last sounds this aircraft would ever make. There was another pinging sound as well. One that started seconds after the helicopter hit the ground. Inaudible to the human ear, its sound was carried on a restricted frequency, it's electronic message carrying out to the infinite vacuum of space, over four hundred miles above the earth's surface. An emergency locator transmitter inside the aircraft had turned itself on automatically, sending a distress signal to one of the twenty-four Nav Com satellites that revolved high above the earth in a wide, circular orbit. Almost half the size of a shoe box, the square, orange colored device had been attached to the bulkhead next to Digger's seat using a wide velcro patch. It had torn loose on impact, activating itself and going into operational mode where it would continue to send out a steady signal until help arrived, or the Ni-cad batteries were eventually exhausted. The signals the transmitter had started to pulse would be the only indication at this time that an aircraft may have gone down. Picked up in seconds by the orbiting satellite, the helicopter's latitude and longitude, as well as the exact time that the transmitter went into operation was then communicated to a search and rescue coordination center located at a Naval Base on the southern mainland.

On this base there was an old red-bricked building that overlooked a long cement jetty where large, gunmetal gray warships were berthed. Two floors up from the guarded main entrance of the building stood a large room full of rows of back-to-back computer screens. Each screen had a plain looking but comfortable high-backed chair, and all the windows in this particular room had been blacked out. Nobody could see in, and nobody could look out. This fact alone suggested the security level designated to the room and that not everybody would be welcomed inside. That's assuming you made it past the armed military guards at their posts downstairs. Against a plain looking wall, dozens of charts and maps had been pinned up, joined together using scotch tape, readily covering the wall from end to end and from floor to ceiling. Where the tidal waters of the coast existed, charts clearly showed the islands and the water depths at the lowest normal tides, and where the salt water lapped against the green land, the maps displayed circular contour lines, indicating the height of every mountain peak and hillock that had been left behind from the glaciers of the Pleistocene age. Virtually every computer screen had a military person working the keyboard, busy scanning their screens while drinking hot coffee from Styrofoam cups. Each person had access to a wide variety of information that they could bring up onto their screens, most of what they had access to was classified top secret. At their finger tips and using the correct pass words, they could observe and track moving weather patterns, search and rescue aircraft, and if they really got bored and nosy, they could scroll through the latest antics of the Soviet, Charlie class submarines that were snooping near the continental shelf out in the Pacific Ocean. At one of these screens sat Lieutenant-Commander Guy, a tall young Naval Officer with a pockmarked face who nonetheless looked impressive in his starched khakis and spit shined black oxfords.

He was in charge of the watch and had promptly sat down at the vacated screen of the Nav Com computer when a tone sounded, alerting him to the activation of an emergency locator transmitter. Normally one of his subordinates would have taken the screen, but the officer had become bored, and a bit of hands on practice kept him current and alert. After poking the applicable keys, he printed off the time and location of the transmission as well as the aircraft's call sign and designate - whether it was fixed wing or a rotor machine. He took his printout then walked over to the wall maps, taking a few minutes to measure the latitude and longitude from the scales at the sides and the tops of the maps. Using a large set of parallel rulers he drew light pencil lines across the maps until they intersected, pinpointing the exact location. Not a very healthy place to park a helicopter he thought, right in the middle of a spire on the coastal range. Guy returned to his desk at the front of the room, and then called the civilian air traffic controller at the large international airport thirty-miles to the northeast. He already knew the signal had come from a private aircraft, narrowing down the search somewhat, but he needed to confirm a flight plan, or lack of one which might suggest the signal had not been set off accidentally. Standing by his desk, the Naval Officer spoke clearly into his telephone, and the air traffic controller who sat in a similar room one floor below the glassed control tower miles away at the International Airport already knew he was speaking to the search and rescue coordinator.

"Good morning Sid, you got a Jet Ranger helicopter, call sign November-eight-four-two-niner-three, inbound from the coastal range?" Guy asked.

"Sure do," the controller replied, "we haven't heard from him yet. Hang on a sec and I'll see if I can raise him on the radio."

Guy sat on the edge of his desk while Sid the controller put him on hold. The other military personnel inside the room remained glued to their computer screens, sticking to their present tasks, oblivious to the drama that was developing around them. Forty seconds later the air traffic controller came back onto the line.

"Nothing . . . they're not responding," Sid reported. "Their radio could still be blocked by the mountains though. Do you think it's gone down?"

"Huh uh. It looks that way. How many on board?" Guy asked.

"Three souls," answered the controller. "Latest weather from a Nimbus satellite shows ten-ten cloud cover throughout the whole area, low ceiling, twelve-hundred feet. However, it's supposed to lift up to two-thousand by midmorning."

"That's good. Well, I can't stand around here wondering whether they've cratered or not, I'm going to roll a rescue rig. Would you call me straight back if you happen to hear from them?"

"Roger that."

"Thank-you Sid."

Guy replaced the phone back on the receiver then picked up a red one that had no dial face, but gave him direct contact to the duty officer of the Search and Rescue Squadron located at an Air Force base further up the coast. Many times these emergency locator transmitters were set off by accident, when they were inadvertently jostled, or some uneducated passenger played with them. Regardless, the geographical location of the transmitting signal put these possibilities in a whole new light. If this aircraft had gone down in the mountains the chances of survival were grim at best, and if someone had survived it would be a cold, lonely place to be lying injured and possibly helpless. Guy made his decision within seconds, and without so much as a gnawing hesitation.

It had been months since they had an aircraft auger in, and even though he didn't like to think about it, the time was close for another bad one. Guy didn't like measuring the odds when it came to human lives, but twenty-six months into a three-year tour of duty at the rescue center told him otherwise. His area of responsibility was long over due for a bit of a tragedy, and these things happened when you flew above the planet in heavier than air machines. What went up had to come back down, and on occasion they came down much quicker than the pilot had anticipated.

Further to these sad, scientific facts, the Naval Officer just had a bad feeling about this one.

Think of it as job security someone had once said. But there were times when the Lieutenant Commander's guarantee of a steady paycheck seemed like it could be a bit of a nasty plague.

*   *   *

Chapter Fifteen

The tandem rotor, search and rescue helicopter was commanded and piloted by an Air Force Captain named Kane, who felt relieved once it was discovered the low cloud had lifted to two-thousand feet above the search area. The wind however had picked up again, a gusting blow that started out in the Pacific, funneling through the deep natural ditch formed by the high mountains. Most of the peaks were still cloaked in thick white but there could be no way the missing helicopter would have been flying that high using visual flight rules. Both the Captain and the copilot, who was a Lieutenant, as well as the flight engineer were seated in the cockpit of the bright yellow aircraft, scanning well ahead through the sectioned windows of the canopy. Stationed behind the cockpit in the fuselage, the load master and the search and rescue technicians watched the flanks through the observation bubbles and side windows. It had taken an hour of flying to reach the search area and Kane checked the coordinates to confirm that they were close to where the emergency locator was transmitting. Observing ahead to corroborate their location with a contour map, the pilot spotted a geological irregularity the locals called the "devils dink." A solid rock spire, it towered straight up, five hundred feet from a flat stony shelf that had been sculpted half way up the side of the highest peak in the coastal range. The walls of the chimney-shaped spire were bare of any ledges or crevices, making climbing impossible, even for the nimble Rocky Mountain sheep who sought out the fibrous mosses that grew around its base. At the top of the pinnacle the rock was virtually flat, offering nearly a half acre for the stand of spruce trees that grew in defiance of the shallow soil and the cold, relentless winds.

Two thousand feet out from the chimney and well above it, Kane suddenly spotted the fluorescent tail boom of the downed helicopter, laying almost dead center at the top of the imposing spire.

"Jesus Christ," she murmured. The whole top of the geological anomaly had been strewn with pieces of the wrecked chopper and her experienced eyes already told her no one could have survived the crash. They were lucky anything at all remained, for had the aircraft been five feet higher, it would have cleared the trees and slammed into a vertical slope located a quarter of a mile on the other side of the devil's dink. Had that happened, pieces no bigger than a human fist would have fallen to the bottom of the deep canyon. Speaking into the boom mike on her flying helmet, Kane advised the rest of her crew that she had found the downed aircraft.

"Target found, two thousand feet, top of spire, zero-zero-zero degree's relative bearing. Looks like a winch job boys . . . probably a body retrieval as well. Three souls we're told."

The two search and rescue technicians abandoned their posts at the observation bubbles and quickly but with practiced efficiency, got their gear ready. Neither one looked at each other, both feeling a sudden let down now that the rescue mission had turned into a body recovery. It was an important part of their job, bringing home the dead to the grieving families but nonetheless it could still be a let down. For all the risks they took and all the danger they faced on a daily basis, nothing made it more worthwhile than bringing the odd one home alive. They had no reason to question the cursory findings of their seasoned skipper, and they would find out soon enough what kind of macabre despair awaited them on the ground. Already suited up in their bright orange flight suits, each Rescue Tech laid out his nylon jump harness on the metal deck of the helicopter and climbed inside, buckling the straps of the rigs to a large round aluminum punch buckle located over their chests. A quick slap and a turn on the buckle and the harness would fall away from their bodies. All the flight crew including the Rescue Tech's was attired with olive-drab flight helmets with boom mikes, so they were ready to go. The load master, a burly sergeant who had to almost fold himself up to climb into the helicopter, had already pulled the top half of the rescue door in, swinging it up against the inside roof of the aircraft. A biting, cold wind howled through the open door, sucking away the warm air produced by the cabin heaters, adding immensely to the deafening hammer of the turbine engines.

Located on the starboard side of the chopper, the electrical winch had been mounted outside on struts above the rescue door and the sergeant cautiously poked his head out, taking the time to scope out the kind of terrain he would be lowering the technicians onto.

"Holy shit," he thought when he spied the lonely, stark spire that shot five hundred feet into the clear air.

Minutes later the helicopter hovered just above the treetops of the devils dink, the nose held stationary in a high attitude position while pointed directly into the wind. Usually about this time Captain Kane would mouth a quick prayer for her Rescue Tech's before they left the aircraft, except this particular operation required her full concentration and then some. Compact and extremely fit, she focused some of her attention on a brown, wilting spruce tree that clung to a slope in the distance. Kane would use this as a reference point as she fought the wind and the mechanical torque from the helicopter, keeping the machine and her crew on station. Perpetually compensating on the controls, she spent the rest of her concentration gently moving the collective and cyclic sticks, as well as applying gentle touches to the foot pedals. Nothing else mattered in the world right now except the job at hand, which was to keep the aircraft in a stable position nearly eighty feet above the flat surface of the pinnacle. Holding the machine so it lined up with the diseased spruce would help Kane achieve this short term goal, although now wouldn't be a good time to get an itch in your crotch or have a large, angry wasp fly into the cockpit. Above her head, the two large rotors spun noisily on their masts in the towers at either end of the bright colored fuselage. The large triple blades pounded the air, causing the tree limbs below to shake violently. It didn't take Kane long to realize their present position was very inhospitable, if not outright precarious. A sudden flurry of descending wind shear, quite prevalent in these mountain ranges and it would be long, breathtaking drop to the bottom of the canyon.

She spoke once again into the intercom, giving the load master the verbal go ahead, and now her sole responsibility would be to hold the aircraft steady as her Rescue Tech's were lowered to the ground by the winch. If required, she would jockey the helicopter on the loadmaster's commands, for he had the best view of the landing zone. The Rescue Tech's preferred to jump with parachutes, but that wouldn't be happening on this particular mission. Not only was parachuting a lot more fun, but they could also record another official jump in their logbooks.

It was a Rescue Tech virility kind of a thing; apparently the Tech with the most para-jumps in a year had the hairiest chest or the biggest bulge in his pants, although only their wives new the real truth. Jumping was also safer than dangling at the end of a long cable, especially when there existed the constant possibility of some sort of a mechanical failure or a sudden wind gust played across the fuselage, bouncing the aircraft around the sky. That said, there were times when they simply couldn't parachute in, like right now, with the wind and the tall trees and the size of the drop zone. Jumping onto that evil pinnacle would be like trying to park your ass atop a button mushroom in a driving hurricane. Some things weren't humanly possible and despite the Rescue Tech's reputation for being the fittest, bravest people in the solar system, they too had their limits and set parameters that they had to work within. Dead Rescue Tech's were no good to anyone, least of all the wives and children they would leave behind at the married quarters on the base.

The loadmaster dropped the lower portion of the rescue door, which swung down on its hinges, snugging up against the outside of the fuselage. Nodding to the first Rescue Tech, the loadmaster handed him the snap buckle at the end of the cable and he clipped it onto the stainless steel "D" ring near the top of his harness. He gave the buckle a firm tug before stepping out the door, swinging slightly on the cable eighty-feet above the devils dink. The loadmaster, his hand on the control panel near the door, paid out the cable as he watched the Tech slowly descend toward the ground. Thirty seconds later the first Tech stood on the ground, standing well away from the cable before giving the sergeant a thumbs up. The load master winched the cable back in so he could lower the second Tech to the ground for they never worked alone, always operating inside the safe confines of the buddy system. After first checking for any apparent hazards to himself, the first Tech walked over to the wreck to check for any survivors, and the scene that played across his eyes was one of the worst he'd ever seen. Two victims were strapped into the front seats of the aircraft, which now lay on its side. They had been decapitated, and their head's lay on one side of the plexiglass canopy below the pilots dangling feet. The pasty flesh on the faces of both heads was almost completely covered in a layer of blood, and it had already started to dry and crack around their ears. Both victims had their the eyes partially open, like a jammed shutter on a camera, freezing in place the final scene they had witnessed before dying. One of heads had a healthy growth of dark hair, the blood matting the fibers into a thick clump, giving him a scruffy unkempt appearance, and the other victim was balding.

Every square inch of the helicopter's interior had been painted with a coating of blood, except for what little remained of the plexiglass canopy where the vital fluids had refused to stick. The whole scene reminded the Tech of his boyhood on the farm, where his father and brother would cull the sickly pigs from the herd every fall. They would slit their throats after hanging them up with a rope by their rear hoofs near the back of the barn, letting the blood flow into a galvanized tub. However, the blood would still splatter everywhere as the pig's squealed and struggled, slowly bleeding to death. Quickly the Tech looked through the destroyed roof of the aircraft into the passenger side of the cabin, and what he saw there brought him the most sorrow, although he soon chased it away. He had to.

Meryl was still in her seat, lying against the thin aluminum door that rested next to the ground, the waist belt holding her body firmly into place. Her skull had been crushed, now appearing brittle and delicate like an inflated paper bag, and a red mask of blood covered her face like some hideous war paint, highlighting her light blue eyes. This young victim reminded the Tech of his own teenaged daughter who would be at classes right now at the Junior High School back on the base. The whole roof of the helicopter had been completely torn away when the drive train had broken loose, and now it lay outside next to the fuselage, all dented and bashed up where it had thrashed itself against the rocky ground. Glancing up to the loadmaster who looked down expectantly from the rescue aircraft, the Tech held up three fingers on his gloved right hand, confirming there were three dead. No survivors.

Scarcely two minutes had passed when both the Rescue Tech's stood near the scene, glancing up as the load master lowered three metal caged litters, each with an olive-drab plastic body bag strapped inside its basket. After receiving the litters they pulled industrial style rubber gloves onto their hands then quickly set about their tasks, each man knowing the drilled sequence for body recovery. First they unfolded the stiff cloth of each body bag, working them flat like canvas tent's that had sat on a shelf for too long. A bag was spread out in each of the litters then zipped all the way open. The Tech's then removed the men from the front compartment one at a time, cutting away their shoulder harnesses and seatbelts using the whetted blades of their survival knifes. Cautiously they pulled them through the open front canopy that had been cropped off by the rotor blades. Together they carried the stiffening bodies, holding them under the armpits and by the legs, lowering each one gently into a bag. They used the utmost caution, trying not to disturb the wreck, keeping it as they found it for the transport safety people who would be descending upon the scene within a day or two.

Even though she weighed next to nothing it took both Rescue Tech's to remove Meryl's slight body as they had to step carefully over the drive train, avoiding the parts that lay strewn about the ground. It pained them that a girl so young and with so much life ahead of her had to die so tragically and violently. Wordlessly they took the young body and placed it inside a body bag, zipping it up over her damaged form, gazing one last time at her strangely peaceful face. Once again they returned to the wreck, looking into the front of the aircraft where the canopy lay open. Body recovery meant just that, so there could be nothing left behind that might belong to one of the victims. Leaning inside, one of Tech's grabbed Elwood's head by the hair, then pulled it out and walked over to the body bags to stow his grisly find. His partner then reached in to retrieve Digger's head, but he really had to stretch to get his hand anywhere close to the unsightly item and then he had to grab the pilot by one of the ears as he was balding.

"Cock-sausage," he muttered, "I always get the one's without any hair."

Dressed in their orange flight suits while carrying human heads around made them appear like some bizarre bowling team. The first Rescue Tech deposited Elwood's head in a bag then passed his partner who still clenched Digger's noggin by an ear. He looked down as his partner walked by with the head, glancing at his ghastly cargo, unable to stay that morbid fascination that dwells inside most human beings. The same fascination that causes people to slow down and gape when they drive by a terrible car accident, hoping to get a squint at something dreadful but at the same time instructing their children in the back seat to close their eyes.

"I'm going to get the emergency locator transmitter," the Tech shouted over the thumping noise of their hovering helicopter.

"Now there's a handy idea," the partner yelled back.

While one looked for the emergency transmitter, the other put Digger's head into a body bag, then zipped the two remaining bags closed. He then unrolled the nylon straps that were riveted to each litter, securely strapping all three bodies into their long, open cages. Once the emergency transmitter had been retrieved from the wreck and deactivated, they carried the bodies one by one to below their oscillating helicopter. Captain Kane had let the aircraft seesaw back and forth over the crash sight to give her limbs and her concentration a bit of a rest. The loadmaster dropped the metal cable down after Kane had steadied the aircraft for the recovery, and the Techs allowed the snap buckle to ground itself against the earth before they touched it. It could carry a hell of a wallop, discharging a powerful jolt of static electricity that had been built up from the beating motion of the large rotors.

After the first body was raised, the operation ran smoother when the flight engineer came back to help the loadmaster with the stowing of the body's. Five minutes later both Rescue Tech's were hoisted up at the same time, and were glad to be back aboard and away from the horrible sights of the crash. Once the crew had strapped themselves back in their jump seats, the loadmaster closed the rescue doors and advised Captain Kane the recovery had been safely concluded. The nose of the helicopter dropped as it moved forward, rapidly gaining altitude and air speed as it set a course for the return trip to the base. It had been another flawless search and rescue operation for the crew of helicopter five-zero-three, adding to their growing reputation that was making them pillars of respect and admiration back at the Squadron. Fifteen minutes after their arrival above the feature the locals called the devil's dink, the rescue aircraft was inbound, returning to the base with its precious payload. No one could criticize the crew on this fine piece of rescue work, executed under extremely dangerous and trying conditions. No one except the pathologist who would be conducting the autopsies. Especially after he found both severed heads inadvertently stuffed into the one body bag.

*   *   *

Chapter Sixteen

Molly Noble had become worldly enough to know that finding a police officer and the elderly Pastor from their church standing on her front door step at four o'clock on a Saturday afternoon couldn't be good news. Judith on the other hand who was less worldly because of her age, had a bit more trouble grasping the gravity of the situation. Dressed in his light blue uniform, the police officer was a roly-poly individual with large round glasses who made Pastor Wilcox look small and wise. Wearing a dark sports coat over his white collared shirt, the Pastor had about him that kind, venerated demeanor that accompanied all people of the cloth. Molly wordlessly ushered them into the front living room and despite being a man in his early thirties, the police office shuffled along like a crippled ninety-year-old with distended balls.

The fact that he preferred to be somewhere else right about now hung accusingly from his beefy face. Both men sat down on the hunter green couch that separated the kitchen from the living room, clearing their throats and coughing anxiously. Judith had been sprawled out on the rug, dressed in blue jeans and an old sweatshirt, watching mindless cartoons now that her father was away from the house. She turned the television off upon Molly's direction, and her first indication that something terrible had happened was when her mother sat in a chair next to the couch, her hands trembling uncontrollably.

The police officer, whose name was Morton, pulled a black notebook from the breast pocket of his patrol jacket. These next of kin notifications had blown-up in police officer's faces in the past when they had been given the wrong addresses or the wrong names. It was always wise to confirm even the most simple facts before you opened your mouth and dropped a stunning, emotional bomb onto someone's life. Morton licked one of his plump index fingers then leafed through the pages of his notebook, searching for his last entry. Visibly nervous and sweaty, bountiful caution and stonewalling was to be this police officer's order of the day. He cleared his throat several times like he was tuning up to give some kind of a goddamned speech, but truth be known he was really hoping the Pastor would seize the moment and jump in with both feet. The police officer had been at home lallygagging in his soiled sweats, off shift but on call when the phone had rung for this death notification. He'd left behind a large bowl of extra buttery, microwave popcorn as well as the first period of the hockey finals. He'd only turned on his brand new, large screen television that had been purchased from flogging the overtime when the phone had rung. Eh, well, no one ever said that police work was going to be fair. Morton looked at Molly through the round, greasy lenses of his glasses, clearing his throat one last time before embarking on his delicate oration.

"Well, eh, uh Molly . . . your husband Elwood and your oldest daughter Meryl left town this morning aboard a company helicopter for a medical appointment in the city?"

Molly nodded quietly to the question, the sparkling tears already pooling on the pink edges of her lower eyelids. Judith stood in the middle if the living room staring at the two men, although the reason behind their afternoon visit still hadn't registered on her young mind.

"I'm afraid we have some terrible news," Pastor Wilcox said, his voice firm but quiet. There was no way that one could dance around these devastating issues, but a proper delivery required the information be released a bit at a time. This allowed time for each segment of the disaster to be fully absorbed and usually prevented outright denial from the immediate family. Even knowing what the victims were wearing could help the next of kin absorb the truth, for the truth was what these sad visits were all about. The messenger had to relay the facts, and stay until the family fully understood the bleak finality of the announcement. There could be no grieving - a natural healing process - until the family had accepted the truth, and there were times it could take a great deal of convincing.

"Uh, ten minutes after take off from the heliport behind the mill the helicopter that Elwood and Meryl Noble were aboard crashed in the mountains." Morton said slowly.

"Search and Rescue were dispatched to the crash site," the Pastor continued, his voice now gentle, "they got there as soon as they could and were lowered down to the area.

Unfortunately . . . there were no survivors . . . I am truly sorry. This doesn't make it any easier, but I've been told that neither one of them suffered. It was all over very quickly."

Molly put her hand over her mouth, "oh, oh . . . my poor baby." The words were there, but it came out as a sob, and the tears were now rolling freely down her face, streaking her cheeks dark with mascara. Judith stood stunned, unable to comprehend and accept that something or someone had taken Meryl from her life. For some reason she didn't think about the loss of her father just yet, somehow viewing his death as more or less a humane and legitimate sanction. A termination to his floundering mind, freeing them all from its rambling despair. Judith looked at the Pastor, her mouth wide open, shaking her head and saying nothing.

"I'm sorry Judith, but Meryl and your father are gone," Pastor Wilcox said softly. "I can't tell you why God allows these things to happen . . . I can only tell you that they do."

Two minutes ago Judith Noble had been giggling at an idiotic, Saturday afternoon cartoon that helped her escape entirely the worries that dwelled in her corner of the world. Two minutes and all that had changed. Now her life appeared to crumble before her astonished eyes as she stood in the middle of the living room, feeling dizzy as she gasped for breath.

"You're a lying bastard," she said to the Pastor.

Molly had become far too mired in her own grief to respond to her daughter's rude accusation but it would have done no good, for Judith was already running for the front door.

She flung it open and was gone, running out into the windy afternoon. The police officer got to his feet but Molly held up her hand, stopping him.

"Please . . . let her go . . . she'll be all right." Molly stood up, watching through the front window as Judith ran down the street. She was confident of where she would find her once the two gentlemen had concluded with their sad business and had left.

Judith ran as fast as she could down the road, her long blonde hair spreading across her face as the wind blew in from the beach. Nearly blinded by the tears, her blowing hair obstructed her vision even further, but she ran on regardless, panting madly as the cruel gusts sucked away the air she was trying to breath. Judith knew where she was running. This trek wasn't one of those mournful jaunts into the great outdoors where the aggrieved ran without purpose or direction.

Judith was running down to her and Meryl's private beach, to be in that safe place where bothersome matters were forbidden to penetrate. The quiet stretch of sand had become a haven for both girls, a place to withdraw when their parents bickering eventually got loud, and Elwood's babbling became too much for them to bear. She wanted to be alone, to watch the breaking waves and gaze at the hopscotch game and the footprints they'd left in the moist white sand.

Twelve minutes later, Judith entered the wide belt of broad leaf sedge, pushing aside the long leaves as she walked down the narrow path to their beach. Another heartbreak fell upon her as she felt the cold, fine sand wetting her stocking feet. Born somewhere out in the middle of the Pacific Ocean, the relentless wind had pushed the water at high tide well onto the beach.

The slender brown pieces of driftwood that Judith had used to create their hopscotch game had been washed away, as well as the footprints that spoke of the simple joy that two sisters had once shared.

Judith felt faint and lightheaded as she plodded slowly over to the log that she and Meryl would lie upon, talking sister stuff while their clothes dried in the hot sun. She collapsed on the flat part of the smooth, weather worn old tree trunk, hiding her face in her hands as she cried. At times the sobs would arrest her breathing for a few seconds, causing her to gasp erratically but she remained very still, even though she was overwhelmed and confused at her loss. Judith lay there for about five minutes, the sound of her sobbing muffled by the roar of the persistent wind and the endless waves. No one knew she was there except for one other person, and Judith could feel her mother's presence as she walked onto the beach and sat next to her. As lightly as possible, Molly gathered her daughter up in her arms, hugging her tightly, using her hand to wipe the stream of mucus that ran from her nose and dripped from her chin. Molly rested her own wet face against Judith's blowing hair, inhaling the clean scent that was distinctive only to her daughter, much like a fingerprint, a unique essence that had come with her joyous birth. She gently rocked her daughter back and forth in that pacifying manner that was an instinctual gift to all mothers. They stayed that way until the cloudy, western skies started to darken in the coming dusk, and Judith looked up into Molly's face.

"Why, mom? Why did Meryl have to die?"

"I don't know honey," Molly replied quietly, "I really don't. The Pastor said something about it being God's will, something that couldn't be prevented, much like the weather. But I really don't know why all this has happened."

Any age was a dreadful time to lose a loved one, but at twelve years old it seemed to cut even deeper into Judith's strained emotions. While she sat there in her mother's arms, feeling helpless and devastated, Judith decided that if this was the will of God, then she never wanted to talk again about such a lordly, uncaring presence. Unfortunately, this would not be the last time Judith Noble would endure such complete anguish, but she would again one day speak of God. That however, would be an occasion many miles down a very long road.

*   *   *

Chapter Seventeen

Doctor Frederick Mallory-Smyth had been cutting into corpses for the better part of a quarter of a century, but he was still intolerant to the sweet, sickly smell of decomposing human flesh. As a Pathologist he had carved up so many cadavers he secretly wondered if he wasn't suffering from a touch of dementia. It wasn't a job for everybody, not after so many years of medical school and internship, followed with the brutal shifts and workload of a residency. Most doctors liked to cure human suffering with their knowledge and skills in modern medicine. Mallory-Smyth was different in that he would cut them open once they had died.

His had become a stainless steel world where cold flesh met cold metal, where human organs including the brain were removed from the people who owned them as they wouldn't be needing them anymore. The Doctor would weigh them to the nearest gram, then slice them open to reveal any secrets that may have dwelled deep inside the fleshy mass. All this refined butchery and analyzing Mallory-Smyth had tempered himself to, an important job that at times could reveal some startling facts; each slice of the scalpel a fascinating story onto itself, a mystery unraveled, or at times a puzzling question fully answered. Twenty-five years of forensic medicine, and one would have though he would have become accustomed the smell of decaying bodies. But he hadn't, nor would he ever.

It was a condition he had managed to hide from the staff at the morgue for all these years.

The arrogant, expatriated Englishman employed a simple, preventive method while in the privacy of his office. Mallory-Smyth had a small jar of vaporizing ointment hidden in his desk drawer, and he would put a couple of dabs of the transparent camphor, menthol, and spirits of turpentine up his nose before venturing down the hall to cut and saw, weigh and measure, scrutinize and dissect. This strong fragrance of menthol would suppress any odors than emanated from the microscopic free-for-all that occurred in any dead body, including a refrigerated one. None of the simpletons that comprised his staff knew anything about his ointment trick and that's the way that he preferred things. The less people knew about him the better, which in the course of human interaction turned out to be a relatively good deal. No one liked Mallory-Smyth, not even his neighbors, so even if he wanted to try and bore you with his life history, very few would have suffered past the part where his mother's water had broken. Tall and thin with short sandy hair and an outdated pencil-thin mustache, he had come to this part of the world during the early sixties when the immigration gates had been thrown open, allowing in a steady stream of eager migrants. Mallory-Smyth had left Britain in a first class stateroom on an ocean liner because a few years after his father had died his mother had married a plain looking, Yorkshire commoner. Therein lay the young Doctor's second good reason for leaving Britain; far too many commoners.

These working folk were found in every corner of the large Island Country, chafing him like an ill-fitting pair of underwear or a confining collar stud. Commoners . . . he detested them.

All of them were spawned from the same dull seed which produced a herd of ill mannered, beer swilling, rutting, profanity speaking class of people that were as provincial as a worn penny.

His decision to abscond from Great Britain wasn't taken lightly however, and not without a good deal of study. Mallory-Smyth embarked on nothing until he'd read about it extensively, and that probably included going to the bathroom, if he even went at all. Having read as many library books as he could about life in North America, which included information on the fat wages they paid to educated professionals like himself, he packed up his pin striped-suits, his medical books, handmade alligator skin shoes, his golfing knickers and porkpie hat, then commenced on his great journey.

Mallory-Smyth left without so much as a cheerio or toodle-loo to his heartbroken mother and simple, kindhearted stepfather. He was indeed a rotter, ripe with his own self-importance as he walked across the passenger bridge that led him to the upper deck of the cruise ship and the first class passenger quarters. Six days later and upon making landfall on the Eastern seaboard , two ocean going tugs pushed the huge liner into its berth on a great river. The eager passengers disembarked and Mallory-Smyth became most annoyed when he had been forced to line up at the customs building with the rest of the common, migrating baggage. Strewth Lord! If some of them weren't brown skinned and couldn't speak a word of the Queen's English. Rest assured though, letters would be written to the Government regarding this abomination; this unruly cattle drive where all men were treated equal by their uniformed herders. Mallory-Smyth was in the first of many rude jolts that hadn't been mentioned in the library books back home. His first lesson regarding integration into North American culture was the lack of any kind of a formal class system, unless of course you were a Negro. In which case they would chase your black American arse out to the ghettos with all the assembled intelligence of a drunken soccer mob. Mallory-Smyth, Oxford University graduate cum laude in the field of medicine and pathology was devastated to learn he was just another white face in the massing crowd. Why, even the men who smoked cigars and rode on the back of those large unsightly garbage trucks dressed in their "Casey Jones" overalls received the same amount of respect as everyone else. Unless of course, if you were a Negro. This disgusting lack of any class system and the simple morals of the people who crowded the cities along the Eastern Seaboard encouraged Mallory-Smyth to seek out more cultured venues. He never found them, although his travels took him to the Pacific Northwest where he eventually settled, much to the mortification of the friendly, easy-going people who inhabited that lovely gem of mountainous rain forests.

Mallory-Smyth relocated to one of the large coastal cities where he soon found himself working for the Regional Coroner's Office on the ground floor of a large hospital. After a few years of apartment life he had a contractor build him a multilevel brownstone home on a forested hill in an affluent neighborhood that overlooked a slow-moving river. The cut, brownstone blocks had to be shipped out from the East, and why he did this when the best timber in the world grew in the surrounding hills was an indicator to his confounding arrogance. He lived alone inside the smooth walls of the brownstone and not much was seen of him, even on his days off, which was fine with the neighbors, though it set their gossipy tongues to wagging about his sexual preference.

Twenty-five years after his arrival to the Pacific Northwest, Mallory-Smyth was now the Chief Anatomical Pathologist at the same hospital, working in the same morgue. The hospital stood only three city blocks from the unassuming clinic that was going to perform an abortion on fourteen-year-old Meryl Noble. Now she lay on a wheeled gurney in a steel-walled, walk-in cooler next to her father and Digger the helicopter pilot. On this particular morning Doctor Mallory-Smyth was in a foul mood, and the three deaths from the helicopter crash was one of the contributing reasons to his ill humor. He had to perform the autopsy's on the three air crash victims at the insistence of the Transport Safety Board, and nothing irritated him more than having other officials dictating to him whom he should be cutting up, and why. The postmortem on the air crash victims would be straightforward and quick; cause of death for each casualty, and drug tests conducted on the pilot. Holding the station of Chief Pathologist usually meant there should have been no need for Mallory-Smyth to perform any more postmortems, but that all changed last night. At that time a roving gang of miscreants had played shoot the turds in an east end crack house. Now the Doctors on his staff would be occupied all day picking forty-five caliber slugs from the collection of street dung that lay cooling in the body locker.

Suddenly the Pathology Department had become very busy, which meant that Mallory-Smyth had to come in on a day off, pull a lab coat over his three piece, finely tailored Steindorff suit and open some people up. On top of all this other marvelous news, he'd found out that his lab assistance would be a sawed-off piss kid named Dwayne, a compact fellow with a disheartening voice and a gimpy leg who followed you around like a groveling man servant. Dwayne had been one of those fellows who never dated much in high school, preferring to spend his lunch hours with the small crowd from the audio-visual club, reading science fiction magazines while placing curses on voluptuous cheerleaders. He was full of harmless inexperience and lived in a hypothetical world, the kind of person Mallory-Smyth really loathed, especially when he would peer at him expectantly through his thick glasses like a begging refugee. This was one of the reasons the Chief Pathologist insisted all the underlings in his working domain address him as "sir." Annoying folk such as Dwayne needed to know where they stood in life, and calling Mallory-Smyth sir could only serve to remind them. After all, it was *he* who attended Oxford to become learned in medicine, not the lowly lab assistant's, and it was he who lived alone in a very privileged neighborhood, not the quirky Dwayne who lamented constantly with his whiny monologues about his sick, elderly mother and her fabulous apple pie. As he stood in his office down the hall from the morgue, carefully applying vaporizing rub to his hairless nostrils, he wondered not for the first time if he should have remained in Britain where people like Dwayne knew where they belonged, and bloody well stayed there.

Haughty, displaced, British Pathologists . . . fear them.

Mallory-Smyth sighed loudly as he pulled a crisply starched white lab coat from his oak and brass coat rack, pulling it on over his shirt after removing his suit jacket. He carefully hung the jacket on the coat rack, and then buttoned up the lab coat that reached to just above his knees. It had the words "Chief Pathologist" embroidered in flowing gold lettering across the white cloth near the open pocket at his chest. The station he held came with few perks, so he had to make his own and insisting the hospital embroider all his lab coats was one such concession. Why, he was even denied windows for his office and if he did have them he would have been treated to a gorgeous view of the back alley and the metal dumpster that was being looted by a couple of starving street people. The Chief Pathologist's office was plain in its construction and furnishings, but like all people who have thus far lived exceptional lives, Mallory-Smyth had the maintenance people style it up a bit and one such addition was the creation of his "me-me" wall. This was located where the windows should have been, and was festooned with wooden framed, old black and white photographs of smiling young men wearing their cricket whites. They all had wide, flat bats resting over their shoulders and had goofy looking hats on their heads. An adolescent looking Mallory-Smyth was in every picture, and somehow managed to appear condescending even amongst his own kind. The Doctor admired these pictures as he reached down to his metal desk, pulling a white filtered menthol cigarette from a square package then carefully screwed it into a long black cigarette holder. Taking a gold-plated lighter from the pocket of his lab coat, he lit the end of the noxious weed. He inhaled deeply on the tobacco smoke, barely getting enough of the calming nicotine because of the suppressive filter built into the cigarette holder.

Mallory-Smyth wasn't supposed to be smoking in the morgue and his offensive habit had become an issue with many of the employees. But they could all rot in hell as far as he was concerned for he *was* after all, the Chief Pathologist. Thoroughly enjoying his illicit morning smoke, he stood alone in his office with his back to the open door, reading the Search and Rescue report that had accompanied the bodies of the air crash victim's. The pilot had been an Army Veteran named Digger with years of experience flying helicopters. Digger . . . Mallory-Smyth thought this over, his face looking contemptuous. Typical, bloody Colonial name. But then they liked to do that. Name their howling, diaper filling male offspring's Buck . . . or Rocky . . . or Slim . . . or heaven forbid, something like Stretch. Colonials, most definitely a breed unto themselves.

We should have trounced their arrogant arses during their Revolutionary War he mused, but then they had the loudmouthed French and the treacherous Spanish fighting on their side. T'was not fair, t'was not fair at all. While Mallory-Smyth smoked his cigarette and became lost in his paltry reflections, his assistant Dwayne padded quietly down to his office. Startling the pants off his boss had become one of Dwayne's most fulfilling hobbies, and he held nothing back this morning as his loud wheedling voice cut the peaceful moment, nearly frightening the philosophical Doctor clear out of his silk socks.

"Good morning Sir!" Dwayne pealed rather vigorously. "I brought you some of my mom's apple pie. She's really sick these days with her bowels, spending a lot of time on the toilet, but she still has time to think about you, sir."

Mallory-Smyth turned slowly to look at his insufferable assistant, his heart still racing from the booming greeting, his stomach already flopping from the ingratiating offer of his mom's stale pie, complete with gray hairs sticking out of the crust. Mother's with apple pie and poor bowels passing hard stools he thought - I truly wish that they, as well as Dwayne - would all go straight to bloody hell. Mallory-Smyth looked down upon his energetic assistant, and the sight did nothing for his plummeting moods. In his early thirties, Dwayne could not have been any taller than five-foot-two, which somehow made him all that easier to dislike. His white lab coat was too big and it didn't fit properly so it hung down around his ankles, and combined with the thick glasses and magnified brown eyes, Mallory-Smyth wasn't altogether certain if Dwayne hadn't been sold from the shelf of some exotic pet store. He always put some kind of goo in his short black hair so it always stuck to his scalp in well-defined parallel lines after he had dragged his comb through it. Dwayne was an aspiring sort of a guy and had his heart set on becoming a doctor, but quite frankly, he had a better chance of becoming President of the United States. He didn't lack any determination, for becoming a Coroner's Assistant had been no easy feat, not with his ailing mother, fallen arches, game hip and swollen adenoids that gave his voice an irritating whistle.

Mallory-Smyth did absolutely nothing to hide the scorn that had fallen upon his face, but it did nothing to deter his animated assistant.

"Sir, you're not supposed to smoke down here," Dwayne chirped, "it's not good for our health you know."

The doctor stood there observing the unbecoming little man, puffing on his cigarette, wondering if all great men like Patton, Hannibal, Churchill or Liberace suffered such mental anguish because of their worshiping minions. When he spoke to the younger man, his dialect was slow, his words carefully chosen, and they held that lofty British accent that seemed only to pervade the lingo of the Royals. His voice had become a refined, class dialect rather than a regional dialect, unlike the East London Cockney's, or the Yorkshire Dalesmen of the Midlands.

"I say boy," Mallory-Smyth began, "you are concerned about a bit of tobacco smoke impeding your health, possibly even stunting your growth, but goddamn it man, use your bloody head. We are at present up to our lips in dead bodies you oaf, and historically, dead people have killed more humans with their filthy plagues than you could ever possibly hope to have for brain cells."

"I know that sir, but those are the union rules. No smoking in the morgue." Dwayne smiled when he said this, ignoring the Doctor's belittling tone and caustic insults. Dwayne might have been short in stature but his shoulders were certainly broad enough, although the Doctor might have been right about the amount of brain cells that occupied his squarish skull.

"Ah yes, the union," Mallory-Smyth continued, "peasant thugs who are wont to lay waste to my knee caps in the parking lot as I climb inattentively into my Jaguar. What is it with *you* people and your plebeian union crowd, and what might I ask, has this union ever done for the likes of you, boy?"

"Well sir, they got me my job working in here," Dwayne answered, his voice happy and effervescent.

"Yes, well . . . rather. One man's unqualified good fortune can undoubtedly become another man's unequivocal pain. Speaking of which, I feel a headache coming on, Boy. Have you prepared the first body?" Mallory-Smyth asked.

"Yes sir, I have," Dwayne chortled, "but you're not going to like what I've found, sir."

"Oh joy. Oh distinct, absolute, bloody rapture," replied the Doctor, "and pray tell, what surprises have you in store for me? And be brief."

"Well sir, you're not going to believe this - "

"You're trying my patience Dwayne. I instructed you to be brief."

Mallory-Smyth pronounced the young man's name as Dooo-waaay-ne, letting it roll slowly off his tongue, all nicely wrapped up in the Received Standard English, something that could only be cultivated in the private schools and hallways of Oxford or Eton College.

"Oh, sorry sir. Well, two of the victims of the air crash were decapitated, and they put both their heads in the one body bag . . . ha hah." Dwayne started laughing, but then he always did when things got really funny. There exists an old world metaphor that could best describe the one-sided, scarcely tolerable relationship between the two men; that message being along the lines of how one man's humor could instantly become another person's lower intestinal cramps. So the look that the Pathologist currently held upon his face might have suggested multiple bowel spasms, or perhaps even some gas distention.

"Just who, pray tell, decided to play swap the heads," inquired Mallory-Smyth, "those gormless

helicopter chaps you call an Air Force? Bloody hell, don't they know anything about body recovery?"

"Sure they do sir. And they liked to be called Search and Rescue Technicians. Best in the world, sir, they really are."

"Yes . . . so you say. Well, come along my little bourgeois friend, let us go and cut, shall we?"

With that abrasive comment, Doctor Frederick Mallory-Smyth, the Chief Pathologist of the city's largest morgue and forensic laboratory breezed down the darkened hallway on his slender legs, his devoted assistant limping quietly after him. It could have been a scene from an old black and white horror film, the one where a crippled Igor hobbled after a rather dashing Peter Cushing as he walked out into a shadowy graveyard. Although Malloy-Smyth was far from dashing. Egotistical. Lordly. Somewhat of an uppish prick maybe. But dashing . . . certainly not.

The Doctor flew through a double set of stainless steel doors that were located at the end of the cheerless corridor, and he did so with all the vigor of a Headmaster whose trousers were on fire. He even allowed the doors to swing back into Dwayne's face as he always did, and the assistant halted his forward motion, proficiently stepping through the narrow opening when the doors swung outwards. Dwayne never even fell out of step as he followed Mallory-Smyth over to an examination table in the corner of the large room. The cutting room was so ancient that one could have mistaken it for a turn of the century abattoir, or even a Medieval torture chamber.

But it sufficed, and most importantly, it was a world where Mallory-Smyth had complete control, a world where he had become the Lord-Master, an office he took rather seriously. When the morgue had been constructed a half century ago along with the rest of the hospital, someone at least had the forethought to design the cutting room large enough to accommodate a half dozen autopsy's at once. Even back then the architect's could predict with some accuracy mankind's mortal devices for escalating death and mayhem.

The walls and floors of the cutting room were finished in large white ceramic tiles that were easily kept clean and dry, inhibiting the growth of bacteria or any virile infections that might spawn from the dead bodies.

Everything else in the room had been constructed of stainless steel, including the six examination tables whose flat surfaces sloped down to a low point at one end where the drain was mounted. Each table had a thick metal dam around the top edge to ensure no body fluids spilled onto the floor or the feet of the people working on them. Controlling the deceased and where their fluids might drip or gush during an examination was paramount to everybody's safety and well-being. All sorts of persons could be present during the post mortem's including police officers seizing evidence, medical students, federal investigators and even an authorized citizen or two. In the center of the tiled floor sat a large workstation, again fabricated using stainless steel. Mounted at intervals across it's open surface were adjustable examination lights, with built in, circular magnification glasses. A number of accurate scales that could weigh an item to the nearest milligram were also placed at the work station, as well as metal trays for dissection and a couple of electron microscopes for those who required a closer look at the cells of a lifeless organ. Tall metal stools with round hardwood tops were pushed in next to the workstation and had been placed there for everyone's sitting pleasure. The examination tables where the actual autopsies were performed had been placed along the surrounding walls, with clean, sharp tools that lay on metal shelving atop neatly pressed green surgical cloth. Above each table hung a garden hose and a microphone, both affixed securely to the tiled ceiling. Each microphone had been wired into a tape recorder and the water hoses had been threaded through a coiled metal spring so that they could retract once the pathologist had rinsed a body cavity or a freshly plucked organ.

At present a body bag sat on top of a wheeled gurney, positioned in one corner of the room where Dwayne had parallel parked it next to an examination table. It was the assistant's job to prepare the bodies for autopsy by stripping them of their clothes and other belongings. He would store their wallets, jewelry, and other personal items in clear plastic bags, placing all the clothing in thick garbage bags that he would then secure with a knot. This would help encapsulate the seasoned smell of decaying flesh that had already permeated the damp clothes. Most of the clothing went to the burner unless it wasn't soiled, in which case the families could claim them along with the rest of the belongings if the police didn't require them for evidence. About ten minutes ago Dwayne had been preparing to strip the first victim from the helicopter crash when he'd pulled back the big brass zipper to find a headless corpse with two heads stuffed at either end. A body bag with two heads was well beyond Dwayne's limited authority and decision-making capabilities. So he pulled the zipper back up, appropriately deciding this was now a job for his repugnant boss. Someone else could sort out which head belonged to which body - union rules you know. At the time of this interesting discovery, the stouthearted Dwayne had been eating one of those glazed, cinnamon twist doughnuts. He'd finished off his daily morning treat before toddling from the morgue to retrieve the Doctor. Unfortunately, large flakes of white sugar glaze had fallen from his lips when he chewed, sending flecks cascading down onto the body bag.

As Mallory-Smyth approached the examination table he soon spied the doughnut castings, spread as they were from one end of the bag to the other. He tut-tutted loudly as he brushed the ample scattering of flakes clear with his hand, sending them onto the floor.

Mallory-Smyth then offered his assistant a painful looking scowl, and wondered not for the first time if his aged mother with her failing bowels hadn't caught Dwayne's head when he was an infant in the door of an elevator or something just as damaging. Nevertheless, the assistant failed to notice the warning frown or else chose to outright ignore it.

"I've told you before boy," Mallory-Smyth remonstrated, "you are not to bring your dreary fodder into the cutting room. I don't need to slice someone open, especially a homicide victim, only to find that your double glaze frosting has fallen in to speckle his or her liver. Is that clear?"

"Perfectly, sir, perfectly." Dwayne piped his response enthusiastically, but those with trained eyes could tell that the Doctor's instruction had gone through one ear and out the other, a simple given when there wasn't much in-between to stop it.

Mallory-Smyth pulled a pair of disposable rubber gloves onto his hands, then leaned over the olive drab body bag, zipping it wide open. Despite the menthol ointment he'd applied to his nose, he still received a feint wafting of the sweet, mawkish, bodily decay. Slowly the Pathologist pulled back the stiff folds of the bag, carefully reaching into the sticky interior, retrieving a human head from between the feet of the cadaver. He placed the blood-covered head onto the examination table, then went snooping around for the other one, which he found in the bag up near the shoulders. Once both heads had been placed on the cold, shiny surface of the table, Mallory-Smyth used the water hose and a thick sponge to rinse them off. The neck muscles on both heads hung below the white skin where they had been severed, and appeared a reddish color like aged beef. Arteries could be seen throughout the muscles, lying collapsed like empty sausage casings and the windpipes on each head were still open, appearing translucent with specks of blood lining the inner walls of each tube.

Once the heads had been cleaned up, the difference in physical characteristics became much clearer. That's better Malloy-Smyth thought as he stood back and studied his cleaning job.

There would be no further dillydallying with this sloppy mix-up, not now. One victim had a healthy head of black hair while the other one was decidedly balding. After giving his assistant some instructions, Dwayne also donned a pair of rubber gloves then quickly sorted through the body bag until he found the owner's wallet in a back pocket. It was a brown leather folding type and the driver's license was in plain view amongst the slits that held the credit cards. Mallory-Smyth took the license from his assistant's hand and quickly identified Elwood Noble's head using the color photograph on the front of the license. The Doctor issued Dwayne with another directive, and the assistant limped down the hall to the cooler to fetch the second male who had died in the air crash. Moments later the assistant returned, rolling in the gurney that held the remains of the other male victim. He pushed it over toward the table, then zipped open the bag, reaching in and feeling around the dead man's waist until he found his wallet.

Dwayne handed this wallet to Mallory-Smyth who immediately searched the contents, finding the drivers license tucked behind a midnight black, extra ribbed condom. Digger's balding pate in the photo was a near perfect match for the expressionless head that stood perched on the examination table. Mallory-Smyth gave the license back to Dwayne, then nodded curtly, indicating that the cutting was to begin. The assistant started to manhandle the first body out of the bag, the one that lay on the gurney next to the examination table. He had to shift it a bit at a time because the rigor mortis had left the corpse, leaving it limp and soggy feeling once again. Of course, Mallory-Smyth looked on as his assistant struggled and heaved on the cadaver, not even lifting a finger to give him so much as some shallow encouragement. Union rules you know. Once the headless corpse lay upon the examination table, Dwayne took some heavy scissors and cut away all the clothing, balling it up before stuffing the wet mess into a garbage bag. The body that lay before them was tall, fairly lean, but well nourished and looking at the physical description on the back of Elwood's drivers license, it became abundantly clear whose head belonged to whom. To be absolutely sure though, Mallory-Smyth walked over to inspect the second body, comparing the remains with the driver's license that had come from his wallet. There could be no doubt, for Digger was described as short and stocky, and those were the physical traits of the body that lay within the second bag. Mallory-Smyth took Digger's head and placed it inside the bag next to his body, then allowed Dwayne to wheel the remains back to the cooler. An earlier call from the police indicated they were still tracking down Digger's next of kin, so there would be no hurry to cut him open.

The deceased father and his teenaged daughter would be another matter, for they had surviving family in a small town up the coast. Most certainly they would be awaiting the conclusion of the autopsies so they could claim their loved one's for a proper interment.

Mallory-Smyth had indeed become what the human race would call a turd, but he hadn't become that large of a turd that he still couldn't show some consideration for a grieving family.

After Dwayne had returned to the cutting room he'd found that the Doctor had changed his mind, which was definitely something of a rarity. Mallory-Smyth had decided to examine Elwood's head after all, a procedure at first he wasn't going to bother performing. According to the Search and Rescue report, Elwood Noble had been a passenger in the front seat of the aircraft, his death caused by traumatic decapitation when the spinning rotor blades dropped low enough to break through the cabin roof. The cause of death was unmistakable, and not up for dispute, but something fussed deep inside of the Pathologist and he suddenly overturned his decision, deciding to have a look inside of Elwood's melon. Mallory-Smyth didn't like to cut open corpses when there existed no real need, but Elwood's head had already been mutilated and dearly departed from his trunk, and the simple dissection procedure would take but a few minutes. Both the Doctor and his assistant took hospital green, disposable rubber lined smocks from packages on the shelf, pulling them over their lab coats. They each took a pair of plastic safety goggles, also from the shelf, and pulled them over their heads, ensuring they were snug over their eyes.

From here on in things would get a trifle messy, and careful you may be, there was always a bit of loose flesh that would find it's way onto your clothing. Or if you were like Dwayne, into your hair. Mallory-Smyth then took a slender hand tool from the metal shelf, passing his assistant the plug so he could connect it to the power outlet that swung freely from the ceiling. The hand tool had a small, serrated disk at the working end, mounted on a shaft the size of a pencil.

After nodding to Dwayne, the assistant grasped Elwood's head in his hands, firmly holding it by the ears with the back of the head against the table. Suddenly the serrated disk spun to life with a high-pitched wailing as Mallory-Smyth applied the power, bending over to his task. Placing the disk against Elwood's forehead, he carefully cut through the skull, causing the tool to shriek with the effort, filling the room with the unmistakable smell of friction burned, finely ground human bone. Moments later a thick dark line could be seen traversing the forehead where the skin had parted, and dark fluid seeped from the open seam.

Dwayne expertly flipped the head over, and Mallory-Smyth continued across the back, cutting through the dark hair, sending small tufts spitting out across the table. Once he had finished with the rear of the skull the circle was now complete, and the Doctor gently pulled the top of the skull away from the head, laying it on the table like a cereal bowl. Dwayne flipped the head over once again and with the staying tension of the scalp now completely removed, the skin on the face sagged down on the skull, looking like some hideous Halloween mask. The top and front of Elwood's brain was fully exposed, the pink-gray of the furrowed cerebrum resembling the massive shell of walnut, it's ridges and grooves curving under a wet, shiny outer membrane.

At first glance the mass of nerve tissue looked remarkable normal, causing Mallory-Smyth to hesitate for a second. This was when he spotted the flesh colored tumor, easily the size of a large grape, growing out of both right and left cerebral hemispheres. It spanned the natural gap of the longitudinal fissure, meeting in the middle, appearing to even force it apart somewhat.

The fissure itself was a physiological normality that bisected the left and right portions of every healthy brain, but Elwood Noble's brain was leagues away from being healthy.

The tumor had been growing in his frontal lobe, the portion that controlled his emotional and behavioral patterns. Mallory-Smyth had seen enough of these cancerous growths to safely speculate that Mister Noble hadn't been too far from a catatonic death. Dwayne had noticed the tumor as well, and forever thirsting to expand his medical knowledge, he had leaned over the corpse's head, taking in a close up of the odd looking growth.

"What's that?" Dwayne asked.

"I would say it's a malignant brain tumor, boy," Mallory-Smyth replied, "I'll take a biopsy and have you trot it up to the lab. They'll be able to confirm it, then we'll know for sure. Very interesting, and would you mind getting your fat hillbilly head out of my bloody light."

"Sorry, sir." Dwayne stood up straight, pushing his glasses back up his sweaty nose with his fully extended middle finger, flicking the Doctor a cheeky, camouflaged jester of defiance.

Dwayne sincerely hoped that one day those Aliens he'd read about in the tabloids would kidnap this stuck-up Limey bastard and use him for a sex slave. The newspapers had said that they had huge sex organs and came from a transsexual universe, which was clear across the solar system.

Dwayne believed in Aliens, but then he was foolish enough to believe in truth and justice, and the inherent right of every child to have a belly full of food as well as a roof over their heads.

"I bet that tumor hurts like hell sir," Dwayne offered, hoping to get back on the Doctors good side.

"*Hurt* like hell, Dwayne, it *hurt* like hell," Mallory-Smyth corrected. "The man's dead so he wouldn't be feeling much of anything. But then I'm just guessing. I *will* tell you this much though boy, he was probably acting a bit potty before he died. However, no amount of cutting or weighing or analyzing his brain will ever confirm that. I shall have to call his unfortunate family to find out that bit of depressing information. This bloody day is just getting worse, eh Dwayne?"

"Whatever you say sir," Dwayne muttered, "whatever the fuck you say."

* * *

Chapter Eighteen

The first big emotional rift to occur between Judith and her mother came about when Molly decided to have Elwood and Meryl's remains cremated. Molly had received a telephone call a few hours after lunch during the third day after the helicopter crash, speaking in length to a Doctor on the other end of the line. Judith had spent the days since the accident languishing in her bedroom, coming out only to use the bathroom or pick at her food while sat quietly at the kitchen table. Occasionally she would wander next door to Meryl's room, lying on the bed and weeping quietly as her sister's scent drifted up from the pillow, filling her nose with a mollifying fragrance, letting her head swim with secret memories. On one such morning excursion Judith had sat at her sister's desk, staring at a framed photograph taken while at a country fair on holidays with their mother last summer. She removed the picture from the pine bookcase built into the back of the desk and examined it closely. In it, Meryl and Judith sat straddling a toffee colored pony, both wearing light cotton shorts and sleeveless summer tops with straw cowboy hats perched on each of their heads. A clown in baggy denim overalls stood by, holding the pony by its bridle. He wore an orange wig with his face painted white and had one of those red bulbous noses. On his feet he wore long, wide floppy leather shoes with holes in them. Meryl sat in front, holding on to the pony's white mane while Judith was snuggled in behind her, her arms wrapped around her sister's waist. Meryl's blonde hair had been cropped short for the hot seasonal months, while Judith's hung well below the cloth brim of her hat, touching her shoulders, curling at the ends and bleached nearly white from the long hours of sunshine. The easy smiles on the faces of the two sisters told of simple, happy times, born from the innocence of sibling closeness and the carefree moods that summer always brought to children.

To a grieving young person like Judith, those were happy times forever lost. A period in her life that could never to be regained no matter what lay on the road ahead. There of course would be good times ahead, but you would be wasting your breath trying to explain this to a twelve-year old who had just lost her sister and father in a horrific accident. Judith had continued to gaze at the photograph of her and Meryl on the pony when she reached inside the top drawer of the desk.

Acting spontaneously and with hurt on her mind, she pulled out a long set of scissors and slowly cut her hair off. Her face remained emotionless as she snipped away at the blonde locks but inside she was seething. Judith had entered that stage of the mourning process when the afflicted person would start to lash out at the survivors, for she now subconsciously blamed her mother for the family's misfortune. She knew that her new hair style would pain Molly more than it would pain herself and it became a quick method to vent some anger, as well as cause her mother some much deserved anxiety. Judith would never grow her hair long again, and whether this act had become a silent, psychological tribute to her dead sister would never be known.

But it mattered not.

What mattered at the time was that Molly was furious when she saw what Judith had done to her hair. It had turned out the way she had meant it to turn out - like a vigilante chop job that no amount of clipping or combing could fix. The yelling started in Meryl's bedroom then moved to the kitchen, escalating into a barbaric shouting match in which both parties leveled some mean, unladylike accusations. Molly Noble appeared to be losing control of her remaining daughter, but then with her drinking and fooling around, it would seem she had lost control of her own life. What Judith really needed right now in her life was room to heal and a strong role model. The role model would come soon enough and from a very unexpected quarter, but the room she would have to fight for, especially with Molly constantly in her face.

Eventually the phone rang, which put an end to the morning's bickering, offering them a much needed break to cool their emotions. As her mother picked up the phone Judith left the kitchen, silently returning to the welcoming confines of her bedroom.

The telephone had been ringing non stop since the accident, the townspeople calling to send their condolences and inquire politely as to the surviving Nobles well being. Pastries and cakes on large platters were spread over every counter top in the kitchen and the refrigerators racks held cooked ham, sausage rolls, pot roasts and piles of sliced cold cuts. The food had started to arrive on Sunday, the day after the accident. It came from neighbors and friends and strangers who knocked on the back door, speaking to Molly in hushed tones as they handed her a plate of steaming food - or something well chilled. This was a social courtesy Molly had explained after one of the many visits, placing more perishables inside the fridge. People usually bring food when tragedy strikes your family her mother had said, although Judith had neither the heart to appreciate the gesture, nor the stomach to eat much of the food. She viewed the exercise as a waste of time as well as a rude intrusion. During mealtimes they sat at the table and took their food together but virtually nothing was said during these moody functions. Molly tried to get the dialogue going but Judith would have no part of it, withdrawing further into herself, adding more bricks to the wall she had started to build.

Unfortunately, the relationship between the two had turned in a direction that made a healthy reconcile difficult, but not totally impossible. Molly had now taken to drinking her tall glasses of orange juice by mid afternoon and Judith had caught her several times topping up the glass with a clear liquid from a bottle hidden at the back of the cupboard. But she was too young to grasp the seriousness of what her mother was doing, and she had become too grief-stricken to care. On the third day of this numbing misery, during the late afternoon the phone rang once again.

Molly picked it up in the kitchen, and Judith could tell it was a different call from the rest just by the formal manner in which her mother spoke. She had been secluded in her room staring quietly at the ceiling, but slid off her bed when she heard the seriousness in her mother's voice, walking silently in her stocking feet down the hall to the plastered archway that led into the kitchen.

Molly was talking to a Doctor of some kind, that much became obvious as she addressed him as Doctor Mallory - something or rather - Smyth. Judith could clearly discern her mother's side of the conversation, and even though the person at the other end sounded like a muted tenor, his voice still reached her, conveyed across the room in a snooty type accent. At the end of the phone call, Molly said something to the Doctor that fell upon Judith like a terrible blow.

"Why yes, Doctor," her mother replied, "Elwood had been acting extremely strange lately, and for sometime now . . . yes, it has caused the family a lot of distress - "

Molly sipped on her drink as she listened for a moment.

"Oh . . . well, for over a year now I should think, I'm really not too sure . . . he had turned very religious, quoting from the bible all the time, yelling at people in the street, calling them all sinners . . . he even did it at home to myself and his own daughters - "

177

The doctor spoke again, and Molly filled the space with another opportunity to brace herself from her glass while she listened. Judith wondered if the Doctor at the other end couldn't hear the tinkling of ice cubes when her mother brought the glass close to the receiver.

"Malignant?" Her mother suddenly asked. "Oh I see, you did a biopsy . . . so it looks like he didn't have much time left anyway . . . Yes . . . I see . . . Yes Doctor, we knew about Meryl's condition, she had an appointment at a clinic to take care of it, that was why they were flying

down there."

Molly glanced through the window over the sink, nodding her head as the Doctor talked with her some more, unaware that Judith stood listening from the entryway.

"Both remains are to be cremated, Doctor . . . yes, that's correct, my lawyer up here has made all the arrangements . . . so they can be released to the funeral home once you are done . . . thank-you for calling Doctor . . . what you have told me answers a lot of questions . . . yes, I'll call my lawyer right away . . . thank-you, good-bye."

Judith stood gasping with shock, feeling betrayed at what her mother had just said, stunned with the calm attitude in which she had uttered that cold, uncaring word cremation. Molly's talk of cremating the remains of Elwood and Meryl came without any kind of a discussion, further entrenching within Judith what would be a series of unwitting fractures. This cremation decision, and other circumstances that were to develop in the following weeks would finally shatter that cherished relationship between most mothers and their daughters. At the time though, and in all fairness to Molly, Judith's mother was just as anguished over the tragic losses. This undoubtedly contributed to her trying to act composed on the phone, the results being she spoke of the funeral arrangements with all the finality an uninterested used car dealer. But when you are twelve years old, and you have just lost your sister and your father, and you were anticipating a sensitive funeral service in which everybody wore dark dresses and suits as they filed past the open coffins inside the flower filled community hall - any talk of cremation would be devastating. Once Molly returned the phone to the cradle, another screaming match ensued. At times it would drop to the level of intelligent conversation as Molly tried to calmly explain her choice to her tearful daughter, but then it would soon escalate as Judith's emotions quickly boiled over. Soon they tired of standing in the middle of the kitchen, and mutually agreed to sit at the table, but this did nothing to curb the peppery accusations. Neither one of them were going to concede as to how *they* felt the funeral arrangements should be handled, and the discussion carried well into the night, until Molly's speech became too slurred to understand, and Judith ultimately surrendered to her exhaustion.

*   *   *

Chapter Nineteen

In the end, the remains of Elwood and Meryl Noble were cremated. This was Molly's unpopular decision, and as she was paying the bills there would be no further talk regarding the matter. The remains were delivered in a timely fashion to the old wooden bus depot downtown, and only one day after the phone call from Doctor Mallory-Smyth. They arrived during the daily scheduled run, unloaded by the driver through the side doors of the bus as his passengers stood yawning and blinking in the rare rays of sunshine. Even though it was a short walk to the bus depot Molly drove the station wagon as she didn't think it prudent to walk through the town toting a cremation urn under each arm. Packed as they were in shredded paper and a stiff cardboard box, she needn't have worried anyway, so she loaded it into the back of the car and drove home. Judith had left the house earlier to go for a walk down the beach, which her mother viewed as an encouraging sign that she might be finally coming around. When she got home, Molly carried the box through the back door and into the master bedroom where she unpacked the contents. Both urns were made of copper, with flowers scribed into the hard round tops, which had been securely screwed into the mouth of each vessel. Square silver plates had been riveted near the bases and had the names of the occupants, as well as the years that they had been allowed to grace the planet. Molly had no idea what she was going to do with them, so she placed them both in the back of her closet behind some clothes, hiding them as though they were children's Christmas presents. She wasn't entirely sure why she hid them, but a part of her feared their very sight might invoke more bitterness in Judith, and part of her was uncertain of what she would do with them if she found them.

The memorial service would be held tomorrow morning at the family church, and large gold-framed photographs of Elwood and Meryl would be placed on the altar for that very purpose. Molly had spent many hours trying to explain to Judith the methods behind the decision for cremation and eventually gave up as talking to a cement no-post would have brought a less aggressive response. She *had* succeeded in convincing her daughter to attend the service, suggesting she do it strictly for the memory of Meryl and her father, rather than doing it for her mother. Judith had renounced God days ago, which meant she'd abdicated places where people gathered to read verses, sing, and celebrate his presence. In the end however, Judith capitulated and Molly felt relieved when her daughter went to her closet to pick out a dark purple dress and a black pair of shoes that she could wear at the service. Pastor Wilcox would lead the memorial service, having been the one who had come to their house days ago to deliver the bad news.

He'd dropped in several times already to check on how Molly and Judith were doing, wearing his white collar and carrying a pleasant smile as well as his thick bible. Most unfortunate though, every time the Pastor had visited the two, they had either just started a heated discussion, were just ending one, or they weren't even talking at all. It was nearly to the point where these spats were getting embarrassing, despite Pastor Wilcox explaining them away as symptoms of stress and wretched grief. On the surface it would appear that the kindly Pastor was disinclined to take sides and cast any oil upon these types of turbulent waters. Maybe his experience told him to leave these things alone as time usually healed all wounds. The Pastor had already commented to Molly during one of his visits that he admired the forthright young lady that was emerging from Judith's desolated soul. Therein lay parts of the problem though, for the strong will that was growing inside of the young girl only helped to contribute to the crumbling relationship.

Once the urns had been hidden away, Molly walked out of the bedroom and entered the kitchen, retrieving her bottle from the cupboard. The time had come to reward herself with a goodly shot of vodka. Once she had sweetened the drink with orange juice and ice, she sat down at the kitchen table, stirring it with one of her slender fingers. She had a dark dress with a short hem to wear tomorrow, with black panty hose and navy blue high heel shoes that would accent her shapely legs. She sorely hoped Jeremy Salter would also be attending the service. He had been invited and she hoped to talk to him in person during the reception for he'd kept a respectable distance since the accident, speaking to Molly only when she called him on the phone. She had a proposition for him, which needed to be discussed in person, and it was difficult to get away from the house while Judith was at home moping. Molly took a long pull on her drink and looked out the window, wondering if she was changing, or if her daughter was changing or maybe they both were changing, maturing like butterflies from a self imposed type of chrysalis. The bizarre cocoon that had enveloped them both would be the ill-fated calamity that had of late tested and played with their low end emotions, binding them in the same confined space together like a couple of stray alley cats. Still staring out the window, Molly continued to sip her drink, watching the fluffy cumulus clouds as they moved across the dusty blue sky, pushed along by the ocean borne prevailing westerlies.

She thought long and deep about the sudden turns that both her and Judith's lives had taken, conveniently freeing one from a loveless marriage, while fettering them both with the loss of a sister and a daughter. Molly dearly loved and missed her Meryl, even though Elwood hadn't been her biological father. Exactly who fathered Meryl was debatable, but the sad fact remained that it hadn't been Elwood, something he had never known, nor will he, or anyone else for that matter.

Many human beings ended up taking secrets with them to the grave, and this would be one of a dozen that would accompany Molly when she went. Meryl had been conceived during Elwood and Molly's carefree, earlier days together when Molly had a rapacious appetite for all kinds of sex, seeking out the evasive orgasm while her dutiful husband toiled at work. Some might have called her sluttish back then, but what about those equally horny men? They had wives at home as well as children, but they hesitated nary a second when they eagerly shucked their shorts to climb on top of an equally receptive Molly. Yes, she grieved for her lost, illegitimate daughter, and the pain wasn't as intense as Judith's, but she knew those feelings were yet to strike, simply a delayed reaction that waited for her at every corner. The liquor had contributed to the stalled emotions as well, setting upon her a numbing, cozy wall that didn't allow too much to get through at the time. Many professionals touted liquor as a depressant, but in the hands of a veteran drinker it could also be an exhilarating, albeit destructive stimulant.

Minutes later Molly finished her drink and went to recharge her glass, moving with the adeptness of a practiced drinker, getting the first few shots into her system in case the bottle were to magically disappear. As she sat back down the silky panties beneath her jeans brushed lightly against the delicate folds of her sex, abruptly awakening another feeling that had lain slumbering this past week. Molly realized she was feeling frisky, her thoughts immediately returning to Jeremy Salter, his muscular body, appeasing lips and callisthenic tongue. She needed to see him, and as she moved her backside over the bottom of her chair the friction seemed to spread the arousal throughout her soft vulva, causing her clitoral glands to harden, making her feel moist and electrified. Molly felt herself flush as her nipples hardened, and she wasn't entirely sure if it was the erotic anticipation that caused her flesh to warm or the euphoria brought about by the liquor. As she sat there considering the immediate future, she attempted to quell the excitement at her mid-section, but instead arrived at another resolution - one that would bring the weekly tally of bad decisions to a total of two in as many days.

The first had caused immeasurable friction when she decided to cremate Elwood and Meryl's remains, whereas the second would be strictly for her own pleasure, but it too would follow with more unintentional conflict. Come the day after tomorrow, which would be Friday, Judith would return to school as the time had come to put the grieving process away for a while and think about her education again. Little time remained until the summer holidays, so Molly couldn't let her daughter falter any longer. It would make for a healthy change, and do her no end of good to get her nose back into a book, mingling once again with her friends at the schoolyard. It would be good for Judith, and it would be good for Molly. With her daughter safely ensconced back into the classroom Molly could see Jeremy Salter and engage in a long, slow romp. Yes . . . things were starting to look up she thought recklessly. Regrettably, it was a reckless complacency that a lot of people lacking in life skills had chosen to practice. Few of them succeeded, and only then on the merits of plain dumb luck, but the majority of them would spiral from the good graces of those who loved them. By weeks end, it would be Molly's wanton desire to have Jeremy Salter lick her nude body that would create the second big rift between a mother and her young daughter. From a distance, and accounting the emotional toll it would cost over the years, one might be at odds to figure out which rift would be the biggest; the one that would develop between Judith and her mother, or the one they called the San Andreas Fault.

*   *   *

Chapter Twenty

On Friday morning Judith arose from her bed and prepared herself for the school day. She looked forward to returning to the classroom and had only nodded quietly when Molly made the proposal after returning home from the funeral service. The service had been well attended, which made it hot and stuffy inside the crowded church. Judith sat in the front pew with her mother and some of the town's dignitaries and even though it had been an emotional day, Judith managed to hold her own which would have made her sister and father proud.

She had decided to be strong that day, there were to be no tears, no solicitation for sympathy, therefore no emotion at all would be allowed to register on her face. Regardless, there was still an incident right after the church service, something with enough potential to make the day turn outright ugly. Although Judith, employing her customary tactful manners concluded the episode before it could gather any momentum. It occurred right after the church service when the crowd started to shuffle from the main hall to the open reception area downstairs. There the women's auxiliary had set up folding tables, first covering them with freshly ironed white linen cloths, then with trays of sticky buns and finger sandwiches. Metal pots containing gallons of hot coffee and tea had also been set out so the grieving herd could properly wash the food down.

The entrance to the basement was outside, and as everybody exited the church the Mayor approached Judith on the front steps, making a grand show of being concerned. A lot of the kids in town called her Worship the old fat broad because she wouldn't answer her door at Halloween, but also as a result of the patronizing behavior she held out to the young people. Near the bottom of the step the Mayor had reached out and clutched Judith firmly by the arm, ensuring to do so in front of a captive crowd of electorates. Her Worship bent down on her thick stumps, putting her face, which was caked with make-up close in to Judith's. She then filled Judith's ears with a trumpeting sympathy, clucking at her bravery as she took a handkerchief she had wet with her tongue, wiping some invisible mark from her young face. Judith could feel her skin quiver as the warm spit was rubbed across her cheek, and she obligingly leaned against the side of the Mayor's head.

"Don't ever do that again, you old cow," Judith whispered into her receptive ear.

True to any politician's deportment, the old Mayor never missed a beat, showing an expansive smile to the crowd as she quickly hugged Judith, "bless you child," she said boisterously, "oh, may god bless you." The crowd smiled and awed at this gracious act, while Judith pulled herself away from her Worship's damp hands and headed for the reception area and the sticky buns.

All that horror had been yesterday, but today would be a new day. Judith thought this as she stood in front of the bathroom mirror washing her face with hot soapy water and a soft cloth.

She thought the skin on her cheek appeared more blushed than normal where the old Mayor had wiped her face with her drool, so Judith gave that area some extra attention. Molly was up and dressed which Judith found unusual, but maybe the time had come for some change in the household routine. When she had walked down the hall from her bedroom she had seen her mother standing near the kitchen sink, humming to herself as she worked at the counter. Molly was wearing a cheeky pair of blue jeans, which stuck to her skin, readily displaying the tight globes of her backside and the satiny shirt left no guessing to the size of her rounded breasts. She had make-up on her face and her blonde hair, clean and shiny, jiggled softly over her shoulders.

The whole scene had become a marked departure from the terry cloth housecoat and the wide yawns that normally greeted Judith every morning.

After she finished washing herself Judith returned to her bedroom to get dressed, thinking once again about her mother. Quite possibly the time had come to suspend their differences, for she was after all the only family Judith had left in the world. Perhaps cremating the remains of her sister and father hadn't been such a terrible idea after all, especially with the urns sitting in Molly's closet where Judith had discovered them yesterday afternoon. At least now she could visit Meryl and her father whenever Molly left the house, but even better, Judith could take them with her when she moved away from this dreary town. She didn't plan on spending her whole life here, living and working at the mill, marrying some guy named Jethro who would drive them to a hootenanny every Friday night in his high slung pick-up truck. No, that wouldn't do for her, not with so many horizons calling out to her from somewhere over a mountain range. Judith rooted through her clothes closet, choosing a loose fitting sweatshirt and a pair of faded denims, which she placed on her bed. From a chest of drawers she retrieved a pair of socks and a pair of underwear, hopping around on alternate feet as she pulled these onto her body.

She paused momentarily, standing in her socks and underwear, looking at the framed picture that now rested on top of her bureau. It was the photograph of her and Meryl seated on the pony wearing their cowboy hats. She felt a squeeze inside every time she looked at it, and this particular time she thought of the friendly advice Pastor Wilcox had given her at the reception.

He had spoken to her as she sat alone at a table munching on sticky buns, and Judith had warned the Pastor the moment he first sat down beside her.

"Pastor Wilcox, please don't tell me that the loss of my sister and father was God's will. I'm sorry but I can't accept that."

The kindly old Minister smiled at Judith's ultimatum, confirming his respect with a gentle nod of his head.

"That's fair Judith. But I do want you to try and forget about your own pain for awhile," the Pastor said gently. He had a soft, lulling voice that could mesmerize you, the kind that you could lay still on a downy bed and listen to all day. "Please try and put aside for now what it is that you have truly lost," he continued, "which is a sister and a good friend, and a loving father. Instead of focusing on your own pain Judith, celebrate and remember the good times that the three of you had together, especially that special time you spent with Meryl. Allow yourself to be buoyed by your memories, and smile at them, if only inside. Please don't let the loss drag you under and make you bitter. I know it's hard sometimes, but I see a resolve in you Judith that I've never seen before in a lady so young."

She had heeded the Pastor's simple advice, and more and more she thought about the good times she and Meryl had spent together, which started to prevail over the periods of grieving; something she now saved for her pillow at bed time.

Still . . . it was hard at times.

Judith left her room once she had dressed and made her bed, walking into the kitchen to find her favorite breakfast food on the table. She poured her cereal from the box into a bowl, adding the milk and eating quietly with a spoon as her mother packed a sandwich and some goodies into a square plastic lunch box. An old stubby thermos with a tartan shell went in last, and Molly snapped the box closed. It was drizzling rain outside and her mother always gave the girls hot soup whenever the weather became inclement.

Summer was only a few weeks away but when the clouds surged in from the ocean they regularly brought the cold moist air with them. Their house had been built within relatively close proximity to the schools, but returning home for lunch hadn't been an option these last couple of years. When Meryl had been alive she preferred to run with her friends at lunchtime and Judith would spend the hour in the library after eating her sandwich in the lunchroom.

As Judith ate her breakfast her mother placed the blue lunch box on a wooden bench under the coat rack near the back door, then leaned against the counter drinking black coffee from a heavy mug.

"I've made you some soup," Molly said, "it's cold outside and there's supposed to be heavy rain later on today."

"Thanks mom," Judith murmured.

She looked at her mother who smiled, and Judith managed a slight smile herself, the closest thing to a truce offering in almost a week. Judith finished her cereal and after placing the bowl in the sink, she walked over to the back door, pulling a bomber style nylon coat from the hooks along the wall. As she zipped it up her mother came over and handed her the lunch box, and when Judith took it Molly put her arms around her daughter.

"Can we be friends again?" Molly asked. "You're all I have left in the world and I don't want to lose you. I promise we'll talk first next time. *Before* I make anymore decisions."

Judith put her arms around her mother's waist and hugged back, taking in the musk of her body, feeling the warmth radiate out from her tummy.

"Yes," Judith replied, "I suppose we should be friends again."

"Good, and promise me you'll never cut your beautiful hair off again. You look like an orphan."

Judith looked up into her mother's eyes, nodding, and they both smiled. Molly kissed her daughter on the forehead then held the back door open for her as she stepped out into the morning drizzle.

It was an easy ten-minute walk through the town and up to the two schools, and Judith took her normal route up the back alley then through the park behind their house. From there she followed the asphalt road as it led up through the surrounding forests to the schoolyards, then eventually out to the mill site. She followed the cement sidewalk that had been built along the side of the road to separate the school-aged children from the constant mill traffic. Judith plodded along carrying her lunch box, enjoying the cleansing smells that were chased from the woods whenever it rained. The turpentine aroma from the resins that seeped from the fir trunks carried out to her nose, as well the odors of the wet earth and soil like scents of the reindeer moss that hung like wispy green beards from the tree limbs. Soon she came to the part of the forest where the trail led off into the gloom, taking you to the fort that Kyle Mortimer and his gang had built deep within the woods. Judith stopped for a moment, looking through the dark pillars of trees, thinking back to the night she had found Meryl in the fort with Kyle grunting on top of her, his small dilly hanging between his legs. It all seemed so long ago now, like it had never happened and even the forest suddenly looked different. Judith made herself a promise as she stood there gazing into the trees; she would never allow a guy to do to her what Kyle had been doing to her sister, not ever.

Turning, she continued trudging up the sidewalk to the schools, part of her lost in the bittersweet thoughts of her sister, part of her happy to be returning to the classroom. Judith couldn't possibly have known it back then, a time when all she could do was dream of becoming a school teacher, but everything that was taking place around her was helping to groom her, helping to make her a stronger and more understanding person. These would be valuable assets for a demanding career in educating mentally challenged children. Halfway up the hill a well-worn trail left the sidewalk, snaking through the thick woods. A shortcut, it led up to the elementary school whose roof line could be seen in the distance, running straight and true across the gray horizon behind the dense tangle of fir boughs. Both the elementary and the high schools had been built on common property, with both a playground and a hard-packed quarter mile track set into the grass in the middle of the cedar-sided buildings. There was something there for every age group to occupy the morning and afternoon recesses as well as the lunch periods, and very few problems had occurred with the two schools being so close together. Today's violent occurrence however, would be the first of it's kind, and would set in to motion a series of new rules that would keep the young adults of the high school well away from the younger children of the lower grades. It would also forbid any further use of the trail through the woods as a shortcut.

As Judith entered the trail the smells of the forest seemed to fall upon her, and the drizzle had brought out the small animals, their foraging sounds reaching to her ears. Frogs croaked from the edge of a far off, low lying swamp while pewter colored Whisky Jacks called out as they scanned the woodlands, perched high among long branches. Small rodents could be heard scurrying through the dead fall that carpeted the forest floor, searching for tidbits dropped by the feeding birds and other animals. The footpath angled well away from the sidewalk and the roadway, cutting deep into the woods, at one point skirting up and around the massive base of a Douglas fir tree the silviculturists from the mill had estimated to be at least two centuries old. As Judith rounded the base of the tree the path leveled out and she glanced up to see Kyle Mortimer standing in the middle of the pathway with his arms crossed over his chest. He had on one of those red and black-checkered work shirts, a symbol of toughness around the high school, and on his face he wore a goading leer, exposing his crooked teeth and the metal braces that lined his mouth. Kyle was with a small horde of his pimply-faced, masturbating followers and Judith had seen prettier expressions on totem poles and she told them this as she eyed them warily.

Kyle Mortimer had been cast from the same mold as all young bullies; a trembling coward when alone and left to his own way of thinking, but in the company of others an instant loud-mouth still lacking any common courage. Had Judith known at the time that Kyle and his gang of hard stools were planning to drag her into the bush out of earshot, then pin her down and remove her jeans and panties so they could all have a good look at her muff, she would have dropped Kyle right then and there. In fact, Kyle's decision to hold a taunting conversation for the sake of his young disciples would be his painful down fall. The original call to action was to jump Judith right away, and had that have happened, things might have turned out a bit different in that there would have only been more casualties. The danger to Judith may have been apparent to anyone else, but she felt no fear and couldn't possibly have known about their nefarious scheme. Kyle began his heckling dialogue with a verbal assault on Judith, attempting to provoke a fight, hoping she might strike out at him, which would justify their peeking down her pants. No one ever said Kyle Mortimer had reasonable thoughts, and no one ever said he was a smart boy.

"Who cut your hair," he began, "or did you get it caught in a blender?"

"Get out of my way Kyle, you whiny little bastard."

Judith's face showed absolutely nothing when she said this, leaving her antagonist's guessing as to whether they were even scaring her.

"You're mother's a slut," Kyle scoffed.

"Have you shown your mindless pals how small your penis is?" Judith asked, referring to the night she had seen him with his pants down in the fort with Meryl. The four of five lads who had accompanied Kyle on this life enriching expedition weren't exactly the obedient flunkies he had hoped they were, for they all started laughing at Judith's comment. Kyle waited until the crimson in his face had toned down a bit and the laughing had stopped before he continued.

"Oh yeah . . . well I fucked your sister," he said flatly.

He turned to his gang who were laughing again, nodding his approval as they acclaimed his right to be their glorious leader. Making such a statement not seven days after Meryl's death wasn't only cruel and spineless, it was also a near fatal error. The poison that spewed from Kyle's mouth had just become the forging factor to an unrelenting determination, a stay and fight reaction, abruptly tempered by the extreme comments made in a wet forest below an elementary school yard. It would be a no nonsense attitude that Judith would carry for the rest of her life.

An attitude that would serve her well.

Kyle laughed at his simple wit, continuing to look at his devoted herd, openly encouraging their support. About this time Judith abruptly swept her arm behind her in a long arc, clinging to her lunch box while twisting gracefully at her waist. Rapidly she returned it in a full roundhouse swing, gathering ample velocity as she guided her lunch box on it's curving path, still holding it tightly in her fingers. One of the young goon's yelped, and as Kyle looked forward the kinetic energy behind Judith's motion slammed the plastic lunch box full force into the front of his mouth. Kyle fell to his knees, blood running down his chin in unchecked streams, dripping stains onto his blue jeans. He shook his head in pain and blew loudly, spitting out blood and at least a dozen good sized white chips of fractured teeth as well as pieces of wire and metal. Some serious damage had occurred inside of Kyle's noisy mouth and it hadn't happened because of the sandwich or the chocolate covered hockey puck with the creamy filling that were packed inside the lunch box.

It had happened because of the miserable weather.

That and the pound and half of weight behind the old tartan colored thermos that contained Judith's hot soup. Four thousand dollars worth of orthodontics and annual adjustments paid from the pocket of big John Mortimer the mill manager, now spewed out onto the forest floor. As Kyle knelt on the trail, gagging on blood and broken teeth, Judith finalized the act with a curt reminder from the past.

191

"I warned you Kyle. That night I caught you in the fort with Meryl I warned you. You ever take another run at my sister and I was going to knock your teeth out . . . remember?"

By now Kyle was crying, holding his hand over his mouth but he managed to nod his head, painfully remembering the cautioning that Judith had given him. It had all seemed so worthwhile way back then, considering he'd just been laid for the first time.

They were now alone in the woods, as Kyle's stalwart crew had fled seconds after the lunch box had kissed their fearless leader's mouth. Kyle had promised them if they came along and helped him they would get a squint at a young girls private parts, maybe even get to touch it if she became horny. But Kyle had said nothing about flying lunch boxes, or games of smash mouth, nor had he said anything about faces being ruined. All this retaliation was an unexpected part of the anticipated peek show and in their eyes this was definitely not a part of the agreed upon deal. The observant gang had spied Judith from the schoolyard through the trees as she entered the winding trail below. They had hatched their immoral plot whilst scooting down to their positions and it seemed harmless enough at the time, scoring a free look without hurting anyone. Troublesome news, for young Kyle Mortimer was a sexual predator in the making but he was now starting to pay for his dangerous urges. This had come from a combination of the manner in which his tyrannical father treated the young man and his mother, as well as everyone else in the town.

The end result was blatantly clear and persisting in its growth, encouraging Kyle to harbor an utter disrespect for members of the opposite sex, and what Judith Noble had just done to him with her lunch box would do little to advance his development into a normal adult.

Had Judith known she was dealing with an evolving pervert she might have left him to rot on the pathway, but she didn't, so after offering him the napkins from her lunch box, she gave him a hand up.

"Come on you stupid shit, I'll take you home."

Kyle placed the paper napkins over his mouth, and walked back down the trail as Judith led him by the arm. He still cried as she guided him down the road in the direction of his house and she felt nauseated and upset with the violence behind her savage act.

The whole thing had been impulsive, and she really hadn't meant to inflict this much damage and as she walked her foe through the falling rain, she promised herself she would never hit another human being again unless it was in self defense. And she never would. Minutes later they arrived at the long driveway that led through a cluster of mature firs and up to the two storey structure that housed the mill manager and his family. Judith walked Kyle up to the front steps of the house and his mother must have been watching from a window because the front door opened wide and she stood there in a housecoat shrieking loudly while coddling her poor little boy.

After leaving her wounded charge in capable but hysterical hands, Judith walked quickly away from the house. She offered no explanation, and placing some distance between the squawking voice of Kyle's mother and herself had just become a priority. Headed in the direction of her own home, Judith sighed, knowing she would have to write off another school day. She would also have to advise Molly about her recent actions, something best heard from her own daughter's lips than from a raving Missus Mortimer. Judith had no doubt that it was only a matter of minutes before Big John Mortimer called Molly on the phone, raising the hue and cry that a marauding blonde girl with a funny haircut had been loosed upon the town site. Carefully, she picked her way down a sloping grassed hill, following a hard packed dirt trace through the tall grass so her shoes wouldn't get wet. The park behind her house was located near the bottom of the slope and as she crossed the deserted playground she could hear the thumping bass of someone's stereo. It sounded like it came from one of the houses that surrounded the park, but Judith was more concerned about her present circumstances than someone's blaring music.

However, once she made it to the other side of the flat lawn that extended the length and breadth of the playground she realized the loud music was coming from her own home. Judith followed the sidewalk through her backyard and climbed the wooden steps to the kitchen door. The door was unlocked as it always was, and as she stepped inside the music seemed to roll over her, dancing across her skull. Molly had some soft rock music playing on the old stereo in the living room and had cranked the volume right up, which was a bit odd. The stereo had rarely been turned on these last few years and only once or twice could Judith ever recall the cassette deck being used. She knew it was a cassette playing because the local AM station would play nothing but that hokey, outdated country and western crap. Judith let out another sigh and after placing her lunch box near the back door she set out to find her mother. The best defense was an unexpected offence, so she would chastise Molly for the loud music, then break the discouraging news about Kyle's ruined teeth. Judith left her coat on as addressing the loud music appeared urgent, now worried that the neighbors would soon be complaining about the incessant, rhythmic pounding.

Leaving the kitchen, she entered the hallway and despite the banging symphony, could hear moaning coming from Molly's bedroom. It wasn't any sound she had heard her mother make before and feared for her, quickening her pace down the corridor. Judith needn't have feared, even though what see saw certainly did very little to gladden her heart. The man she knew as Jeremy Salter was lying naked on his back, his long muscular body spread across the width of Molly's queen sized bed. His penis was long and erect, glistening and blue as an equally naked Molly straddled over him, holding his pizzle as she lowered herself onto the engorged tip.

Molly moaned, fluttering her eyes as Salter reached up and tweaked her swollen nipples between his index fingers and thumbs. Neither one of them had noticed Judith standing in the doorway, for she watched only briefly before turning away. Judith leaned with her back to the wall in the passageway outside her mother's bedroom door, sliding quietly down the smooth surface of the wall, folding her legs close in to her front. She shook her head slowly as the shock of the situation overtook her.

"Will these horrible surprises never end?"

Judith asked this to herself as she wrapped her arms around her knees. But they had already, for there would only be one more surprise left, then all these astounding incidents as well the suffering she could finally put behind her.

Judith's way of life was about to turn a corner, and in the end everything would be fine.

At least for the next few years.

*   *   *

Chapter Twenty-one

Two weeks later Jeremy Salter moved into the Noble household - lock, stock, and big screen color television set. Judith liked the television set as she had never seen anything like it, and the jury would only be out for a short while until she decided how she felt about the strapping Salter roosting under the same roof. The day he had moved in Judith had gone to school as normal, her mother saying nothing to her about what the immediate future held.

She had enjoyed the day, stopping in the library after classes to load up her knapsack with a fresh supply of reference materials. Upon entering the house after the walk home it soon became evident there had been some major changes made; new furniture, hot meal on the table, grinning mother, new father. Just as the rift between Molly and Judith had moved closer together over the past couple of weeks, so could it expand, and expand it did. Immensely. Molly had neglected to discuss with her only daughter her plans regarding the feathering of her love nest with a well-built, younger man. So Judith promptly legislated her no conversation policy with her mother once again, unless it became absolutely necessary, although she found it next to impossible to give Salter the silent treatment.

To her delight, she soon found the man to be a bright, friendly, and caring human being. Whenever Judith spoke to him about the math or the sciences, of global warming, the Cold War, and of the droughts that were crippling the northern part of the continent of Africa, Jeremy Salter would listen, and then make an intelligent observation. It wasn't long before she figured out he was an educated man, for he contributed a great deal to the conversations and would often set Judith to exploring new paths, or at times changing her entire course of thinking. Why or how Salter came to work in the forest industry instead of employing his talented mind elsewhere mattered not to the young Noble. What did matter was the way they would talk away Saturday afternoons in the comfort of the living room, Judith lying on the Rug with an open book while Jeremy sat on the couch watching sports. Molly could have him every night and she did, so she didn't mind sharing her treasure with her daughter. In fact Molly had become ecstatic that Judith had taken such a warming to her lover and her daughter politely ignored the moaning and gasping that would carry down the hallway from the master bedroom every night.

Jeremy Salter took great joy in both girls, treating Judith as if she were one of his own, and he seemed not to be overly concerned or even conscious of Molly's drinking. She now kept her imbibing to the mornings when she had the house to herself, with Salter away working as the bush foreman for a twelve-hour shift and Judith at school. Molly would take a nap at around noon, sleeping off the intoxication until Judith came home from classes. She would then set about preparing the evening meal, all of them sitting down for a late supper when Salter returned from his long day in the forest. Molly became quite adept at hiding her growing taste for liquor from her lover, and she wasn't the first functioning person to camouflage a drinking problem nor would she be the last. Her daughter didn't seem to care either way about the drinking, more absorbed in conversing with Salter and deftly picking his brain. Molly's lover also had a refreshing and sincere sense of humor, something Judith came to appreciate, and the manner in which he handled the Kyle Mortimer facial reconstruction affair made him an absolute Prince in her eyes.

Salter was the kind of person who took the "fight" to his opponent, and when the story of the donnybrook on the trail behind the school finally broke over the town, that's just what he did.

Big John Mortimer came to the Noble house only a day after that unfortunate event, attempting to frighten Molly into paying for Kyle's new teeth and bridgework. When Salter heard about Mortimer's troublesome methods he first gathered all the facts from Molly, then went down to the mill's administration office located next to the employee parking lot. Taking the wooden stairs up the side of the building three at a time, he barged past the flighty secretary and walked into Mortimer's office unannounced, interrupting Big John's afternoon putting practice. Salter wasn't employed by Big John; working instead for the forest contractor so Big John couldn't threaten him the way he did Elwood Noble when he'd been alive. It had been Big John's aggressive attitude and threats that had convinced Elwood to take Meryl away for an abortion, keeping the whole issue an in house secret. Everything from the helicopter flight to the actual abortion was to be paid for by Big John, but in the end, choosing this reluctant option cost the Noble family a dear price. When Salter entered Mortimer's plush office he immediately took the expensive carbon-graphite putter from Big John's hands then embarked on a free law lesson. Quietly, Salter pointed out to Big

John that on the evening that his son Kyle had impregnated Meryl Noble in his sleazy fort built with stolen lumber, he had turned fifteen years old not two days prior.

Meryl was still only fourteen years old the day she had died in the helicopter crash, which made Kyle Mortimer eligible for a statutory rape charge, especially when one considered the elements of the offence. These comprised of nothing more than having sexual intercourse with a female person fourteen years or younger - consensual or not. Kyle's lusting also happened to be a felony, so Salter considerately pointed out to Big John that his only son had a good chance of going to prison if convicted, and that having false teeth in an all male prison might not be such a bad thing, "if you know what I mean."

Big John knew exactly what Salter meant, and the thought of his son in prison with some older boys stifled all thoughts of pressing further for due compensation. Big John would pay to get his son's mouth fixed, as well he would instruct the boy to stay well clear of Judith. He would also conveniently forget about the four thousand dollars previously invested at the Orthodontist.

Before leaving the office, Salter clearly pointed out the damage that would occur should one of these very contentious and sensitive issues be breached. To wit; should one Kyle Mortimer go within spitting distance of one Judith Noble, then Jeremy Salter would most assuredly return to this office where he would take Big John's brand new putter, his calf hide golf bag full of clubs, all his golf balls, including the two between his legs, then shove them up his ass, one at a time.

"Not a problem," Mortimer calmly told Salter.

Big John knew a viable threat when he saw one, and he most certainly realized at that particular point in time that he wasn't the biggest man in town anymore and that years of sitting at a desk had made him soft. Regardless, Big John would have to let this one slide, and he could always recover his orthodontic losses in one month with his unofficial lumber sales through the back gate.

The only thing Judith knew at the time was that Salter had smoothed everything over, and she was to immediately tell him if Kyle Mortimer ever came near her again. Kyle Mortimer never did and Salter had become a conquering hero inside the Noble household. This meant a lot to Judith, giving her the security she needed as she had become a bit concerned about Kyle exacting some sort of a sick revenge. Not only was Jeremy Salter good looking, intelligent, talkative and amusing, but also he had managed to bring some reliability into Judith's troubled life. It was the beginning of a friendship that would span for many decades, but all that aside, Judith had quickly come to recognize the man for what he was - which was supportive and trustworthy. Everything a young person had a right to expect from a caring adult, or even a Father. But as Judith grew closer to her Mother's lover, she seemed to drift further away from Molly, the irreparable damage apparently running deep, the obstinacy willing them both to not forgive, and not to forget. In the end, a lasting but civil understanding fell over the household, and while Salter pushed and stimulated Judith's academic efforts, the Noble girls would only talk if there were a requirement. As the weeks, months, and years progressed, Salter would often sit with Judith at her desk at night, reviewing her homework or quizzing her further on a related subject. She would eagerly take all this extra information in; then file it along with everything else into her expanding memory, allowing her to sprint years ahead of comparable classmates.

When she reached High School Judith filled her roster with a myriad of academic courses, as many as she could cram inside of a day and at night she worked at the Municipal Library where she had managed to get a part-time job. Already planning and saving for university, she had calculated it to be an expensive venture as she would have to live on campus in one of the large coastal cities, and the small rooms with the kitchenettes would not be cheap. During her High School years Judith had been considered by most of her classmates as a bit of a recluse, simply because she was brilliant and refused to run with any particular crowd. Nothing of her could be seen at track meets, school dances or any other extracurricular activities that mostly involved drinking and smoking pot in some student's basement. Nonetheless, Judith hadn't become a recluse, something her teachers readily acknowledged. She had become an individual, a rarity among students who relied heavily on fashion trends and peer pressure. Judith had a purposeful mind and a yearning for knowledge that required a great deal of self-discipline, a regimen that was as natural to her as breathing. Her only friend outside of the house was the little Oriental girl named Susie. Another intelligent individual, she too was scorned by the rest, and quite probably from the same mold as Judith. No doubt a young Albert Einstein was probably ridiculed as he roamed the halls of the high school he had attended in Switzerland, dressed in his leather lederhosen, carrying his pencils and notebooks, his head full of relative theories instead of fancy young women. It became a worthy price, this passion for learning. All good things come from a bit of sacrifice and beneath her head of short blonde hair Judith's intellect grew on a daily basis, which wasn't an altogether bad thing. Beneath the unremarkable clothes she chose to wear, other items were growing as well and like it or not, the young girl was slowly being chased from her mind and body. As if by magic, Judith awoke one morning to notice curves developing around her hips, and her breasts were growing rapidly from perky buds to rounded mounds of soft skin, which wasn't an altogether bad thing either. Half way through High School she made another discovery, something more disconcerting than her maturing body could cause, but nevertheless something that required a closer look.

It occurred during a wet, lazy weekend afternoon while Judith had been drinking lemon tea and playing one of those card games with Salter at the kitchen table. The game had been designed to harvest the most frivolous of information from every region of your brain and it had thus far been producing some mirthful answers. Salter had been teasing Judith having just asked her a question about her early years, but the laughing stopped when she realized she couldn't find the answer. She had absolutely no recollection of her first ten years on earth - she couldn't even remember what dear Meryl had looked like. Molly had gone to the store to get some fresh steaks for supper, so she wasn't there to help jog Judith's faltering memory. Both of them went into the living room, pulling photo albums from the bookshelf before sitting on the rug to flip through the thick binders. Dozens of color pictures featured the whole Noble family from their very beginnings, right up until the horrific helicopter crash. Judith stared blankly at the photographs that had been taken prior to her turning ten years old. She recognized the faces of her father, sister and mother, and of course her own smiling face, but when and where the photographs had been taken and the circumstances behind them only brought a puzzled look to her soft features. Salter suggested she see her Doctor and offered her a plausible diagnosis regarding the memory loss. He was of the opinion that the helicopter crash that took the lives of Meryl and Elwood were the primary cause for blocking out her early years, the same post traumatic stress syndrome suffered by thousands of veterans returning from the Asian conflict.

Respecting Salter's advice, Judith left history class Monday afternoon to walk down to the medical clinic where her charming old Doctor, still capable, still clear thinking and forthright, suggested the same diagnosis. Post Traumatic Stress Syndrome the kindly Physician had called it, and Judith knew all about it because she had researched it in the library during the lunch break. Nowadays the affliction was more prevalent among the emergency services people such as police, fire and paramedic crews, but it could strike anywhere there was human suffering, especially after a large disaster that involved a huge loss of lives. Even though the disorder had existed since the dawn of mankind, along with his appetite for violent ways, it hadn't been totally defined until troops were plucked from the nightmare conditions of jungle combat in Vietnam. Without the benefit of being debriefed, they would find themselves walking the crowded, peaceful downtown corridors of their hometowns some twenty-four hours later. The symptoms were as diverse as the people the ailment could reach out to and grab, causing sleeping disorders, nightmares, flashbacks, and alcoholism and in Judith's case, memory loss. Settled comfortably into a plain wooden chair in the examination room, the Doctor sat in a crumpled but clean lab coat while he spoke softly to Judith. She gazed down at him from where she sat on the crisp white paper that covered the examination table, politely nodding her head to everything he told her. The most likely cause in Judith's case would be the loss of Meryl and Elwood in the helicopter crash the Doctor had said, and not too much could be done about it at this time. Judith could seek treatment from a specialist such as a Clinical Psychologist, which would mean long trips over the long road leading from the town to the big city. Long trips would only interfere with her beloved learning, and might set her back to the point where she would have to graduate with everybody else in her class so she postponed the referral. Judith became hopeful that somewhere along the way something would happen to her that might jostle her memory, and all that she'd lost would return.

The deferral of treatment would be a fair sized concession to make in the eyes of many but one that paid off when Judith and her friend Susie graduated from High School a whole year before the rest of their class. They had completed the requirements for their final year during the evenings and on the weekends, their noses buried deep inside their books. This wasn't achieved on their own of course, for they required some dedicated free time and some lobbying from a few of their most ardent supporters, which were their teachers. The two young girls had their driver's licenses for barely twenty-four months and they were graduating with the highest grades ever achieved in the widely spread school district. Their teachers, justifiably proud of the girl's achievements had arranged interviews and written tests at the biggest University in the region. When the time came in the early spring for their appointments with the faculty, Salter drove Judith and Susie down to the university campus in his pick-up truck. Flying there and back wasn't going to be an option as Judith wouldn't allow Salter to charter one of the company helicopters simply because she refused to climb aboard one. After losing her sister, Judith had promised herself she would never go anywhere near an aircraft, for she had done enough reading to know how those heavier than air machines worked, and didn't work, and that most crashes were caused by pilot error. In her sister and father's fatal case, the Transport Officials had concluded that a series of small mistakes had been made by the pilot, possibly induced by vertigo and the changing weather conditions. Until such time they started producing infallible pilots, Judith wasn't about to sit in an aircraft even if it stood parked on the ground and Salter knew better than to argue. All that aside, the journey down became a bit of an adventure; the two girls, an affable Jeremy Salter, a large lunch packed by Molly, and an endless supply of intellectual conversation and coarse road jokes.

Six hours after leaving the low clouds, drizzle and sad looking buildings of the mill town behind them, Salter deposited the exhilarated girls and their suitcases on campus at the cement steps in front of the granite blocks that made up the administration building. The old building was located past the stone gateway that arched over the entrance to a University grounds that thrived with mature deciduous trees and rolling, spacious lawns. The girl's were to stay on campus for almost a week, exploring the facilities while sharing a two-bedroom dormitory. Little time was spent in the dormitory however, and then only for sleep, but not until after they had talked and giggled in their beds to well past midnight, dreaming and planning their futures. If this collection of old and new buildings were to be part of the horizons that had awaited Judith beyond the wet mountain ranges, she had become hopelessly entranced at what she saw. She felt new emotions and senses she didn't know she had, much like the warm, happy feeling a child gets deep down inside when anticipating Christmas morning. Every turn or short walk among the grounds revealed to them a new sensation, or led them to a building whose halls lay open for them to explore. Judith and Susie took their meals at the main cafeteria where they lined up with the rest of the students, easily becoming lost in the crowds, hardly being noticed for the novices that they were. Both girls were paid guests of the Campus Faculty, and everything would be on display for their close scrutiny. Simply ask, they had been told, and ye shall receive. The staff wanted nothing more than to impress the young ladies, for prodigies such as Judith and Susie were as rare as an inoffensive street gang. Gifted thinkers such as these two would only appear every couple of decades, much like newly discovered comets, their bright lights requiring immediate cultivation while they still shone and could at least share their talents with a tiny portion of the world. If Judith and Susie did anywhere near as well as anticipated on the Senior Matriculation Exams, this University had well-meaning intentions of snapping the pair up for the upcoming fall semester. They of course scored incredibly high on the exams, and the faculty were thrilled at their precious little finds, quickly seating them down with course counselors, nudging them toward the applied disciplines who could best nurture their remarkable talents. On the counselors suggestions, Susie jumped at the opportunity to attend the pre-medical curriculum, but Judith on the other hand - well, Judith became a bit like the handful of sand tossed into the lube oil.

To the chagrin of Judith's counselor, she would have no part of following the rest of the Millenniums great thinkers. Chemical Engineering, Biology, Medicine, Mathematics or Anthropology as a career path was not up for discussion. Judith made it quite clear she had no desires to discover any new medical cures, invent better ways to clone fruit, or unearth the missing link which would assuredly bring her as well as the University a Noble Peace Prize.

If you offered only a choice portion of your stocked goods, or had limited listening abilities then Judith Noble would be what used car salesmen called a nightmare. No thank-you ma'am, she was going to be teacher and she was going to teach special education so all this talk of medicine, scholarships, and discoveries of the decade were a complete waste of Judith and the nice counselor's valuable time. They of course reneged and gave her exactly what she wanted, knowing full well that other universities and colleges would be sniffing around if they got wind that one of the two young sensations had become a free agent. The football, hockey, and basketball clubs on campus weren't the only ones out scouting the high schools for new talent. The academic and science faculties also did their share of grooming - they just didn't make as much noise about the whole thing. By day's end a small scholarship had been awarded to each girl by the University. After enrolling in the fall semesters, the rest of the week was spent wandering around the campus full of blissful joy. Once they had found the library, the exploring had only begun, it was a four story, red bricked building that stood next to a man made lake with friendly white swans. The remaining days ticked away rapidly as each girl became lost among the miles of bookshelves, hiding in study cubicles as they poured over stacks of hard covered manuscripts that took them still further out to a beckoning world.

Judith and Susie would meet at the main entrance to the library after a few hours of reading and would walk together to the cafeteria for their meals, both exhilarated and bubbling over with some new secret the library had surrendered to them. They both realized that one library, on one campus, in their one part of the world would take them years of dedicated reading to study just one portion of one floor. It made them tingle all over, and they couldn't wait to get formally started. Absorbing information was not only a gift to the young ladies, but it was also an addiction; the good, harmless kind of compulsion that became a euphoric catalyst to their young minds. Judith and Susie spent the rest of their five day sojourn inside the library, filling up the nights with walks across the campus grounds, enjoying the warm breeze that blew in from the ocean when the sun went down. To their inquisitive minds the place wasn't a Shangri-La, but they both felt they could almost see it from where they stood. It was their gateway to the world, offering them a key that would unlock any door they chose, giving them the knowledge to walk any path they desired and in their own time. Like everything else pleasant though, one of the finest weeks of their young lives came to an end, but no sadness could be seen upon their faces as they attended to the Administration Building to thank their hosts for the kindness they had shown them. Everybody was happy with the situation, and it would be a few short months before the girl's returned to commence their formal post secondary education. Jeremy Salter met them at the front steps as agreed and after they placed their bags into the open bed of the pick-up truck they climbed into the front seat then drove north through the energetic city. Salter didn't have to ask how things went, for their beaming faces told him the whole story, but they told him anyway, their excited chatter continuing throughout the long drive into the mountains. He didn't mind and genuinely shared in their joy for over the years Judith had become a daughter to him. And like a true father he had made previous arrangements for her graduation present as well as a bit of a party at their home. The surprise celebration would be held near summers end with Susie, her parents, and some other special guests who had already confirmed their attendance. There were to be some other big surprises as well, but they would reveal themselves in good time.

Molly was pleased with the way their trip had turned out, giving her daughter a congratulatory hug as she met the truck in front of the house.

Judith couldn't have known at the time but her mother had been bursting with pride, telling anyone in the town who would listen about how her daughter and Susie had been recruited by a large university. Most of the community's high school seniors, the few that even bothered to graduate usually walked out the main doors of the school and down the road to the mill's personnel office. Once they had filled out the forms properly and had joined the union, they would start at the bottom on the production line, pushing, pulling, and stacking lumber for eight long hours a day. The mill received a steady supply of willing recruits to keep their production lines feeding the consumer demands while the new employees received a steady paycheck and a fairly secure if not dreary way of life. A fair trade, some would say.

So Molly Noble had every reason to be proud and had every reason to brag to the clerk who stacked the canned salmon at the grocery store, or the indifferent old retiree who had parked himself on a wooden bench downtown. By this time the whole village knew of the Judith's and Susie's accomplishments as the editor of the local newspaper had put their pictures on the front page with a shining narrative detailing the lives of two of the finest minds the town had ever produced.

Molly had clipped the article from the paper, clutching it in her hand as she followed Judith from the truck, gushing none stop about the exciting developments, trailing her daughter while she carried her bags into the bedroom. Judith laid her suitcase open on the bed and started to unpack, traversing the floor as she removed her folded clothing, placing it neatly back in the drawers.

She scarcely listened to a word her mother was saying, managing to nod her head dumbly in mindless agreement. Not inside the house two minutes and Judith missed the campus, the lifestyle, and the infinite learning it had brought her. She understood then that she didn't belong here anymore, that home had become a jumping off point for a better life and that now the summer couldn't end soon enough. She also realized that once she had left, she would never be returning to this bleak town. In a few short months the world would open itself up to her, offering countless other roads for her to travel down, and travel meant learning, so now travel would be a big part of Judith's future as well. Unfortunately for Molly, the long road outside the door that led you through the mountains to the village would no longer be on her daughter's travel itinerary as she had harvested everything she could from this town. This would be Judith's last summer of listening to the surf roll in from the Pacific while reading a book and sitting on her and Meryl's favorite beach. She would miss the beach where she and Meryl had played hopscotch above the tide line, but she had anticipated this and had collected an old jam jar of the fine white sand which stood safely in a bottom drawer, all ready to go with her.

After Judith had finished unpacking, Salter ordered Chinese food and they all sat at the kitchen table eating from the little cardboard boxes with chopsticks, laughing and talking to just before midnight. Molly had a look about her all evening that Judith didn't recognize, and mistakenly dismissed it as one vodka too many before she had arrived at home. In fact her mother was glowing - but it was with simple, maternal pride. She couldn't help but gaze at her daughter and wonder what genes had supplied her with such a talented mind, a courageous independence and such an unshakable resolve. Molly easily saw herself in Judith's pretty face, but not even Elwood had been born with such intellect and he had been a steady thinker in his own right. Eventually the conversation slowed to an intermittent trickle and Judith finally submitted to the exhaustion the exciting week had brought her. She trudged off to her bedroom after saying good night, taking her thrilling achievements along with her. Tomorrow morning was scarcely a few hours away and she had a couple of day shifts to work at the public library. Judith would have to work as many hours as she could get this summer, placing every dollar into her savings account for other tuition fees, rent, food and possibly after all that was paid, leave her with some monthly spending money.

A quick glance at her bank book suggested she had no where near enough, but she had been assured of securing a part-time job somewhere in the city once she had moved onto the campus.

It would become a grind, this getting an education, but it was only for five years and she knew she would manage somehow. She always did. As it turned out, the head librarian placed Judith on as many shifts as she could endure and all thoughts of having some spare time to read alone on the beach in the hot sun went the way of the winds. Slowly her savings account grew, and by summer's end she had almost enough to get her through the first two semesters. Two weeks before the end of August Salter had the going away party he'd previously organized for both Judith and her friend Susie. A barbecue, it was held in the backyard with Susie's parents and all the teachers they had become close with through their learning years. Salter had secured a large but tender roast, which he impaled on a spit and placed on the gas barbecue where it would slowly cook the afternoon away. He attentively basted it with his magical sauce as he sat in the back yard in his dark blue Speedo, giving the bored, neighborhood wives a free serving of his hairy chest and substantial pouch. Salter had purchased a few strings of those multicolored, plastic Chinese lanterns from the hardware store and had strung it across the clothesline. Judith figured they looked a bit gaudy being plastic and all, but the attempt to enhance the atmosphere was all that really mattered. When the roast was nearly done Molly and Salter set up a large folding table next to the barbecue, covering its entire surface with several kinds of cold salads, crusty buns, deserts and a plastic cooler filled with crushed ice and chilled drinks. The crowd of about a dozen guests arrived by late afternoon and formed a circle on the grass, sitting in their lawn chairs while talking and admiring the two guests of honor.

Molly became the only predictable smear on the evening. She sat among the guests and talked while drinking fruity fizzes, and as the backyard cooled with the descending sun, she took to giggling at most everything that was being said. Within a half hour Molly had toned her laughing down but then her eyelids began to droop as she fought off sleep, brought about by whatever it was that coursed through her bloodstream. Judith naturally figured her mother had consumed a few fizzes too many between the pulls she'd taken from the pint she had concealed away in Meryl's old bedroom. Shortly before they ate supper Salter ended up walking a very unsteady Molly into the house where he placed her on the bed then closed the door, allowing her to sleep. When he returned to the uncomfortable silence that had fallen over the gathering, he behaved as if nothing had happened and started to carve the slices from the roast as it turned on the spit. As Judith lined up with the rest of her guests for the meal she burned with humiliation, vowing never to forget this one, for now her revered teachers had seen first hand what up until now had been simply a village rumor. Once the meal had been completed and the dishes stacked on the table near the left over food, everybody stood up one at a time to either toast the girl's or reminisce about a long forgotten story. Everybody brought gifts which embarrassed Judith and Susie and the thank-yous and warm hugs went on for sometime as they all talked quietly beneath the Chinese lanterns and an inky sky dotted with the summer constellations.

It wasn't until much later in the evening when Salter disappeared from the backyard, returning within moments, driving up to the front of the house in a late model dark blue four by four pick-up truck. The vehicle was brand new and had a full size, matching canopy over the rear truck bed.

There was an abundance of oohs and awes when Salter presented Judith the keys to the vehicle, which had been hidden a block away from the house. He made a short speech, telling the smiling throng that he'd purchased the four by four so Judith could make the daunting drive home during semester breaks, confidently traversing the unpredictable weather of the mountain passes. As well, the covered rear bed would be able to hold all of Judith's and Susie's personal belongings for their initial journey down to the university. Judith was as stunned as everyone else, but now thankful that she wouldn't have to rely on a transit system in a strange city to get herself around.

She wasn't sure if she could afford the gas and she wasn't about to tell Salter this as she and Susie hugged him long and lovingly. Nor could she tell him of her plans to never return home, especially after Molly's besotted, early evening performance. That heartbreaking exhibition cemented her decision to cut the umbilical cord to the point that when she left she probably wouldn't even bother watching the town as it faded in the trucks rear view mirror. The cluster of close friends circled the new truck, kicking the tires, looking under the hood, and sitting behind the wheel while twisting knobs as they inhaled that satisfying smell that came with every new vehicle.

Inspecting the new truck and playing with all its options became a fitting way to end the farewell party. It was now late but it had been a happy event, so there was a liberal amount of hugging and hand shaking as the guests said their goodbyes before slipping away through the darkness, walking in small groups back to their homes, their talking and laughter carrying back across the clear night. Judith and Salter returned to the back yard, spending a good half hour as they carried the left over food and dirty dishes into the kitchen. The lawn chairs and tables they would leave until tomorrow, wiping the morning dew from the webbing before folding them up and returning them to the metal tool shed that stood at the side of the house. Once inside for the evening, Judith filled the sink with hot soapy water and started washing the pile of plates and cutlery as Salter wrapped the leftovers and placed them in the fridge. When he had finished with the food, he took a dishtowel that had been looped through the door of the fridge and started drying the dishes, placing them in the cupboard once he'd buffed away the drops of water. Moths could be seen in the darkness through the kitchen windows, dancing among the lights from the Chinese lanterns, their tan colored wings flickering as they flew in front of the colored globes. Both Judith and Salter watched them as they stood side by side in front of the sink, lost in their thoughts as their hands performed the mechanics of their simple chores. From a distance, a stranger on the street might easily mistake them through the windows for a handsome and contented couple, although up close the difference in their ages would become obvious.

"Why do you put up with her crap?" Judith asked, suddenly bored with watching the moths.

"Because I love her," Salter said, "and I didn't know she had a drinking problem until a few months after I had moved in here with you guys. You may not believe this Judith, but there are times when you just can't stop loving someone because you discover they have faults. In fact, that's what love is all about . . . dealing with, or helping your partner with their faults, whatever those may be. And to me, that's the true mettle of a devoted relationship."

Salter's reply came without any consideration or concoction given to his answer. It came from his heart, a response that held a simple truth that for some reason gladdened Judith. She thought she didn't care how Salter actually felt about her mother and was confused as to why his answer would please her. It was also the kind of dedicated response that she found impossible to criticize.

Jeremy Salter had disarmed her with a short sappy lesson on commitment, so she responded with the first notion that came into her head.

"You're a very tolerant person Salter, you really are."

By this time he had caught up to Judith in his dish drying, having emptied the plate rack that sat on a rubber mat on the counter. He took the wet, hot dishes directly from Judith's hands as she washed them and he could now turn to face her.

"You know Judith, we all need someone to love, but more importantly, we all need someone to *love* us. Imagine a world where no one cared about you . . . where no one loved you . . . where no one was there to support you or encourage you, or even pick you up when you fell down.

That kind of nurturing every person needs despite who they might be, and they'll need it through the good times as well as the bad times, and I think you're wise enough to know there can be a lot of bad times in a person's life."

Salter could be very reflective, philosophical and absolutely correct when he felt a calling, but none of this surprised Judith for the man was a thoughtful human being.

"What you're saying is true . . . but she really embarrassed me tonight," Judith replied softly.

"Oh?" Salter put his dishtowel on the counter and gazed down into Judith's face.

She saw an emotion flash briefly over his eyes, and wasn't altogether certain if it wasn't anger.

"Well," Judith said defensively, "she went and got drunk in front of all my friends and it was goddamned humiliating, it truly was Salter."

"Your mother wasn't drunk tonight Judith. She's been suffering from clinical depression for the past few months. The doctor only recently prescribed some pills, but she's not supposed to drink alcohol while taking her medication. She only had the one drink. I know; I watched her. But obviously that's all it took to knock her on her ass, and its unfortunate that it had to happen tonight, if it had to happen at all. Please don't take this the wrong way Judith, you're the most intelligent person I've ever met, but you still have a lot to learn about people, especially your own mother."

"Its tough sometimes you know Salter, it hasn't been easy for me."

"Life never is Judith, and that goes for everybody in this world. At least the people I know."

"You say she's suffering from depression."

"Yes, she's terrified that you're leaving home, and she's terrified she may never see you again. That's one of the two reasons I bought you the truck, so you had a way to get back home during the semester breaks. She's your mother . . . she can read you, she can see the yearning in your eyes, your zeal to explore and taste everything that life can put before you. She's devastated at your leaving, but she knows you must go and why."

"I know I should be more loving but it's difficult at times, especially with her drinking."

"Yes Judith, it is difficult, I know. But I promise you one day she will stop drinking, and I'll stand by her until she does. I don't like to use clichés, but there isn't a single person on this planet who isn't without their faults, including me."

"Are you telling me that you actually have faults, Salter?"

She asked this to ease the seriousness from their conversation, now contented with what she had heard, albeit not altogether convinced.

"I know it's hard to believe," Salter replied, "but I do have my faults."

"And what would those faults be?"

"I can't tell you right now, it's a secret . . . but I will someday."

"You promise?"

"Oh I promise."
"And what was the other reason you bought me the truck?"
"You ask too many questions."
"I know, that's why I'm a good student."

*   *   *

Chapter Twenty-two

The day Judith and Susie left for the city with its sprawling university campus, it rained like it had never rained in years. So much rain fell that more than a couple of the wooden truss bridges that crossed the river at the bottom of the mountain passes had been washed over with almost two feet of water. This had happened almost an hour after the girls had driven over their heavy planked surfaces for they had left before the eastern twilight had touched the bloated gray clouds. The back of the truck had been packed with most everything they owned at the time, and even the open space on the bench seat between them held a cardboard box. Although Susie might not have used the box as an armrest had she known it contained the urn that held Meryl's cremated remains. Judith had removed it from the hiding place in Molly's closest a few days ago when her mother and Salter had gone to a hockey game at the local arena.

Susie probably wouldn't have eaten the packed lunch either had she known who was inside the cardboard box, as it had sat atop the folded flaps in a paper bag. But she ate the roast beef and mustard sandwiches and they took turns driving the truck through the carbon colored sheets of falling rain, taking their time as they followed the long road through the coastal mountains.

By early afternoon they had arrived at the front stairs of the old administration building on the campus, the truck still full of their belongings but the gas tank nearly empty. Judith and Susie had been required to register early as they were sharing a one-room suite with a kitchen and two-day beds in one of the permanent student residences. These accommodations were hard to secure, but coming from a rural area had made the process a little easier. It would be better that they had arrived early at any rate, for they had time to set up their suite to their own liking, settling in before the formal classes commenced. One of the newer facilities on the campus, the residence building stood within easy walking distance to the library and the man made lake with the swans, which made life even more attractive. After parking the truck across the street in the student parking lot Judith and Susie walked over to enter the granite faced structure of the administration building, delighted that the adventure had finally begun. The registration office was on the third floor, and as they entered the large open department they were pleased to find no lineups. They approached two of a half dozen desks that had been set up for the registrations, each having an apathetic looking trustee sitting comfortably as they steadily worked on their files.

Judith sat down in front of a desk where a kindly looking older woman glanced up over her half-moon glasses and smiled. She spoke briefly with Judith, jotting down her particulars on a piece of paper, then walked over to the main counter allowing another girl to fetch the file from a long row of metal filing cabinets. While this was going on Judith pulled her checkbook from her wallet, resting it open on her lap, steadying herself, all the while hoping the first hit wouldn't completely empty her bank account. She still had to eat and purchase her books - and fill the gas tank. The lady returned and smiled again as she sat back down in her chair. She placed the manila file with Judith's name along the top on the flat surface of her desk and opened it up. The woman studied the file for a moment then looked up at Judith.

"Hmm, all you have to do is sign some forms Miss Noble, everything else has been taken care of."

"What do you mean?" Judith asked.

"Your tuition fees, residence fees, book fees, everything - its all been paid for."

"Pardon me?" Now Judith was really puzzled. "You mean everything's been paid for?"

"Yes it has."

"That's not possible."

"Oh its possible."

"The whole semester? Paid for?"

"No actually. Everything's been paid in advance and for the next five years," the lady said.

"Until you graduate, plus an account has been opened up for you at the bank inside the school union hall, giving you a monthly allowance to live on."

"I don't understand," Judith said.

The registration lady smiled again; then handed Judith an envelope that had been tucked away inside the file. Judith saw her name on the front of the envelope and recognized her mother's handwriting.

"This might explain everything," she said.

Judith signed the applicable forms, thanking the lady for her time before walking out into the foyer. Susie was still busy registering so Judith stopped near the top of the marbled steps and opened the sealed envelope.

Her heart pounded under her rib cage as she slowly unfolded the letter, finding Molly's feminine and strangely comforting hand inked across the page.

Written in dark blue script, the letter had obviously been mailed long before Judith arrived. She leaned with her back to the metal banister and started to read:

Dear Judith,

I hope you don't mind but I've paid for your post secondary education. Your father had a life insurance policy with the mill that was paid out to me upon his death.

I've been saving the bulk of the money for this day, but please don't worry, there is still a lot of it left for me to get by on.

I took the liberty of opening a bank account for you at the university so you will have a monthly allowance to see you through until you graduate, which I know will be with honors. I have waited until now to tell you about this because I know how independent you are.

If you have problems with this, then simply think of it as a gift from your father. You have made Jeremy and I so very proud, and I am sure Meryl is too, looking down upon you from wherever it is she is at. Both Jeremy and I love you and will miss you dearly. Please come home soon, or at least write so I know that everything is okay.

love,
Molly

Minutes later Susie finished registering and left the main office, looking for Judith in the foyer. She found her friend sitting on one of the marble steps, leaning with her head against the cold metal banister, her back to her. Judith clutched a letter in her hand and her shoulders were shaking uncontrollably. At first Susie thought she was laughing quietly, but soon realized there was no laughter to be found here. Susie knelt down beside Judith and put an arm around her shoulders.

"Are you okay?" She whispered.

Judith shook her head, looking up into her friend's eyes, the tears streaming down her face like tiny rivers.

"Salter was right," Judith said, her voice coming in quiet, sobbing gasps, "I still have a lot to learn about my own mother."

* * *

Chapter Twenty-three

In the warm, still air of the utopian library, Judith Noble looked up from the book she had just finished reading about her sister Meryl. She held it to her chest, her fingers curled around the white leather that covered it. She had started crying quite some time ago, although she knew there was no measure of time here. Focusing her blurry eyes, she looked down to where her tears had soaked the front of her white gossamer gown. She felt small and lost, sitting in the large, high backed burgundy colored chair that nearly swallowed her slender form. Caressing the book she had just read, she thought about her cherished Meryl. Suddenly Judith knew she was alone no longer, and wondered if she could ever truly be alone in this place. She felt the presence, and like a down comforter on a cold winter day, it seemed to fall over her. Judith put the book down on her lap, tasting the salt as some of the tears touched her trembling lips, lost inside the revelations she had only just learned about, wondering why these things had been kept away from her for so long. This was when the voice spoke to her again. It was the same, gender obscure voice that she had heard when she had first arrived here. The measured tones still sounded familiar, a calming voice reaching out to her from somewhere out of her past. Of that she was sure.

"Why are you so upset?" The voice asked.

For the first time since coming to this curious place Judith spoke, surprised that she could hear her own words, sounding as they did, distant and different.

"There were a lot of things that took place when I was a child, and I didn't know anything about them until know. I've just read about them in this book," Judith replied.

"What things?" The voice asked, now sounding tender and concerned.

"I didn't know that my sister Meryl had become pregnant before she died. I'd been told she was flying down to the city because of "girl" problems. They never told me that Kyle Mortimer had made her pregnant, and that she was going for an abortion. I never knew that my dad was dying from a brain tumor, and that was the reason he had been acting so foolishly the last few years he'd been alive. And no one told me that he wasn't Meryl's real father. So many secrets. God . . . I never knew any of this."

215

"Would it have changed anything if you did?" The voice invited. "Would Meryl and your father still be alive? Would you have loved Meryl any less if you'd known she was only your half sister?"

"You certainly couldn't have done anything for your father's brain tumor. If you think about it, its probably better you didn't know any of this at the time."

". . . yes, I suppose you are right," Judith answered.

"You can't change fate Judith, no human can," the voice reassured. "One of the reasons you were brought here is because of the important things that you didn't know. Now knowing these things won't alter the past, but it can change the way you feel about some things, and more importantly, the way you feel about some people."

Judith rubbed the tears from her eyes with one of her ghostly white fingers, surprised to see that her hands weren't wet where she had wiped. There were a lot of things about this place she would probably never figure out - that's if she ever left.

"I didn't think you would be able to cry up here," Judith said.

"You can cry anywhere," the voice offered, "Up here, you can even laugh and sulk, and smile. That's why humans were given emotions. It's only one of two things you can take with you, where ever you go."

"And what would be the second?"

There was no stopping Judith's inquisitive mind. She had her questions, even up here.

"The second would be your soul. But you'll find that out when you leave here - if you leave here."

"Am I staying then?"

"For awhile at least, although they might call you at any time."

Without any further words Judith knew that the voice had left, leaving her alone once again but not leaving her lonely. She reached up to the polished hardwood bookshelf beside her chair, returning the book called Meryl, pulling out the next one that stood upright beside it. Like all the books on the shelf it had been bound in pebbly white leather, the title flowing over the front in swirling gold letters. Carefully Judith placed the book on her lap and opened it to the first page.

Like the last book, this one also had crisp pages filled with bold, gothic font. Judith tilted her head slightly forward and started to read about Iain Andy McVicar, the man who had fathered her twin girls.

*   *   *

216

Part Three
"Iain"

Chapter Twenty-four

It had taken millions of years to evolve and erode, eventually becoming a land of infinite skies, wet marshes, wide rivers and far ranging mountains. A place where in the summer months the skies were generally clear and blue, their invisible bellies constantly tickled by the reaching fingers of the granite peaks. As time progressed to the colder months, the sky would tinge the color of fieldstone and the snow would fall, the flakes floating to every corner of the land and forest. The thick blanket of snow would follow the contours of the earth and weigh down the boughs of the lodgepole pines, making an already enchanting world outright magical.

It was a place that could inspire the heart as well the soul, but it could ruin you as well if you were delicate and unprepared for the land was robust and unforgiving. It would not dally with the weak and this rule applied to every living creature that called the territory home. Only a scattering of colors composed an environment that could still your breath but at the same time numb your sanity if you allowed it. The mountains appeared tinged with gray plum dust where the sparse tree lines ended, turning to a dazzling white in sections where the snow fields began. Forever melting during the warm season, this expanse of snow could be found on every peak within the region for twelve months of the calendar year. What had turned to water under the endless sunshine would be regained in the long dark months of winter. With the summers came miles of green, unbridled marshes that were bordered with coniferous forests whose tree tops extended a simple holler above the land, pointing skyward as you gazed into the endless blue. That was it for color, except during the three weeks in late June when the wild flowers would blossom, peppering the surface of the permafrost with crimson, yellow and purple.

When it snowed, which was a commonplace for nine months of the year, the skies would remain indefinable once the solid gray clouds had moved in. It would be difficult to tell where the land ended and the heavens began but this would change on some evenings when a window would appear in the atmosphere. Then, every creature with a set of eyes could gaze up into the early night sky as the skittish blue lights of the aurora borealis lit up the land as if it were the twilight of a dawning day. The isolated town where seventy-five hundred people lived had been built between two mountain ranges next to a wide river. At one time, when the water had thawed in the spring, it would facilitate the stern-wheelers as they plied the muddy waters with their precious supplies. Now a single ribbon of black top cut through the middle of the valley where the ground was firm, twisting in places as it skirted the open muskeg. This road had now become the town's lifeline as everything was imported except for the moose, grizzly bear, and of course the weather itself. A dirt runway cut a strip on the southern side of town where twin-engine airplanes could land and unload their cargo, taking passengers on before the engines froze in the winter or the black flies had sniffed them out in the summertime. Very few pilots would fly up here with just one engine for if that were to fail then crashing into a remote forest could give the word 'adventure' a whole new meaning - that's if you survived the initial impact. Two of something was always better than one up here and nearly everything that man made had some sort of a back up system should the first one fail. Some of the inhabitants classified the place by using the time worn cliché, choosing to call it "heaven upon the earth," while others called it a "cold, unforgiving Purgatory."

Judith Noble however, simply called the place home.

She lived in an apartment block on the edge of town, enjoying the seasons and the forests that made up this choice bit of hinterland. Everywhere she looked there were mountains, streams, or timberlands where the wild animals could be seen foraging inside the treed borders. Best of all, there was no rain up here. Judith had made the journey north in her pick-up truck, its rear box laden with all her belongings as she traveled for days on the long, secluded road.

It would be her first teaching job after graduating with honors from university, and she'd learned about it from one of her professors. He knew that Judith yearned to put some distance between herself and the city, and she followed up on the job posting right after he'd given her the piece of paper. Her education and training had made her a specialist in teaching the mentally challenged but there had been no such persons living in this town that had been placed near the edge of creation. But Judith required some teaching experience, as well she needed to get far and away from her mother and this job would fill both these conditions.

Molly had slipped further into the bottle these past years and what kept Jeremy Salter hanging around would remain a mystery. Judith never did return to the mill town where she had been raised, primarily because of her mother's drinking, although Molly and Salter had driven to the big city on several occasions for a visit. They would always arrive on the weekends, staying at a nearby motel, and from there they would all go downtown to visit the museums, the theaters, and later in the day, the pubs. This drinking process became too painful for Judith so she ultimately isolated herself, restricting herself to monthly telephone calls and still the slurring that came down the line would upset her. And so when the teaching job in the far north presented itself, it seemed an answer to her problem as well it wouldn't leave any feelings hurt. A lengthy visit to the library told her all she wanted to know about the place and everything she read she liked.

Judith took the teaching job, arriving just prior to the first snowfall, finding an independent town that heartily welcomed newcomers and was proud of all that had gone before them. Each growing tree and metal roofed building had a story to tell for some of them had been standing and watching for well over a century. It was a place that was virtually crime free because most everybody of voting age found employment at the zinc mine that was located thirty miles outside of town. The local police would apprehend the occasional impaired driver or break up the odd bar fight but it was still a place where you could leave your vehicle unlocked while you went shopping.

Judith readily returned the generous smiles of the people, quickly making friends while participating in most everything the village would offer her. In the day she taught at one of the town's three elementary schools and at night she would take courses at the community center, or visit the library. Friday nights she would go downtown to the log cabin pizza place with three friends she'd met at school. After dinner they would walk to the town's only theater and as long as four people showed up to plunk their money down, they would be compelled to run the movie. Less than four patrons and the projectionist would close the doors and go home. That first winter Judith took fly-fishing lessons at the community center. She had already bought a fly rod that would break down into two long pieces for the trips to and from the lessons. In the gymnasium they would form a long line and practice casting while a couple of veteran guides would wonder around, giving advice while patiently correcting their pupils. Her favorite part would be bundling up to walk through the frozen town where the snowdrifts stood ten feet high. The air would chill your teeth as you breathed, numbing your ear lobes as the snow crunched noisily beneath your feet. When the winter months arrived, the sky would skitter a bluish green as the northern lights came out to play, spreading across the atmosphere as far as you'd care to look. These were special times and Judith would spend some of the evenings in her dark living room, watching the nightly display through her balcony doors while sipping hot tea on the sofa.

The whole place was pure. It was calming. And it was one of the nicest settings on the face of the earth.

When the months progressed the cold winter would eventually ease its way toward a much-anticipated spring. The town held a lottery when the weather warmed and anyone who paid a buck could make a guess as to when the ice on the river would crack. This had become an annual event, indigenous only to this part of the country because of the minus forty-degree Fahrenheit weather that accompanied the winters. Hundreds of miles upstream near the rivers head the snow would start to melt on the mountains, turning the river's tributaries into swollen courses of water as they fed into the main channel. Here at the base of the mountains the ice would melt first then finally break apart, drifting slowly down stream as huge blocks more than six feet thick, eventually pushing and grinding against the river's main pack. At the far end of the river, where the wide mouth spilled into the ocean the ice had also been melting. Whenever tons of pressure was involved in a natural setting, something ultimately gave and when it did there was usually quite a show.

As the ice in the middle finally gave with the pressure, a crack would shoot the length of the river for miles in either direction, its unmistakable sound coming like an amplified shotgun blast.

A sound the whole town would hear, even in their beds at night. Instantly the river would break and the pack ice would start to flow toward the sea. Whoever guessed the closest to the actual date and time that the river would break would get to take home the substantial pot.

The following evening they would have a street party where gallons of Moose Milk, a sweet, thick drink made from cream and dark rum would flow freely as the elk steaks cooked on the barbecues. This was the kind of place it had become and there was always some kind of activity taking place somewhere within the town. If you became bored living up here then that would be your own fault.

When summer finally did arrive the face of the village changed once the snow had melted and the grasses greened up and it would be like living some place altogether different. With the changing landscape came many seasonal outdoor activities and Judith pursued them with fervor. She purchased a mountain bike that she had taken to riding in and around the town. It ran a bit rough with the fat lugged tires but nothing else could have done the job, even running a wheelbarrow up and down roads that were humped with frost heaves could be a risky business.

The bike came with a helmet and metal rattrap carriers that the sporting goods store had mounted above both wheels. Just ten miles north of the village lay a small, cold lake hidden in a deep forest where the char could grow to sixteen pounds and could take hours to land on a fly rod.

This place was to be avoided throughout the month of June as the black flies and mosquitoes could drive you to lunacy, the swarms as boundless as the marshes they hid in once the cool evenings had fallen.

Once Judith had waited out that first plagued month of summer, she would ride her bike out to the lake with the required equipment lashed to her carriers. In a wide clearing halfway up the lake a forestry campsite had been built with matching his and hers outhouses set well back into the woods. A thin, forested peninsula jutted out to almost the middle of the lake and Judith spent much of her spare hours casting with her fly rod from the gravelly shore. She caught some real whoppers from that private spot and there were moments she thought her arms would fall off. After the struggle she would carefully pull the barb less hook from the large char's mouth with a set of needle nose pliers then release it back into the lake. Out there with the clear water, the wild fish, and the smell of the pine trees these contests would produce neither losers nor any winners - and that's just the way Judith preferred things.

As the mornings turned into warm afternoons she would lie upon the lichen above the shore and read a book while sipping black coffee from a thermos. Judith still enjoyed books of any kind but she didn't read as much in the summer and for the obvious reasons. The warm months when the sun dropped below the horizon for two hours each night should be spent outdoors, living life to its fullest while enjoying everything the land had to offer. There would be ample chance to read in the winter when the sun would peek over the mountains for a few hours near midday. At least twice a month during the summer Judith would strap her camping gear to her bike and peddle out to the lake where she would spend a few days drinking in the solitude and the clean air.

She would set up her small mountain tent on the peninsula, cooking over a small fire while happily melding into her quiet surroundings. There were times when a girlfriend would join her on these trips and they would skinny dip in the lakes icy waters, talking and laughing afterward as they sat warming near the fire. But for the most part, Judith was satisfied with her own company.

She hadn't by any means become a loner, instead, someone who after her turbulent younger years had finally found peace with her inner self. This state of mind was both healthy and rejuvenating and she recognized its healing properties as well as appreciating them.

While out on one of these camping excursions, an innocent circumstance unfolded that would bring her and a local firefighter named Iain McVicar together. Out of this relationship there would spring more than just a common love, it would also bear life, a gentle reminder for Judith in the coming years of the love she had shared with this man. Iain had been part of a two-person team that worked the rescue truck from the towns main fire hall next to the community center.

Thirty professional firefighters complimented the municipal department, which included the Chief and several operational officers. Seven people were assigned to a twelve-hour watch that manned the hall three hundred and sixty-five days of the year. Iain was a seven-year veteran of the department who enjoyed the challenge of firefighting, especially in the sometimes uncooperative, northern environment. He'd come north for a kayaking trip on some remote river years ago and felt an immediate calling for the rugged country and its people. There had been nothing to hold him back as his parents had both died in a motor vehicle accident shortly after he had graduated form high school. Iain had been born in Scotland where his parents ran a successful, hometown medical practice and when he was seven years old they had immigrated to the land of infinite options.

Here they continued to practice medicine, hoping their only child would one day continue the long-standing, family tradition. The large prairie city they had moved to appeared nearly bleak when compared to the coastal town they had left behind in the old country; a town that had prospered for centuries' in the shadows of the North East Highlands. It would be on these prairies where Iain would become captivated with the openness of the land, drinking in all it had to offer a young man who enjoyed the outdoors. There would be no medical school in his immediate future, nor would there be any kind of an office job - it just wasn't in his blood. Iain had stopped growing once his body peaked at five-foot-ten, but he had developed an athletic physique from all the sports he'd played in high school. A body that hungered for a career that would take him outside and leave him far from any office that required a stifling suit and tie. Right after school Iain took a job at a nearby mill, working the green chain where he sized and graded the wet lumber as it moved past him on a set of metal links. The money was good as well as the benefits and it gave him some breathing room for he had yet to decide what he might like to do with his life.

His parents of course were disappointed with his decision not to attend university, but they had supported him in all his endeavors up to this point and there should be no reason to change now.

Months later there came the tragic accident that claimed his parent's lives and Iain was naturally devastated. He entered the phases of the grieving process and was finally seeking closure
when a friend from the mill invited him on a northern kayaking trip. The decision to go would soon find the lad paddling a kayak through frothy white waters that were situated between miles of slow plodding river. The landscape, with its never-ending mountains and bald eagles that floated high above in the thermals would alter the course of his life forever. At the end of the holiday, Iain and his friend spent a couple of days in town and it was here that he learned the local Fire Department was expanding. They needed six new people, Iain applied before flying back home, and the rest conveniently fell into place. He sold his parents property, took those funds as well as their life insurance policy, and purchased his own land two miles up a secondary road just outside of the town. A beautiful piece of land, it sat in a heavily forested plateau overlooking the river. Iain cleared the land himself then built a handsome "A" frame cabin with wings on both sides and it soon became a friendly hang out for the people on his shift. In the summer they barbecued and drank beer, and in the winter they hot tubbed and drank beer. It became a period in Iain's life when the tranquility ran from his pores and he felt lucky and blessed. He was still unattached but this didn't bother him too much although by the time he reached his twenty-seventh birthday he felt a desire to settle down.

Iain had done his share of dating and hot tubbing naked with some of the town's friendlier girls but that had been strictly for fun - something enjoyed by both parties. He had been a bit of a skin hound ever since his pubescent body had started to manufacture sperm, but all this changed one warm afternoon when he was returning to the fire hall in the rescue truck. Iain's rig, as well as a pumper truck had attended to a motor vehicle accident fourteen miles north of town near a deadly corner. The rescue wagon was a heavy, boxy affair with side bins for all the extrication tools but it usually arrived a good ten minutes before the lumbering pumper truck - at least when Iain drove it. Northern roads did not a race track make, so this style of rushing to the scene while avoiding dozy moose and deep potholes caused his partner Jolene a certain amount of unnecessary stress.

She would casually mention this to Iain whenever he approached the sound barrier, pointing out to him the fact they would be of no use to anyone dead, and who the hell would rescue them if they crashed. They were after all, driving the Fire Department's only rescue truck.

Iain would lightly fob off his partner's concerns with his favorite saying.

"Stressed Jolene? Paah, its part of being a firefighter. Keeps your courage honed."

On this particular day, Iain and Jolene had skillfully freed a mother and daughter from their wrecked truck (everyone in the north drove trucks) and had sent them to the hospital with minor injuries. They were driving back to the hall at a reasonable pace, sweating in their turn out gear but enjoying the sunshine as they talked about anything but work. A mile or so from the outskirts of town Iain suddenly whipped the wheel of the wagon over and stopped the truck in the emergency lane. Before Jolene could complain about her nose being pressed against the dashboard her partner had jumped from the vehicle, returning seconds later with a hardcover book he'd spotted lying near the road.

"Morsey's Guide to Northern Birds," had been printed across the front in prominent letters.

Iain opened the book and found the name "J. Noble," scripted inside in what definitely had to be feminine handwriting. There was also a phone number. Iain still carried a slight brogue from his native Scotland, which thickened whenever he felt the urge, like right now. Whenever he spoke this way, he reminded Jolene of a medieval knight she'd seen in a movie where the god-fearing landlords slaughtered all the miscreant serfs in the end.

"Hoot, mon. Ma thinks I've doth found a bonny lass's book. I will endeavor to return this in person as her handwriting has set mah balls ta tingling."

Iain constantly talked about his testicles, which caused no offence to anybody and if it did you were living in the wrong part of the country. At the Firefighter's Gala Ball last year he had proudly worn his kilt to the occasion, showing up with a date on one arm and a large serving tray under the other. The serving tray was a polished, rectangular piece of silver that became a conversation piece once the required amount of malt whisky's had been put back. Iain would then place the tray on the floor then stand on it with his legs apart, challenging the ladies and anyone else who was interested to "tek a peek at mah harry balls." In no time a line formed with both males and females queuing up to squint into the trays reflective surface where they could indeed receive an eyeful of his "harry balls." Many had to admit that evening the young firefighter had been born gifted, for he carried a truly magnificent set of knackers. This considerate act of sharing his natural wealth even made the front page of the town newspaper for it had been a slow week for any news.

Having glanced into the polished tray herself, Jolene knew her partner like she knew the inside of her own fridge - so well in fact that she could even predict with a certain amount of accuracy when he was going to fart. She liked Iain and enjoyed working with him and together they had built a trust that made their dangerous jobs that much easier. Jolene was an Inuit, so when she spoke her words came out sounding slow, as if she had chosen and mulled each one with care. She was a proud member of a group of people who had lived for thousands of years on the frozen tundra, a place that required all your energy to just stay alive. Consequently, her brown skin, decidedly Asian looking eyes and flat face carried the genes of a race of people who did more thinking and less talking. Jolene only spoke when she had something to say - unlike the white folk who constantly flapped their lips about the weather and other such moronic things like sexual intercourse. She didn't find Iain's comment regarding his tingling balls the least bit offensive but she nonetheless felt a need to respond
"You're a pig McVicar," she said slowly.
"Aye Jolene, but even pigs get the chance to screw."
"There is more to life than sex you know," she offered, "a lot more."
"Nay, dinna tell me that, there kinna be."
"Maybe not for a crotch sniffer like yourself, but there is for my people. Your behavior is enough to make me want to crawl back into the womb." Jolene said all this while looking straight ahead through the windshield. Looking someone in the eyes was disrespectful, the conduct of her culture which had been handed down to her through the teachings of her

elders. Fortunately for the Inuit, many early explorers to the north misread this as the timidity of a simple Nation who would gladly lie down while someone walked all over them. Many soon found out however that if you pissed on an Inuit, they would cheerfully skin you out like a drowned caribou.

These predatory convictions, along with the endless months of crappy weather left them the only First Nations within North America to be unconquered by the migrating, disease riddled Europeans.

"Aye, and I've been inside a womb too," Iain continued, "Tis a grand place - I loved every bloody minute of it."

This banter came to an abrupt end as Iain pulled back onto the road, nearly hitting the pumper truck that had been following some distance behind them. Loaded with seven hundred gallons of water in an internal tank, the pumper nearly went into the far ditch as it swerved to avoid the rescue wagon. The driver of the pumper sounded the air horn and one of the firefighters seated in the jump seats offered McVicar his plump middle finger. That would be as far as any reactions would go and they would all be laughing about the near miss once they'd cleaned and parked their vehicles back in the fire hall and had gone for coffee. In the north, every minute could be an adventure if you would only let it.

After his shift was done in the early evening, and true to his hard earned label of crotch sniffer, Iain called J.Noble from the fire hall, insisting he return the book to her in person. Why, it would be the very least a gentleman could do. He learned on the phone that the book had probably fallen from Judith's camping gear as she biked home from a couple of nights of fishing up at the lake.

"Do you fish?" Iain had asked.

"Yes I do." She replied, "I love fishing."

"So do I," he lied. "I'll drop the book off on my way home."

"How thoughtful of you."

Iain had never touched a fishing pole in his life, but white lies had been the conveniences of some of the world's best lovers. This book could hold the promise of some adventures most sumptuous, he thought as he walked out to his pick-up truck. Still dressed in his dark blue uniform, Iain knocked on the door of Judith's fourth floor apartment and was instantly taken with the person who greeted him. Within seconds, all thoughts and strategies of removing this lady's panties had fled from his mind for he recognized that before him stood no ordinary woman.

Although his biggest mystery was how this charming creature had snuck into town and had wandered about for so long without him ever noticing her.

Oh well, he thought, he could flog himself later.

What Judith saw tweaked something inside of her as well, something she couldn't ever recall feeling before. In the hallway stood a husky firefighter with short hair the color of ripened tomatoes and a freckled face whose smile disclosed a degree of mischievousness lurking deep within. He was neither handsome nor ugly but what Judith saw she instantly liked, so she followed her instincts and invited him in for some tea. Iain could never remember receiving so much joy while drinking tea and chatting with someone and it soon became apparent that this charming lady was very different from the rest. They sat in the living room and talked until well past midnight, the conversation flowing like a bubbling brook once they'd discovered that they had both journeyed a somewhat similar road. The talk led to shared feelings that they had never told another human being and it made them both glow inside along with their hot tea. By the end of the evening there existed no doubt as to where this friendship might possibly go, and Iain secured a further opportunity with an invitation for a Friday night movie and a pizza afterwards.

When he left Judith's apartment, Iain thought that maybe he had finally met the one true person he'd been seeking as of late. The one true person that could fulfill his desire for a long, healthy relationship. He would have to be careful though, for it was a small town and the last thing he needed would be his past conquests telling this delightful schoolteacher what a horny bastard he really was.

"That could spoil everything. Cover your tracks, Iain me lad, just cover your tracks and take your time with this one." This was the promise he made himself as he climbed into his truck for the drive home. Judith had similar impressions as well, after she had closed the door on her guest.

Finally, she mused, and a hell of a distance to travel as well. Judith had met nothing like him in the big city while at university and she realized the time might have come to allow into her life some of mankind's more discreet pleasures. Judith had heard all about this horny firefighter from some her friends at school, but it bothered her not.

"The one with the six-inch hose," they had giggled one day over their lunches.

Judith hadn't decided yet, but she might have some fun and play Iain McVicar like one of the fifteen pounders she'd caught at the lake these last few days. She reminded herself to be cautious though, for when you used barb less hooks you lost twice as many fish as you actually caught and Iain *might* be the one keeper she didn't want to lose. On that particular evening, neither one of them had reason to give any thought to the reality that some species of fish, like the west coast salmon, could travel many hundreds of miles up a long river to find a suitable mate.

Only to die, right after they had spawned.

*   *   *

Chapter Twenty-five

Within weeks, Judith and Iain had been seen together on such a continual basis that they were soon viewed by the townspeople as something as compatible as peaches and cream. When the two weren't working, they could be found playing in almost every corner of the village. One couldn't help but smile at their happiness when they were spied standing in line outside the movie theater holding hands, or laughing like children in their favorite restaurant.

The log cabin pizza place had become their second home, as well, there could be found therein the best french fries west of the great divide. Both Judith and Iain had become well liked and respected for the dedication they displayed in protecting the community as well as in educating the young people. So *their* happiness genuinely became everyone else's. Before long they had taken to retreating to the lake north of town for daily fishing trips. Judith discovered Iain's white lie about fishing, but she thought his fib to be cute and he made a good student as she taught him how to use the willowy rods. They would walk to the end of the peninsula to cast their dry flies onto the lake's crystal surface with only yards separating them as they talked. None of this occurred of course until Iain had purchased a mountain bike, so the first thing he'd learned was that his new girlfriend was no slouch.

The firefighter's days of behaving like a horny slut were over and he accepted this without so much as a sigh. Judith and Iain had yet to make love although this certainly might have happened had Iain a mind to. Judith had become the one he had been looking for, while shamelessly practicing with all those other girls and he had decided from the start to allow this relationship to evolve naturally. Which it did, during a three-day camping trip to their favorite lake. The process leading up to this fulfillment developed as innocently as taking a bath for that's where it all started, in the water. Judith had met Iain at the fire hall in the early morning, right after his last night shift. His bike leaned against a wall in one of the bays, his gear packed and ready to go. Judith greeted him with a kiss and a smile, smelling the acrid odor of burned materials on his skin. There had been an early morning fire at one of the hardware stores and the crew had only just returned to end their watch. Iain's crew had saved the store but they had to enter it to suppress the fire, feeling their way through the thick smoke of burning plastics, backer board, rubber and glue. He truly stunk and should have showered at the hall but they were both anxious to get to the lake and the late August sun had heated the top layer of water so swimming had become tolerable.

As they left town a breeze found its way down from one of the snow fields, refreshing and cooling as they peddled their way north. An hour later and they were riding up the trail through the forest to find the narrow peninsula deserted as it usually would be. Once the gear had been removed from their bikes, Iain pulled a towel and a bar of soap from his knapsack and nodded to Judith as she spread one of the tents out across the ground. He turned to walk through the bush, looking for a private part of water in which to bathe. A gravel beach lay in the midmorning sun and here he stripped off, dropping his clothing and the bar of soap to the ground as he entered the water. Firefighters were very adept at dressing extremely quickly and the same could be said for shucking their clothes. Iain was surprised at just how warm he'd found the water, but it had taken most of the summer to just heat up the top four or five feet. Below this there lurked a very chilly layer that would be cold enough to shrink his "harry balls" to the size of garden peas.

Iain immersed his entire body by dropping to his knees, holding his breath as the water enveloped his head, soothing his entire body as he floated below the surface. It became a private world down there and he enjoyed its silence until the sound of splashing called to him from the shoreline.

Iain felt his pulse awaken as his head broke the water and he gazed quietly at one of the loveliest sights his eyes had ever known. Judith approached him slowly, naked as the lake water surrounded her knees, her skin white and taut over her dainty body. Her breasts were small but firm, and Iain openly admired the smooth pelvic bones just below her skin where they highlighted the inviting, curly blond patch covering her soft delights. Judith looked at him with an odd smile he'd not seen before, but then she dove below the surface of the water and he realized some teasing would be played out here. Her head emerged a good thirty feet out into the middle of the lake, her blonde hair slicked down along the nape of her neck. Judith started to swim for the far shore and Iain set out after her, pacing himself so he splashed and kicked only a few feet behind her ankles. Five minutes of this water tag and they'd reached the other side of the lake, finding a small hollow of shallow water carved into the forested shore. Judith took Iain by the hand as they floated into the little cove where they found the water to be chest deep and as warm as any bath. The little pool seemed to have been placed there as if by magic, offering them privacy and a delightful setting in which to romp.

Iain gave a fleeting thought to birth control, having come prepared but leaving everything back at the campsite. It mattered not though, for there were all sorts of wondrous places to kiss and touch and they had days to explore one another. Gently, he took Judith in his arms, allowing her to float on the surface as he buoyed her body with his fingertips under her hips and shoulder blades.

She felt at ease and relaxed, unlike the awkward occasions with the one or two pimply-faced boys she had allowed to pet her while she had attended university. Iain kissed her breasts and she could feel her nipples gather into tight buds as his mouth formed a gentle suction. Judith flushed with the excitement, feeling the warmth gather in her belly before spreading to her chest in the form of small red bumps. She willed herself not to move, allowing every nerve in her body to enjoy itself as they tingled and danced beneath her skin. Iain took his time as he kissed her, denying his own urges while he searched her sweet flesh, nuzzling Judith under her arms, inside her ears, kissing her neck and even her eyes, tasting the salt residue and feeling her lashes flutter against his tongue. Iain had done some serious rutting in his life, but nothing came close to the intense, delectable feelings that he presently shared with Judith. She had started to moan quietly, it quickly brought Iain to a new plateau of excitement, and he thought he might burst as he stood in the water.

He had every intention of bringing Judith to a climatic pinnacle using his lips and tongue, but she had other ideas and he become so aroused that he made no attempt to stop her, which may have even spoiled the moment. She dropped her legs until her feet touched the sandy bottom, then straddled Iain, hoisting herself up with her arms around his neck, wrapping her legs eagerly around his waist, letting him enter her. Iain hugged her in close as she instinctively set a slow rhythm with her hips. Judith gasped and moaned out loud, never feeling anything so glorious in all her life but there was only Iain and the forest to listen to her rapture. She felt as one with him as their activity culminated in a frenzied delirium that started within her pink folds then spread to every cell in her body, causing her to cry out as the lower muscles in her body and back forced her to arch out as the heady spasms shook her. Iain had a flashing thought about pulling himself away from her but he was too far past the point of any reasonable abstinence and he soon followed her into a draining, emotional bliss, gasping as her warmth squeezed him, encouraging him to let go.

They remained as they were for some period, catching their breath while hugging each other as Iain stood in the water with Judith clinging tenaciously around his waist. Nothing was said as they kissed each other lightly and looked into each other's eyes, happy with their discovery, both anticipating the wonderment of the coming days. Eventually they walked from the hollow of water and up into the forest, lying down near a log on the thick green lichen. The sun's rays filtered down from the lofty canopy of pine trees, its golden fingers warming them as they held each other, face to face, until Iain fell into a light sleep. When the sun's warm embrace left the clearing they both awoke together then walked hand in hand back into the water, swimming lazily back across the still lake. The wakes that flowed out from their bodies was the only other movement that could be discerned for many miles in any direction. Their solitary togetherness was complete and would remain this way for the next three days. In the end, Judith and Iain never did break out the fly rods, falling into the seemingly endless hours as they played wherever and whenever they felt a desire and there had been enough of that to abash a jack rabbit.

But they talked as well. They talked as they held each other, they talked as they leaned into each other near the fire at night, they talked as they skinny-dipped and they talked as they shared two sleeping bags zipped together. Neither one tired of talking to each other nor they never once faltered for things to discuss nor laugh about. Conversation was the foundation of all lasting relationships and this one had definitely started from the ground up. At the end of their camping trip there was very little the two didn't know about each other, and even less to discover about their bodies. As they peddled together from their secluded campsite they both knew just exactly whom they wanted to spend the rest of their lives with and that would be the one topic they didn't need to discuss. They had both come a long way to find someone like each other, and they would have to go further still to find anyone else who could even come close. But finding anyone else was the last thing on Judith's mind as they crossed the bridge over the river that led them back into the town. She had never felt so peaceful before and she wished that the time she had with Iain would never end. Although everything must come to end and anyone with a reasonable mind will tell you this. Life, prosperity, and even the mountains themselves would erode away to nothing given enough years. There also existed times when unfortunate incidents could happen much quicker than one had a right to expect. These hardships would occur when your guard was down and you were not expecting them. This is when they can, and will, hurt you the most, and there could be no exceptions to this undignified rule.

*   *   *

Chapter Twenty-six

The one constant to all tragedies is their extraordinary tendency to strike without warning, to sneak up and devastate a person and then roll cruelly over them when they are down, weakened, and emotionally defenseless. Most tragedies reach beyond their initial victims, involving bystanders or those who are committed to helping, which only proliferates the misery further and this is the part they call the "domino principle." All these factors together, and all of them occurring within a short period - at times in only mere seconds - would be the primary reason mankind called them tragedies.

A pity, but there it was.

Autumn had already arrived in the valley, cooling the land while turning the leaves that clung to the branches in the small patches of deciduous trees the color of cornmeal. Soon they would fall, then the winter snows would arrive. A month and some days had passed since Judith and Iain's blissful camping trip and this brought them to the time of the year that heralded the night of the Firefighters Annual Ball. A much anticipated, semi-formal event, the evening started with a meal of grilled moose steaks or baked salmon filets - the choice was yours - then moved on into the wee hours with a lively dance. Every bit of the celebration, from the food to the live band that had been flown in, right down to the napkins you dabbed your lips with had been paid for by the firefighters. One did of course, have to purchase one's own drinks but that would be a trivial inconvenience. The party was held above the main fire hall in a large open room that served as an off duty club and was by invitation only. In one corner stood a large bar where volunteers served your drinks and they even had a room to check your coats at the top of the stairs. This room had been planned as a gathering place, so when the hall had been constructed the living quarters for the on duty personnel downstairs lay in a smaller, separate building that had been joined to the vehicle bays by a short hallway. Iain and his partner Jolene had to work the night shift as part of the minimal crew of four firefighters. The full strength of a watch was seven members but it would be allowed to run with only four. Any less than that and attending fire calls became outright perilous.

Iain and Jolene had been given the night off last year to attend the celebrations so it was their turn to work the shift, allowing others to go. Three firefighters on their watch booked the shift off so they could celebrate at the Ball, which left a skeleton crew in the quarters below. Iain and Jolene were assigned to the pumper truck with the two remaining firefighters, one of whom was a Lieutenant. If the rescue wagon were needed they would attend the call in that particular vehicle, and if things really fell apart then they knew where they could find the rest of the fire department. At least those who hadn't been drinking. Iain had asked Judith to attend the Ball on his behalf and she'd agreed with the idea. She could meet all the wives and everybody who thought they might be someone and all in the same, eventful evening. It was now a certainty that Iain and Judith had started that blessed slide of a couple in love which now included their attendance at certain social obligations.

With summers end came the start of another school year and the two were now inseparable, spending their evenings and days off together. This was when they weren't locked away inside the bedroom at Iain's cabin, for his house in the forest brought them the least amount of interruptions. His watch now had to seek out another location in which to drink beer and someone else's hot tub in which to lollygag. The hot tub still witnessed a fair bit of action, but not from Iain's crew. Although Judith and Iain had yet to discuss anything permanent, it had become obvious to both of them just where all this was going, which was the main reason she had agreed to go to the Ball alone. She decided to wear a Royal blue, mid-length dress with a front bodice and a sweetheart neckline. After hugging Iain good-bye in the vehicle bay at the fire hall she climbed the back stairs to join the festivities. Judith sat at one of the round tables with a Fire Department Captain and his outspoken wife whom she quickly took a liking too. The meal was well prepared and Judith chose the salmon with roast potatoes and steamed fresh vegetables.

She had never taken a real liking to liquor, but a couple of glasses of the cold white wine calmed her nervousness and made the meal all the more enjoyable.

After the meal there came the traditional speeches and the annual awards that were given out for various off duty sports as well as some on duty shenanigans. Long winded as these talks were wont to be, the dancing didn't start until after nine-thirty and Judith politely declined all offers for an escort to the floor. She enjoyed talking to the Captain's wife, who had relocated from the Midwest to take a nursing job at the local hospital. She was another person who had journeyed many miles from home to the isolated town, only to find someone compatible. The band was good as they plucked and strummed through their sets and Judith found herself daydreaming whenever they played their slow songs. If the Captain's wife wasn't up dancing with her husband, she would sit and laugh with Firefighter McVicar's handsome new girlfriend, telling each other insignificant secrets as the evening helped them to form a friendship.

The night moved on as the partygoers reveled in their fun and the duty personnel in the hall below watched a boring video. Everybody was now relaxed and indifferent, a minimal fire crew were on shift so the principle ingredients for a tragedy were now in place. All it lacked was a fateful push to set the first domino into an irreversible tumble. This came come from a blameless, four-year old boy named Bryan Parkin. The Parkin family lived in a large, five bedroom home on the town's municipal limits and the location of their house became a contributing factor to the grief that would follow. This, and the irresponsible manner in which Buck and Terry Parkin raised their two children came together to cause a lot of people, a lot of anguish. The Parkin couple should never have been allowed to reproduce in the first place but some things humanity simply had no control over. For a start, they were both stricken with alcoholism but they could still function as the disease had yet to spill over into Buck's job. On this fateful evening, Buck had left hours ago for his night shift at the mine. Terry had sat alone at the kitchen table drinking the remains of a bottle of vodka while her two children had been playing in the warmth of the rec room downstairs. The house had been built on a parcel of land that was set well back from the main road in a forest of Jack pines. A dirt track wove its way through the forest to the front of the house, offering the family privacy, although parts of the roof could be spotted from their nearest neighbor. Once Terry had finished her bottle, she felt soothed as the liquor took hold and exhilarated her into that dopey sense of euphoria.

Moments later the stupidity set in and she felt an urge for company and some more drink, something she knew she could find in Kirby's trailer at the bottom of the dirt road. Terry put on a warm coat and had enough mind to embrace a certain amount of responsibility before she left the house. She went downstairs to the rec room to check on the children who slept soundlessly on a massive, grizzly bear skin rug that lay in front of the wood stove. Terry covered her children up with a blanket from the old couch then opened the stove to put a couple of more logs onto the embers. Buck kept a steady supply of split wood in a box in the corner of the rec room along with kindling and newspapers for the rare occasions when the stove was allowed to go out. Terry took one last glance at Bryan and his two-year-old sister Sophie, then went upstairs to walk through the cold night to the neighbors. She was drunker than usual, and as she staggered down the dirt road she reminded herself to eat supper next time, although food only inhibited the alcohols intoxicating affects as any drunk will tell you. On several occasions Terry wandered off the road and found herself lost amongst the trees, but had the persistence to find her way back to the trail. I shouldn't have taken those codeine filled painkillers either, she thought.

Fifteen minutes of this meandering, Hansel and Gretel stuff and she finally found the steps to Kirby's trailer - although much like the fairy tale, she would in fact be the only witch in the forest tonight. Kirby had rented a piece of the Parkin's land near the main road and had lived there for more than a decade in a winterized travel trailer that he'd hauled up from somewhere. It was quite long and cozy and he'd built a Joey shack with a wood stove against the side door to keep the weather out as well as adding an extra room. Kirby was as ancient as the glaciers that carved their way through the mountains, with a withered face that reminded Terry of a dried up apple.

But he had a good heart and the beer in his fridge would be cold and there was lots of it.

Kirby had been watching through the front window of his trailer as Terry staggered down the road, finding it slightly more entertaining than the show they presently had on the television.

A battered up kitchen table had been pushed up against the front window of the trailer and the small television sat buzzing at one end. Kirby had already opened a bottle of beer for his guest, placing it on the table opposite from where he sat. What did he care, it wasn't his liver that was being tarred.

Terry carefully navigated the wooden steps to the Joey shack as the old man stood waiting in the doorway. She nodded to him as she entered the trailer, going directly to her regular chair in the corner by the table. Terry took a long pull on her beer, swigging half the contents as her throat pulsed with apparent delight. When she put the bottle back down on the table, this was the signal to start the conversation and it started the way it always started nearly every other evening.

"My but we're good and pissed tonight Dear," Kirby would say,
"You betcha ole man," Terry would slur.

Once the niceties had been dealt away they would talk about everything including the weather and Kirby appreciated the company, for he found that being old and lonely could soon wear him down. While Terry enjoyed her visit with the old friend who happily contributed to her liquored delinquency, terrible things were happening back at the house. Bryan had woken and laid still for a few minutes, bored and pondering whether he should cry out for his mother or go look for her. He crawled out from underneath the blanket, leaving Sophie to sleep, and toddled over to the wood box picking up a piece of newspaper the way he'd seen his father do countless times. Bryan walked purposely over to the stove, taking the insulated latch in one hand and easily flicking it ajar, pulling open the small-hinged door.

The flames inside captivated the child, and he couldn't have possibly comprehended the danger of what he was about to do next. Bryan held the newspaper just inside the door of the stove, just the way he'd seen his father do time and again. He gasped with delight as the flames jumped magically to the loose ends of the paper, quickly dancing up it as he held it to his front. Bryan was about to holler to his sister when the flames licked at his fingers and he dropped the burning paper onto the bearskin rug where his sister still dozed. The flames instantly ignited the coarse ruff of fur along the neck of the bearskin, spreading frighteningly across the rug, consuming the hairs with deadly speed. Bryan was mindful enough to reach down and grasp his sister by the hand, dragging her from the fully engulfed rug. Sophie had been startled from her sleep, crying out with her brother's rude tugging, trying to understand what had happened when she saw the burning rug, the flames now as high as her chin.

Her brother took her by the hand and pulled her down the hallway that led to the steps, but instead of turning to go up the wooden risers Bryan sought safety inside the bathroom at the end of the hall. He closed the door behind them and even locked it. The child couldn't have known any better nor should he have. By now the flames were consuming the old couch, scorching the particleboard on the wall behind it. If any good were to come out of this fire, it would be the long prison sentence a Judge would eventually hand out to the children's mother. That and the fact that Bryan and his sister would die of asphyxiation long before the flames ever got to them. The course of events that would quickly follow would change the lives and the innocence of a small northern town forever, for the dominos had now fallen, and there could be no stopping them.

*   *   *

Chapter Twenty-seven

A fire requires fuel, oxygen, and a continuous heat source to keep it burning and there existed plenty of that inside the Parkin household. Buck had left the ceiling in the rec room unfinished and in five short minutes the fire was free-burning, swiftly igniting the two by ten wooden floor joists, providing an open path as the flames convected rapidly across the ceiling. The walls in the rec room and the hallway burned next as the heat radiated down from the ceiling, causing the upper portions of veneer to burst instantaneously into flames. Hot gases rose rapidly up the stairs as the open door at the top acted like a chimney, allowing the heated vapors to collect along the ceiling of the upper floor. One of the last things to burn in the basement was the stairs and these became a direct source for the super hot gases to vent directly to the second level of the house. Now starving for air, the fire in the basement sucked the oxygen from the bathroom where Byran and Sophie huddled together inside the shower stall. Moments later they lost consciousness, then drifted peacefully, but not alone to their deaths. On the stairs the fire had nearly burned out, leaving the steps a charred skeleton.

Along with the rising gases to the upper floor went the excessive heat that accumulated against the ceiling, rapidly reaching down along the walls of the living room and kitchen. As the temperature rose, the man-made products on the second floor reached their ignition point and the upper floor became fully involved as the flames flashed over the ceiling and down the walls. It was at this point of the fire that old Kirby noticed something wrong from the window of his trailer. Terry had passed out in her chair, snoring quietly as Kirby stared vacantly at his television.

A flicker of bright orange from up the dirt road caught his attention as the flash over inside the Parkin house lit up the front yard through the living room window. Kirby moved quickly through the Joey shack and out his front door to get a better look from the road. He felt sick as he saw bursts of orange flame flickering from parts of the living room window. Kirby ran back into his trailer and dialed 911, then went over to shake Terry who mumbled briefly before slumping her head onto the table. The old man left his trailer a second time, making his was up the dirt road, wheezing with the effort and the dread he held for Terry's two children.

The call came into the fire hall fifteen seconds after Kirby had hung his phone up and the people at the party in the room upstairs knew about it because the floor rumbled beneath their feet as one of the electric doors opened up. Nearly a dozen off duty firefighters' left the dance floor to look out the windows to the street below. It was a force of habit, they couldn't help themselves and some of their wives joined them as they gazed out into the night. Judith walked over to join them, her curiosity calling out to her. Seconds later, a lime green pumper truck rolled out from its bay below, the red lights and siren piercing the stillness of the night. Judith saw Iain and Jolene sitting on a bench seat in the "dog house," a cab that faced the rear of the truck located directly behind the driver. They appeared calm, fully dressed in turnout gear as they strapped themselves into the breathing bottles that were mounted on a quick release device at the back of their bench seat. Seconds later the truck disappeared from Judith's view but she could still hear the siren, until it became muted, fading into the distance. She continued watching out the window until she could hear the truck no more, then returned to her table and the Captain's wife.

Kirby had given explicit instructions regarding the location of the Parkin house and when the pumper truck turned off the main road the driver followed the dirt trace right up to the darkened house.

"No hydrant," thought the Lieutenant as both he and the driver jumped from the cab.

All four firefighters gathered briefly at the side of the pumper with Iain and Jolene ready to go. They looked expectantly through the clear visors of their breathing masks having already cracked open the air bottles on their backs. Both of them were now inhaling uncontaminated air and they took a moment to check one another over, making sure their helmets were secure and no skin remained exposed. Wide collars and cloth flaps protected their ears and necks and everything else was wrapped inside their heavy turnout clothes. While they were doing this, an old man came huffing up to them, the fear evident in his voice as he announced that two children were most probably trapped inside.

"Anyone else?" Demanded the Lieutenant.

"No." By now the old man was shaking he had become so distraught.

"Where the hell are their parents?"

"The mother's drunk, the father works at the mine."

"Do you know where the children's bedrooms are located?" The Lieutenant asked.

"Upstairs I think," replied Kirby. "I'm just a neighbor."

The Lieutenant nodded to Iain and Jolene and they immediately set to their tasks. The driver had climbed up behind the doghouse to work the levers and watch the glass dials that ran the fire trucks internal water pump. As the Lieutenant called for a tanker truck, an ambulance, the police and more personnel on his portable radio, Iain reached up to one of the hose beds located along the side of the pumper. Quickly he pulled a flaked length of inch and a half hose down onto his shoulder, jogging up the stairs to the front door as the hose paid itself out behind him.

Jolene was right beside Iain and they crouched down on either side of the front door.

They had both seen the deadly signs of the impending back draft, the blackened front window with no sign of any flames anywhere inside. The fire had entered the smoldering stage, having used up most of the available oxygen inside the house, and it waited like a hungry animal, hovering in the air below the ceiling at over one thousand degrees Fahrenheit. Its food would be the oxygen that would rush into the structure when Ian and Jolene attempted their entry.

They prepared themselves for the back draft, eager to work through it. Seconds later Iain could feel the woven jacket of the hose expand in his hands as the water from the pumper charged it. They would have to be very careful as the seven hundred gallons they carried in the tank wouldn't last more than a few minutes with the nozzle wide open. Jolene had removed a glove from her hand, feeling the door then yelling to Iain that it was hot. She replaced the glove then crouched even lower onto the front porch.

It was Iain's turn on the nozzle, so he would be the one to pop the door and all Jolene could do was wait. Both of them were concerned about the children in the house, neither one holding out much hope, dreading when they eventually felt their way to the bodies. It could be the worst thing a firefighter could endure; finding small, lifeless bodies inside a charred bedroom.

Iain reached up to the doorknob, turning it as he pushed it open, abruptly falling to his belly as the loud whooshing sound filled his ears. The outside air rushed in over their prone bodies, sucked in through the open door and the whole front room became an instant fireball, the flames blowing like an explosion back through the front door and out over the yard. Iain rolled onto his side then pulled back on the U-shaped bail that controlled the water flow. He had already adjusted the nozzle to send out a wide, shielding fog and he made a circular motion with the hose as he sprayed a short burst of water from where he lay. Within seconds the flames had nearly dissipated as the water droplets absorbed a great deal of the heat, turning to steam as they extended into every hot corner of the room, a dampening action that would allow Iain and Jolene to enter the building.

When the flames died so did the light they created, replaced with a thick, slow-moving smoke that blinded the rescue team. They would have to work without seeing until another team arrived from the fire hall to chop a hole in the roof, which would ventilate all the smoke. Flashlights were useless as the white beams would dazzle them as they reflected off the smoke particles and they didn't realize at the time that a lot of the smoke was pouring up from the ruined basement.

Iain led the way, with Jolene snuggled in close to his body as they both pulled on the hose, crouched down on their hands and knees, entering what they believed to be the living room.

This was an instinctive drill that let them know the other was there as well it kept them down low as the steam and gases above them were still simmering at a deadly temperature. The living room was huge, and after touching helmets they had a brief conversation then separated as each one crawled along opposite walls on their hands and knees, feeling as best they could out into the center of the room. Iain had left the hose behind to expedite the search that he would pick up once they met again at the entryway. Any furniture they came across would have to be physically checked, every inch felt with their hands both on top as well as underneath. Terrified children had been known to climb into cupboards during a fire so they could be anywhere. It would have been nice to go directly to the bedrooms but they had no idea where they were located, so this was the standard procedure when you were blind and in a strange building.

Time would also be an enemy as the air bottles they carried on their backs were constructed of aluminum tubes wrapped in woven fiberglass. This made them extremely light and portable but they could only carry fifteen minutes worth of air. *Fifteen minutes* - if the wearer were sitting comfortably at a table playing cards in a nice cool room. Considerable less if the stress level had become elevated because you were moving around in a hostile environment, your breathing and pulse picking up as you blindly searched for two children whom you hoped to find alive.

The bottles were also fitted with low air bells that would ring when the air supply was nearly exhausted, giving the wearer approximately three minutes to evacuate the building to get a fresh bottle. *Three minutes* - if you were sitting passively in a nice quiet room. About half of that time if you were deep inside a burning building and if you didn't follow your hose back out in the required time you would most likely die. After searching the living room Iain and Jolene met back at the nozzle, then continued down a hallway, dragging the hose with them. They found three bedrooms along the outside wall, methodically searching under and on top of the beds, including the crib that sat in one of the rooms and all the closets and furniture they could find. Nothing.

Professional they may be, both of them were now starting to feel a bit frantic for the missing children as they realized the situation was nearly hopeless. They crawled back down the hallway then turned left, feeling their way to a room they thought must be the kitchen.

Speaking briefly once again, they would each follow an opposite wall, checking the kitchen cupboards and even the sink before moving to another room. Iain inched his way along the left side of the kitchen, running his hand along the wall while reaching out across the floor with his other hand. He had gone about ten feet when he discovered a doorway in the wall. This was when Jolene's low air bell started to jingle loudly through the impenetrable smoke.

They would both have to leave.

A firefighter never remained in, or entered a burning building by themselves.

Iain took a couple of seconds to explore the doorway, hoping it would lead them to the basement.

He leaned out a bit to feel for the step and he soon found it as he placed a gloved hand onto the top riser. The charred step collapsed beneath his hand and Iain fell into space, somersaulting through the air, crashing through what remained of the burned stairs, hitting the cement floor nine feet below him. He fell onto his back, feeling his lower spinal column snap viciously over the rounded bottom of the air bottle.

Iain lay momentarily stunned, listening to the bell ring on his own bottle. He realized he was in grave danger if he didn't find a way out quick enough but when he went to move he found he couldn't. He had been paralyzed from the neck down, an acute condition when he'd broken his back in the fall. In the kitchen above him, Jolene searched quickly for her partner having no idea what had happened to him, her own low air bell effectively muting the sound of Iain's. She called out through her mask, spreading herself out into the center of the kitchen with her feet against the floor boards, feeling with her hands, hoping to find Iain, her breathing becoming ragged as the adrenalin charged through her body. Then her air was gone and she could feel the rubber mask suck against her face in mid breath. If she didn't leave now, she wouldn't make it and even that possibility was debatable as she felt her way toward the nozzle. Jolene fought the impulse to rip the mask off and breathe the highly toxic smoke and gases, which would have seared her lungs in a flash of choking pain.

She crawled down the length of hose through the smoke, willing herself not to panic, her lungs only half full, stinging with her last breath. She only just made the door where the Lieutenant waited, kneeling beside the hose as he peered through the dense smoke. Jolene collapsed near his feet, blacking out as her lungs sucked instinctively against the rubber mask. The Lieutenant pulled the helmet from her head, using his fingers to break the seal the mask had formed around her face, relief flooding over him when he heard her gasping for air. Gently he removed the mask and gazed down at her face.

"Where's McVicar?"

Jolene shook her head slowly, and the entire bottom fell out of the Lieutenant's evening.

The young firefighter that lay at his feet was one of the departments best, and her coming out of a smoldering house alone while sucking on an empty air bottle could be a very bad sign indeed.

As the Lieutenant frustratingly raced through his options he sadly understood there was nothing he could do until another team showed up from the fire hall. Many firefighters had died returning alone into burning buildings to find missing or injured partners, only to perish along with them.

In the end it was a good thing the Lieutenant stood by his decision for Iain McVicar had already lapsed into unconsciousness, the air from his bottle now used up. Immobilized and in the gutted basement, he began the slide to a lonely death. Although it was never meant to happen, firefighters quite often died fighting fires and no amount of training or safety equipment was likely to alter this cheerless fact. This would be one reason they all bought life insurance. Something to help ease the suffering and hardships of the loved ones they were forced to leave behind.

*   *   *

246

Chapter Twenty-eight

Six days after the death of Iain McVicar and the Parkin children, the town held a funeral for the fallen firefighter and a memorial service for the two tots. Someone once said that misery loves company and the whole community joined Judith in her grief although not to the degree that she herself may have suffered. She refused to leave her apartment for the period leading up the service, preferring to remain a shut-in after booking time off from her school. Judith hadn't felt such devastation since the death of her sister Meryl and her father in the helicopter crash of so long ago. The fetus that had started to grow in her womb saddened her even more, for she knew how hollow life could be growing up without a father. She thought briefly about terminating the pregnancy but soon dismissed those thoughts as too many emotions burdened her as she struggled with her sorrow. Judith had already surmised that the conception had occurred the first time she'd made love with Iain in the tiny cove at the lake. They had used no birth control upon their initial intimacy but Judith had roughly calculated herself to be in the infertile stage of her monthly cycle. She had been wrong with her reckoning, and allowing herself to be swayed by the exquisite intensity that Iain had brought her with his gentle touching would now prove permanent. Over a week ago she had missed her period, the first time since she had started to menstruate. Judith had immediate suspicions and confirmed them with a kit from the local drugstore. She felt overjoyed in the beginning, sitting on the toilet seat as the paper wick turned the color that according to the instructions, suggested new life was growing within her.

Judith wasn't entirely sure when she would tell Iain, but she knew him enough to predict the delight it would bring to his freckled face. During their long hours of talk, they had approached the subject of raising children on several occasions, each knowing how the other felt so there could be no unforeseen surprises hovering on the sidelines. Not a bit of this mattered anymore, not since her life had collapsed with Iain's untimely death. Judith was once again alone in the world. Pregnant and alone, at least for the next eight months or so. Jolene herself had come to tell her the terrible news, scarcely four hours after Judith had left the annual Ball. A half dozen firefighters had left the party when the call came in for more personnel, but the Captain's wife had reassured Judith that this was a commonplace, a simple requirement for more hoses before any more property could be lost.

The party had finished up shortly after two in the morning and Judith drove home feeling happy and content. She had just made a new friend in the Captain's wife and the unpredictability of a common life had favored her with a pregnancy and a caring mate. All that ended when a fire truck had parked on the street in front of her apartment building. By then the deadly fire had been extinguished, the bodies recovered, and the local police and coroner were conducting an investigation. Traditionally, the Fire Chief would attend to tell a widow or surviving family member that a loved one had died while attempting to save lives and property, but Jolene had insisted on being the messenger. Judith didn't know the Chief very well and it would be the least that Jolene could do for Iain. He had been a wonderful partner, complete with his unbridled laughter and raunchy talk about his "harry balls."

The crew on the fire truck watched in silence as Jolene entered the apartment block, all of them secretly glad they were returning to the fire hall, all of them respectful of the courage she was now displaying. At just after six a.m. on a Sunday morning Judith opened the door to her suite to find a firefighter dressed in blackened turn out gear standing in the hallway, the odor of smoke almost overpowering. Still half asleep, she thought it was Iain standing before her but then she recognized Jolene's face beneath the black smudges that marked her skin. The firefighter didn't even get a chance to utter a single word for the expression on her face and her very presence said it all. Jolene shut the door behind her and held Judith as she wept, walking her gently to the couch in the living room where they both sat hugging each other. It would be the most emotionally taxing act that Jolene had ever performed in her whole life, something she wished she would never have to do again.

The firefighter stayed with Judith until exhaustion overtook her emotions and she fell asleep leaning against Jolene's soiled coat. Jolene eased Judith down onto the couch and covered her with a blanket. Before she departed, she kissed Judith on the forehead and left a note on the coffee table to call if there was anything she could do to help.

"He didn't suffer," were the only words that Jolene had said during those hours she'd spent consoling Judith, and she felt a bit guilty at telling this lie as she walked from the building and down the street back to the fire hall. Her crew had long since returned to the hall as there were hoses to hang and equipment to clean and it all had to be done before the next call.

Judith called Jolene a day later to thank her for what she had done, but politely refused any offers of company. The drapes were drawn on the windows of her suite, and the phone had been unplugged and things would remain that way for a few days. Judith felt the need to be left alone, to course slowly through her grieving process while deciding what her next move might be.

She called the school where she taught and they had arranged for a substitute teacher to take over her class. "Take your time," had been the Principle's soothing message. The despair that followed Judith around her apartment over the next while seemed never ending and overwhelming to the point that she ate next to nothing and didn't even bother bathing. She would constantly wander aimlessly throughout her apartment, the anxiety fueling her plodding, and confused movements.

Five days of this activity and another knock came at her door, but like the rest she decided to ignore it. Moments later an envelope was pushed under the door and inside there was a note from Jolene. Iain's funeral would be tomorrow morning and a vehicle would drop by at ten o'clock to pick Judith up. The time had come to muster the inner strength that had thus far taken her over a life that had been fraught with disasters. Judith had to be strong again, and if not for herself then for the child that grew inside her. The child she had now decided to keep.

On the day of the funeral, Judith Noble's life took another unexpected turn, another change in direction that among other events would ultimately redefine her future forever. At precisely ten o'clock she was picked up by three firefighters in a crew cab pick-up truck. They all wore their dress uniforms and Judith felt relieved when she saw Jolene sitting in the rear seat. Silently she took the seat next to Iain's partner, feeling her warmth when Jolene reached across to grasp her hand. Judith wore a navy jacket and matching skirt - the darkest clothing she had in her closet. Judith and Jolene spoke quietly as they drove through town under a gray sky that held a threat of the season's first snow. The service was held in the fire hall, which could hold a lot of people once the vehicles had been driven from their bays and parked out back. Nonetheless, the people attending had spilled out onto the street and they left the rolling bay doors open so everyone could listen to the service. Iain's polished hardwood coffin had been placed on the rear hose bed of the pumper truck that he had traveled on to his last call. The hundreds

249

of feet of six inch, red highball hose that fed the water from the hydrants had been stripped from the truck, leaving an open-ended box in which to place the casket.

A minister in white robes stood near the truck which had been parked inside the hall, speaking to the gathering in a clear voice, reading passages from his bible before talking about Iain's short life. He then went on to talk about the even shorter lives and the innocence of Bryan and Sophie Parkin, condemning society's inability to look after its helpless charges, a guilt that possibly the entire town should carry. Once the service had finished, Judith and Jolene walked slowly behind the fire truck with the minister as it moved through the town to the old cemetery located near the high banks of the river. Iain's fellow firefighters marched behind these three solitary figures, and they all gathered around the gravesite once the casket had been unloaded and placed above the freshly excavated hole. Despite the pressing embrace of the crowd, Judith felt a deep loneliness and it was here, as she stood next to the grave, that she finally considered her pregnancy a blessing. Only eight months of being alone and she would have a child in which to share her life.

Lost in her thoughts at the grave side she heard very little of what was said as the Minister sent Iain on his way, bidding him a quiet sanctum at his journey's end. Judith, for the first time in a week stood reminiscing about one of the happiest periods of her life, wondering if they could ever be replaced. She had also decided at that point that she had finished with her crying, except for some private moments that would occur in her future, moments when she was alone and scared in a world that had left her feeling vulnerable. After the graveside service, the congregation walked back to the fire hall as the sky opened up and the snow began to fall.

Judith had hoped for one last visit to her and Iain's secluded lake, but that appeared impossible with the large white flakes that now fell to the earth. The rough trail leading down to the water would be inaccessible within a few hours, the forest floor resting once again beneath a thick layer of white for another long winter.

A reception had been planned in the large room above the fire hall and a local bakery had provided finger sandwiches and fresh coffee, all of it laid out on cloth-covered tables. Judith was never left alone during the reception, and she became glad for the company. Many came up to offer her condolences and one individual embarked on a little business once he'd shaken her hand. He was a roly-poly man with loose jowls that nearly hid the tie he'd worn with his three-piece suite, one of two lawyers who practiced their vocations within the town. Marty Dempster took care of all the civil litigations while the other lawyer handled all the criminal matters, a mow your own lawn agreement that kept them both well paid but might have failed anywhere else.

Marty had a good heart and his smile was sincere as he spoke to Judith.

"Could Miss Noble attend his office sometime this afternoon?"

"What would this be about?"

"Mister McVicar's estate."

"What has this to do with me?"

"He registered you as the sole beneficiary more than two weeks ago, he has no other family you know."

The two worked out a time just after lunch that gave Judith a while to reflect on this latest development. Iain owned the cabin and the land he lived on outside of town but Judith already knew she couldn't live there, not with all the memories that dwelled inside of those rooms.

Judith didn't bother having any lunch, preferring to walk home through the snow that fell steadily over the village. Her dress shoes weren't the best footwear for the weather but she arrived home before the snow had started to really collect on the ground. After changing into some seasonal clothes and with mukluk's on her feet, Judith walked back downtown for her agreed upon appointment. She was ushered into Marty's small office on the main street by his secretary and she sat quietly waiting as the barrister sat perched behind his desk. He had a manila colored folder sitting on the blotter and he wasted not a moment with the disbursements.

Some of which left Judith speechless.

When he had finished with his short, legal talk, Marty's pudgy fingers slid a certified cheque across his desk for two-hundred-and fifty thousand dollars, the total sum of Iain's life insurance policy. Wordlessly, Judith signed for the cheque that had her name printed across the top, then Marty had her sign for the chattels and property that Iain had owned. Everything would be registered in her name at the land titles office by late this afternoon.

"Do you have any questions?" Marty asked.

Judith shook her head . . . no.

"If there is anything I can do, anything at all, please call me."

Judith thanked the lawyer then left his office, walking through the heavy snow to her bank six blocks down and on the other side of the street.

Inside of two short minutes, Judith's net worth had amassed to just over four hundred thousand dollars and it would be safe to say she was still in a mild state of shock.

As she walked through the center of town, it once again became a battle to keep her emotions in check. The man standing at the service counter inside her bank couldn't possibly have known the feelings that were surging wildly through her soul as she opened a special account and deposited the money. There had been no problems as Marty had called the bank before lunch to advise them of the impending deposit. His client didn't need any humming or hawing while some bank clerk scrutinized the cheque then made some imposing phone calls to confirm its authenticity.

As Judith walked home, people nodded and smiled as she went by them, and all of them thinking how bravely she carried herself. But not one could realize the pain she suddenly felt, at least not by the neutral expression upon her face. A neighbor stopped to talk to her in the foyer of the apartment building and Judith nearly didn't make it to her suite, jogging the last few feet to her door. She fell apart once she had closed the door behind herself, leaning against it while she knelt on the floor. It felt to her as if Iain had touched her one last time from his grave, providing her and his unborn child with the means for a secure life. All she had to do was provide the child with a mother's love and simple nurturing, never having to worry about money. This latest sequence of events had given Judith's future some much needed stability, for the road ahead of her promised at times to be a lonely struggle. Although there would still be one more surprise yet to come.

It would be this revelation, combined with other reasons, that would influence her decision to leave behind this friendly, close knit, northern community.

*   *   *

Chapter Twenty-nine

The decision to leave the town did not come easy for Judith, even though she had started considering the idea right after Iain's death. Her tummy had been growing steady, already starting to round out and it was her Doctor who first suspected a multiple pregnancy just three months into her term. An ultrasound at the local hospital confirmed this and the news brought Judith great joy and to this day she's not sure where this wonderment had come from. Raising one child as a single mother in the north would be a challenge; bringing up two held the promise of an honest struggle. Although, it would be the haunting reminder and the emptiness she felt whenever she entered a store or a restaurant where she and Iain had shared a moment that would eventually provide her with the decision to move. Wherever Judith traveled within the town she would be reminded of Iain, and of the special times they'd had in a particular place as well it would trigger the pain of his sudden loss. These memories would niggle away at her, causing anxiety and even though she never wanted to forget him, these stark recollections made the healing process all that much harder.

Judith had to remain healthy for the birth of her twins, and she had to remain strong if she were to raise them in a wholesome environment. She had known herself the despair of an unstable childhood and she wouldn't have wished that upon anybody. A change of venue made the most sense, a new life without the constant memories of what she once had and the short period in which she had been allowed to hold it. Judith knew that if she stayed, she would never again venture out to the small lake with its private peninsula and cool waters.

Far too much heartache could be found out there.

By the end of week though, Judith would know where she would be going and exactly what she would do when she finally got there. The staff room at the school had been empty one lunch hour as there had been a pep rally going on in the auditorium. As Judith ate her lunch alone, she read one of the Union newspapers that were published monthly and it was here she found a job posting for a teaching position in the gulf islands of the Pacific Northwest. They preferred a teacher who had the special education required for dealing with and instructing mentally challenged children.

A telephone sat on a coffee table in the lounge and Judith called the number provided. She had simply been seeking an information package with this call, but it became apparent after a short conversation that the school was having difficulties attracting a teacher with the specified training.

Property on the island was expensive; especially on a teacher's salary and apartments were virtually none existent, which had also been scaring away any prospective hopefuls. One day after this initial call the chairperson of the local school board had a telephone interview with Judith, and thirty-minutes after it had begun, they had reached an agreement. The school board required a teacher with specialized training who could afford to live on their fair island, and it just so happened that their new teacher needed a dramatic change of scenery. They had discussed everything including salary and the chairperson had even agreed to pay the moving expenses if Judith could take her post in the classroom as soon as she had arrived. Later that day, Judith found herself once again in the law office of Marty Dempster where she reached an agreement, regarding the sale of the property that Iain had owned outside of town. Marty would see the deal through from start to finish, securing a reputable real estate agent who would list the cabin and once sold, wire the money to the island that Judith would soon be calling home.

The next few days were busy as Judith gave her notice at school then arranged to have her furniture and belongings placed into storage until she had purchased a new home on the island.

Her evenings were filled up as well as she carefully packed any household items and clothing she would need for her long trip. These were placed in cardboard boxes then stowed in the back of her truck. There would be a period of time that she would spend living in a local motel.

The school board had recommended a nearby resort on the beach with house keeping cottages, a quiet place to live until she found a suitable home to purchase. When Judith called the resort, they offered her one of their secluded units in a fruit orchard above the beach. It had an unobstructed view of the coastal mountains and a covered porch to sit under while enduring the rainy season.

The day before her departure, on a cold, snowy afternoon, Judith's friends at school held a combination going away party and baby shower in the staff room. They knew she was expecting twins so they gift-wrapped two of everything that they'd purchased for the expectant mother, solving the gender issue by obtaining one blue set of baby clothing as well as a matching pink set. After a few hours of laughter while drinking chilled, de alcoholized champagne, Judith's friends helped her load the gifts into the back of her truck, then they said their last good-byes as the snow fell gently around them. There was one last stop to make before Judith returned to her apartment for one final evening and she left her truck running as entered the fire hall through a side door. Judith could never forget Jolene, or that morning many months ago when she had arrived at her door to deliver the shocking news about Iain's death. She found the firefighter cleaning equipment next to the rescue wagon and they stood talking in the bay for about twenty minutes. When Judith hugged Jolene it became a sad moment for both of them, for they each felt as if they were saying good-bye to a family member as they had both shared Iain, but in entirely different ways.

They wished each other luck, making a promise to write and it would be one of those hasty vows that both of them would manage to keep.

Judith left the fire hall feeling drained but full of hope for a new life in a new town, as well for the life that grew inside of her. Once back in her empty apartment she took her clothes off and climbed into the sleeping bag in the middle of the living room rug. Gazing through her balcony doors she watched as the aurora borealis frolicked its way across the cold night sky, changing shapes and colors as it spanned from one horizon to the other. It appeared to Judith as if the northern lights were saying good-bye as well, and these were her final thoughts before she drifted into a contented sleep. She would rise in the morning long before the town had stirred, climbing into her truck for the long drive over the hard packed snow that covered the highway. As Judith slept under an animated sky, many thousands of miles to the south a young man named Ben Trilby had just started his rookie year with a large, metropolitan police department. This young man and Judith were now traveling parallel paths that would one day intersect, although this would not occur for at least another decade. It would take at least that long for Judith's wounds to heal. The coming together of these two people would not be a mere coincidence, but rather something that had been intended from the day they had both been conceived. Something that no amount of tinkering would change. Try as you like, you can't ever tinker with fate.

*　　*　　*

Chapter Thirty

Judith ran her fingers over the white leather covering of the book, feeling its pebbly surface with her fingertips as she stared straight ahead, almost as if she were reading brail.

She had just finished reading the book about Iain McVicar within the transcendent parameters of the library. It struck her that there had been only one, minuscule item regarding his life that she had not known about and even that was directly linked with his death. Judith and Iain had shared everything in the short time they had been given together. During their long discussions out at the lake they had talked for hours about their innermost thoughts and secrets, their goals and aspirations, even the past misfortunes that had affected and shaped their lives. There was very little that Judith didn't know about Iain. Until she had pulled his book from the shelf to read about his story and the true manner in which he had died. Judith wasn't sad though; just mildly surprised as it had been more than ten years since his death. The reading of her close relationship with Iain came more as a refreshing elixir than as a melancholic reminder.

She seemed as if she could feel everything all over again as her eyes held every word that had been boldly printed onto the pages. For the first time in more than ten years Judith wondered if the time hadn't arrived that she should love again while at the same time allow herself to be loved.

Many years had passed without sharing the physical proximity of another man, many years devoid of not laying together like a set of spoons beneath the covers as they whispered to each other their naughty thoughts. Judith was about to replace Iain's book on the polished shelf when she felt the familiar presence of the voice once again. And now she was absolutely certain that the reassuring voice had come from somewhere out of her past, although she still couldn't say exactly where.

"You have found something about Iain that surprised you?" The voice asked.

"Yes. Jolene told me that he had died instantly from his fall in the house fire. His back broken."

"Yes," the voice replied.

"But it would appear from this book I've just read that he had suffocated after he ran out of air. That would have been a horrible way to die."

"No," the voice said, "Iain didn't suffer. Jolene only told you that to ease your own suffering, for she couldn't possibly have known what Iain had felt. No one there at the time could have. If it is decided that you will be staying here, they will tell your twin girls precisely the same thing - 'your mother didn't suffer, it was over very quickly.'"

"How do you know that Iain didn't suffer?" Judith asked softly.

"Your body is simply an instrument in which to carry your soul, which is the true heart of every human being. An instrument that enables you to touch, feel, taste, savor and even reproduce life itself. Iain's body may have suffered in that burned out basement, but his essence wouldn't have. His spirit was gone before his body had even hit the cement floor. Look at yourself. Did you feel any pain when the power pole fell down and its lines electrocuted you?"

"No, I didn't."

"Then believe me when I tell you that Iain didn't suffer. After reading about Iain, do you think you're ready to love again."

"Yes . . . I think I am."

"Good, for love is something that is very natural to you Judith. The time *has* come to love again - any longer and you will be denying yourself the one true pleasure of living. Please continue reading Judith. I will return to let you know when it is time."

"Time for what?" Judith asked.

"The time for whether you stay here . . . or leave."

The voice left as abruptly as it had sounded and as Judith replaced the book of Iain back onto the shelf, she took another one down. This book was identical to the rest of them, bound in white leather with gold lettering spread across its pebbled front. Judith read the name "Grace and Uncle Walt," then opened the book to the first page. Before she started reading, she'd noticed that only one book remained on the shelf beside the deep chair in which she sat. Judith reached up and turned the book so she could see the gold title embossed upon its front. She let out a quiet gasp.

This last book had *her* name printed across the front.

*   *   *

Part Four
"Grace and Uncle Walt"

Chapter Thirty-one

The only other person on the face of the earth to ever know the truth behind
the ruination of Private Walter Matthew Brem's features was First Lieutenant Grace Looby.

To anyone else who might have been nosy enough to ask as to how a handsome young man could acquire such a Quasimodo type-face - the answer was simple and succinct.

"I caught a bullet from a machine gun while storming a cement bunker in France."

"Oh, how terrible," the rude inquisitor would reply.

"Yeah, it was a real piss cutter."

If the truth need be known, the crater in Uncle Walt's face had been fashioned some eight hundred kilometers east of the sandy beaches of South Western France. The bullet however, did in fact come from the weapon of an enemy soldier.

It occurred during the waning days of the last Great War in Europe and why they would call any war great was a baffling contradiction. But nonetheless, the end of this one appeared to be in sight. People on both sides of that horrible debacle were getting tired of the fighting and the killing and all the other atrocities that would haunt a comparatively peaceful world for decades to come. Walt Brem was especially sick of the fighting, for he had been a gentle person all of his life and the brutality of combat would leave him marred forever. Another sad fact was that Walt really didn't need to be fighting over in Europe. He should have been back home helping his father run the families thriving hardware store. All this changed when his high school sweetheart Sally dumped him one fine sunny day. Sally enjoyed drawing attention to herself, so she picked the town's main street near about high noon to end the relationship with Walt, entertaining the shopkeepers as she wailed away her complaints.

"Why, she'd called that little turd all sorts of rude names," the Butcher had chuckled later.

Sally had been Walt's first real love and they were even talking of marriage, children and a quaint cottage near the beach but then it all headed for the toilet. Everything fell apart after she left the island to travel to the mainland for a few days, only to return with the realization that there was more to life and boys than just what the local crop had to offer. Within the big city there dwelled an endless smorgasbord of virile males running through the nightclubs. They all had high paying factory jobs, expensive suits and convertible motorcars with an infinite supply of condoms in the glove boxes.

A teenaged Walt was both devastated and lost for the break up came without any warning although the whole community seemed to know about it days before he'd had been so tactlessly informed. That's the way it was on the island back then - an intrusive but friendly community where discreet love affairs and family secrets were essentially none existent. Oh, the fooling around was there as well the family secrets but make no mistake, everybody knew about them. In the end, Walt Brem handled the Sally problem much the way he handled all his other problems, a process that required two definitive stages and usually ran the course of a few weeks. He would first withdraw into himself like a turtle, pulling all his emotions back inside so they weren't out on his sleeves for everyone to gawk at. He still lived at home and had been an only child, the product of an accident, the locals would smile, and right after dinner he would go up to his bedroom in the attic to mope as he lay on his bed staring hopelessly at the ceiling. This would be the deny-his-parents-his-cheery-face-I'm-mortified-beyond-reach-leave- me-alone, unless you knock on my door stage of the grieving process. The second stage could at times be somewhat impulsive, although this time it would become a bit more permanent, if not outright dangerous. During the third day of his bemoaning, Walt Brem took the ferry over to the mainland with some well-intentioned thoughts about doing some whoring around himself. Life would be wonderful if he could bring back some colorful stories to regale loudly up and the down main street in hopes of rubbing Sally's nose in it. But Walt really wasn't the whoring around type, so alas, this just was not to be.

Once Walt had walked off the ferry he took a bus downtown where he sat next to a uniformed paratrooper who had returned home on convalescent leave. He had only one arm, but the soldier's chest was covered with ribbons and his mouth rattled off an endless supply of tales about his combat exploits and feats of masculine, daring-do. Walt couldn't have known that the soldier had lost his arm in a jeep roll over while driving back to his unit after a drunken furlough in a French town. Nevertheless, a wholly misguided Walt Brem shook the paratroopers remaining hand, bid him good health then got off the bus to go find the army recruiting office. All thoughts of exotic, sexual conquests with strange ladies had left his head as he entered the recruiting station to join the army to do his part in ending the war in Europe. Three days and three nights later, after spending quiet evenings in an outhouse of a hotel staring dreamily out the second floor window, Walt Brem had become a soldier.

Yes sir, the smallest lad to ever graduate from the islands only High school would show Sally Thornby that a real man lurked beneath the crew cut and scrubbed face and through his body there flowed, rampart, undiluted testosterone. She would be begging him to father her children when he returned in a few months with a sizable pension and four pounds worth of medals pinned to his by then hairy chest. Walt's parents were naturally a tad miffed at this news but there wasn't a lot they could do about it for their only child was of legal age and if he wanted to join the war effort they could only hope he would at least write them.

"Walter, you might get hurt," was his mother's only admonishment before she thoughtfully washed his clothing and darned his socks for the trip to boot camp. Barely had the laundry dried on the clothesline and he was out the door and off to recruit training. The Brem's prayed nightly for Walt's safe return and although the elderly couple couldn't have known it at the time, their son would come home from the war, but he would not come home unscathed. He would bear marked changes both inside and out but would nevertheless return to the family hardware store with a new bride and a Purple Heart medal pinned to his chest.

The next morning found Walt in the city where he boarded a train that took him on a three-day journey across the country he had just sworn to defend. He read books or watched the golden fields of wheat roll by as they traversed the Midwest and the other recruits played cards or entertained themselves with fist fights in the open aisles of the coach. It would be an idealistic young man - a man full of vigor and fantasies who would arrive with the rest of the herd at the recruit training base in the east. All of Walt's comrades in arms seemed to know the delicate intricacies involved with surviving in a modern army, well versed to the man about the subtle tricks as well the most important decree of soldiering which was you never volunteered for anything.

Not ever.

Not even if it sounded like a good idea for there could be no such thing as a good idea in an army that was at war. Unfortunately, someone had neglected to share this information with Walt Brem and he never did twig to the fact that he was one of the few recruits with his hand up at boot camp whenever they'd asked for volunteers. He simply wanted to show the drill instructor's that he was there to do the job and that he could be relied upon whenever they came calling.

"Who here can drive?" The Drill Instructors would ask.

"I can," Walt would eagerly reply.

"Very good Private Brem. Now drive your body up to the Headquarters building and pick up the mail."

"Who here wants to clean the shitters?"

"I do," and Walt would put his hand up again.

After the recruit training had finished, they came around once again soliciting for volunteers.

"Who wants to join the Airborne Regiment and jump from a perfectly serviceable aircraft then float to the ground under a white canopy while the enemy finds the range to your unprotected balls?"

"I do," Walt said, putting his hand up once again.

Some Psychologists compared this pick-me behavior to "the whipped dog syndrome" in that no matter how many times the dog would be beaten he would still return devotedly to his Master's side. So off he went to jump school after the graduation parade and subsequent beer bash in the junior rank's mess. Sadly enough, Walt Brem, given his gentle disposition should have been at home on the island putting nails into the metal bins inside the family hardware store instead of nailing soft bodies with metal bullets. Those soft bodies that he's shoot on the battlefield belonged to people he'd never met before nor would he ever be given the opportunity to know them. Behind every face of every person, both military and civilian that had died in that horrid war, there lay an untold story. A story of whom they loved, whom they cherished, what made them happy, what brought them sadness, and who was left to feel empty and hollow after Walt had done his duty by ending their lives.

Years of living, years of memories, all gone in a fraction of a second after the trigger had been squeezed and Private Brem put a copper jacketed bullet into their visible center of mass.

He would scope them out over his open sights, centering on whatever part of the enemy's form happened to be exposed, then he would send the bullet cracking down range a second later.

Mild mannered though Walt Brem might have been, he had also turned out to be a wicked shot, something that always came from a certain amount of natural talent. He had never been overly good at anything in his life and had usually been the first boy to be beaten up and the last one to be picked on the playground for a pickup game of baseball. The army quickly discovered his hidden talent and wasted no time in cultivating it beyond the normal realms of a marksman. Walt simply wanted to show his Sergeant as well as himself that he was truly good at something, but what he'd become efficient at came with a terrible price. In time he would be issued with a .30 caliber, bolt action rifle with a Weaver telescopic sight and be designated as one of the Platoon snipers.

Walt could blow a nasal ball from a man's nostril at a distance of five hundred meters, a rare talent and highly valued commodity during a war. Although Walt wasn't the least bit smug about his lethal skills and he had in fact become shameful of his unique job. There were occasions when a man he had just shot would lay moaning in the mud, the pink coils of his intestines spilled across the dirty front of his uniform jacket. This would be the gruesome result whenever he used a dum-dum round, a bullet whose pointed metal tip had been filed blunt so as to cause maximum carnage when it butted its way through human flesh. Used by all sides, these bullets were illegal but just who the hell would you call when the medics pulled one from what remained of your buddy's leg? Walt soon learned to shut out the sounds of his wounded victims as they bawled pitifully for their mothers for in most incidents he'd been ordered to forgo the delivery of a killing shot.

A wounded enemy soldier would require two fit men to drag him from the battlefield and until that happened, the sight of his raw guts and ceaseless moaning could rattle the sensitivities of even the hardiest troops. It got to the point where Private Brem would pray for a clear, unobstructed head shot for regardless of his orders he made the final decision as to the fall of shot. Then he would allow the bullet to crease their brains and they would drop soundlessly to the ground. Visible center of mass - that had become the training standard. Walt had to shoot the dead center of whatever they had inadvertently exposed to the cross hairs in his scope.

Some of the other sniper's within the unit kept a score of how many "pumpkins they'd popped," and when they asked the diminutive Walt he

263

could only shake his head then shrug his shoulders. He never kept count but he already figured he would be going straight to hell. There were many unsuspecting enemy soldiers he'd sighted and shot, appearing larger than life through the magnified lenses' of his scope before he dropped them. A sniper also led a lonely, furtive life.

A life that required him to sneak around with another soldier who would provide cover until he found an optimum position in which to carry out his tasking on an unsuspecting enemy. Some of them he'd shot while they had been reading letters from home, the crisp whiteness of the paper contrasting with the dun colored earth to draw his attention. Many he'd taken out while they were having a peaceful piss in the bush or a quiet but quick bowel movement. If you were new to this game and still ignorant about the rules of concealment then you could be in for a deadly surprise whenever you dropped your drawers to expose your bleached ass. Leaves and twigs don't stop bullets and the only target a good sniper required was a glimpse of white skin as it flickered amongst the false security of a lush green forest. There were more shameful ways for a human being to die; this war had certainly shown the world that. But when they fell with their pants down around their legs or with a letter from a loved one in their hands, a part of Walt Brem always went with them.

Bit by bit, month by month, the sensitive young man started to unravel each time his rifle butt slammed into his shoulder with the violent recoil, and another enemy soldier would drop from his sights. And still Walt volunteered, jumping up like some drunken yahoo in a coonskin coat at a college football game. It would be this inability to keep his hand down and keep his mouth shut that placed him in his present position on a bench seat aboard a twin-engine, C-47 Douglas Skytrain as it flew North East of the Ardennes. Below the cloud cover at fifteen hundred feet, thirty of these aircraft were dismally off course as they carried a Battalion of men toward a covert mission. The lead aircraft was designated the pathfinder and the navigator on board used dead reckoning to find his way as a star shot with his sextant was out of the question because of the clouds. Using a combination of speed, time and distance in the black of night could be dangerously inaccurate in a steady crosswind. Especially when the pathfinder's navigator had more confidence in his coffee thermos than his own piloting ability and he still tallied single digit numbers using his fingers. Many small things do a tragedy make and this secret operation would be no different, as it had already started to come apart with the errant navigation.

The Allies had been on a sweeping roll across the European Theater when winter and its ensuing mud had bogged them down. Their momentum stalled, they allowed their ambitions to slip to the point that they figured they might just have a quiet Christmas before being ordered to press on toward the Rhine. This indifference fostered a counter attack that would prove a serious mistake and would cost two-hundred-and-twenty-thousand lives for the enemy alone. So as the Allies cleaned weapons and wrote Christmas letters home, twenty-four Divisions of opposing troops rolled out for one last desperate attack, attempting to strangle the Allied supply line by seizing the nearest deep water port. A "bulge" nearly ninety-seven kilometers wide at its base was formed as ten armored divisions with infantry support punched through the Anglo-American lines. The very weather that kept Walt Brem's Skytrain flying at fifteen hundred feet also kept the Allied aircraft from strafing and bombing the advancing enemy as they dashed up the center of a now widely divided front.

If someone didn't get off his or her collective asses and in a hurry, a lot of hard-fought ground would be lost and the goddamned war would drag out for a few more years. It would take about nine days of dirty fighting for the Allies to eventually push their foes back from where they had come.

In the meantime however some bright spark had hatched the idea for an airborne assault behind the lines. It was hoped that such an operation might speed things up a bit but unfortunately you can't speed a war up and some people will never learn that. They speculated that if a relatively large group of eager soldiers were to parachute to the rear of the enemy and pick away at their backsides they may just think they'd been surrounded. This might cause enough confusion and buy some more time as the Allies moved reinforcements into the area. Like all plans though, it looked sweet and easy in a warm command post when all the lines and tactical doodads had been drawn across a wrinkle free map. Pathetically enough, and in reality, there existed a very thick, imaginary line that could be drawn between the word theory and common practicality. Although the most unfortunate thing about these two designates was the amount of lives lost in any attempt to prove that very point.

And so after the plan had been approved over a cup of coffee with a brace of rum, word was sent out for volunteers from Walt's Airborne Division, a part of which had been garrisoned in an abandoned monastery.

"We need some volunteers," the Lieutenant had stated, addressing Walt's platoon. They lay casually about on the stone floor in some straw deep inside a wine cellar. Finding shelter in buildings wasn't a common practice during the war but the Allies had air superiority, which gave them one less concern regarding their choice of accommodations.

Once again . . . Walt Brem's hand went up.

Others offered their services, and from an entire division of some fifteen thousand men, there would be enough fools to take a nice clean theory and possibly turn it into a practical objective. Later that afternoon, Walt and hundreds of his fellow but willing soldiers gathered in the courtyard of the monastery for their operational briefing.

The brass did not expect many of the paratroopers to survive and when the time came to notify their next of kin on the other side of the world they could comfortably say to the grief-stricken family members, "he volunteered, you know." They main reason they had asked for volunteers was because of the vast distance found between the principle of a military plan, and its probability of a successful execution.

"And speaking of execution," the briefing Colonel had said, "don't get caught because the enemies have their backs to the wall and they no longer have the luxury of taking prisoners. If you're caught, you might be interrogated and then most probably shot. Questions?"

Several hands shot up out of the hundreds of now concerned looking paratroopers, and one particular hand was being waved vigorously, doing its best to catch the Colonel's attention.

"Yes," the Colonel said, "the short guy down in front. What's your name soldier?"

"Private Brem sir."

"You have a question, Private Brem?"

"Yes sir, could I possibly give this operation a skip please? I don't feel so good anymore."

The Colonel waited until the raucous laughter had died down before answering Walt.

"No you can't Private. You know too much about the operation to turn back now, otherwise we'd now have to shoot you. Ha, ha."

By the powers of piss, Walt thought, it sounds like I'm going to get shot anyway.

By the time Walt's platoon of paratroopers had boarded the Skytrain near midnight and had taken off, he had also volunteered to carry a bazooka and four of its heavy rounds. With ninety-five pounds of extra equipment now strapped to his body, he couldn't have even carried a thought for very far. On top of his present, discouraging situation, Walt had to urinate and he already knew he wouldn't be able to pee in the tiny head that lay enclosed in a dark cubicle at the back of the aircraft. Not with all this crap tied and strapped to his combat uniform, not while inside an aluminum aircraft that vibrated and bucked all over the night skies. By now though the strike force was miles off course, which no one could have known at the time and then things got worse as they usually did in wartime. This was when the starboard engine of the aircraft that Walt was on overheated then caught on fire. He hadn't seen such a fire since his Boy Scout days when they'd burned the hall down during a massed camporee on the island. The leaders had blamed a gaggle of rogue scouts from the South for causing that little weenie roast, but unlike that fire of so long ago this one didn't appear to want to burn itself out. And it wasn't like someone could walk out on the wing to the radial engine and snuff it out with a fire extinguisher. Bright orange flames lit up the inside cabin of the aircraft and you could see the fear on the paratrooper's faces as they realized this couldn't be an altogether healthy situation.

One of the three aircrew members came back from the cockpit to tell the paratroopers to brace themselves as they were going in for a crash landing. Telling thirty soldiers wearing parachutes who despised the Army Air Corps - complete with their warm beds and dry mess halls - that their plane was going to crash was definitely the wrong thing to do.

"What's our altitude?" The Platoon Lieutenant yelled.

"Twelve-hundred-feet," replied the flyboy.

"Tell the pilot to hold it level for one minute, that's all we need. We're out of here."

The flyboy nodded then returned to the cockpit. Before the Lieutenant could even issue the order, Walt and his fellow paratrooper's were on their feet having already snapped the nylon webbing of their static lines to the cable that ran the full length of the ceiling inside the fuselage. When they jumped from the aircraft, the static line would pay itself out until it automatically pulled the paratrooper's canopy and rigging lines from the packs on their backs, which would fully deploy their parachutes. The chutes could be pulled manually but this self-operating method eliminated any need to count to five to ensure they had cleared the aircraft before they hauled on the ripcord. As well, the chute would still deploy should a soldier be injured upon exiting the aircraft. Safety had become a paramount concern during this war.

As the Lieutenant moved to the rear of the aircraft he snapped on his own static line then pulled in the rear, port side exit doors as the soldiers formed a single line. They immediately started jumping from the airplane without so much as a threatening holler from their leader. The fire burning in the starboard engine was rapidly worsening, with flames now running the length of the fuselage as they were sucked back into the aircraft's slipstream. Thirty-five seconds later the paratrooper's had vacated the Skytrain and the Lieutenant figured they'd set some kind of a record for exiting an aircraft. Walt Brem had been one of the last to leave, feeling the icy air as it sucked him roughly into the night sky, the static line jerking then straightening his body as it pulled the chute from his pack. As he floated silently beneath his parachute, he watched the Skytrain as it quickly lost altitude, the yellow flames from the fire reflecting off the bottoms of the low clouds, the aircrew struggling valiantly to control the doomed airplane. A millisecond later the aircraft detonated brightly as the fuel tanks in the wings ignited.

"By the powers of piss," Walt whispered as the airplane turned into a fireball, arcing into a steep bank as it turned back into the direction it had just come. Then it broke apart, falling to the ground in burning fragments, taking the aircrew, who were still strapped inside the cockpit, to their deaths. The aircraft tumbled from the sky, falling into the edge of thick woodland, sending out shock waves as its main body struck the forest floor. Burning fuel erupted from the wing tanks, spreading like flaming waves over the forest floor, instantly igniting the lower boughs of the timber. Immediately the fire spread to the upper limbs and in seconds that whole part of the forest was ablaze. When those fly boys crash a plane, Walt thought, they really put on a show.

But the aircrew wouldn't be the only casualties suffered during this rapidly souring operation. Miles off course and with a forest fire lighting up their drop zone, the men of Private Brem's Platoon now had their own unique problems.

For this was when they heard the tanks.

And there were lots of them.

The throaty roar of the diesel engines and the shrieking of metal tracks reached up to the paratrooper's as they approached the earth at seventeen-feet-per-second. Most already knew the tanks moving below them belonged to the enemy as there existed no diesel powered armored vehicles in the Allied inventory. A handful, including Walt Brem, who hadn't slept through the armor recognition portion of their training, knew that the sounds of the vehicles moving on the ground were made by the brutish, fifty-ton Panther tanks. There could be something frightfully compelling about heavy armor grinding its way across a battlefield, especially when you were swinging above them on a parachute made from forty pounds of silk and nylon rigging lines. Even worse, where there were tanks there was infantry and this combination was not a good thing for a section of lightly armed paratrooper's to be dropping into without being invited. This whole scenario held the promise of an unhappy ending Walt thought, and it was enough to take the curl out of ones pubic hair.

A number of the enemy troops on the ground had spotted the parachutes as they neared the earth, their canopies glowing rosily from the forest fire, which had consumed an acre and was still spreading. Tracer rounds started to lace the sky as the machine guns mounted atop the turret roofs of the Panther's opened up, seeking the range to the exposed paratroopers. Many of the tanks had stopped along the road as the crew commanders swiveled their machine guns skyward and the infantrymen who clung to the square turrets aimed their rifles into the night sky, joining in on the melee. Many of Walt's Platoon members died while still swinging in their harness' and all he could do was watch in horror as the blazing tracer rounds streaked up to puncture their bodies, the bullets exiting on the opposite side, developing a wild trajectory after striking firm flesh and hard bone.

Walt studied the ground as he got closer, and in the illumination cast from the forest fire he could see a long armored column in either direction moving up a dirt road that snaked through small copses of pine trees. Infantry rode piggyback on the outer shells of the turrets and packets of support vehicles moved along the road between the tanks. Walt had drifted quite a bit from the main group of parachutes, having being one of the last to leave the aircraft and this placed him several hundred meters away from his Platoon. Not a large distance, but enough to save his life as he had yet to be noticed by the soldiers on the ground. Now he needed a place to hide for once he landed that would be his only chance for survival. Walt spotted a nearby copse of tall pines and steered himself toward it by pulling down on one side of the rigging above his head. As the air dumped from the opposite side of the parachute he rapidly sideslipped in the direction of the small forest.

Walt harbored not one misconception about firing upon his adversaries once he had touched down, for there lay many pages in a dictionary between the words courage and stupidity.

This was one scrap they wouldn't be winning.

In fact, they had already lost it and without firing a single round. Nearly half of Walt's Platoon were dead as their bodies hit the ground, collapsing like wooden marionettes whose strings had been clipped, the white canopy's of their parachutes floating down over their bodies like huge bed sheets. Those who were still alive upon landing struggled to their feet, trying desperately to shuck their jump harness and bring the barrel of their weapons to bear but they were all too late.

Squads of enemy infantry converged onto them as they hit the ground, firing into them at point blank range. Others got close enough to the scrambling paratroopers that they could beat them with the stocks of their rifles. The whole miserable scene chilled Walt's soul as he watched his fellow Platoon members get summarily shot or brutally pummeled to death. There could be nothing honorable about any soldier dying, but what was happening on the ground became a horrific reflection of a World War where chivalry had become nonexistent and the pages of the Geneva Convention were used as toilet paper by both sides. Walt hoped that he would be able to shoot himself before the enemy got to him, politely saving them the effort of beating the shit out of him - something he'd experienced enough of while in high school.

"Don't get caught, you'll be shot," had been the briefing Colonel's grim warning.

At least they weren't being interrogated, Walt thought as the deep copse of trees rushed up past his jump boots. It could be foolhardy at anytime for a paratrooper to land into a forest but Brem required immediate concealment if he wanted to see another day. Pine boughs broke his rate of descent as he plunged through the upper branches and the sweet smell of the sap touched his nostrils, reminding him of his home on the island. Queer time to be thinking of home Walt figured as his parachute became snagged in the upper limbs, suddenly arresting his fall. He found himself suspended about four feet above the forest floor and it appeared as if the opposing troops moving down the perimeters of his forested sanctuary had failed to notice him. Seconds later Walt had freed himself from his jump harness, landing upright as he fell the short distance to the ground.

He took a moment to scope out his situation, confirming that no one had spotted him. The copse that Walt squatted in was only about fifty meters wide, its center slightly illuminated from the forest fire that still burned from the downed aircraft. Leaving the two-piece bazooka and its ammunition behind, he took his rifle and crawled through the ground foliage, getting closer to the outer fringes. Walt had to put some distance between himself and the incriminating parachute as well the time had come to go to ground and stay there until this column had cleared the area. He would attempt to get his bearings during the daylight hours, but until then hiding was the handiest idea he could think of.

Most of the tanks and the support vehicles in the convoy had started to move again, their outlines casting long shadows over the ground as they rolled past the burning woods. The tanks sent out gray plumes of smoke as they accelerated, vibrating the earth beneath Walt's belly, reinforcing their impenetrable might as champions of the battlefield. An enemy crewman wearing a wedge cap had dismounted from one of the Panther's and was walking purposefully among the moving tanks, a dark, shimmering silhouette against the moving flames in the background. As Walt watched, the task he was carrying out sickened him to the point that he threw up the corned beef hash he'd eaten earlier that evening for dinner. The crewman held a pistol in his hand, moving among the supine forms of Walt's Platoon, spread out where they had landed across the open field that skirted both sides of the road. As he got to each one he shot them in the head. They all had their combat helmets securely strapped on and if they lay on their backs the enemy crewman shot them in the face, and if they were prone on their belly's then the bullet was put through the back of their necks.

What disturbed Walt was that some of them had survived their beatings, moving and moaning gently until the crewman came over to dispatch them. Shocked though he may be at what he was witnessing, the same thing had occurred when his own army had advanced across France.

Many times an impulsive decision had been made by the Platoon Leader that they wouldn't be taking any prisoners and Walt had seen enemy soldiers shot right after a fierce spell of street fighting. Shot as they walked from a bunker with their hands above their heads but you won't read that in any history books. Many might call the crewman's actions cold retribution, but what he was doing was a simple fact of war.

After every seven or eight shots the crewman would stop to reload a fresh magazine, pushing a loaded clip up into the pistol grip before recommencing his grisly chore. This morbid tactic of a single bullet to the head was known universally as a coup de grace, or "stroke of grace," but Walt didn't consider anything graceful about it. He watched on for at least ten minutes, unable to take his eyes away as the soldier moved over the field until he had shot the last of the paratroopers. Walt Brem was now alone and in a pine copse that would be no more than a tiny dot on a map - that's if he had a map. And if he did manage to get one from the body of his dead Platoon Leader he had a better chance of growing a third arm than of orientating it to the point that he could figure out just where the hell it was in Europe he might just be. Realizing the hopelessness of his circumstances, Walt trembled with a suffocating fear that he'd never felt before. One that reached deep inside of him and when his bladder let go he didn't even notice the warmth as the urine pooled around his crotch, darkening his combat pants and the front of his jump smock. Bigger problems than pissing his pants now abounded his present situation, for as he watched on, things became progressively worse.

Most of the convoy had moved on, disappearing beyond a low point between two small hills, but a few of the tanks still straggled, moving slowly forward with their main guns swung out over their back decks. This should have told Walt Brem plenty about what was going on but little registered in his mind he had become so terrified. One of the heavily armored Panthers had separated from the rest, sitting stationary as its engine thumped away, idling just this side of the road and almost within spitting distance of the concealed paratrooper. Walt could see a crewman standing through one of the top hatches of the turret, exposing his body from the waist up. The forest fire threw enough light that Walt could see him picking his nose and he could have put a bullet into his head with his eyes closed at that range, but then he might just as well stand up and shout hello for all the good it would do him. This was when his predicament took a ruthless slide, taking him from the lows of a very bad but possibly survivable dilemma, right down to the basement where things became outright perilous.

The enemy crewman who had put the final bullet into each one of the paratrooper's had holstered his pistol then walked over to the lone Panther tank. Walt suddenly realized that he was the Commander of the tank crew as that particular open hatch was vacant. The Tank Commander removed a wooden handled shovel from its mounting place along the side of the vehicle just above the tank track. The crewman who'd been picking his nose tossed him a rolled up newspaper he'd fetched from inside the turret and now the Commander walked directly over to where Walt lay hiding in the low brush. After all that killing the time had come for a peaceful dump while there remained a lull in the action, and the soldier even had enough light from the forest fire to read his newspaper if he so desired. At that particular moment in the war, Private Walter Brem hit that invisible bump in life when his cognizant reality informed his sensitive conscience that this lunacy had gone on long enough. Every human being had a level where their faculties would finally bend to the point of breaking, although many in this war had been allowed to forego this unnerving experience because they had died first. Walt was nearly hyperventilating as the enemy Tank Commander walked to within a foot of where he lay in the scrubby undergrowth.

He could count the eyelets on the Commander's boots, right up to where his black coveralls were bloused around his ankles and the triangular chevrons on his sleeve designated him a Feldwabel (Field Corporal). The only reason the enemy Corporal hadn't seen Walt was because his night vision had been ruined by the brightly burning forest fire. Turning away, the Corporal dropped his belt with the holstered pistol onto the tall grass, then pulled his coveralls down to his ankles then squatted low to the ground. Quickly, (there was a war on you know) he evacuated his bowels loudly onto the tall grass and the moist, pungent smell nearly set Walt to retching and he'd wondered why the Corporal had bothered to bring a shovel if he wasn't going to bury it. The young paratrooper had never given religion much thought until now but he found himself saying a prayer, begging for deliverance if only he could live long to smell the salt air and see his island home once again. Walt dared to look up as the Corporal tore pieces of the newspaper off, scrunching it up before applying it to his backside. Things were looking fairly grim if the enemy lacked toilet paper he thought, but apparently they still had lots of ammunition and there were plenty of them still running around to cause grief and that had now become Walt's only concern. He was badly outnumbered and with his bolt action sniper's rifle he wouldn't be able to shoot them very fast so that made him outgunned as well.

Once the Corporal had finished wiping himself with the newspaper, he turned around once again and looked down at his own stool, admiring his creation while Walt vibrated silently with fear, not even a foot away.

"Mein Gott," the Corporal stated proudly, "ein grossen scheisse. Das stinkt . . . ya. Ho ho."

Walt remembered reading in high school that a great philosopher - Plato, or someone like that - had written that all men had three things in common; they all peed in the public baths, they all played with themselves and they all looked at their own stools. He thought once again what a queer thought to be having while his life hung on such a fragile precipice. This was when the enemy Corporal spied the white parachute hanging in the middle of the copse with its empty harness. He still had his coveralls down around his ankles and this little faux pas would give Private Brem a wee bit more time to react. Squatting back down, the Corporal reached for his holstered pistol and this was when he looked into Walt's terror-stricken eyes. As he fumbled for his pistol Walt struggled to get to his feet, bringing his ungainly snipers rifle up to his front so he could defend himself.

They both stood at the same time, the enemy soldier with his pants and underwear looped around his ankles, and the teenaged paratrooper who the Corporal himself considered a sworn enemy. Two young men that might have been good friends if only circumstances and a different decade had allowed it. As the Corporal brought the pistol up, Walt swung the rifle up under his chin in one fearful motion. Nine pounds of wood and steel were kinetically transferred as the rifle butt slammed into the enemy soldier's lower jaw, splintering bone and shattering teeth.

Not a sound was made other than a dreadful crack as the man collapsed to the ground, dropping his pistol as he fell. Walt had the presence of mind to reach down and grab the semiautomatic pistol, a much handier weapon than his rifle, especially at close range. As he stood up, he felt a pair of hands grab his ankle and he looked down to see the Corporal, dazed and bleeding from the mouth, reaching desperately for Walt's legs as he choked on his broken teeth and blood.

"Leggo," Walt urged, "Jeezus, leggo of me."

Confusion and fear were portrayed in the Corporal's eyes and as his grip became tighter, Walt would never know that the man had been blindly reaching for help. Terrified as well as cornered, Walt brought the pistol up and shot him in the face. Now dead, the Corporal relaxed his solicitous grip but the snapping sound the pistol had made alerted the rest of the tank crew.

Shouting came from the stationary tank, and Walt wasted not a second as he fled into the woods, tears blurring his vision as he stumbled for the center of the forest. He had never killed a man at such a close range, and it grieved his sensitive nature to the point that his brain decided this had been one violent episode too many. The man he had just killed, the man whose name he would never know, would be the last human being that Walt Brem would ever shoot again. His days of killing were about to come to an abrupt end and had he been aware of that cheery fact he might have been able to garner some comfort. But there was no time to think of anything for as he ran through the trees the crew in the Panther tank had swung the turret around so the main gun pointed in the direction of the fleeing paratrooper. The gunner inside the turret opened fire with the 7.92-millimeter machine gun that was mounted coaxially beside the long barrel of the main gun. Walt had nearly made it to the center of the copse when he heard the rapid "braaaap" of the machine gun, the bright tracers from the bullets flashing out into the forest to his front. He then felt a burning sensation in his outer leg just below his right hip and he fell to the ground as the pain sucked his breath away. Glancing toward his leg, Walt knew he'd been hit by a bullet, because of the black stain that soaked his combat pants, near his outer thigh.

He now lay prone just under a thick tree trunk, suddenly startled when the machine gun from the tank turret hosed off another burst of rounds. A few of them thudded dully into the trunk above his head, causing pieces of bark to salt his face. Walt heard many voices that signified more troops had dismounted from the few tanks that still remained in the area. It would be a matter of minutes before they flushed him out and if they caught him alive he had no preconceived notions about how they would treat him. Walt had just shot their Tank Commander in the face and he feared he wouldn't be as fortunate to die so swiftly. More bullets punched into the tree trunk above his head. Bad news, for they knew exactly where he had gone to ground. Wounded, and with no hope of survival or escape, Walt had become a man in frantic need of a miracle and right there in those lonely woods an astonishing phenomenon did in fact occur.

It was delivered to him quickly. And it came from his own hand.

Walt had shot many men because it had become his sworn duty but that alone couldn't make the killing a just cause. Walt decided that the time had come for his own death and he briefly hoped he would go to some place better but he rather doubted it.

Private Walter Brem pointed the pistol he'd taken from the enemy Corporal at his face then pulled the trigger with his thumb. A blazing flash and a stunning wallop from the nine-millimeter bullet was all he would remember about this pitiful and most extreme act. Walt had done the right thing though, for moments later three soldiers from the Panther tank had crept up onto his position and found the paratrooper with his face and chest covered in blood that had flowed from a bullet wound just under his left eye. Because of the shadowy darkness and with his shallow breathing, they assumed him dead, the wound caused by a round spit from their own machine gun. They never saw the pistol in the grass by the paratrooper's feet so they weren't given cause to assume that anything else might have happened. Nor would they have cared for they were on a very tight schedule, a schedule without plans or any regard for time appreciation and they'd wasted enough time on these piffling airborne troops. With this on their minds, the three soldiers returned to their tank then hastily climbed aboard. The Panther's engine roared and the tracks screeched as they moved past the burning forest toward the twilight of a dawning day.

They followed the rest of their convoy through the draw between the two hills and approximately five miles past this point they started to run out of fuel. As the vehicles sputtered the last of their diesel they were abandoned and the tankers became infantry as they quickly stripped whatever weapons and ammunition they could carry. Many of them would be dead within two days, but most of them would be captured, feeling relieved and blissful, able to sit out a war that could have no happy ending, leaving in its wake a ravaged and divided continent. Had Walt's Lieutenant the chance to get his compass out before he died he would have noticed that the enemy convoy was heading toward the East. They were not moving to the front as reinforcements to assist in the attack and expand the bulge further into the Allied lines - they'd already attempted that and it had faltered miserably. This armored convoy was retreating because the one, final blitzkrieg of the war had been halted by the Allied Forces and in some ten short days. They were retreating in contradiction to the strict orders they'd received from a mad man. They were moving fast to avoid certain annihilation from the overwhelming armies of their determined enemies and who the hell could blame them?

Nevertheless, word from the front lines of this monumental shift had been received slowly. Reports that the fighting had changed to once again favor the Allies and their offensive push had trickled slowly into the main command posts and then down to the many units including Walt Brem's Airborne Division. The same Division who had just sent hundreds of volunteer paratrooper's on a mission behind the lines. A mission where thirty of them had jumped into a retreating section of the opposing army and consequently to their deaths. An overtired, underfed, and frazzled wireless operator had failed to send a runner from the main command post to Walt's unit until the following morning. Six hours after their C-47 Skytrain's had taken to the air with their cargo of airborne soldiers. This, combined with a nincompoop navigator who'd led the fleet of airplanes wildly off course, and an engine fire had ended as well as altered the lives of many men that cloudy, cold evening. Because of these series of events, three aircrew and twenty-nine men had died, many before they had even landed on the ground. Only one would survive, but then he would have a hideously scarred face for the rest of his days. All these mishaps had united to generate this small tragedy and very few of the surviving family's could take heart that something good would someday arise from this frightful mess. It would send Private Walt Brem down a long path of restoration - a path that would allow him to take a good look at himself, as well as a path that would allow him to meet his future wife.

*   *   *

Chapter Thirty-two

It would be a long, trying, few months before Walt Brem would totally accept the fact that his survival had become every bit a deliverance, and then some. Even then, the Psychiatrist at the Veteran's Hospital admitted this to be an incredibly short period of time for a patient to appreciate the hand he'd been dealt. Three months of surgery, convalescing, counseling and careful reflections of the true person who dwelled inside of him would be required to assist in this healing. Walt, like legions of other soldiers would spend the rest of his life secretly agonizing about the men he had killed during his service in the war.

Normal people don't kill other people then walk away unscathed.

That sort of crap only happened in the 'B' Westerns at the Saturday matinees.

Private Brem's mental rehabilitation process with the Psychiatrist seemed to touch on every emotion he had, and much like everything else that occurred through the course of those healing days, in the end, they would have a purpose in his therapeutic strides. Walt spent many daylight hours searching for his inner vitality while at the same time looking for a way to deal with his anguish. At night he would vent his torments by weeping silently in his hospital bed in the semi-darkness, a shaft of moon glow cast through the window above his head and a solitary, burning light bulb at the nursing station the only witness to his misery. All this focusing and recognition of these very human sensitivities, plus the soft presence of a nurse named Grace Looby would convince Walt Brem that being alive with a ghastly face was far better than being buried with somewhat boyish good looks.

When the enemy tank crew had left Private Brem for dead in the pine copse, he was in fact very much alive. The instant after he had shot himself using the captured pistol, the nine-millimeter bullet had rendered him unconscious, saving his life but at the same time destroying his youthful face. Two hours after the incident an advancing Troop of armored Staghounds from a British Reconnaissance Squadron had found the wounded paratrooper. The fast, four-wheel drive vehicles with their boxy turrets had been reconnoitering the roads and the land well forward of the advancing Allied Armies. As another day broke under a now cloudless sky

278

the Troop went to ground for some rest, using the pine copse where Walt lay as their daytime hide. As per the standing operating procedures for all reconnaissance units, the seven vehicles of this particular troop had backed their vehicles deep into the small forest to get the most available cover from the winter foliage. With their thirty-seven millimeter turret guns pointing outward and their .30 caliber, pintle mounted machine guns tilted skyward, they could give any opposition enough worry that they would choose to go elsewhere to pick a fight. It was just after the Troop had backed into the woods and had shut down their engines when they found Private Brem lying in the grass beneath a bullet scored tree trunk. After dismounting, some of the troop went out to inspect the stiffened corpses of the paratroopers while the troop leader and his noncommissioned officers squatted on the ground to have an orders group not twenty feet from where Walt lay. They assumed him dead, given the amount of blood and the nasty looking hole in his face but that all changed when he started to softly moan halfway through their operational meeting.

"Bloody hell," said the lanky Troop Lieutenant. "I rather think that Colonial chap is still alive, say what? Sergeant Mollins, do give him a prod and stick a bandage on him whilst I shout for some help."

A radio call went out and thirty minutes later a box ambulance with medics arrived to cart the lucky paratrooper away to a Battalion aid station where a fresh surgical team patched and stitched his smashed face and torn leg as best they could. Nothing fancy was ever performed at these aid stations - there simply wasn't enough time and the sheer volume alone could be daunting.

Stop the bleeding, stop the pain, prevent any further injury, tag them and then send them up the line for some intense treatment. The further from the battlefield a wounded soldier was taken would be a direct reflection on the degree of medical attention he would require. This was of course due to the obvious, logistical reasons; you don't set up a mobile hospital where it and its valuable medical staff might likely get bombed. It was here, at his first stop in a virtually demolished building that Private Brem drifted in and out of consciousness and realized for the first time that his attempt to kill himself had been bungled. Whether this was good or bad still remained to be seen.

There had been a lull in the fighting and all the wounded from the previous days had been transported to safer locations. The surgeon at this particular unit had some time so he stitched up the furrow in Walt's right leg then he deftly removed the nine-millimeter bullet using long forceps. Carefully, the Doctor followed the narrow furrow from the entry point to where the lead bullet lay at the lower back portion of Walt's skull. Self inflicted wounds would send a soldier straight to the brig once they had healed enough for a Court Martial. But the enemy round pulled from Private Brem's noggin would hardly cause a second glance, let alone foster any suspicions. The Doctor wrongly assumed that the paratrooper's chances for survival were slim, but he nonetheless forwarded him up the line for further treatment. Walt soon found himself bouncing around his litter as he was transported in the back of another box ambulance over a muddy road to a field hospital far from the front lines.

Located in a winter pasture on the outskirts of a French farming town, the olive drab tents of the field hospital is where a now cognizant Walt Brem received a little more in depth medical attention. Once he'd been anesthetized, a portion of the shattered cheekbone beneath his left eye was removed and the remaining edge of the bone filed down so it was smooth. The surgeon had feared infection so he had been meticulous when he had picked the bone splinters from the pulpy flesh. Lacking structured bone and with only soft tissue to now support his eyeball, the Doctor had saved the eye but his actions had allowed it to migrate to the geographical center of Walt's cheek. Heavily bandaged and riding a euphoric wave of morphine, it would be sometime before the injured man would see and feel the terrible implications of his desperate actions in the pine copse. Four days later, Walt Brem and dozens of other walking wounded were helped from their cots inside the large tents and walked out to a convoy of awaiting box ambulances. After being helped up through the back doors they sat on bench seats and chatted quietly, and smoked issue cigarettes while they were driven to a local airfield. From there they shuffled over to board a specially rigged, Catalina flying boat.

The aircraft had been painted white with large red crosses stenciled along the wings and fuselage; simple markings that would be respected by all pilots of the Axis forces. It sat perched on its tricycle landing gear, appearing ungainly as well as out of its elements, but once the gear was retracted up flush with the hull, the boat like bottom smoothed over and it became the graceful amphibian it was designed to be. The only thing that concerned Walt was another fire in one of the two engines and when he climbed aboard through the side door he asked the pilot about this but the pocked-faced Captain got all pissed and threw him a vicious scowl.

This goddamned war had made a lot of people irritable Walt thought as he found a seat by one of the windows.

The aircraft was soon rumbling down the dirt runway, climbing into the morning sky to fly west, quickly putting some distance between its towering tail section and the affliction that had become the European Theater of war. Three hours later the flying boat's hull kissed the flat waters of Dublin Bay on the East coast of Ireland. As the aircraft slowed, it wallowed as it plowed through the water toward a waiting motor launch and Walt craned his head around to look through one of the side bubbles. His exposed, good eye revealed a massive hospital ship at anchor in the distance. It too had been painted white and with a huge red cross on either side of the hull would assure an unmolested crossing of the Atlantic ocean. Behind the ship stood the sharp, symmetrical silhouettes of a city that had not been razed and bombed into depressing rubble of submission. Untouched, Dublin looked friendly and welcoming through the side doors of the aircraft and Walt could hear the seagulls as they sailed through the crisp air, crying out for food scraps, instantly drawing his mind back home to his own small island in the Pacific Northwest. As Walt waited to be helped from the Catalina he wept quietly, the tears soaking his bandages for it was then and there that he realized his part in the war was now truly finished. His personal suffering however was far from over for he would be carrying the marks of his contribution for many rears to come. He had still yet to see the damage to his face and once he did he would take to shaving without the use of a mirror. No man needed that kind of a reminder every morning for the rest of his life.

Once they had boarded the hospital ship, the soldiers were placed into expansive wards that were dimly lit but well ventilated as the open portholes on both sides allowed a steady flow of the clean, salt scented air. The next morning the vessel weighed anchor then followed the coastline south and then out into the open Atlantic. Despite some of Walt's ward mates missing entire limbs and many living with a constant, throbbing pain, the atmosphere on the ship became holiday like and not even the pompous, military protocol was going to spoil this voyage. Those patients who weren't ordered to bed rest or invalided would wander about the decks with their duffel coats draped over the pajamas they'd been issued. Outside they could enjoy the sunshine as they smoked or sat in pairs on huge rusting capstans while playing cards. The convalescing soldiers quickly realized they could stop casting a wary eye skyward for an approaching enemy fighter plane and the medical staff soon learned not to approach them unannounced and from their blind side.

Four days out into the Atlantic Ocean and Walt decided to take a peek at exactly what lay beneath his dressings. They had of course been changed several times by the nurses but he had never thought to seek out a mirror as they checked the stitches and the healing skin for any infection. The doctor's had warned him several times during these examinations that plastic surgery would be required as well as some skin grafting before his face could be restored - but it would never quite be the same.

"We're doctor's . . . not magicians," the last one had warned.

This comment about not being a magician set Walt to thinking so shortly after that particular bandage change he scurried off to the head to have a squint for himself. As he stood in front of one of the mirrors above the rows of sinks, he gingerly peeled back the white hospital tape that kept the bandages from slipping down his face. The gauzy material had been wrapped around his head, completely covering the whole left side including his cheek, and he carefully pulled it up with his fingers to expose the damaged portion. His left eye stung painfully, the eyesight dazzled as his fully dilated pupil became suddenly exposed to the bright, white light.

Walt let out a gasp and his body shuddered involuntarily as he glimpsed in the mirror at his face. His left eye appeared to now sit in the middle of his cheek, surrounded by angry red skin and numerous laces of black stitching. He couldn't stare for too long though because within seconds he had fainted, collapsing onto the tiled floor of the deck but not before driving his chin into the painted iron sink. This created another lovely gash, opening the skin, which further managed to enhance his already botched appearance. This was probably a good thing for during that brief peek at what remained of his once smooth, innocent mug, Walt Brem fully understood that he would never be dating Prom Queens like Sally Thornby again. Nor even girls that remotely looked like her. Walt's mother had preached to him as a lad that good looks were only skin-deep, but that adage didn't hold for much on a hospital ship in the mid Atlantic. Those beauty and the beast fairy tales were written for the simple reason that they were fairy tales; relegated to the dreams of young girls where they rightfully belonged. Within that brief period of ruthless discovery, Walt embraced a serious consideration about throwing himself overboard into the cold waves of the Atlantic Ocean. He wouldn't have been the first badly wounded, misshapen and forlorn soldier to go missing from a hospital ship.

But splitting his chin wide open would be another one of life's flukes, a chance accident that would offer Walt an unwanted alternative, something that in the end would help secure his existence for a very uncertain future. He was found moments later by a burly orderly who carried him back to the ward where a doctor stitched up his chin and wrongly assumed that the fainting spell had something to do with possible head trauma suffered from the bullet wound. This doctor ordered Walt moved to a secure ward where his movement would be severely restricted unless he had an escort, as well he would be under constant observation. The doctor didn't want Private Brem passing out in any more unsightly places such as the communal washrooms. The Army Medical Corps with its ninety-six percent patient survival rate hadn't brought the wounded paratrooper this far to have him crack his head open in a ships toilet and do himself further damage.

There was already enough work involved with the plastic surgery they had planned, which entailed numerous operations and long hours of painful recovery so they could have done without any additional mutilation to their charge's face. This action unintentionally put an effective damper on any plans Walt may have harbored about going for a fatal swim. The only cold water he would see for the rest of the journey would be delivered to him in a glass by a rather large but friendly orderly. A good thing in the end, for our hero would not be able to leave the ship until it docked in a large city on the Eastern Seaboard eight days later, and even then he was escorted down a long gangway to an awaiting bus. The next time Walt Brem saw any deep, cold water, it would be the friendly, constantly moving tides of the Pacific Northwest . . . and he would not be alone when he once again beheld those clear waters.

*　　*　　*

Chapter Thirty-three

The Veteran's hospital was, and still is a three-story brownstone sited at the end of a quiet street in a small city in the lap of one of the Great Lakes. Most buildings in the region were constructed of stone, or brick and mortar as suitable timber for building was much more prevalent and indigenous to the west. Although the shores of the lake were a few miles to the west of the hospital grounds, those patients who were fit enough to wander the asphalt paths that took them through the leaf bare poplar trees could feel its biting wind as it blew through the corridors of the city. Many patients would be confined to the hospital when summer arrived, and they would suffer none to gladly the humid, stifling air as it wafted in from the lakes surface like a moist breath. Walt Brem had arrived at the hospital during the last winter of the war in Europe, a time of year, which many agreed was more tolerable than the long days of summer. But more importantly, he arrived four months before Lieutenant Grace Looby had been set to receive her military discharge.

Grace was one of the nurses who worked on the ward where they had placed Walt. All the wards within the hospital were long, wide rooms that had rows of beds running the length of each wall with baths and toilets located at the far end. These rooms could easily have been an army barracks except the walls were painted white, there were no lockers or barrack boxes and the blankets on the beds were a gentle blue color. With as many as twenty-five soldiers on the mend in any one of these wards, it would be a good place to muster together the remnants of one's health. Here, all the patients naturally bonded having first hand knowledge of the horrors of war. The hospital was quiet and somewhat sane but more importantly, it was located at least a world away from the bombing, the screaming, and the filth of the European battlefields. And then there was Lieutenant Looby's warm smile and endless cheer as she moved around the ward during her shift, attending to her list of never ending duties. At least a few times a day she would be required to take many of her patients temperatures - a reading she would obtain by inserting the applicable thermometer in to which ever end had suffered the least amount of damage. If she wasn't recording temperatures, then she was taking blood pressure or emptying bedpans or answering the many questions that flew her way and she did all of this with a winsome smile on her face. Not too bad for a Commissioned Army Officer. It would be her smile that caught Private Brem's attention and not the gold bars on the shoulders of her white nursing uniform. She would first notice his candid innocence and how much he differed from the rest of the loud, horny pack of wounded soldiers. For if they weren't comatose or hadn't lost their peckers to a landmine they had one thing on their mind and it involved one of the nurses and a few minutes in a toilet stall. In this war, the draft board had gone for quantity and not necessarily quality.

However, the teenaged man who occupied the seventh bed on the left was very much different from the rest and it would be his simple demeanor that would separate him from the herd. The first time Grace had approached his bed with her wheeled trolley laden with medical instruments she found a man both unique and sincere. She had taken his pulse and blood pressure, recording both readings on the chart that had hung at the foot of his bed on a clipboard. Grace then took a mercury filled thermometer from a row of slender tubes that lay on a thick bed of gauze atop a tray then shook it vigorously. As she leaned over to insert the instrument into Walt's mouth he hesitated, appearing unsure as to what she was doing.

"That ain't been up somebody's ass has it Ma'am?" Walt asked quietly.

Grace was about to scold the soldier for his language and ignorance when she looked down at him and saw that his question was serious, his face appearing child like and full of genuine distress. Her smile quickly returned when she noticed his worry and his heavily bandaged face.

"No soldier," she reassured, "we're very careful to keep the oral thermometers separated from the rectal ones and they are all properly sterilized before each use."

Grace knew Walt's history quite well from his chart - the young man who would be requiring a few sessions of plastic surgery to take a deformed face and make it appear less distorted.

Although no one including the surgeon would be holding their breath. Plastic surgery, a discipline now over two-thousand-years-old, still had many bounds to go so the prognosis discussed by the Doctors who reviewed the chart at the nurses' station didn't sound very heart lifting. One of the resident Psychiatrists had been seeing Walt on a daily basis, laying the groundwork for the difficult adjustment period that lay ahead for their patient. Inexplicably, Grace had become instantly charmed with the compact man who was both quiet and polite and like millions of other people could have done without the tragedies of a world at war. And despite his own injuries and depressed state of mind, Walt felt a strange chemistry whenever he gazed over to admire this dedicated nurse. She was about the same height as him, with a round face and a smooth complexion that highlighted her vibrant, brown eyes. Her chestnut colored hair was long and curly when it wasn't pinned up under her white cap and her build was decidedly roly-poly. Or full-figured if you wished to be polite and mindful of other peoples feelings. A few years older than Walt, Grace had led a basically sedate life because of her physical size, unable to fit the vogue fashions of an era where slim had become the ultimate institution and big boned was to be outright ignored or ridiculed. After finishing high school she had consequently directed all her time and energy into her nursing studies while those around her socialized on the weekends and went out on dates. Sock hops and watching the submarine races while parked at lovers' lane could be found nowhere on Grace's Looby's social resume. She had enlisted during the latter part of the war in hopes of at least expanding her mind by seeing another part of the world. Her first and last posting after Officer's Basic Training would be the Veterans Hospital with its scrubby lawns and plain rooms. But within those walls there now lay her key to a long and fulfilling future.

It would be because of Lieutenant Looby's figure that the majority of the healing soldiers on the ward would save their hubba-hubba's for the slender, more attractive nurses. They would leave Grace and her effortless smile unmolested for the enjoyment of the more reserved patients like Walt Brem to fully appreciate. Grace had already resigned herself to the cruel fact that she would never be asked out by any virile looking movie star types, and even though she shouldn't have thought this way she nonetheless did. People will be people and no amount of reassurances about beauty being on the inside will change that bleak fact. With that said Grace soon started to look forward to her daily rounds as she enjoyed the conversations with the honest paratrooper who'd had part of his face shot away with a bullet. She had changed the dressing enough times to observe the damage. She'd seen first hand what a well-meaning front line surgeon had left behind when he had removed a portion of Walt's cheekbone to prevent any infection. Grace Looby was by no means a plastic surgeon but she knew enough about medicine to know that the plastic surgeon at best would only be able to smooth over the horrible mess. Conversely, Walt already knew that if he was to ever marry and enjoy a normal life it would be with someone he had met *after* he had shot himself. No high school sweetheart that he knew back on the island would look at him now.

A week or so before Walt was to begin his series of reconstructive surgery, his relationship with Lieutenant Looby had already started to flourish but in an innocent enough fashion. Within that secretive consciousness where crushes and first loves are usually generated, flames had already been kindled inside of them. So a small part of Grace's daily routine easily set the scene to allow for its comfortable fruition. With the war still running at full throttle there lay a shortage of capable men to call upon to work the Nations industries and hospital care would be no different. The shortage of orderlies shifted some of the burden onto the nurses and this, combined with the Doctors prescription for fresh air brought the two together as naturally as a hummingbird to a summer flower. Grace started escorting Walt on his daily walks around the hospital grounds and the physical contact came under the wonderful guise of a nurse's practical care.

She would assist him as he got into his duffel coat and with herself properly bundled against the chill air they would venture out to the grounds and enjoy the colors of a Midwest winter. Grace would loop her arm through Walt's and with her other hand pressed reassuringly against his forearm, there could be no possibility of him tripping because of his wounded leg or blind eye. They would walk over the crunchy brown grass as innocent looking as the rest of the patients who required escorts, breathing the cold clear air, numbing as it touched their teeth when they spoke their easy words. Walt found Grace's touch comforting as they walked and his arm seemed to tingle where she lightly grasped him and when the wind was light and from the right direction he could inhale her delicate scent. Her light musk caused him a healthy excitement, something he hadn't appreciated or felt in quite some time. In return, Grace received a heartfelt respect and some witty conversation from a disfigured but honorable man who had every right to wonder just where it was in this screwed up world he might eventually fit. This would be their common link; two people concerned they may be shunned by a society where physical looks counted for a lot if you had any hopes of running with a crowd. Neither one of them were much for running with crowds and this only enhanced the instinctual pull that brought them together. When they walked they spoke of everything from steamed crabs and country fairs to the Pacific Northwest and the natural intoxication brought about by living there. Grace had never ventured any further than a thousand miles in any direction from her home, not even for Nursing School and Army basic training, but Walt's island home sounded every bit like a beckoning Utopia.

Within weeks Grace started to plan her schedule so she could be available to escort Walt for his walks and no one seemed to notice this nor would they have cared. Both of them looked forward to the pleasures of these walks and the wondrous thing about all of this was that they now truly realized that attraction could indeed be born from within, and this would be all that mattered to Grace and Walt. Her friendship also put to rest any plans Walt may have had about jumping into any fast moving and very deep rivers. But more importantly was the fact that he wouldn't be alone when all the plastic surgery was completed. When the bandages were removed to reveal either a medical masterpiece or a cruel aberration - whichever way one chose to view it - Grace would be there for him and she'd already told him this.

Walt had his very own personal cheering section once the surgery began and life couldn't get any better than that. Not when he would climb from the confusing depths of anesthesia to find Grace's smiling face close by in the ward. She would come to his bed within minutes but it was all-professional as she took his temperature and checked his pulse, which probably raced as her warm fingers held his wrist. Walt was now hurting at both ends for they were grafting skin from the smooth globes of his buttocks to use as patches on his face and all this could best be described in his own words as "a real pain in the ass."

The first order of business was to completely smooth out the skull where the field surgeon had removed the fragmented cheek bone. Normally they could build on this missing piece of skull by grafting and shaping a piece of rib or a part of the pelvic bone but this kind of reconstructive surgery was usually reserved for the rich and famous paying high prices to private clinics. A sad social comment to be certain, but Walt Brem was a Private in the care of the Department of Veterans Affairs. This amounted to dedicated and relatively skilled plastic surgeons retained on monthly salaries, who hoped at best to obtain acceptable results. It would be a band-aid solution meant to inspire the wounded servicemen more than it was to reinstate any good looks. The effort was made however, and it was made with all sincerity and just who the hell could criticize that.

Next the surgeons had to purposefully "rough up his face" to the point that it became a raw, weeping injury so the new section of skin from his buttocks would readily adhere to the new site. Once they had removed a partial thickness of an epidermal patch from Walt's smooth and hairless backside, they would place this layer of skin over the roughed up portion on the left side of the cheek, just under the eye. At first, the grafts were nourished by the serum that oozed from the roughed up tissue, but in time they would regenerate by feeding from the capillaries that thrived in the healthy skin. These operations were conducted several times until the surgeons were satisfied with the thickness of the regenerated skin, carefully monitoring the process until the patches had completely grafted onto their new home. If Walt wasn't recovering from surgery or being pushed around the hospital grounds by Grace in a wheelchair, he would be nursing his sore face and ass while entering into long, private discussions with the resident Psychiatrist. It would be here, during these quiet hours in the sun filled room on the other side of the hospital that the thought provoking exchanges would demonstrate to the young soldier that the feelings he'd taken away from the war were perfectly normal. The Psychiatrist also prepared Walt to help deal with his disfigured face but not to the point that Grace Looby would ultimately take him.

Days after his final session with the plastic surgeon the bandages came of so the air could speed the healing process. To say the end result was thing of beauty would be an outright lie. Even though the surgeons had made great progress in removing some of the divots, Walt would definitely have drawn less attention had he lost a limb or two. Living during a period of time and in a society that still regarded Black people as something other than human was a terrible social comment, an atmosphere that assured Walt Brem and his botched face years of open contempt. But where Walt considered himself a physical disaster, Grace saw a uniqueness now highlighted by these special features, particularly when she combined this with the uncomplicated personality that dwelled just beneath the damaged face. Walt's eye hadn't relocated to the center of his cheek despite the fact that it certainly appeared that way. The missing cheekbone caused the left side of the face to collapse around the eyeball and just below it lay a large but new triangular patch of skin as smooth and as glossy as a frosted light bulb. The edges of the triangle were white and acute where they had knitted to the surrounding tissue and when Grace managed to get him laughing, the tears would flow uncontrollably over the polished plot of skin. Within days Walt realized he couldn't cover up the spot with a beard, as no facial hair would grow there so with just the one side to drag a razor across he stopped using a mirror for this morning ritual. Very soon he took to avoiding mirrors entirely, much the way an arachnid phobia would detour from a translucent web with a fat spider suspended in the center.

On the day of his nineteenth birthday, Walt was given a day pass to leave the hospital grounds and the Psychiatrist thought a day on the town would be a hurdle he best get over much sooner than later. As he put on his khaki dress uniform in the change cubicle at the end of the ward he wished Grace had been working that day. He needed her warm, cherubic face to encourage him in this lonely venture, these first steps into a world where there were no bombs exploding or bullets flying but where there stood the critical eyes of an insensitive public. Once Walt had buttoned up his brown dress tunic, he left the cubicle with his duffel coat over his arm then left the sanctity of the ward for the stairwell. In the main foyer downstairs he signed out after showing the sentry his leave pass and service identification. Beside the main entrance doors to the hospital stood a full-length mirror that allowed departing servicemen to check their dress before leaving the building. Walt avoided his reflection altogether as he pulled his forge cap onto his head then walked through the double doors and down the steps, hesitantly following the side walk to the front gates.

The morning was cold despite the clear skies and the sun had already completed its short ascent toward its zenith. It was the kind of morning when a young soldier, alive and home from a catastrophic war should be glad to be alive and looking for inspiration to the paths that lay before him. This certainly was the feeling that flowed through Walt's senses as he showed his pass to the military policeman at the main gates. He almost marched, happy for the first time in weeks as he moved in the direction of the tree lined avenue that led to the bricked buildings of the city's downtown area. Half way downtown and Walt had already noticed that very few people offered him any more than a passing nod as they walked by him on the sidewalk. Most of these were young mother's pushing strollers - some with toddlers clinging tenaciously to their long, wool coats. Nearly all able-bodied men were either fighting the war or working in the factories that fed the gargantuan effort, so there was very few of them to make comment. Only the toddlers looked at him with their large blinking eyes, their innocent scrutiny's borne from the stories of the bogey men and the trolls that lurk in the darkness under every child's bed. What Walt failed to realize at the time was that the majority of the towns folk were used to seeing scarred and badly disfigured soldiers wandering the streets of their city. Another young soldier with a face that looked as if someone had run a lawnmower over it was no longer a novelty.

The open ridicule as well as the revulsion would come soon enough, once he had returned to his island home. There, everybody knew him so it would become their inherent right to offer their verbal critiques and simple-minded scoffing. But that would all come later on. For now, Walt had become emboldened with this initial testing of the waters so he decided to visit some shops once he'd wandered further into the city's core. Hopefully he could find a suitable gift to take home to his parent's on the island. His mother had been extremely supportive of him in her weekly letters.

It was surprising how efficient the postal service could be when there weren't any eruptive front lines to courier the precious mail through. She knew all about his hideous wounds because Walt had described them to her in a letter the Psychiatrist had urged him to write home. A job at the hardware store as well as his inheritance to the business awaited him upon his return. The old truism about "having a face only your parents could love" certainly resounded loudly in this particular situation. The only other order of business planned for his short furlough was to find a restaurant that served greasy hamburgers with hillocks of french fries and rich brown gravy. Army, and Army hospital food had been Walt's fare for much too long and he salivated just thinking of something other than powdered eggs and instant mashed potatoes.

As he walked slowly among the red-bricked buildings of a tidy city that restricted the erection of any structure over four stories, he eventually found the café that would cater to his culinary yearnings. Walt stood on the sidewalk and peered through the steamy windows, taking in the booths that lined both walls with the required jukebox standing brightly in one corner. The odors from the deep fryer floated out onto the street, the hearty smell of fried sausage calling to him like a beckoning wisp. Walt decide then and there that a late breakfast followed by a much later lunch would do his soul some much needed good, and as he walked over to the door he heard a familiar voice.

"A home cooked meal would taste much better. That I can promise you."

He turned to see Lieutenant Looby standing in front of the antique store located next to the restaurant. Walt had seen a woman looking at the knickknacks on the shelf through the stenciled lettering on the window but he hadn't paid her much attention. Grace stood dressed in a long coat with pants to keep the chill from her legs and she looked warm, soft, and every bit like the woman she was. She looked altogether friendly, far away from her starched skirt and nursing smock with the gold bars affixed to her shoulders. She had gloves on her hands and carried a box-like Brownie camera clutched to her front and she readily admonished Walt with a smile when he accepted her offer of a meal, then called her "Lootenant."

He considered this chance meeting a bit of good luck for he really liked the woman. Walt had never felt such comfort around someone before and her being a nurse had nothing to do with it. Moreover, this hadn't been a chance meeting, even though it had been meant to happen right from the very start. Finding a soldier on a day pass with a healing face while dressed in uniform was detective work of the simplest order. Grace had known days ago about Walt's pass and every soldier who left the hospital for the first time always sought out a diner for some real food and then a bar to fortify his sorrows. After that most of them would stagger over to the local whorehouse. Walt wasn't the drinking type as well he would be the last person found in a whorehouse, so tracking him down hadn't been much of a challenge for Grace. One might condemn her behavior, saying it a bit straightforward for a lady living in a time where social rules were quite strict. But she knew enough about life to know that the spoils usually went to those with the audacity to dare. As for fraternizing with a Private, this bothered Grace not in the least - not with a few months to go until her discharge and not with this friendship having already passed several awkward milestones. They came together, and chatted and walked in the direction of a nearby park where tamed ducks had lost the instinct to fly elsewhere for their winter foraging.

For years the locals had taken to hand feeding the birds bread and roasted peanuts and the need to join any kind of a migration had become a distant memory. Grace threaded her arm through Walt's as she did when she walked with him on the hospital grounds and the couple looked as natural as two youngsters on a sandy beach.

As Private Brem walked with Grace he felt a warmth simmering inside of him and all thoughts and nightmares of the terrible war seemed to be whisked away on the lightly blowing wind. He couldn't have known it back then, but Grace Looby would be the single most positive factor to helping Walt accept his disfigurement; steps he had to take if he were to have any hope of moving on with his life. The park they entered had a lake that lay in the geographical center of the town and to say the least it had become a picture, bordered on three sides by well-kept houses. But first they had stopped at a corner store to purchase a bag of roasted peanuts before crossing the street to wander through the tall maple trees that gave the park its name. The lake had a sheet of ice that reached out from the entire shoreline for at least twenty feet where it gave way to the deeper water that refused to freeze. As Grace and Walt approached the sandy shore a flock of Mallards forgot all about their dabbling in the water and moved quickly in the direction of the twosome. They knew that where people stood, there would be an abundance of food and the couple laughed as the ducks skidded gracelessly over the surface of the ice with their webbed feet.

There were both males and females in the gaggle, and they quacked excitedly, stretching their necks as Grace and Walt offered them the warm peanuts. The males, with their iridescent green heads were both pushy and aggressive as they chased the intimidated females away from the proffered fodder. But the lake was one of Grace's favorite places and she had been here before on countless occasions, so she knew how to play the feeding game. The greedy males were easily defeated with a simple tactic. Grace would now demonstrate this slick move to Walt, who stood enraptured at her side, holding the peanut bag. She cast a handful of peanuts out onto the ice and the female Mallards - marked with their mottled gray plumage - scattered and slipped out to get their fair share while the males remained staunchly at her feet, being fed from the other hand. Both sets of ducks were fed in this manner and Walt soon observed that the females were getting much more food than the males. While the males still pushed and fought as they gathered around his feet, Walt couldn't help but ponder if the same irony couldn't be applied to the misery of the war. He soon chased the thoughts away for there would be no considerations given to the war – not today, and not while he stood there with Grace.

When the peanuts were all gone Walt stuffed the empty bag into the pocket of his duffel coat and the couple moved on, now holding hands despite the cold. As the ducks quacked loudly in protest, Walt realized he had just experienced one of those special times that are hoped to occur in everyone's life but seldom do. One of those exceptional spells that you wished would never end but they always did. Although when they did end you could always take them away with you in your minds eye, a memory you could pull out, something to make you smile whenever you felt the need. The couple walked over the grass, away from the lake and stopped when they came to a bronze statue that stood on a round, concrete base near the edge of the park.

It was a memorial erected in tribute to the seamen who had died while shipping a nation's wares across the immense and weather ravaged waters of the great lakes. Standing twice as high as a normal man, the bronze figure depicted a sailor standing at a ships wheel. He leaned forward into an invisible wind, dressed in a slicker with a wide brimmed southwester capping his long curls. Oxidized to a bluish-green, the helmsman had one hand gripped firmly to the wheel of the imaginary ship as he pointed with his other hand, his index finger fully extended over the compass binnacle mounted to the front of the spoked wheel. A square plaque riveted into the base of the statue had raised lettering that simply read "The Rescue."

Grace and Walt stood and admired the monument even though Grace had seen it a dozen times before. It made Walt speculate as to whether a grateful nation would ever erect such memorials for those who had died in the war he had so recently left behind. As he stood reflecting this, Grace had stopped a young black mother with a pair of tots in tow. She politely asked the mother to take a picture of her and Walt using the Brownie camera. They stood under the reaching arm of the bronzed mariner and smiled contentedly, holding hands as the mother held the camera in front of her chest, gazing down through the square lens mounted on the top. She clicked the photograph, capturing the happy poise for eternity in what would become a scalloped edged, grainy black and white picture. Grace thanked the mother who then returned to her tots and she and Walt continued their walk, crossing the street and returning once again to the appeasing hustle of the city.

They made only four brief stops before going to Grace's apartment. The first place was a Ma and Pa jewelry store owned by an attentive old couple who didn't care if you purchased anything as long as you spent some time to chat with them over the display cases. Grace helped Walt pick out a cameo broach made from white coral. It was surrounded with delicate gold fluting and it would look pleasing once pinned to his mothers dress. A pocket watch with a tiny latch was chosen for his father and both gifts cost nearly forty-dollars. This amounted to a couple of months of service pay but Walt had plenty of money. There hadn't been many places to spend it while on the battlefield and he had refused to gamble with the other soldiers. Four doors down from the jeweler stood a butcher store that didn't have too much to offer because of the war rationing. Grace picked out two thick pork chops that the Butcher wrapped in brown paper, paying the man before Walt could get his money out. He sensed that arguing about the chivalrous notion of paying for the food would be futile - especially in a world where it had become fashionable for women to wear pants due to a shortage of rayon and silk stockings. He did however offer to carry the package, which was accepted with a smile. A couple of blocks further down the street was a grocer who had a limited but fresh supply of vegetables. Grace picked out several dark skinned russets and a handful of carrots that the shopkeeper placed in a paper bag. The last stop had been a bakery where Grace purchased two cup cakes with chocolate icing and a fresh loaf of white bread.

They walked quietly the few blocks to Grace's apartment, enjoying the afternoon sunshine and Walt felt like bursting every time he glanced over to admire the clean complexion of Grace's round face. Someone, somewhere, as of recent, had been smiling down upon him, that much he was now certain of. Walt had played his hand against incredible odds, only to be delivered from a lethal caldron then returned from one side of the world to meet someone like Grace. The time had come to look to the future and to stop entertaining anymore foolish thoughts about ending it all. For if Walt gleaned anything from this delightful day it was the fact there still existed hope, even for a mutilated young man. These were his very thoughts as they entered the back alley that took them to Grace's apartment. The entrance stood at the top of a flight of wooden stairs, leading to several suites built above a downtown variety store. At the top a landing fronted all the suites, running the full length to serve as a balcony where the tenants could enjoy the fresh air during the humid months of summer. Grace shared her furnished apartment with a civilian nurse who worked at the General Hospital across town. She could have taken quarters at the Military Hospital but her Officer's Commission granted her the privilege of living elsewhere.

Once inside, Walt found a suite that was sparsely appointed with plain but functional furniture. The dining area featured a table with chairs made from chromed tubing with yellow vinyl coverings and the tiny living room was nearly overwhelmed with a fabric covered chesterfield and matching chair. One main room formed the living, dining and kitchen areas with perimeter doors that led to the bedrooms and the bathroom. The whole place had a feminine ambience to it, further enhanced by the lace doilies placed on the coffee table and over the arms of the furniture. Being single and living in an age of celibacy before matrimony, Grace was taking a chance by inviting Walt into her suite without a chaperon. But she cared not, for the worst she could suffer would be some vindictive gossip by the intrusive neighbors. A pittance when compared with what she had seen and heard while working a hospital ward that contained a steady supply of wounded soldiers. Walt sat on the chesterfield after he had given Grace his duffel coat and he gazed out the front window that looked out onto the back alley. In the distance a flock of seagulls circled, white and gray dots against the blue sky, soaring above the nearby shores of the Great Lake. Grace hung a brightly printed apron over her neck and after tying it around her waist, went into the kitchen area to prepare the meal.

They talked effortlessly as Grace butterflied the pork chops then fried them in a cast iron pan on an old gas stove. She quickly peeled the potatoes and the carrots then got them boiling in separate pots and the smell of frying meat reminded Walt of his mothers kitchen back home. Within half an hour the meal was on the table and they sat down to enjoy the hearty fare. The mashed potatoes were creamy and delicious and the carrots sweet and glistening with a coating of melted butter. Grace had cut the loaf of bread into thick slices and as they ate they smiled quietly at each other.

Walt realized then and there that he'd probably found something he hadn't even been looking for. Grace Looby's smile was comforting and attractive and as he ate his dinner he knew inside that this relationship would be going someplace reassuring. She knew it too, especially when his face glowed like a child when she put the cupcakes on the table then wished him a happy birthday. It would be one of the kindest things any girl had ever done for him, for Walt himself had forgotten hours ago the true meaning of this special day.

After the meal they drank coffee with real cream and talked about the homes they had left behind. Grace had been a service brat, her father a flying instructor at an Air Base in the south, and one military base with its married quarters was much the same as any other. Army, Navy or Air, they were all unremarkable with their white painted rocks and unappealing, featureless buildings. When Walt again spoke of his home in the Pacific Northwest, the conversation quickly became focused on the island and Grace clung to every word as he described the coniferous forests, the rolling hills and the clean breaking surf. She had never given thought to living on an island before, thinking only of palm trees, straw huts, desert sands and half naked aborigines. Walt's picture of island life was much more appealing with its cedar sided cottages, gravel roads and Sunday afternoons spent at the local farmer's market. When they had finished at the table Walt helped with the dishes and his lack of familiarity with basic kitchen skills became the brunt of some well-intentioned humor. They both laughed as Grace took a wet plate from his hands then demonstrated the proper method of drying it with a tea towel.

Far too quickly, the day had come to an end, its demise governed by the time that had been typed on Walt's leave pass. If he hoped for more days like this one, he must return to the hospital on time. They said goodbye at the door and Walt left with the promise of another day pass and a matinee movie the following weekend. As he walked the downtown streets under the cold twilight of an early evening, Walt considered his good luck as well as the overwhelming chances of running into Grace during his first day downtown. He never did suspect a conspiracy by the nurse to find him that cold morning when he had left the hospital, nor would he know the truth until over a half century later when the couple would each trade a life long secret as Grace lay dying from ovarian cancer.

Their meeting on a cold street in a city where wounded soldiers were sent to heal themselves put into motion the last variables needed to bring the two together. This uncomplicated, teenaged man with the ruined face considers this 'chance' meeting in the coming weeks as something extraordinary. Just as he would soon come to accept what he done to himself with the captured pistol in the pine copse while surrounded by men who were just as desperate as himself. There, he had full intentions of taking away a life and in his failure he had unwittingly blessed his own and that of one other.

Private Walter Brem had survived one of the most devastating wars ever started by mankind and that alone had to be an accomplishment; particularly in a conflict where millions of others had perished. During the next few weeks Walt would finally come to terms with the consequences of his own actions, as well he would put behind him the reality of what should have happened back in that bleak forest.

He should have died - is what *really* should have happened.

It would only be then that he would make great strides toward becoming whole again. Best of all, he was not alone when he started that long walk to a full recovery. Something good had emerged from Walt Brem's predicament; a redemption of sorts, as well as something he could hold and cherish for nearly a lifetime.

Walt and Grace had become perfect for each other.

Two imperfect people, brought together in an imperfect world, and absolutely nothing bad could come from that.

*   *   *

Chapter Thirty-four

When Walt Brem departed the Veteran's Hospital near the Great Lake he took three very important gifts with him - a new bride, a will to live life to its fullest, and a Purple Heart medal. Grace Brem also gained many wonderful things but to do so she had to leave behind her Army Commission and her maiden name as well as any reservations she may have held about herself. Nearly two months to the day after they'd fed the mallards in the park, Grace and Walt became husband and wife. It all happened during a ceremony in front of a Justice of the Peace in an office located within the marbled walls of the city hall. There were no bridesmaids nor a best man or any witnesses other than the Justice, but that detracted nothing from the true meaning of their avowed union.

Walt and Grace genuinely loved each other and only wished to spend the rest of their lives together so they dispensed with all the flowery pageantries that marked traditional nuptials. More to the point, neither one could afford a big splashy wedding with a foot long guest list, besides they didn't know that many people in the first place. Both wore their dress uniforms to the occasion and once everything became legal, Walt performed the noble custom of carrying Grace across the threshold of their apartment above the variety store. They still did traditional things like that back then but the undertaking became touch and go as Walt's wounded leg was still weak where the bullet from the Panther tank had torn through his muscle. In spite of this, Walt performed the chivalrous deed even though it didn't appear from a distance as an altogether elegant act. It did bring smiles to the newlyweds' faces and that's all that really mattered.

Grace's roommate had vacated days ago to take up residence at the hospital, leaving the couple to gasp and giggle on their wedding night as they played on the old double bed in the back room. Two days after the wedding Walt took his discharge from the Army, but not before he had marched into the Hospital Commandant's office to receive his medal. He had worn his dress uniform for that occasion as well, but he felt a bit of a phony when the Colonel shook his hand then presented him the Purple Heart for being wounded in combat. Walt reassured himself as the Colonel thanked him for his patriotic sacrifices, for he most certainly had been wounded in combat. By his own hand and with an enemy pistol - but regardless, still wounded and on a battlefield. Some things in life are best left alone he eventually decided - left to appear as they should, and the incident in the pine forest would be one such event. Like most other humans who walked through life Walt now held his own timeless secret and it would remain such until the day he told someone. Grace continued her nursing duties at the Veterans Hospital, taking the bus to work everyday while Walt managed to find employment at a nearby lumberyard. The owner didn't consider him much for the customer's to look at with his face all buggered up, but he was relatively fit and had a good working knowledge regarding the hardware end of the business. So he hired him and six days of the week Walt walked to and from work with the lunch Grace had made for him the night before. When their days off coincided - which became a consistent rarity - they would walk to the park to visit and feed the ducks.

Very soon, Lieutenant Grace Brem took her discharge from the Army and quite happily made the transition to Missus Brem, civilian wife of Mister Walter Brem. The time had now come to leave the town and transit clear across the country to Walt's home in the Pacific Northwest. They had very few effects to take with them, fitting all their belongings into a couple of steamer trunks and the only thing they left behind were memories and a forwarding address for their military pension cheques. Walt's parents were aware of the changes in their son's life and had made all the preparations, having redecorated his attic bedroom in anticipation of the arrival of their new daughter-in-law. Gone were the hotrod magazines and baseball pennants and up went the lilac paint, lace curtains and four-poster double bed with the patchwork, down filled quilt. To say that Walt's parents were overjoyed would not have been an exaggeration. Not only was their only child returning home from the war, but he was also bringing with him the daughter they never had. On the day of Walt and Grace's arrival the elderly Brem's got dressed in the best clothes they could find in their closets then drove the family station wagon over to the mainland.

The reunion on the platform at the train station was an affair both joyous and awkward. Mister and Missus Brem were meeting a total stranger who had just joined the family as well their Walt had changed both inside as well as outside. His face now hideous, this made for some very clumsy greetings but the change in Walt's personality became an unexpected treat; no longer stood the sensitive, fidgety young son who used to react in desperate ways to the uncertain world around him. Returned was a married man who behaved with confidence, someone who accepted what he had been through - even emerging somewhat appreciative of his present circumstances. Once the hugs and handshakes had been dispensed with, the men loaded the steamer trunks into the back of the station wagon and the return trip to the island became a happy, family outing. The Brem's were soon enchanted with their daughter-in-law, falling into easy conversation with her as if she'd been a dear friend while Walt held her hand in the back seat. Aboard the ferry they ate sandwiches in the sunshine on the outer deck and Grace felt like a child at a country fair. After the picnic lunch she walked the open decks with her husband, watching a habitat that thrived in clean air and clear waters. This was a place far from any sprawling industry, impeding skyscrapers, and large population densities. As they stood at the rail, Walt pointed out the surrounding islands of the Gulf as the vessel moved past them at a steady fourteen knots but Grace forgot the whimsical names the moment they rolled from his tongue.

Once the ferry had docked they drove down the loading ramp and Grace kept her eyes to the windows and felt warm and intense when she realized the island world she had just entered could only get better the more of it she beheld. There were more bicycles than vehicles moving over the quiet roads and in a lot of the fields there grew orchards - their rows of fruit trees uniform and already starting to blossom. Rocky cliffs formed the foundation of the island's stubby mountain range, capped with its lone peak to the south. Native arbutus trees with their red peeling bark grew defiantly around the base in the soil that spotted the rock shale. As far as Grace would care to look in any direction stood countless green smudges of pine forests, amber meadows, and wave washed beaches. Grace had never seen anything like it, having spent most of her life on military bases. As she gazed around she realized she'd found a cornucopia of ideality. She wasn't sure just what excited her more, the man she recently married, or the island he had just brought her to.

After they had parked the station wagon at the end of the long gravel driveway the two women entered the multistoried white clapboard house while Walt and Mister Brem went for one of those father/son strolls around the property. Missus Brem proudly walked Grace through the comfortable, lived in rooms that would make up her new home and the pair talked and laughed, like sisters sharing secrets. Walt and his father entered a forest where the ruins of a tree house Walt had built years ago stood rotting high above the forest floor. They talked a bit about the war as well as the changes that had occurred on the island during Walt's absence. His old girlfriend

Sally Thornby, the one who had so cruelly spurned him on main street in what seemed like a decade past had been killed in a boating accident. She had taken to running with the athletic, disgustingly handsome son of one of the islands richest families. They were part-time residents with enough money to buy all the toys required to move fast and foolishly over both road and water. Sally and the rich boy had left one early evening in a cabin cruiser out of Balford, having throttled the vessel onto a full plane before they had even left the confines of the harbor.

Witnesses said the vessel tore off into the darkness without its red and green running lights
on - a dangerous practice in the days before readily available marine radar. Their naked bodies were washed up onto the shore the following morning as well as bits of wooden flotsam. The Ferry Captain who had commanded the last sailing to the mainland the previous evening had noted a muffled thump at mid channel. He had entered the event into his logbook on the bridge and he and his First Officer had erroneously concluded their eight hundred and fifty-tonne vessel had struck a deadhead. As his father told of Sally's death, Walt felt sadness instead of joy, something of a puzzle for when she had first dumped him, he could have cheerfully have shot her. The war, and all the killing he had been forced to do on the battlefields had indeed mellowed him.

Within days the newlyweds settled into the dawdling lifestyle of island routine, not surprisingly, Grace found she rather liked it. Walt returned to work with his Father at the hardware store. There, the smell of linseed oil, paints, and moist lumber, as well as the sound of the squeaky floor joists touched all his senses with their comforting familiarity. Grace took a job as a day nurse at the small hospital in Skinny's Reach, located just a block from the Hardware store. They walked together everyday to their jobs, rain or shine, while Walt's aging father preferred to drive the car. On the weekends they would explore the island on bicycles and if it rained Grace would help Missus Brem with canning or other domestic chores while Walt and his Father sat in the living room listening to the ball games on the Motorola. Their lives became routine but happy and nothing overtly eventful happened which at times can be a good thing.

The only blight would be the open contempt and senseless torment Walt endured from some of the islander's who felt it their place to comment about his deformed face. This kind of behavior turned into an oft talked about incident one day when Walt had been sorting wooden pickaxe handles into an oak barrel on the boardwalk in front of the hardware store. One of the town Goon's had stopped by to remind Walt just how ugly he had become but he didn't get very far with his venomous discourse. He stood belligerently on the boardwalk with his muscular arms boldly crossed, wearing a loose fitting pair of farming overalls and using words he couldn't even spell. Walt, the ex-marksman, listened patiently for a moment before wordlessly hammering him in the testicles with the thick end of one of the pickaxe handles. It was a beautiful sight to behold as the Goon staggered down the street in the direction of the hospital, gasping for air as he cupped his bruised rocks. The damage to the Goon's testicles wasn't permanent but moreover, Walt's reputation for not suffering any more hurtful narrow-mindedness soon was. After the "crushed nuts" episode, the rude comments ceased almost immediately.

Within a year of marriage it became apparent to Walt and Grace that conceiving a child might take a bit more than just a yearning although the practicing certainly went well. Fourteen months after settling in to their new lives, a tragedy struck and Walt would be most thankful for Graces's supportive presence. Mister Brem suffered a stroke at the store one afternoon and wasn't found until Walt returned from lunch with Grace. He lay on the floor behind the counter, saliva drooling from his mouth and they immediately took him to the mainland in the back of the Island's antiquated ambulance. He died peacefully two days later and they buried him at the community's only cemetery, a large patch of grass on a gently sloping hill with tall stands of Gary Oak trees. Whoever sited the graveyard chose it well for it looked out onto the constantly moving waters just beyond the shores of Balford. After the graveside service a reception was held at one of the town halls where many gathered to console the family while drinking tea and nibbling on donated pastries. Having Grace to snuggle close to in their bed at night during this sorrowful time didn't make Walt's loss any easier, but the warm consoling did take the edge off his bereavement.

With the Hardware store now his absolute responsibility, Walt applied much of his energy into running the business and after weeks of this solitary toiling he realized he would need an assistant. He knocked on the door of another war veteran - one who had turned his hand to the land by planting apple orchards on several fertile acres a few miles from Skinny's Reach. Myron Bandie had bought the land with a veteran's loan but it would be sometime before the spindly seedlings would produce any fruit or profit.

Myron had lost most of his right leg fighting in the South Pacific and had chosen a wooden stump over a modern prostheses. A good choice in the end as he could pirouette his slight frame on that carved chunk of spruce better then any jointed, artificial piece of molded plastic. There being no such thing as a perfect person, Myron Bandie wasn't to be the exception, so he too came with his small problems. When Myron left a part of his tattered leg behind on that sweltering tropical island they had fought so hard for, he'd brought home with him a distressed soul as well as a penchant for Dark Rum.

Despite his agricultural venture, he still lived in town and he hoped to build a house out by his orchard one day. Myron and his quiet, mousy wife rented a cottage near the water and they became a harmless enough couple. They had an infant son named Wally who in twenty-five years hence would sire a vicious little goblin named Martin. Martin Bandie would of course live a short life but in that period he would become the utter bane of the island's populace. Myron's wife Beatrice tolerated his nightly drinking as he'd always been a peaceful type and would fall asleep in his chair once he'd finished with his cups. Walt knew that Myron had three mouths to feed as well he was good with a pencil and a ledger - a necessary talent when running a business. So Walt set him to work in the office in the mornings where he would show up around nine o'clock, bearing some degree of fragility and with liquor breath sour enough to curdle a glass of milk. All the heavy lifting and customer servicing would be handled by Walt until just after lunch, at which time Myron would vacate the office and the ledger to join Walt on the floor. By this time Myron's malodorous breath would have mellowed somewhat although it mattered not for the whole island knew about his drinking problem.

Grace continued her nursing duties at the local hospital while Walt ran his Hardware store and nothing of any significance happened until nine years later when Walt's mother passed away in her sleep one summer evening. She'd had a good run but the whole thing was naturally upsetting to Walt, and Grace felt as if she'd lost a dear friend. Once again a close group gathered to mourn, standing around the freshly dug gravesite next to Walt's father. The death of Walt's Mother brought about another major change in the Brem's lives and unfortunately it still didn't involve the birth of a child. Walt and Grace would never have children and some things in life you cannot change and brooding only brought you bitterness. Grace did however feel the need to move from the old house that had been in the Brem family for years, so they sold the property and purchased a large log house that stood on a bluff overlooking a rocky beach. This part of the island's shoreline offered fine, white sand at low tide so one of the first job requests Grace made was to have Walt build a flight of stairs that led from the back door down to the beach. The house also came with stables that were set away from the main residence with a two-bedroom suite built into the second floor. The place was far too big for just a couple but it did Grace's heart good and they off set the mortgage payments by renting out the apartment above the stables to Myron and Beatrice. Myron still worked at the store with Walt and not much had changed there except their son Wally had grown into a ten-year-old who liked to play with matches and peek up the girl's dresses while on the school bus.

The decades moved on as they always do and thirty years after they'd purchased the log house, Grace convinced Walt over supper that the time had come for them both to retire.

They had aged harmoniously, as well it should be with lifetime couples, and neither one really noticed the delicate changes to their bodies. Myron and Beatrice Bandie had long since left to do whatever it was one did with orchards and there no longer remained a mortgage on the log house. Selling the thriving hardware store would give them a comfortable retirement fund but more importantly, it would give them time to relax and enjoy the years they still had left before them. Grace and Walt discussed these plans at the dining room table that evening until the moon rose high and shimmered down on the flat surface of the straits. Had they a crystal ball though, they would have known that only twenty-three months remained in their devoted union, for the cancerous tumor growing inside of Grace's ovaries had already spread to her stomach and intestines.

Far too often this debilitating and lethal disease would course undetected through the human body and this was the case with Grace Brem. The first indication of her failing health was the chronic diarrhea and stomach pains that had started to plague her. Weeks of tests as well as numerous trips to the mainland hospital finally brought about an agonizing diagnosis; ovarian cancer which had spread to the point that it had become terminal. There remained little time for Grace but the Doctor prescribed chemotherapy for this kind of disease should never be allowed to proceed unchallenged. Grace and Walt were heart broken, but plans had to be formulated and adjustments made. First they would put their beloved log house up for sale, as soon enough it would become a large, joyless shell for

307

Walt to wander through with anguish as his only companion. Walt painted a large "for sale" sign on a sheet of plywood and nailed it to a fence post out by the road. He'd misspelled the word acreage but the few people who came to view the house hadn't the heart to say anything for the whole community was aware of Grace's ailment. Over the years she had treated or helped deliver many of the island's young inhabitants during the course of her nursing duties at the hospital.

Their plan was to live in the suite above the stables should the house sell quickly. Grace preferred to die on the property she had so much come to love and Walt would turn rock salt into gold if that's what it would take to grant her last wish. If need be, they would write this condition into any offer to purchase that might happen their way. But nothing happened for well over a year other than the lettering on the "for sale" sign fading from the weather and Grace's health from the cancer. Then one day a young pregnant schoolteacher named Judith Noble drove up to the house in a pick-up truck and knocked on the door. By this time Grace was bedridden and under the care of a nurse who visited daily and administered the morphine injections for her constant pain. No matter the suffering, she still insisted on meeting the island's newest schoolteacher and shook Judith's hand as she lay propped up in her bed. Grace knew then and there that the property would be sold even before Walt had shown Judith the house, the forests, and the outbuildings that would accompany the acquisition. After the walk through an offer to purchase was written up on the dining room table over a pot of tea and Judith graciously agreed to allow Grace and Walt to live above the stables for as long as they chose.

Thirty days later Judith took possession of her new home and the Brem's made the short pilgrimage over to the two-bedroom suite above the stables. Walt continued to be with his wife as much as possible and Judith wouldn't bother to scold him whenever she found him doing odd jobs around the place. She knew full and well the feelings involved with losing a loved one so she left him alone to his daily distractions. Judith took to visiting Grace on the weekends or after school and the two formed a close but brief friendship. Grace had lost considerable weight with the illness, her white arms nothing more than rake handles but her passion still remained despite the narcotic effects of the painkillers. She passed away late one evening as Walt lay on the bed beside her, but not before they exchanged two life long secrets. Grace told Walt in a strained voice how she had known about his day pass from the veterans' hospital so very long ago, and how she'd purposely gone looking for him after he had walked downtown. As he hugged her Walt became truly grateful for her bit of scheming for it had brought him a life of peaceful unity. Then he told Grace about the circumstances surrounding that cold night when he had parachuted behind enemy lines during the war, and how he had shot himself with a captured enemy pistol once hopelessness had set in. Grace became fully appreciative for that desolate act, as it alone had set into motion the events that would eventually bring Walt into her friendless world. Now Walt Brem's secret about how his face had come to be ruined was no longer a secret because he'd just told another human being. Furthermore, Grace never repeated it because it was personal and private and because she'd slipped away with it still on her lips. Walt lay with her for a while longer then made a brief phone call and an ambulance crew arrived to quietly remove her body.

Judith knew that Grace had died during the evening when she saw Walt in the early morning hours, standing like a lost child in the wet dew on the lawn in front of the stables. She'd taken to sitting on the balcony of the master bedroom in the log home to enjoy the morning sun when it rose from behind the coastal mountains. Judith left her balcony, got dressed, and then walked out into the chilly dawn to be with the old man as he stood on the grass. He said not a word and neither did she as she hugged him, feeling his body tremble, when the grief finally overtook him. Judith herself had only recently felt the same, lonely heartache with the loss of Iain and she had the birth of his twins still ahead of her. It became a poignant gesture to be sure, holding a stricken old man but consoling was one of the countless things that good people did well. They stood there for quite some time, motionless as the sun rose and a small herd of deer grazed on the clover, working their way slowly across the wet lawn.

Judith then took Walt into the house and made him some coffee and they sat and talked, and eventually started to laugh lightly at the kitchen table as Walt reminisced about Grace and what she had meant to him. Judith's simple offering of comfort became the foundation of a friendship that would be long lived and devoted. Within months, Judith would give birth to her twin girls, experiencing one of the most painful feats of womanhood, but when it was over she would not be left standing alone. Not with Uncle Walt around. Even though Judith was about to be a first time mother, her instincts as well as her inner strengths would see her through her tiring responsibilities and sleepless nights. Now Uncle Walt would help temper her to some of those maternal obligations by doing whatever tasks he could, so she could attend to her newborn's. On that morning after Grace had passed away, Walt Brem inherited the daughter he and Grace could never have and Judith Noble regained the father she had lost as a child. It was one of the rules of mankind and his affinities; when one relationship ended, another would surely begin, unless of course if you were a hermit.

*   *   *

Chapter Thirty-five

"You seem surprised once again," the voice in the sublime library said. Judith looked up from the book she'd finished reading about Grace and Uncle Walt, even though she instinctively knew she could never see the speaker's face. She closed the book and allowed it to rest on the lap of her thin gown.

"I didn't know Uncle Walt had shot himself," she said quietly, "what a terrible thing for a person to have to do."

"Yes," the voice replied, "but he really had no choice as the soldier's of the tank crew would have killed him - as he would them, if given the chance."

"Yes, I suppose," Judith offered. "All that killing . . . all that suffering, how very dreadful."

"It was, wasn't it? Although you might take some comfort in the fact that there will never be another war like that last, big one."

"It would certainly make for a better world to live in," Judith agreed.

She put the book back on the polished shelf then retrieved the one that had her own name printed across the front. It was the last book to remain on the shelf. Judith's hands shook discernibly with anticipation as she opened the white leather cover to the first page. She exhaled abruptly when she saw nothing but a clean whiteness, then flipped through the entire book, finding every page void of any print.

"The pages in *my* book are empty," Judith said softly.

"That's because you have to fill them yourself Judith," the voice replied. "You have to live your life to its fullest to make a complete story and you haven't been doing that."

"Is that why I've been brought here?"

"That would be one of the reasons," the voice answered. "Another reason is because of a lonely person who lives on the fringes of your existence. He is a good man Judith, and you need him as much as he needs you. You must find the courage to love again, to allow yourself to be whole and to let your twin girls experience the joys of having a father. And you must trust me when I tell you this."

"Yes, I know the person you are talking about. I've actually liked Ben Trilby for some time but I have been afraid of his friendship. I don't think I could bear to loose anyone else."

"I understand that. You must take little steps before you can find the confidence to increase your strides. But since the loss of Iain you have been floundering far too long. The time has come to live again. Do you understand me Judith?"

"Yes, I think I do."

"It is important that you touch those around you. Look at your mother, Molly. You haven't spoken to her in years. Could you bear to loose her?"

"No . . . I suppose I couldn't."

"She has quit drinking, although her struggle continues. Did you know that?"

"No I didn't."

"You must reach out to her again. You're all that remains of her true family."

"I will, I promise. But these can't be the only reasons for bringing me here."

"That's true. You're also here because of the mentally challenged young boy named Brodie."

"What has Brodie Bandie to do with me?"

"Brodie had to be saved from his father Martin, who would have killed him five days from now in a drunken rage. Martin needed to be stopped but unfortunately this required an extreme measure.

You are to be Brodie Bandie's mentor. For now, and in the coming years he will need a kind and patient tutor as well as a suitable role model. That is one of the things I must task you with."

"What is so important about this little boy, Brodie?" Judith asked.

"Like all children, he is important and must be cherished," the voice replied, "but his importance will come to pass with the son he will sire twenty-years from now."

"I see."

"Yes . . . and so shall the rest of the world."

The voice went quiet for a few minutes and Judith gazed into the infinite blackness while she pondered the implications of the conversation. When the voice returned it was no longer soft and in proximity, it now sounded distant but still very certain.

"They are calling for you Judith, it is time for you to go back."

"To go back where?"

"To return home."

"Will I ever speak to you again?"

"Not for many, many years. And before you go, there is one more undertaking that I must ask of you. You have your dead sisters ashes in a cremation urn in your closest at home. It's been many years since she perished in that helicopter crash in the mountains. Please take the urn Judith and cast its contents onto the sea near your house. That is how she remembers you Judith - as two sisters playing hopscotch in the sand next to the ocean. Will you do this for her, Judith?"

"Yes, yes I will."

"Good-bye then Judith, and please do my bidding, for the turmoil in your life has finally come to an end."

"Good-bye . . . and who are you?" Judith softly asked, "I feel like I've known your voice all my life."

"You have Judith," the fading voice replied, "I'm someone who loves you."

*   *   *

Part Five
"Ben"

Chapter Thirty-six

Exactly seven minutes had passed since Fred and Barney, the paramedic's with the rumpled uniforms had left the scene of the motor accident with a clinically dead Judith Noble. While Ben Trilby drove the ambulance to the hospital the two medical technicians worked nonstop, attempting to resuscitate her lifeless body under the bright white lights in the back of the vehicle. Once they had started rolling Fred requested Ben call his dispatch on the radio to update them of the situation as well as have them notify the on call Physician. The vehicle had been driven at a steady pace through the rain, but not with such haste so as to impede the paramedics in their job. Judith Noble was in knowledgeable hands and her chances of survival had risen dramatically once the paramedics had taken over the cardiopulmonary resuscitation that Ben and Cheryl the Police Officer had started.

There was no de-fibrillator inventoried to the island's ambulance service so they would have to wait until they reached the hospital to try and electrically jump-start their patient. Time would still be crucial though, for they needed to bring her life back before brain damage occurred from a lack of oxygen. It had happened before and there could be nothing more heartbreaking to a paramedic than resuscitating a fellow human being, only to revive them as a vegetable; a drooling face, a diminished mind, all locked within a healthy body that they could never use again. The work Fred and Barney were performing on Judith as the rain drummed a cadence on the metal roof of the ambulance was sensitive enough and they both knew it. Not a lot was known about this very private lady, but she had become a touted notable among the community for her dedicated, patient work with the island's young people. She had caused a sensation with the locals when she really came into her own, which was educating the tiny population of mentally challenged children.

All anyone actually knew about Judith was that she had come from the north, and why she had chosen this particular island from the dozens that

315

spotted the gulf waters had never been discussed too much. The fact that the small group of disabled children bubbled and chirped, and spoke more about their teacher than they did about Santa Claus or the Easter Bunny best summed up how they felt about their solitary school ma rm. She had become *real* to her kids and their grateful parents - tangible, and touchable, easily loved for her simple caring ways and brilliant mind. Barney thought about his own young daughter as he looked down into Judith's blue, lifeless eyes, squeezing the rubber am/bu bag that forced air into her lungs. His only daughter had been born with Downs Syndrome and was one of the pupils in Judith's class.

She spoke of nothing else but school and her teacher when she came home and wasn't sound asleep in her bed. If they lost Judith it would break his daughter's heart and the program for the handicapped kid's would assuredly loose the momentum that the lively educator had put into it. Barney sat near Judith's head on a folding jump seat as Fred kneeled on the edge of the gurney, applying the chest compressions, counting out loud so Barney would know when to squeeze the rubber ventilation bag.

Judith Noble would certainly be a hard one to lose, and the atmosphere in the back of the ambulance made Barney's skin tingle, almost as though someone was looking over his shoulder, urging him on like a small voice, telling him that this particular person *had* to be saved. Fred felt it too, like a warm sigh as he leaned over his patient with his elbows locked, even taking a second to quickly gaze around the back of the vehicle, almost expecting to see someone standing in a corner watching them. They were both doing their best and they treated Judith no differently if she had been a starving, stinking beggar plucked from a frozen dumpster. Fred and Barney were professionals' whose primary purpose was to do their utmost to save lives.

They couldn't care less if you smelled nice or stunk like a pair of old work socks or came from the wrong side of the island or couldn't pay your bills. Your particular rung on the social ladder was of no consequence to them, for saving you was all that mattered. It was what they were paid to do and it was what they did best.

As their ambulance moved under a darkening sky over the wet asphalt toward the island's only hospital, their thoughts remained focused on resuscitating this young, single mother. A teacher whose enchanting graces had cast a spell of sorts on a whole community of children, a resourceful teacher that the parent's had come to hold in high regard. For some reason

316

though, Judith Noble *had* become different from the others and when Fred and Barney finally got some free time after what would be a busy evening of calls they sat in the coffee room back at the hall doing the required paperwork, debriefing and discussing the peculiar feelings they had both felt when in the back of their own ambulance attending to Judith. They had both seen and felt strange things in their line of work and undoubtedly there would be stranger things yet to come, so they shrugged the whole episode off as too much coffee and not enough sleep.

The Island's hospital had been sited on a grassy knoll above the town of Skinny's Reach and it offered a sweeping vista of the harbor through the large windows but at the same time exposing the building to the relentless winter gales. It had been named in memory of a Korean War Veteran who had apparently sported a sharp bayonet on the battlefield and an even sharper tongue when he had returned home after the conflict. A cement driveway led up to the back of the cinder block, single story building where the main entrance to the emergency room was located. Ben drove up this short road and stopped the ambulance next to a set of automatic double doors; automatic if someone were inside the hospital working which wasn't the case on a Friday night. The structure had a sloping metal roof with aluminum window sashes painted the color of ripe cranberries and the handsome building would still be standing long after the present generation had come and gone. They had spared no expense with its construction, having been built during an election year, but the flow of money slowed to a copper trickle right after the ribbon cutting ceremony. Not soon after the grand opening the hospital took a quick, unprincipled slide to the status of community medical clinic and the four neatly made beds in the small ward gathered dust without so much as a patient ever gracing the clean, pressed sheets. The clinic would be open Monday to Friday to serve the community's health needs, but anything after those hours would require the attendance of the on call Doctor and at least one trained, emergency room nurse. Fiscal restraint, they said.

As the ambulance came to a gentle halt by the glassed doors, Barney gave Ben some quick instructions about accessing the building. Ben grabbed his cane and slipped from the front seat, limping through the rain over to the doors, gladdened that someone had at least left some lights on in the building. He inserted a key into the metal cylinder; the double doors slid open with an audible hiss, riding quietly on their electric rails. Ben then hobbled to the back of the ambulance and opened the wide doors so they could remove their patient. As Barney took a firm grip on the head of the gurney Ben placed his cane over his wrist then pulled the lower end straight back, supporting the weight with his arms until the wheels and metal legs fell into place and locked. His hip socket ground murderously and he clenched his teeth, managing to swallow the pain and keep the grimace from his face. Once the gurney stood firmly on the ground Barney pulled it in the direction of the doors while Fred continued with the chest compressions, walking in close to his patient. Ben limped after the gurney and soon fell behind, finding himself standing in a darkened waiting room with chairs and coffee tables that had magazines scattered across their veneered tops. Fred and Barney had gone straight through the swinging doors of the emergency room, which was fully lit up, its light casting through the cracks of the doors into the waiting room. Ben remained standing in the middle of the waiting room, unsure if he should follow or allow Judith the courtesy of some privacy but then one of the paramedics called out to him.

Ben shuffled in as fast as his ruined hip would allow, his pupils burning as they adjusted to the intense lights. The gurney had been parked near a corner where glassed cupboards lined each of the white tiled walls, their medical supplies easily spotted and readily available. Barney beckoned Ben over, showing him how to ventilate Judith by squeezing the am bu bag, instructing him to do this every time Fred nodded his head. Fred was still busy with the chest compressions, maintaining an audible count as Barney stepped over to a wheeled tray that had a red metal toolbox sitting on its top shelf. Atop the large toolbox was a cream-colored piece of equipment with small white knobs and a small black screen that looked much like a television set.

This machine was a combination heart monitor/de-fibrillator and would play a major part if Judith were to be brought back from the abyss. Barney quickly fetched some packaged items from the rolling metal drawers of the toolbox, knowing exactly where to find what he needed. He returned to the gurney, placing the handful of items next to his patient's head, then took a pair of scissors and cut through the front of Judith's light blue sweatshirt, snipping the front of her bra at the same time. Barney pulled the clothes away, tucking them close into Judith's body, and as Ben glanced down he couldn't help but notice Judith's nipple's pucker with the cold, and he hoped it was a sign there was life somewhere deep inside of her. As Ben watched for Fred's nods, Barney started to rip open the stiff plastic bags, carefully pulling the foil backing from three round adhesive pads. Each pad had a white metal nub mounted into the fabric and without interfering with Fred; Barney placed one pad just below Judith's right collarbone, pressing it firmly against her skin with his fingers. Another he placed in the same position on the opposite side of her body and the third one he attached on her left side near the edge of her rib cage.

Reaching back over to the toolbox, Barney gently sorted three plastic coated wires that hung down the side of the tray. Each had a small metal alligator clip attached to its end and he carefully affixed a wire to each of the pads that were stuck to Judith's skin. He then reached over and turned on the heart monitor on top of the toolbox. A bright dot pulsed in a straight line from one side of the screen to the other, something that even a novice like Ben didn't find altogether encouraging. They all heard the sliding entrance doors swish open, and Ben looked up expectantly to see one of the local doctors walking into the emergency room. Tall and thin looking in his comfortable sweats, his name was Todd and Ben thought he looked a bit like one of the marijuana growers from the cooperative with his long brown hair tied behind his neck in a pony tail; although that would be where the similarities would end. As Todd walked over to the gurney he took the whole situation in, analyzing and making decisions in the time it took a normal person to draw a breath.

"Full arrest," Barney said, "electrocution, high power lines came down at a motor vehicle accident. CPR started and sustained since the incident, about eighteen minutes now."

"I.V. saline wide-open Barney," Todd said flatly.

By the time he got to Judith's side the paramedic was already preparing the intravenous, peeling the sterile wrapping away from the thick needle.

"Stop CPR," Todd ordered, "I need to establish her rhythm."

Fred stopped his compressions as the Doctor glanced at the screen of the heart monitor, scarcely regarding it for more than a couple of seconds.

"V- fib," Todd announced calmly. "Lets shock her boys, start it at two-hundred."

Fred reached for a set of flat paddles that lay in front of the defibrillation machine and handed them to the Doctor. The paddles had a square contact surface almost the size of a slice of bread with cylindrical handles for the operator to grasp. Coiled insulated lines like those found on a telephone led back to the machine where Fred stood adjusting a dial. Once Todd had the paddles, he held the flat surfaces toward Barney and the paramedic squeezed clear jelly from a plastic tube onto the smooth contacts. The ointment would prevent burns when the electrical current transferred from the paddles through Judith's exposed skin. All three of the medical staff worked quickly and wordlessly as they prepared their patient and the machine for its life-giving jolt. They had all done this kind of thing many times before and the calm manner in which they conducted their business told Ben they knew what they were doing and he took this as his cue to leave. The Doctor had arrived and Ben had done everything he could to assist the paramedics up to this point. They wouldn't require his untrained hands anymore, but more important, he could turn his back on the tension involved as they attempted to bring Judith back to life. Half naked and unofficially dead, she at least deserved her dignity and the fewer people who saw her like this the better, so the ex-policeman limped noiselessly through the swinging doors, pushing them closed behind him.

As he ambled over to a chair in the dark waiting room a young woman whom he recognized as a nurse came jogging lightly through the doors of the hospital, going straight into the emergency room. Ben eased himself into a comfortable looking chair and rested his cane across his lap, picking thoughtfully at a piece of lint that had stuck to his blue denim overalls.

He looked out the main glassed doors to the rain bouncing off the asphalt around the parked ambulance. Lost in his apprehensive thoughts and with nothing else to do, he allowed his mind to drift, knowing that sitting alone in a dark room with his thoughts could be a reckless thing.

A picture soon formed in his mind's eye and he attempted to chase away the past before it formed a disturbing recollection but it was too late. The antiseptic smell of the hospital had filled his nostrils, touching every cell that lined his nose, weakening the determination that helped keep the memories at bay, or at least keep them where they belonged - which were in his nightmares when he slept.

The last time Ben Trilby had been in a hospital emergency room he had been laying on a gurney himself, his patrol partner Lisa Carmaducci laid out beside him in the next treatment bay, part of her face shot off. Ben had a one hundred and fifty grain hollow point lead slug buried in his hip and the medical staff were fighting to prevent further blood loss. He had fallen into a delirious shock and was trying to tell the doctors working on Lisa that they were wasting their time. Ever the dedicated bunch though, they decided to make the effort and were preparing to de-fibrillate her with the paddles when a nurse drew the drapes around her gurney. Ben never saw his partner again, and couldn't even remember what she had looked like - until tonight, when it all came back to him. This time it had been triggered by the sights and sounds and smells of another lifeless form and with yet another journey to a hospital. Another trip in an ambulance where it was hoped that once again the spirit and energy of a vibrant young woman could be restored to her dormant soul.

Ben suddenly thought about those tickets he had for the concert at the old playhouse in Balford two weeks coming. He'd left them sitting on the till back at his store. He had asked Judith to go with him while she and her daughters had been in the store just this afternoon but she had said no. Ben had told her he would keep asking her to go and she had said she wouldn't mind, even though the answer would probably be the same. He believed he would get the chance to ask Judith again, and something told him that unlike the last time he'd been in a hospital, this particular young lady was going to make it. Ben truly hoped so, for he really admired the sparks that flew along with her no-nonsense attitude, her delightful intellect, her knowing smile and the two little gems she had for daughters. Judith would live and she would say yes to the concert because Ben would be goddamned if he was going to ask one of those hairy-legged, pot smoking granola type girls out. He'd burn the tickets and turn gay before he forced himself do something that drastic.

Ben looked back outside, watching the rainfall as it formed a pewter-colored wall, just the way it had the night when he and Lisa had been so cruelly gunned down. With the skies so overcast, night would come early this day and already the dusk had started to fall. The Doctor had warned Ben that smells, sights, sounds and even the weather could bring the memories back, washing over him, seizing his moods, and that trying to ignore these thoughts would at times be like stopping the wind itself. The Doctor had warned him that moving to this island might be a healthy change of venue, but the past could still chase him down and find him unless he chose to deal with it. Ben had to put the incident to rest in some manner best suited for his own particular psyche if he hoped to carry on. He had to flush the disturbing event completely from his mind and soul. Unfortunately for Ben the Doctor had been completely right, for as he sat there in that lonely waiting room he found himself thinking less of Judith and the concert in Balford - and more of that *other* night when it had pissed rain and bullets cracked the darkness.

*   *   *

Chapter Thirty-seven

By the time Ben Trilby had graduated from High School he hadn't accomplished an awful lot he could genuinely brag about. His grades had been below average, he had lost his virginity that "certain summer" to another graduate named Margaret and he had been a capable defensive lineman on the school football team. He didn't talk too much about his grade point average, said even less about his first tryst with a woman (the actual copulation which had lasted all of eighteen seconds) but would ramble on about the last home game if you prodded him in the right place. Ben loved football. He loved playing football and he loved watching the game. It was too bad because not a lot of people wanted to hear about the last home game and with low grades one wouldn't get very far in life riding on one's football laurels. Not a tall man, Ben was nonetheless built square and solid and he appeared appealing enough to the girls with his dirty blonde hair, west coast tan, and shy attitude. But much like a fully laden herring punt pushing full throttle against a rip tide he moved with more purpose than with speed. Had Ben not been on the football team he might have made it through high school altogether unnoticed - just another face in the crowd. However, his performance on the football field throughout his school years appeared in nearly every edition of the school newspaper and these accolades steered him in a direction he ought not to have been headed in the first place.

Ben's father Emmet liked the game as well, and his deluded counseling didn't help with the situation and important decisions that had to be made. Ben subsequently placed all his academic eggs inside a gridiron basket, as well as a football scholarship, much to his father's proud nods and his mother's utter mortification. Ben's mother Bea had performed most of the nurturing and guiding when it had come to raising their only child. It was she that had lovingly suffered through his growing pains, pimples, strange new hair and the various other speed bumps that accompany every teenager who travels the rough road of puberty. Accordingly, Ben should have set his sights on becoming a dentist, or a gynecologist, or something a bit more noteworthy than carting an inflated pigskin up and down a piece of astro-turf. Bea had single handedly weaned Ben, changed his diapers and had raised him by herself and this was not the direction she wanted him to go. She wanted her boy to enter the medical profession or at the least become an x-ray technician or one of those people that give vaccinations. Football was for hooligans in her opinion, and her boy wasn't going to be a hooligan. At the time, Emmet was a long haul truck driver who constantly traversed the country in a magnificent looking midnight black conventional Kenworth tractor with a queen-sized sleeper mounted behind the cab. The truck had become a source of pride for Ben's father and he even had those large rubber mud flaps with the chromed silhouettes of naked women mounted behind each set of dual wheels. Emmet had also become a walking cliché, wearing cowboy boots, tight blue jeans, and one of those huge metal belt buckles that sat half hidden under his belly while the crack of his ass rode prominently exposed on the opposite side. The baseball cap with a rival's truck emblem sewn above the peak and the toothpick that constantly hung from his lips completed the standard ensemble.

A trucker through and through and if his manner of dress or his breezy deportment didn't alert you to his vocation, then the way he spoke to you certainly would have.

"Money don't grow on tree's Woman," was a favorite saying to his wife, "and if it did I'd have to shake the goddamned branches."

To Ben he would impart the end all solution to every young man's problems: "Don't take no shit off no one boy, not even your teachers."

Now there was absolutely nothing wrong with being a truck driver. In fact it could be a noble profession that kept the vital wares of a nation constantly moving to the consumers.

The problem here was that Ben's father was just too much of a "meat and potatoes" kind of a guy - your basic gap between the upper front teeth, bellowing like a moose and permanently in rut. Driving his hallowed rig made Emmet extremely contented as well it kept him conveniently absent during Ben's critical teenaged years. Ben saw even less of his father once Bea had found a pair of crotch-less panties behind the mattress in the cab of the sleeper. She had gone out to get the fuel bills from the sun visor so she could update the books when she noticed the black lace waistband peeking out from a corner of the bed. Emmet had just returned from a long trip and was snoring gently inside the house and as a result Bea ended up learning more about her husband of twenty years than she might have cared to ever know.

Ben's mother was a 'forgive and forget' kind of a woman and might have overlooked one misgiving with a ribald scolding but then she found the photographs in the glove box.

And there were dozens of them.

All done up with a nice matte finish, each one featuring her naked husband in some hot tub surrounded by bimbos who were just as naked, except they all had large breasts and saucy red lips. Some of the photographs clearly displayed Emmet and the buxom flock engaged in some shocking pornographic acts and the less said about those the better. The stupid bastard had written the dates on the back of each photograph and Ben's mother didn't need a calculator to conclude that her husband's cavorting hadn't been a misguided, isolated, wandering incident.

So numerous were the photographs that Bea was puzzled as to when Emmet found time to drive his truck, and possibly eat and sleep.

Soon after this perverted disclosure the senior Trilby was given his marching orders while Ben's mother sought out a good lawyer. The last Ben saw of his father was when he drove off into the sunset in his hand polished black tractor, the naughty chrome mud flaps swinging in the breeze, waving a cheeky good-bye. Never one for complete abandonment, Emmet would however continue to champion and support his son by sending him encouraging post cards from all across North America. Why, even the odd collect phone call would come into the house to Ben from his father, persuading the lad to pursue his football career and drop all these silly notions of obtaining a useless degree. It was Emmet after all who would be paying the post secondary bills and appeasing the hand that fed you was the least the strapping young man could do in gratitude. If the football thing didn't work out and Ben wasn't rich and famous within a few years then he could always drive a rig with his old man and go hot tubbing during their lay overs. As Bea watched on from the sidelines, she appeared a trifle miffed at this talk of becoming a professional athlete and her face became all blotchy the day Ben announced he would be attending the local college on a football scholarship. And who could really blame a mother for wanting the best for her only son? Unfortunately, Emmet would indeed be paying the bills and more unfortunate would be the fact that *nobody* was going to steer her son from his present course of playing professional football.

Nobody . . . except his college football Coach. Although this devastating revelation didn't present itself until Ben's second year at college, during one of those coach/defensive lineman counseling sessions.

Ben had been focusing a little too much on his play book and not enough on the blackboard, so consequently he was failing Political Sciences as well as a host of other subjects. One of the terms of the sports scholarship was that each candidate maintain a respectable grade average, a begrudged concession that was dutifully enforced to prevent the coaches from recruiting any brainless ringers. During this man-to-man discussion Ben defended his commitment to football, but then the Coach very succinctly and without a lot of compassion tossed Ben's career ambitions and dreams out onto the dung heap of ill sought endeavors.

Ben Trilby would never be a professional football player the Coach had told him. True enough, the lad had become a gifted athlete but he moved on the playing field a lot like those timbered fishing vessels did on the water - plowing doggedly through the brine instead of skipping over the surface like a planing speed boat.

Ben would be a valuable asset in helping to bring the team to the coveted college finals, if not this year then maybe next year but that would be as far as his dedicated head butting and predatory tackling would get him. "Sorry son," the Coach had said, "but you'll never make it as a pro, you're just not fast enough." The Coach then leaned forward with his elbows on his desk, his hands clasped together, his face a fixture of serious concern. Now that he had compared Ben's single-minded aspirations to common ditch litter, the time had come to embark on his initial intentions of giving Ben a motivational pep talk regarding his grade averages. But he had already lost the young man. Ben had faltered somewhere back between "timbered fishing vessel" and "speed boat." He sat motionlessly in the oak chair in front of the Coach's desk, fighting back the tears that stung his eyelids, allowing his mentor to drone on about the world being Ben's oyster and that all he needed was a shucking knife and a fresh lemon. By the time the Coach had reached the lip worn part of his spiel wherein the brawny young man would have to start pulling his socks up in the lecture halls, Ben was destroyed and started shuffling for the exit door.

It would be a pathetic looking young man who traveled the halls of the college from class to class the rest of that week, walking as if entranced, his head drooping toward the floor.

What really hurt Ben was the fact that deep inside he knew his coach to be right. It had been something he suspected all along but had become fearful of addressing the issue and for several good reasons. The biggest of which was his love for the game. His second biggest fear was the fact that he had no alternatives put into place, no back-up plan. Oh sure, he could pull his socks up and start applying himself but the courses he had signed up for were haphazard and willy-nilly at best. After a few years Ben would be a tad smarter regarding the political sciences and he could certainly join in on a discussion at a party regarding the evolution of European clay pottery. But that would be as far as his post-secondary education would get him once outside the college. None of the courses he had signed up for were actually occupationally motivated. They were all regarded by the faculty as tedious fillers, a place that Ben could sit to use up his precious time when he wasn't on the football field or running around the quarter mile track, or working out in the weight room. Despondently Ben realized that he would have to take up that offer his father had given him driving tractor-trailers, but first he would have to locate Emmet and he had no idea which of the whorehouses he should call first. Driving the trucks would be something he could handle, but the thought of joining his father's hot tub parties during lay overs was enough to make Ben's toe nails curl. He knew he would have to lay down some firm ground rules and if that meant throwing cold water into his father's overly stoked furnace then that's what he was prepared to do.

Ben might have only been "just" a good college level football player, and he might "just" have only been a borderline student, but above all this he was a decent and respectable human being and he never hesitated to reciprocate in kind return. To his way of thinking, using women the way his father did was the lowest form of human indignation, an act lacking even the slightest molecule of human dignity. All these good qualities Ben had gleaned naturally through the decent upbringing and sustaining love of his good-hearted mother. The only thing Emmet had ever done for the boy aside from paying for his football gear and tuition fees was to show him the crack of his ass as it left home on another long journey. Bea of course was wholly thrilled with these recent developments of Ben never playing professional football, although she successfully hid her glee as she could easily see the misery that clung to her son's face. This welcomed development had rekindled Bea's dreams of her son going to medical school and she cared not whether he became a Proctologist, a Gynecologist or even a dentist. Ben wisely said nothing to his mother at the time about his plans to drive a truck with his father, which was probably a good thing if he still wanted to be fed. Even though Ben was now over twenty-years old, had Bea known of his nomadic intentions she would have cornered him and given him an ear full and offered up cold cuts for his supper fare. He still lived under her roof so that gave her the basic right to voice her opinions and state any, if not all displeasures she may have had festering. This was after all, a single mother's inherent right, a state that Ben cautiously and wisely acknowledged.

So Ben went quietly about his business; albeit wearing a career-ending frown but nonetheless forging on with his ill conceived plans to join his father Emmet in the brotherhood of the Nation's truckers. However, before he could drive one of those big trucks he would first require the proper accreditation. His first formal hurdle would be to take a sanctioned driving course, which would help him obtain the appropriate class permit. Apparently the Department of Motor Vehicles and law enforcement officials frowned upon unlicensed people driving these eighteen wheeled behemoths on the Country's highways and Ben had no intentions of breaking any laws. Through this process would lie an ironic turn of events that would greatly alter his course and lead him on a journey that would eventually change his life forever. It all happened on the main floor of the metal and glassed building that the Motor Vehicle Branch had for their offices in the downtown core. Ben had wandered in to pick up a few brochures regarding driving courses, but found the place to be a spreading panorama of human bodies, with a continual low roar emanating from their ceaseless chatter.

People of all shapes, sizes and ethnic backgrounds were packed like cord wood into the large main plaza of the license office, all of them looking bored and thoroughly frustrated.

This immense throng of people formed the lines that eventually led to the wickets and the equally bored and frustrated looking government employees. Not easily swayed from any task, Ben joined the line-up, and resigned himself to missing lunch and possibly even supper and all of next week. After a few hours he hadn't moved very far but was at least in a part of the line that skirted one of the walls. Here someone had been accommodating enough to tape up a diverse selection of the FBI's most wanted posters. Ben found himself reading the absorbing criminal biographies that accompanied each black and white photograph and even thought he recognized a few of the instructors from the college. He had secretly hoped that his football coach might be found somewhere within the collection and that he could turn him in and there would now be two ruined careers. But that tidbit of vengeful fantasy wasn't going to be, at least not today.

An hour later Ben had finally made it down to the end of the wall where he quickly found he still had a long way to go to the service wickets and his driving brochure. He also found a picturesque recruiting poster for the City Police Department, placed on the wall in both a colorful and satiric contradiction to the wanted posters. Ben found himself admiring an impossibly handsome police officer wearing tall, spit shone black cavalry boots and dark blue riding breeches with a thick red stripe stitched to the sides of the pants. He had a white and blue helmet over his head with a gold crest in the middle and soft leather straps were cinched up under his chin. The curved visor on the helmet touched the top of the policeman's sunglasses as he leaned against a Harley-Davidson Electra glide motorcycle that sparkled in the pure sunshine of an early morning. Ben Trilby was the kind of young person the marketing people intended the poster to reach out to, and reach out to him *it* did. He was fascinated with the authority and the respect that had been emblazoned across the poster and rather thought the man looked like a football player except he carried a gun. He certainly played on a team of sorts, and wore a neat looking uniform with a helmet and got to butt heads with the opposing team who happened to be the malcontents who lurked on the fringes of a fast paced culture. Playing for keeps would even make this kind of game all the more fulfilling. It got better though, for the address at the bottom of the poster was just across the street and unless someone in this crowd farted or rolled a hand grenade onto the floor there remained an enormous likelihood it would be shifting nowhere fast. Ben looked at the recruiting poster one last time then made a decision that instantly set the gears of his own fate into an irreversible motion. He stepped from the hot stuffy line of humanity and pressing body odor and jaywalked across the street and into the Police Headquarters Building - and he never looked back.

The men and women of the police-recruiting unit liked everything they saw in Ben and then some. He was built like a pallet load of bagged cement mix and had the reasoning and common sense of a life wizened elder. Inside of two weeks Ben had breezed through the written entrance exams, answered all the questions correctly during the extensive interviews and had been declared a healthy specimen by the Department's Medical Officer. His only flaw was that he couldn't skate so he wouldn't be much of a benefit to the Department's numerous hockey squads. But that little drawback they decided to overlook. On the Friday he was sworn in as a Peace Officer he wordlessly left the house dressed in the navy blue three-piece suit that Bea that had bought him as a high school graduation present.

Ben drove his pick-up through the morning rush hour traffic, humming and tapping his fingers thoughtfully on the dashboard as he listened to the local country and western station on his truck radio. He had no problem finding a spot at the Police Headquarters parking lot as the shift change was already a few hours old and they had issued him a permit for this very occasion.

Ben found twenty-three recruits sitting nervously in the main waiting room outside the Police Chief's office on the fourth floor of the headquarters building. They eyed each other with mounting respect, wearing neutral smiles as they evaluated the individual competition that would form their troop at the Police Training Depot. They would be living together in a barracks on a corner of an Army base for nearly six months of extensive training and when it was all done they would come to know each other as a family; more like brothers and sisters, but in many ways much closer than any of own kin. One-hundred and eighty-days of pushing oneself to the ends of one's physical and mental capabilities did that to a team of people brought together for the common purpose of law enforcement. The twenty men and four women who made up Ben's training roster would view the world they had come to know quite differently at the end of the six months, and not even their old their friends would ever seem the same again. In fact, most police officers made new friends after they had become badge carrying, working members of "the blessed chosen."

Although Ben and his small fellowship couldn't have known about these subtle changes in their lives at the time of their swearing in, nor would they have cared, so nervous with anticipation had they all become. Every move they made from here on in, every twitch of the face or hesitation in a decision, every itch they scratched or uniform item out of place or unpolished would not go unnoticed. When you wore a uniform and went out into the public eye to keep the peace, very few seconds went by without some form of respect being shown or disdainful scrutiny being leveled at you. The sooner a recruit learned to treat his every action as if it were being recorded on a video camera, the better they and the Department would be. So after the required time of sweating in their suits and adjusting their neck ties, the recruits were finally ushered into a small media theater where they sat in folding wooden chairs until their names were called out. One at a time they approached the front of the theater after an officer spoke their names from a list he held on a clipboard. The Chief of Police stood next to a mahogany dias wearing his dress blues and swore each candidate into the Force as they each held a thick bible in their right hand, repeating the oath of office as the baritone words rumbled from the Chiefs mouth. After they signed a formal document, they were sent on their way with instructions to report to the Training Depot first thing Monday morning next week, and don't be late.

When Ben had finished, he exited the police building whistling a detached tune to himself, neither proud nor humbled by the huge step he had taken. He was going to be a cop, something he hadn't even thought about three weeks ago but sometimes the job comes to you. One month ago you could call him Mister Trilby, professional football player hopeful, but now you could address him as Officer Trilby, peace officer and that was a certainty. The pay would be fine and the benefits were hailed as the best even though Ben was still too young to care much about pensions and indexing and all the rest of that old age stuff. He would be working in the fresh air and he would get to meet a lot of interesting people although some of these people he realized he would have to fight with. It shouldn't be a problem though, not when you're built like a defensive lineman. Ben climbed into his pick-up truck still whistling, and removed his necktie as he drove from the Police Headquarters parking lot. He followed the busy downtown streets eventually turning onto a four-lane, one-way thoroughfare that took him in the direction of the college where he had planned to meet some of his football pals. They were going to treat him in a local tavern where they would hoist a few brews, eat some pizza and then send their ex-teammate on his merry way down the road of good fortune. The tavern was quiet but it soon turned into a jovial afternoon with much vocal reminiscing, back slapping and colorful character assassinations. Shortly after six o'clock Ben said good-bye to his football brethren then drove home under a dusky sky. He still had to tell Bea about his recent career developments and he truly hoped she would be proud of him. Ben parked his truck in the driveway then stood alone under the twinkling stars, smelling his mother's fabulous cooking as it wafted from the house.

Friday evenings meant two glorious but simple things to Ben Trilby. The last dinner of the week always hailed meatloaf with creamy potatoes mashed with sour cream, buckets of thick brown gravy followed by the evening football game on the television. It couldn't get any better than this Ben thought as he entered the steamy kitchen through the back door and kissed his mother on the forehead. She stood standing near the stove wearing a red and white gingham apron, watching her son as he took his tweed jacket off, draping it neatly across the back of a chair.

"Did you have a nice day son?" Bea asked.

"I sure did mom."

"You've been up to something these past couple of weeks Ben. You keep disappearing and I don't think you've been going to school. You know how I don't like secrets. And this morning you left the house all dressed up and smelling nice without so much as a word of where you where going. Did you go for a job interview or something?"

"Yes Mom, you could say that."

"And did you get the job Son?"

"I did at that, mom, and all by myself," he beamed.

"What about college?"

"I quit college."

"My goodness, what a pleasant surprise."

"I had to, Mom."

"Please tell me it's not football Ben. I don't want you being a professional football player. It's too dangerous. They're always getting hurt and breaking their limbs and you might get crippled up and then you'll never be able to work again."

"Don't worry mom. It's nothing as dangerous as football. I've joined the City Police Department. I start training Monday morning next week up at the Army Base. I'm going to be a cop."

"Oh dear," was all Bea said.

Ben reached into the fridge and pulled out a frosted bottle of beer, heading for the living room and his football game without further word or discussion. His mother didn't appear to have much to say about the breaking news, which could be a good thing so he might just as well catch the opening kick-off and leave well enough alone. There would be enough opportunity during the halftime show for them to discuss Ben's present calling. Bea stood alone in the kitchen and suddenly didn't feel so well. Silently, she undid the loop on her apron at the small of her back and slipped it over her head, hanging it on the handle of the fridge door. She then walked down the hallway to her bedroom and quietly went in, closing the door behind her. Bea sat on the edge of the bed in the darkness, remaining very still as she looked straight ahead and thought about what her son had just told her. She wasn't sure if she liked this news at all. Even worse though, an instinctive foreboding known exclusively to the mother's of this world fell over Bea as she sat there in the dark room. She'd much rather Ben now become a professional football player or better still, just got a paper route. At least there were rules and referees in football and his opposition wouldn't carry all sorts of sinister weapons that could be used to try and kill him. There were no rules in street policing unless you caught the criminals, and very few of them were these days. A quick browse through the daily newspapers would easily tell you that score.

The bad guys always seemed to be winning, particularly the drug dealers and street gangs.

No, Bea thought, this news about being a police officer wasn't good at all.

*   *   *

Chapter Thirty-eight

More than a decade after Ben Trilby had joined the Police Department, Officer Lisa Anna Carmaducci received a posting to the Uniformed Patrol Division, District Number One. It had been a hot spring morning just after her passing out ceremonies from the Police Training Depot and the whole world lay before her. The downtown Riverside district was never a recruit's first choice for a posting, but if you wanted to be a police officer you would go where they needed you and you kept your lips still. The Depot Commander had told Lisa that her field trainer would be a capable, dedicated veteran by the name of Ben Trilby. Ben had been policing the Riverside district for over a year now and had made some remarkable progress with the residents - both good and bad. The neighborhood lay in the shadows of the busy office high rises on the edge of the downtown center and had become a bit of an enigma within the city . . . but then so had Officer First Class Trilby. He was the lone police officer assigned to look after the inhabitants and patrol the small area that made up Riverside's streets. When Trilby wasn't on shift the officer's from the neighboring districts would take the calls, but one could see their hearts weren't into it - they had enough problems in their *own* precincts.

They called it a community because it was a residential collection of a turn of the century, two story clapboard-sided houses although others preferred to call the tiny section of town something else altogether. Almost half of the structures backed onto the wide, slow-moving river and true to the era of their construction, they all had gabled peaks over the porches with intricately detailed, arching fretwork that covered the open fronts of the gables.

All the yards had mature pine trees and many had the hearty, grow anywhere poplar trees that were as abundant as the sunshine. Some of the elderly residents had nurtured sugar maples until they were full-grown but the lack of any sudden cold snaps on the coast curtailed any yearly flowing of the sweet saps. Most of the houses were well cared for with trimmed lawns and fresh paint covering the porches and square wooden posts that supported the gables that held high their steep shingled roofs. On the other hand, a high percentage were neglected flop houses with paint peeling like

335

cancerous sunburns and lawns that were more weeds than grass with fibrous stalks that reached as high as your waist.

In the nicely cared for homes there lived mostly elderly people who had been raised there, inheriting the property as their families had passed on. These people had a voice but it was rarely heard among the council chambers at city hall, their tax base not being big enough to justify the volume required for a political ear. Residing in the run-down, poorly cared for homes were people of all ages and from every ethnic diversity known to North America. The landlords of these homes didn't live anywhere near the neighborhood (not a good place to raise a family you know) and chose to divide the old multi-storied houses into small apartments which they rented to the people who whether by cultural design or by bad luck, had no other place to live. They were a collection of drug users, alcoholics, prostitutes, pimps, impoverished single mothers and some of them were just plain, honest losers. The one social common denominator that bound most of these people together was the rotten start that most had received at the beginning of their lives.

Many had virtually come from dysfunctional families where the violations of their bodies, minds and souls had been fostered from their parents' substance abuse, and the poor start that their generation had received. A lot of these people were simply carrying on the family traditions that had been tattooed into their genes, born like their parents, highly prone to substance abuse and never really knowing right from wrong; screwed the first time they put a liquor jug or smoldering joint to their curious lips. Although much like their elderly neighbors, who probably weren't much better off economically with their meager pensions, these people, because of their status in modern society lacked a voice at city hall as well.

All this changed however once Officer Ben - as the neighborhood had come to call him - had been posted to the neighborhood as a patrolman and had soon obtained a feel for the streets and the people who lived there. It is impossible to police a community if you didn't know anything about them and making arrests and breaking heads wasn't always the answer either, at least to Ben's way of thinking. Ben liked to solve problems, not scoop them up and throw them in jail where they would appear a day later as if by magic, the same problems in the same place doing the same goddamned thing. The Inspector in charge of the Ben's watch had a noodle for a backbone and even less for a brain so he wasn't interested with his beat cop's solving neighborhood problems. Neighborhood problems didn't hold for much on a shift report.

He wanted arrest sheets and he wanted lots of them. He also wanted to see possession of narcotic charges, drunk driving charges, drunks arrested as well as a few dozen street gang members taken in for loitering, picking their noses or whatever it took to bag them. This kind of stuff impressed the Mayor and the Police Chief when they received the monthly statistics report, which in turn would be proudly turned over to the media.

When all these figures finally went to print or aired on the nightly news, it would appear to most residents that the Mayor, the Police Commission, and indeed the Police Department itself had a firm choke hold on the hordes of urban ne'er-do-well's. And so the taxpayers, ensconced safely at home in their scotch guarded easy chairs would watch and read all this tripe and wrongly assume the local constabulary was winning the war on street crime when in fact it could be compared to bailing a stricken ocean liner using a shot glass. The Police Department had neglected to tell his worship that a routine, possession of a narcotic charge took a cop off the street for a minimum of two hours while he or she processed the prisoner and did all the seizure reports as well as the endless prosecutor information sheets. Double that length of time to wade through the paperwork involved with a drinking driver who would most likely get off on a technicality the day he received his due process in a courtroom. These were only misdemeanors that the average uniformed police officer encountered during a regular shift, but when you considered the man hours spent on the more serious crimes (and rightly so) then the statistics and solve ratio representing the side of the moral majority became outright scary. Crime and/or evil, as well as violence and the various cottage industries that had spun from these ad hoc enterprises - such as prostitution and burglaries - were sadly holding their own in the constant battle for a safer humanity.

Another discouraging tidbit the Mayor hadn't been appraised of was the fact that the average possession of a narcotic charge nets a convicted offender a fifty-dollar fine with scads of time to pay while the investigating officer is testifying on a day off which means double overtime for him or her and the sixty or so other police officers also attending court on that particular day. In all fairness though, this whole process had become a victim of an already overworked system that appeared to be bordering on collapse. Unfortunately, it would probably keep running as it did until something terrible happened, or someone chanced along with the truckload of political resolve required to rebuild the program and overhaul its laws. As most politicians were lawyers, the hopeful forecast of a systematic renovation was at best a predictable dream, or at the very least an acquired fib. Most lawyers and their fraternity knew better than to mess with something that bought them new sports cars and funky apartments near their practices where they could keep their lovers - both male and female - far from their wive's searing eyes. All these roadblocks aside though, there did exist an old saying that you can't change the world or even your little corner of it for that matter. But if you tried really hard you could make a difference, if only on one street, in one neighborhood, in one city, and to hell with the rest of them. That would be just the way the streetwise, veteran Officer Trilby would tackle these policing issues. One neighborhood at a time.

It hadn't taken Ben Trilby long as a rookie police officer to realize that the statistical rules his own Watch Inspector imposed upon his subordinates and the general anarchy of the booking in and court systems were only hindering his ability to deliver a quality police service. Once Ben had completed the mandatory one-year probation period of all new police officers and was a card-carrying member of the Police Association, he made up his own rules and played the streets the way they should be played. Piss on his Inspector, piss on the defense lawyers and piss on his ass kissing colleagues. Ben was there for the people, the ones who paid his wages, the ones who couldn't afford to and the ones who lived in the streets on a daily basis. Unlucky enough with life, these social castoffs were nothing more than a quick tick on a statistics sheet to most of Ben's compatriots; an easy manner in which to beef up the arrest figures as well as their annual assessments. A limited amount of arrest reports at the year's end meant the Police Chief and the Police Commission would have to do a fair bit of groveling for additional funds or at least embark on a minimal amount of whining just to maintain the status quo. "Do a lot more, with a lot less," was the inspiring ditty found at the bottom of the Police Chief's monthly newsletters, which incidentally cost about three-thousand dollars a month to publish. These days the whole thing had become a money issue, a degenerating state of affairs that sickened Ben because it changed absolutely nothing. With that in mind he soon twigged to the fact that arresting the same people who dwelled near the bottom of the barrel day in and day out did nothing to alleviate the street crime and accompanying social problems.

Now this wasn't to say that Officer Trilby didn't arrest anyone or didn't lay any charges. Nothing could be closer to that certainty, but Ben had become more interested in quality than quantity and he wasn't about to start dancing every time his Inspector or Administrative bean counter pulled a fiddle out. His style had become innovative and new, and the Neanderthal hierarchy at the police department wasn't fond of it because it didn't produce any tangible statistics they could give to the politician's who pulled on *their* strings. Why, if all their officers employed this style of policing then certainly the streets and back alleys' would be a safer place to be, but what the hell would they give the Mayor at the end of each month? Which became the second reason Ben liked to practice his unique style - if it kept the people he policed happy but rubbed management a bit raw, then it had to be a good thing. So when he first received the posting to Riverside (basically unsupervised except for an overweight zone Sergeant who never left the office) he immediately applied the simple ideas that had worked everywhere else for him.

Ben would drive down to the Riverside neighborhood from Headquarters after the watch briefing, and park his blue and white marked patrol car next to an old stone church and get out. On foot with his portable radio, he would spend the shift walking around the neighborhood, knocking on doors and talking to the people who lived in the freshly painted homes, as well as the people who lived in the flophouses. A large portion of the inhabitants who lived inside any of these dwellings were more than a little shocked to find a Police Officer standing on their doorstep with a smile and an affable greeting. Had to be an election year most thought at first. The majority of police officers balked at this extended foot patrol crap and well they could for it really didn't even exist in most of the operational manuals. Ben rightly surmised earlier in his career that he would be surprised at what he saw and heard if he got out on foot and policed his district without being surrounded by the recycled metal and glass of his patrol car. What wasn't surprising of course was the way people, good or bad, drunk or sober, would talk to him when he took the time to greet them and speak with them face to face.

They would *slowly* open up and talk once they were secure in the knowledge that they could trust him and their complaints wouldn't fall on detached ears, (even the bad ones had complaints, especially if they just got stiffed by a drug dealer) or found they wouldn't get their asses kicked if caught behind a brick wall smoking a joint or sucking on a bottle of cheap hooch. Ben wasn't after the poor slobs who drank the Apple Jack down by the river bank, or sold their wasting young body's for their next drug fix, or fell asleep on a wrought iron bench in the neighborhood's only park, shivering in the falling dew until he drove them to a warm bed at the Sally Ann across the bridge. He only wanted to make his neighborhood safe for *everybody* who lived there and it wouldn't cost the Department a lot of money. In fact he saved them money every time he parked his police car and conducted his shift on foot. Within two months of his transfer to the Riverside district Ben's face had become as familiar and as natural looking as the manhole covers on the streets. People from all walks of life spoke easily to him and soon forgot that the ex-football player with the short curly blonde hair even wore a police officer's uniform.

Ben had become a good listener and it didn't matter who would be talking and just what their station in life had become because they all got the same empathetic young ear and the same courteous attention to their problems. When a police officer roamed the streets of a community on foot, and treated all the locals with dignity and respect an incredible amount of useful information could come his way. All one had to do was simply listen. Not only was Ben getting to know the residents of the district who in turn learned to respect his fairness and trust ability, but he was slowly gathering important information, always adding to his growing list of intended targets. These were the people that Ben was after. These were the turds who would get the single mothers hooked on heroin, then force them into the sex trade so they could afford to feed their habits. These were the low life traffickers who came into the area with a recognizance of bail stuffed in their back pockets from a previous offence, duly signed and promising to keep the peace and be of good behavior, yet with vials of crack cocaine hidden in their socks. These and many others were the one's selling the highly addictive crack cocaine and heroin to the already down-and-out people whose livers could have done without the introduction of something else to ingest into their already failing systems.

These were the people Officer Ben Trilby would target and arrest and with an uncommon zeal. He would relentlessly chase them a mile or two along the riverbank and although he was built like the heavy planked fishing boat or a fully laden herring punt - he was steady but sure.

The skinny drug-pushers who chain-smoked and ate nothing but garbage when they did eat, were no match for Trilby who moved in on them like a runaway boxcar. Every single time he would eventually catch up to them, scooping up their discarded drugs like a fumbled football without so much as a check in his pace. Ben would usually snatch them in his massive hands as they neared collapse, wheezing and fighting for breath, terror sculptured onto their faces as they feared the impending beating that usually came when they made the other cops run. Even though he was capable of ripping their faces off, folding them up, and tucking them into their wallets, this wasn't his style or a part of his gentle personality. He would however, crank his stainless steel, Smith and Wesson handcuffs onto their bony wrists, adjusting the tightness in direct proportion to the distance he had to run after them. Locked metal on a wrist bone with only a layer of skin for a cushion could hurt like hell but did no damage and the more the prisoner squirmed and struggled the more intense the pain would become. Handcuffed and searched and out of luck, Ben would escort the prisoner downtown to the booking office in the back of his patrol car, then wade through the mounds of required paperwork after lodging them into the city cells.

Possession for the purpose of trafficking in heroin or cocaine was a much more serious offence than standing goofed on a street corner and howling at the traffic lights. Even a few liberal judges recognized these sub-humans for the blight they truly were so there was never usually a problem asking for and receiving a remand into custody until their first appearance in their courts, which kept them out of Ben's thinning hair for at least a month or two. Ben also had tenacity for search warrants and he liked to execute at least one during a five-day shift. Notwithstanding, the Department's required Policies for obtaining search warrants might just as well have been inked onto toilet paper for all the attention Trilby gave them. All search warrants were to be approved first by the Zone Sergeant's and then initialed by the Duty Inspector's but Ben considered these procedures to be a complete waste of time, as well as undue wear and tear on the soles of his boots as he walked the papers from office to office. After that he still had to get the warrant signed by Judge and with that in mind our stalwart young police officer once again seized the initiative and bypassed these two trivialized figureheads. He rightly assumed his work was on a need to know basis and there was really no need for the fat Zone Sergeant or his Inspector to know what he was doing. Besides, obtaining their approval was not a legal requirement, only a bureaucratic department policy.

Ben soon discovered that finding out where all the traffickers lived and the kind of dope they peddled was the easiest part of obtaining his search warrants. The completing of the information to obtain a search warrant was another matter, but he always forged on and got the goods even if at times this did require a little "creative license." Ben's evidence to obtain the warrant always came in the form of "information received from confidential informants known to him, who in the past has proven knowledgeable and trustworthy." Should the facts be known, the information Ben received from the streets could be scanty at best, but he was guaranteed to find something hidden away in the pushers stinking grottos. This information was good enough for the Judge signing the search warrants, it was good enough for the people Ben policed and more importantly it was good enough for Ben. Albeit it had become a nightmare for the trafficker's behind the doors he would be soon breaking from their hinges. Each search warrant proved productive and within short order word was on the streets that Officer Ben was more interested in the people dealing the drugs than the people consuming them. The time had come to break camp and move their goods; setting up shop in a more accommodating neighborhood would be a healthier alternative to jail.

Using simple police techniques like walking the neighborhood and constantly speaking to the people who lived there, as well as ignoring antiquated department policy, Ben slowly plucked the foulness from the streets and alleys of a district where the others had long since given up. Bit by bit he managed to get the streets of Riverside back to its nineteenth century lifestyle, but his dedicated efforts hadn't come without a price. At least once a week he would be summoned down to his Watch Inspector's office where this oddity of a senior Police Officer would have a run at him about following rules and procedures. Ben would sit quietly in the chair in front of his desk, putting on his very best naughty boy face while saying with as much sincerity as he could muster, "sorry sir, it won't happen again - I promise." The white-shirt officer would look smugly at Ben, pacified with the knowledge that his verbal reprimand had effected the desired results.

He would then write Ben up a "shit-chit," which he had him sign like a truant school boy before dismissing him back to the streets. All would then move along nicely as it should, until a week or two would pass when reports of ignoring procedures would once again filter up to the irksome officer who would in turn send out another bidding for Ben to attend his office. Whereupon the Inspector would go through the same chastising routine where Ben would once again apologize to his patronizing nods, reassuring him that it "was an oversight this time, won't happen again, scouts honor." Although Ben was never a scout, these visits in themselves were becoming bothersome and the brutal pace that Ben had set himself to clean the neighborhood up that started to wear down his resolve.

The posting to Riverside was generally a six-month tour due to the high stress rate suffered from carting human trash around on a continuing basis. It wasn't until Ben's eighth month that he realized he was probably going to be left there because of the manner in which he conducted his daily police work. Unofficial word made the rounds of all the districts that his work frustrated some of his peers and drove his Watch Inspector to the point that he would keep this unyielding black sheep posted to the beat-your-head-against-the-wall Riverside district. There was indeed a quality of truth to those slanderous rumors, albeit something one could overlook, but the unfortunate affair surrounding the gorilla with the two-foot penis was the one that really frosted some people's backside and put the seal to Ben's posting ambitions.

Shortly after the gorilla suit went missing, every corner of every office in every district was ripe with the hearsay that Ben had been the perpetrator of the evil deed and subsequent fall out. Nevertheless, no one had a smattering of proof other than to say that Trilby had been in the general vicinity when the suit had literally walked out the door of the main booking office and down the street. Trilby had already been cast as an odd one by the rest of the street cops, which did nothing to stem the gossip and its impromptu heralding. Some of the Department's lower ranking fellowship had grown extremely leery of Ben for when it came to street level policing as no one could recall him ever losing his temper. Not once. Not even for a little bit when he was out of sight of the general public. Not even when a drunken fat biker had bitten him on the arm during the annual Sea Festival riots of two years past. Even the Department's two clergymen were known to get slightly miffed from time to time as members of their law enforcement flock strayed where they ought not to have strayed. But not Ben, he would never get angry and would even take his morals a step further, becoming quite vocal about his feelings regarding any illegal street justice.

Almost every officer at the patrol level knew about Ben and knew he wouldn't tolerate any brutality nor would he be a party to any such behavior. Regardless, once the dust of rumor had settled, Ben was in fact the one who had filched the gorilla suit, complete with its twenty-four-inch pecker. But he had done it only to prevent the fool who utilized it from bringing any

343

further discredit upon himself and the Department - and because the gorilla had paid Herb Twinkle a visit while the poor old man had been held in custody on a psychiatric remand. Old Herb was Ben's prisoner, and he was Ben's case and the booking office crowd should have known enough to stay clear of him. So Ben's presence in the booking office area when the gorilla suit went missing, as well as his perplexing viewpoints regarding "attitude adjustments, street justice and elevator rides," made him a likely candidate for expropriation of the now famous, great ape.

Street justice had become daily reality of take it or leave it, for there usually came a time in every Police Officer's career when some mouthy, vile smelling, urban miscreant pushed that invisible button that eventually led to a well timed and long overdue attitude adjustment. Ordinarily, these attitude adjustments were administered during the elevator ride to the third floor booking office. Mister Gorilla, as he had been so aptly named, had evolved from and had become a natural extension of that elevator ride from hell. Regrettably, some prisoners refused to close their beaks once they were lodged into cells, so some quick manner of quieting them down was required and why not have a little harmless fun in the process. The bulk of all people arrested were usually taken into custody during the weekend, which meant they were intoxicated by liquor or drugs and had been acting up in or near some kind of a public place. Copious amounts of liquor did strange things to some people, but the golden amber did even weirder things to the young, single white male with long hair wearing blue jeans and their trademark black tee shirts. After hours of swilling high-test beer and stuffing cocaine up their noses in a trashy nightclub on a Friday night, a very strange metabolic transformation would frequently occur. Many associated these transmutations with a full moon, although they generally did commence near midnight as the subjects mouths as well as their muscles and ego's seemed to swell to super human proportions, bringing about a form of behavior that only ended when a half-dozen police officers arrived.

Once the uniforms had entered the establishment, the mouths of these besotted rubes would get bigger still, urged on by the presence of the voluptuous female bystanders who had spent the evening spurning their drunken advances. There would then be a minor scuffle on the dance floor followed by much screaming and spitting as one or two of the disgruntled hooligan's were removed in handcuffs from the premises. With his hands manacled behind his back, there was little the detainee could do except spit vigorously at the arresting officers. In a day and age when Hepatitis "C" and other infectious diseases were as prevalent and as certain as the winter tides, this wasn't always such a good idea. Not when you're being escorted by a couple of exasperated, overworked police officers who each have a kid requiring seven-thousand dollars worth of orthodontics and you still had the impending elevator ride to the third floor booking office.

Once arrested there would follow a short, noisy ride downtown in the back of a marked patrol car to the Headquarters building that was quartered in the old section of town. This building backed onto a narrow alley where high-bricked walls skirted both sides of a timeless lane constructed of cobblestones, long since eroded from an era when the prisoners were first carted in on horseback. One-hundred years later only the mode of transportation had changed, and with that the arresting officers would park their patrol cars in the darkened alley which lacked any amount of natural light during the day due to the high walls on both sides. It would become even blacker at night despite the flickering white neon light mounted above the wide metal door that formed the back entrance. This location was also conveniently far enough away from the sensitive eyes and ears of the public who would stroll the downtown area looking for a bistro after the theaters had cleared. At times the prisoner would become so out of control that a tune-up just couldn't wait for the elevator ride. So the less the general public saw and heard coming from the shadows of the back alley, the better off the whole world would be.

Depending where in the lane the officer's might find a vacant place to park, the prisoner would then be walked or dragged, generally kicking, yelling and spitting through the door and up to the back counter where a frazzled Duty Sergeant approved the arrest report. From here the caterwauling citizen was taken for a short walk across the tiled floor to the dreaded "elevator," where upon the flying sputum and hollering would cease the moment the double doors had closed upon the prisoner and his two escorts. This would be the time when a belligerent, mouthy, in custody client who freely shared with his police escorts his gobs of bacterial loaded saliva received his unspoken, unauthorized, none bruising but highly deserving attitude adjustment.

The booking office, or 'bucket' as it was referred to locally, incorporated the whole third floor of the Headquarters building and was accessed after a short (or long) ride up in the elevator.

It was your standard service lift with room for about six people, with a buffed metal panel near the sliding doors, which had three black plastic disks and a red emergency stop button whose surface had become worn from frequent use. This little red button held the secret to a quiet, short ride to the third floor, or a long, painful ascent up to the cells. It was within this mobile little room painted the light green of a fresh melon that the attitude adjustments would unofficially take place. Suffice to say that when Monday mornings would roll around a janitor would spend a good half hour scrubbing the elevator walls to remove the impressionable motifs of human lip, head, hair and ear marks ;all beautiful imprints, all made with human blood and mucus, although some were nothing more than crude smears running the width of the wall across the shiny, enameled paint.

When the doors opened on the third floor, the occupants of the elevator were treated to the smell of urine, feces, sweat and vomit. But on a cheerier note the prisoner was no longer hawking phlegm and screaming about his constitutional rights. He would have quieted right down as the blood dripped off his chin from a split lip, limping painfully as his testicles started to swell. A stiff pair of designer blue jeans offered little protection to his sensitive plums where the flick of an oak nightstick had parted the soft flesh of his scrotum. All of these injuries occurred of course when the prisoner fell inside the elevator as it lurched up to the third floor and it will continue to happen until they get the union boys in to fix the goddamned jerking, which wouldn't be for a couple of years they were so busy.

Time in custody would eventually soak away the pain and sober him up, but the odd one would press forth with his outlandish allegations of police brutality. But as a god-fearing taxpayer just whom would *you* believe? Some drunken, cocaine snorting, unemployed shit-rat who has sexual designs on your daughter and has just been booked for causing a disturbance in a public tavern. Or two decorated veterans of the police department who risk their necks for little glory and even less on their paychecks. What takes place inside that elevator after the emergency stop button has been activated may truly never be known, but what is surely known is that the prisoner's attitude is almost subservient as he is walked up to the wire mesh cage encircling the booking counter where the handcuffs are removed. Here he is ordered to forfeit everything he owns to a plastic property bag including his large wallet with the nifty chrome chain, his money, jewelry, shoelaces and gaudy, leather waist belt with the huge buckle. From here on in he is nothing more than common barnyard offal and the men and women pulling a shift at the booking office make no attempts to alter these very real facts. Intoxicated persons don't even get a phone call, as they tend to rip the instrument from the wall when the harried lawyers hang up on them in the middle of the night.

After the prisoner is searched, he's then escorted down a long corridor in his stocking feet, his sweaty pads leaving moist footprints on the polished linoleum. The cell area stood behind a vault type door with a small sliding portal at eye level so you could see who stood on the other side.

To gain access to the bucket, this door required a half turn from one of those large, solid brass keys with Joliette, Illinois stamped into its handle. As the door swings silently open on its long strap hinges you enter the bucket which has remained unchanged in more than twenty years except the smell of human filth seemed headier than the last time, as if it has now saturated the impervious cement and gray metal bars of the holding areas. If you were an unlucky detainee and up until this point nothing so far has happened to make you feel otherwise, then you were placed in one of the drunk tanks with three dozen or so other sad cases. Each tank had three cinder block walls with bars along the front and a drain in the middle of the floor to gulp the gallons of hot water and disinfectant used during the daily wash downs. Unfortunately, the occupants relieved themselves and dropped whatever came out of their bodies through that small grated opening for there was no other place to go. If you passed out with your head near the drain and some individual had to urinate, well, your face was going to get wet and that was life in a big city pokey. On more than one occasion the prisoner's were herded from the cells after many hours of sobering up, some of them finding their faces and backs covered with someone else's excrement.

Shame could be the only sensation a civilized man would feel in the drunk tank as your presence along with your fellow inmates was indicative enough that you'd already hit bottom.

Most of the stink that festered the cell area came from the three drunk tanks that were habitually full during the evenings. These holding tanks were a statement in simplicity and were designed with the sole purpose of safely holding the highly inebriated people who were lodged there. Some drunks preferred to make malicious statements by attempting to rip sinks and beds from their mountings along the walls. Still others could fall the foot or so from their bunks in a catatonic stupor or trip over a stainless steel commode where upon the city could be quickly slapped with a lawsuit for not properly looking after their charges. The less that adorned the walls and floors of the drunk tanks in the way of toilets and bunks, the less likelihood of any injuries or willful damage.

Smaller cells were built on either side of the tanks, their bars symmetrical and cold looking as they ranged single file down one side of the long narrow hallway that ran the full length of the cell area. Against the far wall of each cell stood a plain metal door that allowed entry to officers from a darkened catwalk that also traversed the full length of the cells. This door offered the officers a tactical advantage, allowing them to enter the cell from both ends at the same time to surprise and remove an uncooperative prisoner from his cage, usually to drag him over to the courthouse across the alley. These smaller cells were deluxe accommodations when stood next to the drunk tanks for each had a stainless steel toilet in the corner that you flushed by pushing a button and a set of metal bunks bolted into one of the cinder blocked walls. A thin, vinyl-covered mattress and a wool blanket made all the difference between a tolerable occupation and the stinking chill and filth of the floors of the drunk tanks.

If you were lucky enough to be placed into one of these cells, you were either sober or the tanks were stuffed to overflowing. Unlike a school bus or an elevator that was allowed to carry a maximum capacity, the drunk tanks weren't full until the jailers decided they were. At times it would become a sort of college game where the freshmen would try to stuff as many students as possible into a phone booth or a compact car. So during the odd occasion they had more than thirty sweating bodies packed into one tank while the other two remained vacant, just in case there was a riot downtown or something. No matter though, a visit to the city cells could be unnerving for the uninitiated for the bucket could become an extremely noisy place until everybody had passed out or had become too hoarse from threatening to have their keeper's jobs. By about three in the morning, the rush of human trash being delivered to the bucket would slow to a manageable trickle, and the officers working the bucket and counter could go for a pee, or have a sandwich, or sit quietly staring at a wall, wishing they had a clean shirt to replace the one someone had puked on. The important part about this time of the evening was the luxurious silence that seemed to hang in the stifling air along with the acidic stink.

Silence could indeed be golden and the officers would enjoy and relish it as they sat on their stools behind the caged counter, dreaming of the day when their posting to the bucket would come to an end and they could return to the streets where the air was clear and some of the people they dealt with had the decency to at least bathe every other day. Golden it may be, the silence would frequently be short lived as one of the jailed reprobates would eventually wake up, the swill or illegal drugs still clouding his mind, unsure of where he was or which solar system he was even in. Eight times out of eleven it would be the single white male who would start the noisy hubbub. The one who had been picked up spitting and fighting at the tavern at around midnight. The one with the crushed nuts and the split lip who had fallen during the elevator ride up to the third floor bucket. You know the one. Now his yelling would start all over again and if he wasn't quickly stopped he would soon be joined by the others, their combined chorus quickly escalating into a plastered cacophony of utter belligerence. The key here of course would be to stop the dissatisfied prisoner *before* he awoke the hundred or so other people presently incarcerated. Timing and style was essential here, for a verbal disturbance could easily escalate into a riot of sorts, especially in the drunk tanks where they lay stacked like two-by-fours on the befouled floor.

So evolves our hairy primate, for this was when Mister Gorilla would make a terrifying appearance to the holding cell of the chanting rebel. The huge monkey would say very little and always give the immediate impression that the purpose of his visit was to engage into some interspecies intercourse. Coming down from a continual crack cocaine high, or a week long bender on the bottle, the last thing anybody wanted to see was a six-foot-four-inch gorilla with a two-foot long schlong enter through the back door of his jail cell from the gloom of the cat walk. Mister Gorilla would employ all the tactics available to him, often sneaking up to the prisoner who would be pounding on the bars at the front of the cell, raucously challenging the no-ball's head jailor to a fist fight. All these fearless threats would disappear in a loud gasp as the gorilla slid up and tapped on the shoulder of the braying internee, who would almost always fill his drawers as he gazed up into the gorilla's leathery black face. Some would even faint once they took in the long black appendage that hung between the ape's hairy legs. In short order the prisoner would be reduced to a whimpering mass as the ape cuffed him about the ears, then put a black index finger to his licorice colored lips, indicating it best the inmate remain silent or some very unnatural and very unpleasant things may just occur. Just as fast as the simian had appeared, he would glide quietly back through the rear door and disappear into the catwalk. Silence would once again fall upon the snoring prisoners and cold cement walls of the inner city bucket.

Nobody, not even the seediest, most ambitious ambulance chasing, or the most corrupt criminal lawyer in the city would believe a client's story about a nocturnal visit by a huge gorilla with an even proportionally bigger dink. One would be better off telling his counsel about a horde of naked, buxom elves dancing on his stomach as he lay on his bunk in the city jail.

The fact that the gorilla did exist was something known only to a handful of Police Officers working the night shift in the bucket, although half the beat crew in the Police Department had their suspicions. Word soon drifted onto the streets that such a creature lurked within the shadows of the catwalks, waiting for some mouthpiece to start crooning long after everyone else had the decency to pass out or go to sleep. There occurred here a bit of an irony in that the gorilla suit itself had been purchased by the police association for a parade a dozen years back and had been forgotten about until a huge cop named Oliver Ginty had become a permanent, hulking fixture inside the bucket.

Officer Ginty had lost the hearing in one ear after becoming involved in a very untoward and nearly fatal incident. He'd chased down a career criminal into a downtown alley who in his desperation to avoid arrest had discharged his stolen revolver a bit too close to Ginty's exposed ear. Both Ginty and the criminal went to the hospital with related injuries. Ginty was driven in a patrol car with a loud ringing in his head while the criminal traveled unconscious in the back of an ambulance with a smashed in face. Still, it could have been a lot worse. Ginty was out of shape and overweight from all the years of soft living and scoffing free grub offered to uniformed police at the Burger Barn. He nearly lost this fight and had been a mere rasping breath away from taking a thirty-eight-caliber bullet in the head, although those who truly knew him doubted that would have done much damage. Oliver Ginty was an old guard centurion the new breed of Police Officer's had labeled "strong like a farm tractor, clever like a garden rake." Pitifully enough, this proof lay in his daily actions.

There were a few like Ginty who breathed the fetid air in the booking office on a continuous basis. All of them sick, lame, or just plain slackers devoid of any drive and for whatever reasons were restricted from doing active police work. Like most of the booking office crowd, it only took Ginty a couple of shifts before the persistent clamor that accompanied a weekend night shift started to rake his nerves just a little. One rare and quiet evening Ginty had found the discarded gorilla suit in an equipment room down a hallway behind the caged booking office.

It lay all forlorn looking, tucked away in a plywood box, stacked among similar boxes that contained the section's riot gear. Now as previously mentioned, Ginty was an enormous man but the same couldn't be said about his brain, which was thought to have suffered some damage after he cross-checked the side of a moving zamboni a few years back. He had done this between periods while the machine's driver laid a new sheen onto the surface of the ice during a hockey tournament with the Regional Police Force. Ginty had been half drunk and full of piss and vinegar but obviously not full enough as the zamboni went on to clean the ice without so much as a dent and the dozy Ginty was carted from the rink atop a canvas stretcher.

Many will say he's never been quite the same since the hockey accident and the ruined part of his head may just be the cluttered portion where he acquired the plans for the black, dusty gorilla costume. Nonetheless, one night Ginty removed the suit from its plywood box and shook the dust from the matted hair then pulled it on over his uniform. Mister Gorilla soon became a howling success just minutes later when it debuted inside of cell number seven, which held a deranged and yapping sex murderer who had raped and choked to death three young women. The serial killer's name was Kyle Mortimer and he felt for once the kind of fear his victims felt before he strangled the life from them, but he did become a changed man after the gorilla's visit.

Mortimer in fact hung himself after being sent to a Federal Penitentiary so you couldn't say that Ginty's heart wasn't in the right place. Always one to build on an idea, Ginty started to add bits to the gorilla suit and his first addition was a black nylon, knee-high dress sock that he filled with rolled oats and sewed to the crotch. Now Mister Gorilla was indeed a Mister and with a wang like that he wasn't one to be trifled with. The attire was complete, and the great ape was indeed ready for action with any obnoxious and impertinent shit-rats who wished to yodel away their night of incarceration into the wee hours of the morning.

Alas, but all good things do come to an end, and to everything upon this earth there is an apparent purpose . . . except of course for our friend the gorilla. With it's rather manly looking phallus swinging in the breeze and with Oliver Ginty parading secretly around inside of him, its demise became sealed the night it paid a call to the cell of old Herb Twinkle. There lay no real purpose nor any intelligent meaning behind that particular visit and Ben considered it an outright pox upon the Department and human dignity in general even though few people knew about it. Upon Herb's arrest by Office

Trilby of the Riverside District, the starving old man was nothing more than a lonely bag of flesh, left to mutter quietly to the walls as he lay curled up on the bottom bunk in his cell, willing himself to die. They say that to every beginning there is an end and the leathery-chested gorilla would be no exception to that century's old proven rule.

Upon the night that Oliver Ginty, alias Mister Gorilla, dropped in on Herb Twinkle would herald the beginning of the end for the well-endowed hairy monster. Thou shalt not screw with Officer Ben Trilby's prisoners, especially the ones who were faint of mind and held even less in their waning hearts.

Herb Twinkle was one of the saddest cases Ben had seen in his ten years as a police officer.

So despondent that the cruel story crept into Ben's dreams as he lay slept at night in his apartment. Sleep would usually come easily after a grueling day shift fraught with crack dealers and gang members who were finally becoming an extinct species in the Riverside area. One was supposed to leave the street work behind in his locker at the end of a shift but everything about the Herb Twinkle file bothered Ben. For the first time he disregarded the code of conduct and became personally involved in a criminal file. Ben had too. He couldn't stand by while the lonely soul that was all that remained of an old man was eaten up by an unfair system then spit out the other end without any regard for the cheerless facts.

People like old man Twinkle would mark Ben from the rest of his fellow officers as well as taint him badly among his superiors. Ben had become an idealistic young police officer but idealism became a mute and frustrating standard when it came to the so-called balance of law, order, and social justice. The Twinkle file developed into a pitiful travesty and it was all Ben could do to stand on the sidelines and watch as the full letter of the law was brought down in its entirety. He had been working on the file from it's very the outset, putting in many of his own hours at the typewriter, sending out letters to lobby the District Prosecutor, even hoping to obtaining an audience with a Supreme Court Justice in his chambers. The final outcome and the fact that Ben had come to know the Twinkles quite well made it even more of an emotional burden. When the elements of premeditated murder was existent and undeniable then no amount of crusading or outright pleading was going to change those facts or the mandatory sentence of life imprisonment.

Herb and Mira Twinkle had been a kindly old couple in their late eighties who lived on the lower floor of one of the rooming houses that backed onto the river. Herb was a decorated veteran of the Second World War who had endured the heavy fighting to recapture the Philippines and beyond. He had been one of thousands of soldiers who had breathed a sigh of relief when Colonel Paul Tibbetts dropped the first atomic bomb "little boy," from the belly of his B-29 Superfortress onto an unsuspecting Hiroshima. The planned invasion of Japan had been conservatively calculated to cost at least one million allied soldiers, something the politicians lacked the stomach for, not to mention that it would prolong the war a few more costly years. Everybody had become sick of the brutal fighting in the humid jungles, including Sergeant Herb Twinkle and the crew of his M-4 Sherman tank. When Tokyo capitulated and the remnants of the Imperial Forces of Japan submitted to the inevitable surrender, it allowed Sergeant Twinkle to rotate home with his skin as well as his limbs and all digits intact. The Pacific Northwest never looked so beautiful and if he ever saw a jungle again with it's suffocating heat, deadly vipers and spiders with bodies the size of kiwi fruit he would cheerfully shoot himself with the M-1 Garand rifle he'd surreptitiously liberated as a keepsake.

He married Mira shortly after his return home, in a backyard wedding with a few close friends in attendance to help celebrate the bonding. Mira had been a petite girl with fresh, clean skin whom Herb had known in high school and their union seemed as natural as the clouds and the sky. The contented couple settled into a rented house on the outskirts of what was back then a rapidly growing city. Herb labored in a local fish canning plant for the duration of his working days and collected a small pension when he eventually retired. The military supplemented this allowance with a small monthly annuity but it didn't amount to an awful lot of money. Herb and Mira had never been blessed with children for some biological reason but it hadn't occurred through a lack of trying. In the end it would probably be a good thing with the borderline poverty that had stalked their simple lives. A savings account held a bit of money that would see them through their golden years, as well they had managed to buy the house they had rented all these decades.

Life appeared to be acceptable if not somewhat plain as the couple drifted in the direction of their twilight days. Then Herb's brother-in-law entered the picture with a boneheaded scheme about investing into a vending machine company that would be coin-operated and dispense everything from cold sodas to condoms. Apprehensive at first, Herb eventually gave up his cautiousness, hoping to buy his wife a better house and more deserving lifestyle; months after handing over to his brother-in-law his entire savings and the deed to the couple's small house.

The deal, which had never been anything more than a tempting mirage, fell apart and blew away along with all the relinquished money and the deeded property.

Destitute but still having each other, Herb and Mira rented the lower half of a house in the quiet Riverside District and Herb took a job as a night watchman at the nearby rail yards to pay the rent and put some food on the table. They had lived in this same house now for more than thirty years even though the neighborhood had taken a terrible slide and the house now boasted peeling paint and damp, grease stained walls. Ben had taken a liking to the old couple and would stop by to drink steaming mugs of weak coffee with them in the bare kitchen before going upstairs to pick the brain of the drug addict who lived in one of the rooms above.

However, their meager existence took a bad turn when Mira had been stricken with a massive stroke that had mercilessly failed to take her life. Once stabilized and without the benefit of medical insurance, she had been discharged from the hospital as nothing more than a drooling turnip, given over to the care of her aged husband. Some warm hearts in the community had supplied the couple with a wheelchair they'd found in a second hand store and this certainly helped Herb with his daily toil.

But Mira could no longer speak or eat by herself, nor even recognize the man she had shared a life with and her broken body eventually taxed what remained of Herb's declining limits. He now dressed her in adult diapers and a housecoat as this made cleaning up after her easier on his sanity and his own failing body. He would never have made it this far without the wheelchair but enough was enough and twelve weeks after his wife's stroke Herb one day decided to take himself and Mira to a place far better than the one that lay before them. It had been a warm, sunny morning when he got out of bed, and poured the last of the oatmeal into a pot and fed himself and his wife one final meal of hot porridge. Herb then pulled the gray, pinstriped suit that he'd been married in from the closet and heard his tired bones creak and click as he labored to put it on. He didn't bother with shoes or socks and hobbled into the bathroom to wet and brush his shiny gray hair, returning to the bedroom to retrieve his military service medals from the drawer of an ancient cherry wood dresser. These he pinned above his left chest in a smart, even row, carefully adjusting them as he stood looking into a full-length wall mirror. He appeared almost comedic standing in his pinstriped suit, the luster of his long yellow toenails peeking out from beneath the long cuffs of his trousers. Either Herb had shrunk with the years or else the pants had grown longer while hanging all but forgotten in the closet. Once he was satisfied with his turn out, he struggled for about a half hour as he put Mira into a fine pink cotton gown then combed her hair and wheeled her into the living room near the front window where he kissed her good-bye on the forehead.

Herb Twinkle then mouthed a quiet prayer of forgiveness as he walked with purpose back into the bedroom to get the equipment he would need to take them on their final journey. Returning to the living room, his knotty fingers pained as he fed three brass rounds through the top of the breech and into the built in magazine of his treasured M-1 Garand rifle. He still handled the weapon like it was an extension of his own body, pulling back on the scribed metal nubs on either side of the blued, steel bolt, letting the springs drive the breech block home while simultaneously chambering a round into the dusty maw at the receiving end of the barrel.

Taking careful aim from a distance of only three feet Herb took one last look at his wife as she slept peacefully in her wheelchair, the sunshine falling upon her restful face. He slowly squeezed the trigger, just the way the Army had taught him those many years ago, so as not to anticipate and cringe at the approaching discharge, a sure way to pull the round off its intended target.

When the booming report and kick from the rifle butt ultimately came, it startled the old soldier exactly the way it was supposed too and he knew intuitively that the bullet had found its mark.

Ben had been working the day shift on foot patrol, talking to a derelict in the park when he heard the muffled shot coming from more than two blocks away, somewhere out on the eastern edge of the Riverside District. Trilby was gone in mid sentence like a charging receiver after snatching a punted football, lunging over the crumbly surface of the sidewalk in the direction of the shot, his mouth dry with fear as his massive legs pumped him along at speed. The front gardens of the houses he sped past seemed to fly by timelessly from the corner of his vision and before he was halfway there the portable radio hanging on his Sam Browne crackled with an address and a complaint of a shot fired. Ben's throat choked involuntarily as the address registered in his mind and he gave the telecom operator a ten-four into the microphone that bounced from the leather strap below his epaulette. "Christ no . . . the Twinkle house," he thought as he ran.

Ben was nearly upon the residence when he heard the second shot from somewhere inside the house, and he took the front wooden steps in one leap, disregarding all the sneaking and peeking rules practiced in officer survival. He hadn't even bothered to un-holster his nine-millimeter pistol nor advise the telecom operator that he'd arrived so sure that only carnage awaited him inside the house. Ben knew all about the tragic stroke that had afflicted Mira and had watched Herb's predicable slide toward a miserable surrender. He had contacted the Social Services Department, who already strained to their budgetary ends had managed to supply a home nurse for three days of the week. But it couldn't possibly rekindle the spirit for life that had seeped from the now defeated Herb. When Ben crashed through the flimsy door of the lower floor apartment he instinctively panned the scene with his eyes and later wished he had simply just walked over to the residence instead of running. This would have given the elderly soldier a little more time to carry out his final mission.

Ben took in the whole devastating scene within the common blinking of an eye, analyzing everything that lay before him while at the same time coming to a logical conclusion. Mira sat slumped over in her wheel chair in the warm sunlight by the wooden panes of the front window, her face serene looking as she lay in a final peace. A plum colored entry wound formed a small dot the size of a garden pea in her temple below her straight, silvery hair. A trickle of dark blood found its way down her white skin and dripped slowly from the bottom of her chin, blotching the wrinkles of the cotton gown that covered her lap. The round that Herb had used was a factory load, military point-thirty-caliber bullet with a full copper jacket which meant the lead slug would have traveled clear through Mira's brain before making a clean exit wound on the other side. Ben confirmed this in a millisecond by the spray of blood that had pocked the greasy wall on the other side of Mira's wheelchair. A small black hole in the center of the blood spatter also told Ben that the bullet had shot through the thin walls of the house and had followed an unpredictable trajectory down the street. An old black cat the couple had named Twiggy lay motionless in the middle of the water stained hardwood floor with a pool of dark blood encircling her furry head, which accounted for the second shot Ben had heard. The third bullet had yet to leave the barrel but it was dangerously close as old Herb sat on a musty, rose-colored divan with his transparent blue lips around the hot muzzle of the rifle. He struggled to get one of his big toes into the circular metal band of the trigger guard so he could apply the required pressure to discharge the weapon then follow his cherished Mira into the hereafter.

It was a piteous sight; one that had become instantly engraved into Ben's memory. One of those scenes that would make him shiver with despair every single time he thought about it. Herb was dressed in a tatty, pin-striped suit as he sat concentrating on his mortal task, his eyes focused through the lens of the thick glasses that must of weighed more than the ancient warrior himself.

Ben covered the distance across the floor within the period it took for the third precious second to tick over. He snatched the wooden stock of the rifle in his hand as it discharged next to his face. Like a small explosion the last bullet was sent harmlessly into the ceiling at a speed of over two thousand feet per second. The shock wave from the muzzle blast left Ben stunned as its force pushed his head back on his shoulders; the thunderclap giving his ear drums a harsh pounding as the ringing brought on a wave of nausea. It required a couple of more seconds before Ben realized that he hadn't been hit with anything other than the loud, high velocity muzzle gases. He looked down to check on the trembling old man who sat weeping, mired in his own failure to join his precious wife.

The room seemed strangely still and quiet considering what had just happened, then the microphone below Ben's left ear squawked to life, cutting the abrupt silence, startling him to the point that he jumped reflexively as the female telecom operator checked on his status.

He took a moment to speak into the mike and advised her that everything was fine although it would appear that he had a homicide. Ben immediately reflected on just how profound and relative that statement of 'everything was fine,' could have been taken by an untrained observer.

There was absolutely nothing fine about the events that had taken place inside this damp living room. Keeping a firm grip on the rifle stock, Ben then took a few mandatory seconds to breeze through all the rooms of the suite to secure the entire crime scene, touching nothing but ensuring no one else was present. The back door that led from the kitchen was bolted and all the windows were latched shut. Upon his return to the living room Ben viewed the crime scene once again and the sheer misery that engulfed the room could best be described as absolutely depressing.

It became a bad taste that touched the tongue as well as the soul of the young police officer who now fully regretted the expeditious manner in

357

which he had attended to the house. Ben already knew where this tragedy was heading and just exactly how it would end, realizing that two or three seconds in the right direction would have made all the difference in the world.

He laid the rifle on the floor behind the divan, well out of Herb's reach and knelt down beside the shaking old veteran, looking directly at him.

"Jesus Christ, Herb . . . why?" Ben wasn't totally sure himself why he asked the question for the answer was more than just a bit obvious. Herb looked up into Ben's eyes, rubbing his bony fingers together, his thin lips trembling as he shook his head slowly. He opened his mouth to speak but heavy footsteps from the front porch broke the numbing spell, stopping the words before they were ever spoken. Ben glanced up to see a couple of "plain wrappers" enter the living room and he could feel the resentment rise inside him along with the other emotions that now roiled around his stomach. The whole time that he had been policing Riverside he had yet to see any of the city dicks from the plain-clothes units even drive through the district. Now a desperate, sickly old soldier with very few options attempts an extreme exit, a citizen calls in a shots fired complaint and the boys in their polyester suits fall on the place like blowflies on a dried stool.

These two wrappers Ben especially despised for they were a regular pair of test pilots and the most obnoxious of their bunch. They were large men and each packed a belly or two stuffed beneath their colorful wash and wear shirts and they both held a condescending manner toward any living creature other than a fully qualified detective. Every Police Department in the Northern Hemisphere had a few just like these two - it had become an allotment kind of a thing that no one could ever figure out. The two that stood before Ben were especially insufferable. They both came equipped with booming voices, drinkers faces, and a fierce common loyalty onto themselves as well the ladies they took outside of their third or fourth failing marriage. This pair went by the names of Fenton and Darby and they were both Detective Sergeants, which disadvantaged Ben even further, although it didn't change the open contempt he held for the two. Darby spoke first, looking at Ben over his half-moon glasses, a long cigarette with at least an inch of ash wagging in his puffy lips, disregarding all the basic rules for preventing a crime scene contamination. It was obvious to all three police officers they had a smoking gun homicide, but one of the most basic rules of elementary police work was never to assume anything. Not ever.

"You okay, Trilby?" Darby barked.

Fenton had pulled his black issue notebook from somewhere inside of his sports coat and had started to make a rough sketch of the living room.

"Yes, I'm fine. Listen, Sergeant, can I park Mister Twinkle in your patrol car? I think it best we get him out of here. I'll warn him and read him his rights."

"Where's *your* car?" Darby demanded.

"Parked a few blocks away, down by that ancient stone church."

"Oh yeah . . . I heard all about you. You like to walk around so's you can *greet* the people." Darby's voice came heavy with sarcasm but Ben ignored it, knowing there would always be a later. There always was.

"Something like that," Ben replied quietly.

"Is the scene secured?" Darby grunted.

"Yeah, but there's a druggie named Mike who lives upstairs. I'm not sure if he's home right now and I didn't get a chance to look."

"Sounds good," Darby said, "we'll take over from here, take the prisoner downtown and book will ya? We'll interview him later."

Ben nodded at Darby as he tossed him the keys to his unmarked patrol car. Ben caught them in his open hand as he stood up, then leaned over to gently help Herb to his feet, slowly walking the frail veteran along by an arm as he escorted him to the door. Darby stood watching as Ben patiently shuffled Herb for the door, his fleshy face a fixture of malignant arrogance and, despite the anguish of the situation, he just couldn't help but set his tongue into motion. There was no need for any verbal judo, but veneration be given to the badge carrying almighty wrappers, for Sergeant Andy Darby didn't much like the attitude of this uppity, oft heard about as of late, uniformed minion from the lowly rank and file.

"You know something Trilby . . . as members of the Serious Crimes Unit we handcuff *all* our prisoners," Darby scoffed. "Department policy you know."

Darby put the emphasis on the word all, and Ben thought this to be a hell of a place and time to get into a pissing match about putting the cuffs on a broken old man so he decided to cut the head from the beast right here and now.

"Sergeant, I'm not a member of the Serious Crimes Unit, and if ever I do become one, I'll forgo the optional issuance of the extra paunches that you two choose to drag everywhere you go. You're a disgrace to the Department you're so out of shape. If ever I got into a brawl and you two are in the area I would thank you kindly to stay well back and take good

359

notes because that's all you'd be good for. That's assuming you can both spell."

This outburst was very un-Trilby-like to say the least, but the long hours of policing a vermin infested neighborhood as the lone cop was starting to niggle at Ben's stout determination.

The horrible crime scene in which he now stood, and the annoying wrappers didn't help the situation much either. Truth be known, it was long overdue. Some tempers snap sooner than others, while some never snap at all. For the record though, Ben's temper hadn't snapped.

He was only giving Darby, one of the celebrated 'Prince of Pricks,' his honest consideration.

While a more suitable location for this verbal barrage might have been while hanging a helmet at a row of urinals in a cop's bar, sometimes the place just picks you.

Ben turned away from Darby and walked out the door, taking his prisoner with him. Darby's face mottled into a deep purple as the veins in his neck became engorged with a rapidly building wrath. His mind suddenly became more occupied with the insubordinate Trilby than with the stiffening body of Mira Twinkle and just how she came to be that way. Fenton stopped sketching in his notebook, looking into Darby's face, knowing he had to curb his partner's famous temper before it flew out of control. A curious crowd had gathered on the sidewalk outside the house and the last thing the Department needed was a plain-clothes dick venting on a uniformed officer in the middle of a serious crime scene. Or worse, an outright fight, and most everybody carried around those goddamned video cameras nowadays and it wouldn't be the first time Darby had picked a fight with another Police Officer. Strange things indeed were bound to happen when some individuals couldn't properly handle the stressors that pervaded daily police work.

As Fenton regarded the younger, fitter cop his main concern lay with his unit's integrity rather than with any public humiliation a fight may bring about. Trilby would eat Darby for breakfast then spit him out without so much as a gas cramp, which wouldn't do the dignified, plain-clothes unit any good. Fenton walked over to Darby who was about to trundle after Ben and promptly pointed out the gathering crowd.

"We'll get him later Andy," Fenton muttered, "we'll do up a proper report and have him disciplined."

"Asshole," Darby growled.

Darby lurched over to the front door, unable to resist a demeaning, parting shot at Ben, especially in front of a pack of craning taxpayers.

"Hey Trilby, this is a crime scene, get them lookie-looks away from the front of the house," he bellowed.

"Sorry Sergeant Darby, I can't do that," Ben answered pleasantly. "I have custody of the prisoner and he's my first priority. Department policy you know."

Darby slammed the door shut in his frustration, knowing full well the gathering herd were not all of Riverside's finest citizens and nothing short of a mounted unit would shift their indifferent asses regardless of the fact they had every right to gather on the sidewalk

Ben took his time walking Herb out to the brown unmarked sedan as the old man slowly picked his way across the cold cement walkway. He still lacked any shoes or socks as nothing could be removed from the house until the scene had been cleared, and all the evidence collected and even Ben understood that rule. A white panel van pulled in behind the unmarked car, and a uniformed Sergeant named Lidster stepped onto the sidewalk after shutting his vehicle off. The Sergeant was a friendly fellow from the Forensic Identification Unit who took professionalism and his unique craft to new levels, which could be an altogether bad thing if Herb Twinkle's predicament went to a jury trial.

"Why it's young Ben," Lidster stated with a slight smile. "And how are you doing son?"

Ben nodded at the Ident Sergeant, then stopped briefly with his prisoner to speak to the technician.

"Hello Sergeant Lidster. I'm fine, thanks. Looks like a smoking gun, the weapon's inside behind the divan in the living room. I had to touch it to disarm the suspect so you will want to check a set of my own fingerprints for elimination purposes on file at Headquarters. A couple of wrapper's are already inside. They've got the ball."

"Who are the wrappers?" Lidster asked.

"Darby and Fenton," Ben replied.

"Christ, one of those days."

"I'm afraid so . . . and I've already got Darby warmed up for you."

"That's very thoughtful of you son."

Ben nodded to Lidster then placed Herb into the back of the unmarked car while the Sergeant walked around to the back of his van to fetch the numerous cases and bags he would need for his investigation.

Sergeant Lidster would be spending the rest of the day inside the house, going over the entire lower floor with every technical piece of equipment his van could carry. He would dust the weapon as well as the spent brass cartridges and nearly every surface inside the house, searching for fingerprints of both the victim and the suspect. Hard surfaces like glass and smooth metals were the best for retaining fingerprints, while woods and other porous materials would usually reveal nothing. Full, or even partial prints left from a person's body oils he would lift from a smooth surface using rigid, sticky on one side, clear cellophane squares that had been designed for that very purpose. But only after he had circled and initialed the squares with a yellow grease pencil and photographed them in their original locations. The couple's fingerprints would prove to a criminal court that they did indeed occupy the suite and any prints on the weapon and the spent brass casings would hopefully prove the obvious. Every obvious place within the apartment, such as doorknobs, glossy magazines, table tops and even cutlery would be dappled with the fine, blue dust. Lidster would then take dozens of photographs using rolls of high-speed thirty-five millimeter color film. He would photograph every room of the dwelling and from every angle, including the cooling body of Mira Twinkle who had ripened the stale air when her bowels had evacuated seconds after her death. Hours would then be spent by Lidster as he took meticulous measurements of each room of the house so a bird's eye planned drawing could be produced for the courts and a jury to have a setting in which to wrap their pondering heads around.

Once the Coroner had shown up and consented to the body removal, Mira Twinkle would be placed in a heavy clear body bag once an exhibit tag was tied to one of her toes. At this particular stage of the investigation she was nothing more than a piece of physical evidence to a crime. She would remain as such until the autopsy had been conducted in the presence of Sergeant's Darby and Fenton. They would seize anything extracted from her body that ought not to be there while another Ident Officer photographed the whole procedure; anything that would help build them a solid homicide case. After the postmortem Mira could then be turned over to any family or in this case the state, who would pick up the cost of her cremation. While Sergeant Lidster poured his trained eyes over the entire crime scene, he would quickly track the trajectory of two of the three bullets that Herb Twinkle had fired from his rifle.

The bullet that had killed Twiggy the cat had gone safely into the basement. After figuring out a rough fall of shot, Lidster would send some uniform officers out to knock on some doors.

This wouldn't be an option. They had to ensure there were no further victims sprawled out down the street from any of Herb's stray bullets. It had happened before and it will undoubtedly happen again and failure to check could be quite embarrassing to say the least.

Regardless of whether the crime had been a smoking gun, a freshly imbedded knife, or a baseball bat crusted with the victims dried blood, with a suspect days on the lam, a tremendous amount of dedicated work went into every one of these investigations. The wrappers and the Ident people performed the majority of this work and were there for the sole purpose of supporting the uniformed men and women who patrolled the streets of every community. Their services freed up the uniformed Police Officers - the backbone of every department - so they could continue to answer the routine calls. These support Units were very good at what they did, all pursuing one common goal and only after spending years on the streets as well as attending numerous accredited police courses. They analyzed mutilated bodies and every square millimeter of a crime scene on a daily basis; some of the victims were found aged and dead in their own homes after living a full life, some of them were very young, their soft bodies violated and dumped in some distant field, years before they could even count the syllables in the word pedophile. The men and women who wore the suits and took the calls at their desks behind the frosted windows of every district office had one common goal that haunted them every day they carried a badge and drew a fresh breath. They all carried a pressing need to solve every serious crime that took place within their jurisdiction but they all knew that the odds of that happening were equivalent to initiating a full sixty-seconds of global peace.

The people in the Serious Crimes Units were also trained to anticipate that each case would go before a Jury Trial and that each minuscule piece of evidence would be scrutinized and even ridiculed by the defense lawyers. Many would dedicate up to a quarter of a century of their lives investigating these kinds of crimes that entailed endless hours and too much deep fried food. A lot of them would retire to floundering marriages and with bodies that were starting to fail under the constant pressure. Some said all that would change with the new breed of Police Officer's who ate carrot sticks and wheat germ, and were aware of the job pressures and held firm the knowledge that they could overcome these daily nuisances. The old guard however, a little more circumspect to these new beliefs held close the opinion that father time would be the best judge of these healthy ideals.

New breed or old guard . . . it mattered not for the job needed to get done, and it did get done. Nevertheless, some things will never change and that's the road that life followed sometimes so there still existed a healthy resentment between the plain wrappers and the uniformed Patrol Officers. This kind of light conflict plagued every Department in the free world and wasn't likely to change anytime soon. The Officers who policed the streets felt quite capable of doing these complicated investigations themselves and most certainly were. But Missus Smith's dog was barking again and five people had already complained including an Alderman as well that rowdy party at Fifth and Dogwood had just spilled out onto a quiet street and some of the revelers were flashing some rather sharp looking knifes. That's just the way it was when you lived in a city and the inhabitants young and old had every right to expect someone to attend to these complaints. That aside, attending these incidents had become the main stay of good basic policing and besides that it was Department policy.

Another piece of department policy, as well as an integral part of the Constitution was the endless rights that an accused person had entrenched on his or her behalf. Herb Twinkle was no different and his rights were read to him only seconds after Ben slid behind the wheel of the unmarked car. He peered back at the old man through the metal cage that separated the front seat from the back, which kept the rear occupants where they belonged, reaffirming their lofty status of prisoner. Despite knowing the constitutional rights back to front, Ben still read them out from the plastic card all police officers carried. This way there could emerge no insinuations into what he said or didn't say to an accused when cross-examined by a defense lawyer at a trial. If asked in a courtroom he would simply pull the same card out and read from it verbatim. Herb, like every other suspect, had the right to an attorney at taxpayer's expense as well as the right to keep quiet or chirp like a caged songbird and receive back rubs every second evening of his incarceration.

Unlike every other criminal although very much like any decent constituent, Herb didn't quite understand all of the legal talk about these rights that allowed him to waive this and stick that.

To most normal people like Herb Twinkle, having your rights read was like watching one of those old Japanese monster movies where the actor's lips didn't quite synchronize with the English voice-overs. You heard every word that was said but failed to comprehend the full meaning, if any at all. To get a full interpretation of his constitutional rights Herb would have to consult a lawyer or talk to a seasoned criminal, the kind who has just been caught walking out the back door of a family home with a brand-new CD player and a laptop computer. Every criminal offender who desecrates virtually every community in North America can recite their legal rights the way a young child can peal off an innocent nursery rhyme . . . just ask them.

Ben read the Charter of Rights from his arrest card three times for Herb's benefit, but still the devastated old man shook his head as he wept quietly in the back seat. It took awhile but Ben finally got his prisoner steadied to the point that he held his full attention. Wiping his runny nose on a sleeve, Herb nodded at Ben, his eyes wide as he looked at the Police Officer through the smudged lenses of his thick glasses.
"Listen to what I'm about to tell you Herb - "
"But it wasn't supposed to happen this way, Ben -"
"I know. It seldom ever does Herb. Now listen to me carefully, please. You're in enough shit already and you're probably looking at a premeditated murder charge. There's no point in calling it a mercy killing Herb because from here on in nobody else will; except maybe your court-appointed lawyer. It's very important Herb that you say nothing at all about what happened to Mira to any other Police Officers because now that I've read you your rights because anything you say from here on in can be used as evidence against you. They already have enough evidence to fry you, so there's no point in stuffing an apple into your mouth and climbing onto a platter. Do you understand me Herb?"
"Yes Ben, I think so."
"Good, now not another word out of you about what happened back there in that house, alright?"

The old man nodded, offering a disheartened look as Ben started the engine then drove the car for the ten-minute trip to the downtown bucket. Throughout the whole booking in procedure and during the elevator ride to the third floor not another word was said about the terrible incident, which suited Ben just fine. As soon as Herb had been searched he signed over his pocket full of worldly belongings then a booking officer walked the broken old man back to the heavy door that led into the bucket. Ben took a few minutes to sit on a stool behind the cage and make some detailed notes regarding his involvement about what was said and when. He would have preferred to leave the pages empty but telling the truth was one of the things that Police Officers did best. It became a difficult task as he wrote because his eyes kept stinging, wanting to let go with the tears. For the first time in a decade of policing Ben Trilby became cognizant of the fact that his rotten job was finally starting to wear him down and rightly so. What the average onlooker would fail to notice through no fault of their own was that out of this whole Twinkle calamity there had emerged three victims. Four if you counted Twiggy the cat. Mira would have to be the first with a bullet in her head and her loving husband of more than fifty years had become the second. Ben of course would have been the third. No Police Officer, regardless of how solid they may think their character to be, could walk away unscathed after witnessing something as painful as the event that had taken place on the main floor of that dirty old house in Riverside. Many fooled themselves into thinking they had, but they usually ended up paying the piper come pension time with a thinning wall in their aorta, a booze soaked liver or long, rolling nightmares.

By the time Ben had arrived home that evening to sit in his living room with a cold bottle of beer, the Twinkle homicide had become a lead ball of emotions growing somewhere at his mid section. Seeking a diversion he reached for the remote and turned on the television set but the whole event reappeared in living color as each channel strove to make it a local headline.

It sickened Ben when Sergeant Darby's varicose face filled up the full twenty-six inches of the screen, appearing in front of the Twinkle house as he called the crime "despicable, horrendous and cowardly." Those plain wrappers certainly like to chortle their Godlike opinions when they had a microphone held in front of their lips Ben thought as he flicked the off button on the remote. He watched in silence but seethed inside as Darby's face shrank to a meaningless white dot on the television screen. It was during this short news broadcast that Ben decided the time had come to drive the wrong way down a one-way street and if someone's toes got stepped on then that would have to be someone else's problem. Officer Ben Trilby was going to rally behind Herb Twinkle and support the soon to be condemned old soldier because sending him away for ninety-nine years or worse would prove absolutely nothing. He reached this decision partly because the old man was already circling the drain with little time left in his miserable life but

mostly because it seemed like the right thing to do.

His letter writing blitz was well on its way and all these ideas of lobbying the District Prosecutor, the media and the Social Services people had become true and firm when Ben went to visit Herb in the bucket

366

seventy-two hours later. He dropped in after a long day watch, finally submitting to a quiet relentless voice inside his head that insisted he visit the declining war veteran and at least let him know that someone still cared. Before he went up to the bucket at shift's end he changed first in the locker room on the first floor of the headquarters building. He always enjoyed the comfort of a pair of jeans and a sweatshirt after eight hours in a pressed uniform and the confining thick leather of a stiff Sam Browne.

It was early Friday evening, and by this time fresh blood had been smeared across one wall of the elevator, and the booking office was nothing short of organized bedlam. About twenty uniformed officers were standing around with handcuffed prisoners, waiting to lodge them into the bucket. Most of the detainees were intoxicated which meant they were all headed for the cold embrace and concentrated stench of the drunk tanks. The booking officer staff as per standard procedure were in no particular hurry to wade through the paperwork required to book the prisoners, so it would be a goodly wait before the uniforms were free to return to the streets. Ben went into the caged area behind the long counter through the open half door and plucked a spare set of door keys from the key press on the back wall. As he walked down the long hall he passed Oliver Ginty who offered him a surly nod. Ben let himself into the bucket, walking slowly down the front of the cells, breathing through his mouth to filter off as much of the offensive odors as was possible. Herb had been remanded on a fourteen-day Psychiatric warrant to assess whether or not he had both feet on the ground which would be bad for Herb if the Doctors decided he did, in which case his case could go directly through the court system. Whether or not there would be a trial would be Herb's choice, depending of course upon his plea. Either way, it wouldn't be too long before he commenced down a road that at the very least would bring him a life imprisonment but justice would be served and that's all the milling flocks cared about.

Ben entered the cell and sat on the end of the bunk as Herb peered at him like a frightened waif, curled up and shaking beneath his blanket. Ben chatted with him for about ten minutes, bringing him up to date on the letters he'd written on Herb's behalf and how a reporter named Griffin from the daily newspaper had also taken up the cause not two days ago and had started to churn out some scorching editorials. Meeting the reporter had been an incredible coincidence Ben told Herb. One of those strange things that just happens; something you have no control over yet seemingly defies all explanation. This Griffin fellow had been doing some research into the affluent East Hill assembly, a community of people who lived in one of the most expensive neighborhoods within the city. The journalist had been taking a shortcut through the rundown Riverside area hoping no one would steal his hubcaps when he noticed Ben standing on a wet street corner having a hot drink while chatting amiably to an out of luck drifter. It struck the investigative newsman a bit odd that any uniformed cop would bother spending his coffee break standing in the rain with a social outcast so he stopped his car to get out and chat.

Griffin had a nose for news that tended to stray from the norm and he immediately recognized Ben's unique qualities as well as an untapped source for countless human-interest stories. Ben of course was cautiously optimistic as he saw a possible ally in the reporter, a possible torchbearer for Herb Twinkle as well as a useful medium in which to leak information that could be advantageous to the common cause. While Ben recounted these recent developments Herb appeared preoccupied with other things, staring unfocused into Ben's hopeful eyes. One didn't have to be a scientist of any kind to realize the loss of Herb's dear wife at his own hands and his failure to join her would have to play heavy on his soul. Right or wrong, the poor bastard had simply been trying to seek some salvation for his wife and now he stood accused of murder.

And whether he heard what Ben had to say about these recent developments regarding his consequences mattered not at all, for the final destiny of the tired old man had already been decided.

At the end of the visit with Herb, Ben shook the old man's hand, and wished him good luck and told him how sorry he was that his life had taken such a vicious turn. By this time Herb had perked up a bit and this was when he told the young Police Officer about the huge gorilla with the "big cock" that had come to visit him each night as he cried under his blanket. The cheeky beast had even cuffed him a few times when Herb wouldn't stop weeping. Ben's vision darkened as he listened to all this, feeling the adrenalin surge through his system, his emotions building into an apoplectic rage. Like all the other uniformed street grunts Ben had heard about the gorilla and his nightly shenanigans and held a deep suspicion as to just who wore the suit and his name would be Oliver Ginty. After locking the cell door, Ben said good-bye to Herb Twinkle then stood in the walkway, allowing a few minutes to compose himself. If he lost his temper in front of the booking office crowd and awaiting Police Officers they'd throw the book at him page by page and this was just the thing the Duty Inspector would be waiting for.

Something substantial like punching Officer Ginty in the face in front of about forty witnesses would bring about the hearty hoorays as well as the discharge papers and the loss of a pension. Ben was in enough trouble having received written notification only this morning from his Watch Inspector that he was under statutory investigation for his open disobedience while at the Twinkle crime scene. The whole thing was an orchestrated sham and when Ben attended to the Inspector's office the cowardly turd had fled somewhere for his coffee break and one of his underlings had served Ben the notice. "Gross insubordination toward Detective Sergeant Andrew Darby, a Senior Member, while at the scene of a serious homicide investigation," had been the exact wording of the service offence charge. Ben had signed the bottom of the form to signify knowledge of the charge, then couldn't help but wonder about the formal wording regarding his act of defiance. If all this back talk had taken place while at the scene of a stolen bicycle complaint would that have made any difference to the severity of the charge? Was there such a thing as a non-serious homicide?

All this he would double check with the local Police Association President but in the interim it would almost appear to Ben that the Department couldn't help themselves by making the poor Twinkle's a part of his mutinous misdeeds. With that bit of drama added to the pot Ben would have to be very careful as to how he dealt with the gorilla although within the suit itself lay the answer to this now out of control problem. Ben could have taken the whole thing up to the Duty Inspector but that might appear a bit like being a snitch to his fellow officers and no hard evidence had as yet surfaced. He had to do something, that much he already knew for only a heartless moron would tease a shattered old man who had lost everything including what little remained of his dignity.

Ben left the cellblock, checking that the heavy door had locked then he returned to the caged booking office. Perfect, he thought as he scanned the area. The place had become as busy as an outhouse at a beer garden and a window of opportunity might not present itself again for weeks. While everybody appeared to be busy writing, or searching or restraining, Ben walked down the darkened back hall to the equipment room and did so strictly on a police officer's hunch. He immediately found that the instigator of the marauding gorilla to be a positively sloppy individual. Part of the furry costume hung over the edge of the lid of one of the plywood equipment boxes and Ben easily pulled the gorilla costume from its secret hiding place.

Within seconds Ben had formulated a plan of action and quickly pulled the suit on over his body, carefully pulling the black nylon zipper up over his chest and snagging it amongst the fur under his chin. Anonymity would have to be absolute if Ben were to successfully cull the great ape so no part of his body could be exposed.

His vision had become somewhat restricted through the eyeholes in the rubber mask but arrogance and surprise would be the key to a safe departure. Ben was about to turn and leave the equipment room when he decided if he was going to wear a monkey suit onto a stage of sorts then he might just as well take along a prop. Besides he reasoned, things could turn a bit ugly as he tried to make good on his escape. He leaned over and pulled a four-foot long, solid American white oak riot baton from one of the other plywood boxes. It had a thin leather thong attached to one end so the user could loop it securely to his wrist but Ben had every intention of discarding the club long before he left the building if not sooner. Stealing a gorilla suit that had been used to traumatize prisoners was one thing; stealing police gear was another.

Ben was now ready to execute his simple plan, but he ran into a hurdle before he had even left the equipment room. When he turned around, he found what little light that flowed down the hall from the booking area was now shadowed by the bulk of someone very large. This person stood in the only doorway of the small room, effectively blocking Ben's escape route. It was Officer Oliver Ginty and Ben could just make out the brutish smirk he had fixed to his beefy face.

He wore no side arm with his uniform, as service pistols weren't allowed in the bucket, so all he had at his disposal were his bare hands and what little matter had grown between his ears. In one massive paw he held a greasy chicken leg that he had ordered from some deep fried bird joint and it had left a clear gloss of fat across his bloated lips. They looked downright revolting, especially when they moved to form some words.

"I dunno who the fuck you are, but - "

That would be as far as the gorilla would allow Ginty's lips to flap for the time had come to abscond wholly from the crime scene while there was still time aplenty. Ben drove the butt end of the baton into Ginty's ample mid section with both hands, driving the wicked stick deep into his gut. This force, spread over the small area at the end of the baton compressed the large man's diaphragm and forced the air from his lungs. The whoosh of expelled breath and a sickening smack was the only sound heard as Ginty dropped his fried chicken leg then collapsed to the cement floor. He fell like a colossal sack of composted steer manure, and there probably wouldn't have been much difference between the chemical make-up of the two.

Ben leaned over the gasping heap, looking down at the fallen officer as he spoke, his voice sounding distant and muffled because of the mask.

"You should lay off the fried chicken and the doughnuts . . . you lazy prick."

The gorilla, or Ben, or whatever you wish to call it tossed the oak baton to the floor then stepped over Ginty and walked down the hall to the booking office. If Ben had any intent on seasoning the pot to the point of poisoning the soup he couldn't have picked a better time. As the gorilla lumbered through the open area where the prisoner's and escorting officer's awaited to be processed, at least four of five police careers were heading for the toilet. Not only was the room full of uniformed Police Officers and drunken wretches looking forward to their long walk to the cells, but there also stood therein some very prominent people. A trial lawyer who was awaiting an escort to interview a prisoner and a Justice of the Peace who was to be conducting a bail hearing for an "in custody," watched with no amount of amusement fixed to their faces. Two of the prisoners who sat handcuffed on a painted metal bench started crying wolf the second the great hairy beast crossed the floor while everyone else stood and watched, their mouths dropping onto their chests. The lawyer, a grandstanding gentleman in a twenty-six- hundred-dollar morning suit who called himself R.Caldwell Holdner, opened an appointment book that was eloquently wrapped in supple eel skin and started taking highly detailed notes. Like other solicitors, he'd heard about this big chimp from some of the pro bono clients he was obliged to defend as an assignment from the courts.

Holdner had discarded these previous stories because he knew from his high school biology that a male gorilla's penis couldn't be any longer than a couple of inches, so he had taken to nodding politely as these disheveled legal aid types recounted what was surely a product of the delirium tremens. However . . . *all* this changed as he watched along with a gaggle of other notaries what would later be described before a jury during civil litigations as a huge person in a gorilla costume with what appeared to be a two-foot long penis. R.Caldwell Holdner at that point in his life had said good-bye to his thirty-six-foot sailing ketch moored at one of the exclusive and very private yacht clubs on the downtown waterfront. As well he forgot all about his mewling wife and the nice post and beam cottage he had perched above a sandy beach in the gulf islands.

All that had become window dressing in a mere flash as the person wearing the monkey suit stepped onto the elevator and disappeared behind the closing double doors.

Holdner now saw himself as a rainmaker of sorts, an easily attained title once he became counsel for all the poor slobs the gorilla had terrorized. He was already planning to file a class action lawsuit that would set him up nicely in a stuccoed villa on the French Riviera with a skimpily clad, well-tanned concubine. This roving simian would put Holdner on the globe as well as give him the funds to abscond to the *other* side without so much as a dusty trail, or one single alimony payment. The civil justice system had suddenly become the best thing since the evolution of oral sex and this is exactly what coursed through the lawyer's mind as he scurried about the booking office taking the names of Police Officers and the prisoners he would subpoena to the impending civil trial. R.Caldwell Holdner had never been much of a religious type, but the seas might just as well have parted when a dazed Officer Ginty staggered out of the booking office cage, holding his belly, and complaining loudly that "some asshole had just stolen *his* gorilla suit." Holdner was silently elated about Ginty incriminating himself and asked in a rather glib tone if his name was spelled with a 'y' or with an 'i e'.

Ben Trilby on the other hand, couldn't have cared less about the little melodrama that was developing upstairs as he walked off the elevator and out the back door past an astonished Duty Sergeant. Just minutes ago the sun had dropped below the western horizon, making the dark alley even blacker and Ben melted quickly into the inky night as he jogged over the cobblestones.

He continued jogging until he had crossed at least two main streets then stopped by a dumpster to quickly peel off the stifling hot suit. Ben dropped the costume into the large, square trash can then dropped the lid on what would develop into a very agonizing and embarrassing era for the Metropolitan Police Department. He left the alley walking slowly back to the headquarters building to retrieve his car, stopping only once at a phone booth located next to the parking lot. Ben pulled a card from his wallet then deposited the required coins. Moments later he spoke briefly to Griffin the newspaper reporter, apprizing him of the mysterious gorilla's adventures and the most recent developments, including where the incriminating costume could now be found. Griffin affirmed Ben as a confidential source then said good-bye to the Police Officer, bent on securing the suit before another reporter did. Newspaper work could be a dog eat dog world and this story would be one of the biggest of the year so Griffin couldn't afford any slouching when it came to securing the evidence to back-up his story.

In the next couple of weeks much was written on the front pages of the daily paper regarding the gorilla affair and the sad circumstances behind the Twinkle homicide. The sadly misinformed upper echelon of Police Management was livid when some extremely ripe and truthful information was made public - complete with a color photograph of a smiling Griffin with a gorilla suit spread over his day desk. This picture became an instant broadside, initiating public calls of a cover up regarding the Department's official statement that all this talk and threats of law suites about some whimsical gorilla were just that - sheer whimsy. Unfortunately, some of those occupying the middle ranks of the Department had foolishly chosen to cover up the monkey business, regarding the whole matter as nothing more than a "little harmless fun."

They might just as well have whacked a nest of African killer bees' with a stout stick for upper management responded with their full wrath. The all-accountable Police Chief unleashed the headhunters and Internal Affairs soon fell upon a deceitful and untalkative booking office crowd. Like all good reporters, Griffin took great joy in his immunity and continued to tip the apple cart using sensitive information he'd received from a "delicately placed mole." By week's end the official statement from the Police Department had been altered to reflect the fact that Officer Oliver Ginty had been suspended and that more heads would roll as the investigation by the Internal Affairs Unit continued. And much like a hound on a fresh blood scent, Griffin didn't stop there with his snooping and humiliating accountings of public discovery.

He studied the monthly police reports that were given to the Mayor - the ones that were proudly published in the papers for all to see. Griffin had been quite astute at high school math and he soon discovered a disparity or two. According to these all-trumpeting statistics - along with the telltale population to Police Officer ratios - the largely overlooked Riverside District should be policed by at least seven point four peace officers; not the solitary, overworked and highly dedicated Ben Trilby. Once again the

Department brass was caught with their misinformed pants down and the Deputy Chief could only sputter "we're looking into it" when he was ambushed one evening by a television crew in the parking lot.

"Tisk, tisk. Why wasn't I informed?" was the Mayor's official response, shirking his accountability by suggesting that the sad Twinkle case may never have occurred had there been enough cops on that street. In all fairness to his worship, he did however authorize more police into the oft-neglected Riverside Community. When this Mayor spoke, his orders were rarely ignored. So not three weeks after the unfortunate gorilla business had pinnacled and one day after old Herb Twinkle died peacefully in his sleep in his cell at the bucket, Officer Lisa Carmaducci found herself transferred to the Uniformed Patrol Division, Riverside District.

Someone once said that out of every tragedy there comes some good and if that were true then the only good thing that came out of the Twinkle incident was Officer Carmaducci. This would be the kind of screwed up world that she had been posted to. Fresh and vibrant from the ranks of the training depot, she came prepared to take on anything the Riverside residents could throw her way. She would become a competent partner for Ben Trilby and in four short weeks she would become even more than that to him. The harsh reality of street policing was a seedy world filled with violence, endless paperwork and a limited amount of gratification, which at times could draw together people of a common purpose. It was a world they had said very little about at the training depot for fear of intimidating some of the recruits. A world like any other in that the clocks would always continue to tick over the seconds, the minutes, and the hours of the days.

In Lisa's world the clock was ticking as well, counting down on what little time remained of her delightful tenure upon the earth. Even though the policing world she joined with Ben Trilby had become a much better one - especially now that the sorry gorilla matter had drawn to a successful conclusion - her violent death would nonetheless be a cruel reminder that fate was the number one item in any of the rule books of human existence.

*   *   *

Chapter Thirty-nine

Ninety-six percent of all police shootings take place at a distance of seven to ten feet and occupy a time span of only three seconds. That is a callous reality. Why the hell someone would compile this kind of information could be debated for days but nevertheless these facts surfaced at most Police Academies during the officer survival portion of the training. The shooting that involved Officer's Trilby and Carmaducci would be the only incident regarding their close relationship that had really followed any of the basic rules or predictions. Everything about the two much like real life, just sort of fell into place and would be no one else's business although the rude and the curious certainly tried with the prying questions.

After the smoke had cleared and all the finger pointing that needed to be done was done, the shooting was analyzed from a different point of view and some bright spark civilian employee did up a report for the Police Chief and the Mayor. This mathematically cold report clearly showed that the lopsided gun battle had taken place over a distance of eight feet and the actual conflict which left one maimed and one dead lasted closer to four seconds than to three.

The report ended with a pompous referral that police shootings would probably remain a "predictable element" and future training should remain guided by this enlightening disclosure. The proclamation had been signed with a swirling, effeminate and totally unreadable signature. Had the author of the report been present when Ben had read it on the fourth floor of the General Hospital, he quite likely would have taken the statistician's solar powered calculator and shoved it up his nose, capping each nostril with one of the pen light batteries that came as a back-up should there be a need to work in the dark.

Thankfully, this didn't happen because the stat man hadn't been there when Ben had read his report. As well, one of the first things that Doctor Deirdre Bonson, Clinical Psychologist, went to work on was the readily ignited temper Ben had acquired out of the shooting. She had been sent to salvage Ben - not so much because he was considered a valuable resource in so much as there lay both a legal and moral obligation to set him right. Tall and elegant with long flowing blonde hair, Doctor Bonson gave fine dress skirts and leather pumps a new meaning, especially when you caught her out

375

and about in the public eye. Rude as it may sound, when Doctor Bonson was out of her office taking a second look had been relegated to the back of the English language and replaced with the words outright ogle. In her late forties, she made her maturity look outright sensual and consequently couldn't go anywhere without attracting attention from the opposite sex as well as some dreamy looks from her own gender. But she might just as well have been wearing a clown suit when she first visited Ben in his private room on ward Four-B. Here would begin the long, painful therapy that would hopefully return the caring, sensitive person that had been chased from a young Police Officer's soul. Ben had become so lost in his own affliction and survivor's guilt that dancing Martians' with bongo drums would have failed to catch even a glimmer from his dimming, Jack Frost blue eyes.

The therapy was conducted within the convenience of Ben's hospital room so he wouldn't have to hobble far to the comfortable chair and the sunshine near the window. Deirdre forced him from the hospital bed as the surgeons had trouble shifting him which would be good for his recovery as well he would nod off constantly from the steady prescription of pain killers.

Doctor Bonson was a civilian member on permanent retention to the Metropolitan Police Department. A Department unfortunately, who still had one or two upper management types who would only go kicking and screaming into the twenty-first century. A small, elite boy's club who viewed posttraumatic stress syndrome as if it were a form of uncontrolled menopause.

These failings became most apparent when Deirdre had a meeting with the Staff Sergeant in charge of the human resources section. She had gone to his office to receive a briefing on Ben and found a man in his late fifties who was borderline neurotic although still a somewhat understanding person. Why a man that age would hang around a Police Department for so long was beyond her reasoning although the truly sad part was he'd probably blow a valve one day while he sat fidgeting with his pen at his desk. Deirdre wondered if he even went home at night he looked so much like a permanent part of the office. In all fairness though, the Staff Sergeant had survived a rough career, which would have broken others, and it showed in his sunken eyes and withered face. He had joined the department when you had to fight your way onto your beat then fight your way off; all of it done without the reassuring benefit of modern radio communications or readily available emergency response teams who were armed to the nuts.

The Staff Sergeant had told Deirdre that Ben's Watch Inspector hadn't considered Officer Trilby much of a team player - a black sheep of sorts. In fact, this management drone didn't believe in all this critical incident stress crap, even suggesting that leaving Ben alone without sympathetic visitors would speed up his recovery. The Department's Padre had been into see him on a daily basis but that was the extent of any kind of moral support. Ben's mother Bea had remarried eight years ago and lived on the Eastern Seaboard. She planned to fly out in a day or two to visit her son and they couldn't find Ben's father who drove trucks and lived a nomadic life without any permanent address. If things could get worse for the young Police Officer, they were certainly going to as they had yet to tell him the really bad news. This insignificant item they withheld, as they didn't wish to take everything away from him in one heartless swoop so they had decided to leak it to him a bit at a time. Of course this manner of thinking infuriated Deirdre, but she held her tongue and listened politely as the damage had already been done. The assailants who shot Ben and Lisa had used controlled expansion bullets that were strictly for law enforcement purposes only. Regardless, this restriction changed nothing, as criminals weren't supposed to be packing firearms when they committed crimes so the whole issue was moot.

Ben's right hip socket had been destroyed by a horrible, one hundred and forty-seven grain nylon-coated bullet, that spread into a six-fingered star with slender razor tips when it struck human flesh. They could rebuild part of the hip using nylon and stainless steel for new sockets and joints. However, Trilby's police career was finished and he would be pensioned off once his rehabilitation had been completed. No one had told Ben this yet, and only a handful had knowledge of it for news like this could be devastating to an already wounded psyche.

"Could Doctor Bonson advise the soon to be Mister Trilby during the soon to start therapy that after his recovery he would soon be discharged from the Police Department . . .?" asked the Staff Sergeant.

Deirdre only nodded to the request and its lame excuse.

"Splendid, Doctor," smiled the Staff Sergeant. "That would be very much appreciated."

Deirdre returned the smile in full, but the word coward danced across her mind's eye.

"Oh, and one more thing Doctor," the Staff Sergeant said quietly, "we think Ben and Lisa might have been diddling each other."

"What has that got to do with anything?" Deirdre shot back at him.

"Just thought you should know," the Staff Sergeant replied, shrugging his shoulders.

Deirdre stood to leave but the word fool now skipped across her mind's eye.

Doctor Bonson thanked the Staff Sergeant for his time and walked down the busy hallway of the headquarters building, making mental notes as she headed for an elevator. The information about her new patient being described as a black sheep was indeed very good news. Not only did she have a survivor in which to apply her skills and knowledge to, but she also had a fighter. Deirdre had been around long enough to know that describing Ben as a black sheep simply meant that when someone barked "sit, boy, sit," he most likely trotted over and pissed on their pant legs. She considered this a strength, not a weakness. And where there lay strength, lay hope. At this point, and even further into the long therapy process things could go in one of several directions. Two of which she didn't even want to think about. If Doctor Bonson could keep Ben Trilby away from the deceptive embrace of a liquor bottle as well as keep the muzzle of a loaded pistol from his mouth, she will have succeeded in bringing him home.

That's how the healing began, with Doctor Bonson entering the hospital room every second afternoon and waiting patiently in her chair as Ben limped painfully in his housecoat over to his own chair by the window. Deirdre would have him sit with his back to the window so he couldn't be distracted by the outside world but could still enjoy the fine weather. She would pull a small butcher's block bread board from her briefcase then lay it over her lap with a pad of foolscap, her pen ready to write. She always left a lag of twenty-four hours between visits so Ben could mull over what had been discussed as well his mind would naturally explore and sort through the emotions that troubled him. Ben was well aware of why the Doctor was visiting him and knew that if he ever wanted to laugh again, or enjoy the cool evening breeze with a lady's smile or anyone else for that matter, he would have to get himself over this terrible pain. He also knew that this regeneration would have to come from within, coaxed out by the understanding Doctor who would dissect the trauma while allowing him to set the pace.

More important than easing himself out of the despair was regaining his will to live, for Ben knew deep down that if his handgun had of been anywhere near him he might just have used it a few days ago . . . *might* have.

To every end there is a beginning, so during her first visit Deirdre asked Ben to talk about the start of his relationship - professional or otherwise - with Officer Carmaducci. The part of Ben that wanted to live and love again had grown bigger than the part that wanted to dry up and blow away, so he agreed to the Doctor's suggestion and started the therapy with the entrance of Lisa into his life. He held nothing from her, for Deirdre had a trusting grace about her that defeated any hesitation and Ben even told her about some of the sore points from his childhood. It all came out so easily which would be very crucial if there were to be any hope of healing, although the sorrow that fell from his words even reached out to Deirdre herself. Ben would talk and the Doctor would listen, and write, and ask questions and offer guidance as well as explanations where she thought they were needed. There would be nothing mystical about the treatment. No spells cast or wands waved. It would be talk, steady guidance, suggestions, relaxation exercises, a caring ear and nothing else. Ben had never been much of a talker until he met Lisa or trained a recruit. Except now he would talk about everything he'd shared with Lisa and he would do so to Doctor Bonson who at first had been a perfect stranger. They say that the past and the present are directly connected. A truism to be sure, for Ben would have to once again relive the immediate, tragic past, if he was to have any chance at a future.

*   *   *

Chapter Forty

Ben Trilby took an instant liking to Lisa Carmaducci and immediately enjoyed her presence despite his constant concerns regarding some very untoward events as of late. Ben needed a real friend after the fall out from the monkey business as it soon became apparent that horrid little incident would take months to die a dignified death. There had been a handful of suspensions without pay over the gorilla suit incident as well as a lot of unfavorable national and international media attention. Civil litigations had been filed and would undoubtedly drag on until the last six-figured check had been cut and issued to the last incredulous victim. Ben had been labeled as the likely instigator as he had been in the bucket when the suit had walked out the door. His "do-right," unrealistic attitude toward policing the general public hadn't helped his cause much either. Rumors regarding the gorilla's demise were as free as the coffee the men and women of the Department drank at the Burger Barn and they all pointed in Ben's direction. Lisa's arrival had become a healthy diversion as well a hopeful light in the distance. She was posted to the Riverside district, at the Mayor's, insistence for immediate training and deployment to the streets. Ben welcomed her as a friendly and yet to be swayed, able-bodied Police Officer. If Lisa Carmaducci had known she had inherited the Department's whipping boy as a field-training officer, she either didn't care or failed to show it. She knew all about Ben though, and liked him as well as admiring the fact that he had chosen to be different. It would be a good partnership from the start as she perked Ben up with her lively personality and solid sense of humor. She was also nice to look at despite the police uniforms ability to make some people look rather dumpy.

Compact and fine boned, Lisa's long dark hair was pinned into a bun at the back of her head so there was less for a criminal to grab in a fight. Like a hot pot on a camp fire she had a scalding energy that would burn you if tried to mishandle her, something that could cause you more distress than any bulky, muscled physique. Her brown eyes constantly danced with mischievous flickers and her Italian heritage shone in the smooth, walnut shell color of her skin. Lisa was a focused listener without presumption that would make the involved, six-month field training a pure delight. Most of the general public was unaware that a Police Officer's formal training continued long after they had graduated from the Police Training Depot. Truth be known, the learning process never really ended. The half-year spent during the field training was every bit as important as the time spent in the classrooms and gymnasiums at the depot. Like a lot of trainer's, Ben would tell his energetic charges that a lot of what they learned in training should soon be forgotten. Much of what they had absorbed in ideal classroom conditions with respect to self-defense and crisis intervention didn't hold for much out on the street. Out here there were no rules and if you had to think about matching up a tactic to a particular situation for longer than a split second you were screwed anyway. He had informed Lisa of his thoughts during their first day on patrol, virtually the same speech he had pealed off for all the other recruits.

"Forget about the 'who flung pooh' and the 'fuc dung young' you learned in self defense classes. Unless you practice that stuff every day you'll forget all those moves within a few weeks. The biggest muscle in your body is between your ears and if you get into a fight, you do whatever you have to do to win because the public expects that from you. We are paid to win, even though you and I both know that's not always going to happen."

Lisa nodded quietly as Ben laid this realistic advice upon her as she drove the patrol car slowly through their district. Another quiet day, it gave them time to talk while attending complaints or stopping to chat with the locals. It became a one sided, running monologue. It always did in the beginning with the rookies. Ben would talk and Lisa would listen, interrupting only when she had a question or a suggestion to a certain topic. The process could be educational for Ben as well, for many techniques and equipment changes had developed over the past decade and Lisa surprised him on more than a few occasions. As the days and the learning curves progressed, Ben would speak less and their communications would graduate to a balanced, easy conversation. They talked everywhere they went while working together on shift; in the coffee shops while taking a break, in the car as they moved through the neighborhood to a complaint, even calling out to each other as they chased a drug suspect full out along the river bank.

At first, both of them were completely unaware that they were laying the footprints for all successful relationships and had they known it probably wouldn't have changed a thing.

Lisa's progress soon became quicker than any previous recruit's, which pleased Ben as well as made his extra tasks much easier. She made every practical hurdle that lay before her with a running jump and had effortlessly passed her first big test by winning over the Riverside residents with her dry wit and caring manners. While conducting a foot patrol days ago Ben had introduced her to one of the neighborhood inebriates, a short, elderly fellow with a crew cut and wizened round eyes who went by the name of Scooter. They had found Scooter sitting on top of a round, aluminum garbage can with a magnum of "cherry plonk" nestled in his lap on the greasy fabric of his worn trousers. Half the contents of the bottle had already been consumed even though the sun had only climbed halfway into a clear morning sky. The old bastard was in a cheery mood, which could change to a spiteful anger once he'd finished the bottle of strong, crimson colored wine. If he failed to pace himself and got too shit-faced he would then start howling furiously at the crows in the trees until the time came to seek out a covered place to sleep, which would be just around the time the rest of the city would be going for lunch.

Scooter was harmless enough and in the overall picture he was but a speck on the canvas so Ben routinely left him alone.

At first Lisa had wondered why her new partner hadn't seized Scooter's wine then hauled his drunken ass off to the bucket then she remembered Ben made his own rules, preferring to spend his precious time chasing bigger game. On this particular morning Scooter had been very pleased to meet Officer Carmaducci, so pleased that he had tested her mettle with a personal question regarding her ethnic background. He leaned forward atop his metal perch to address Lisa, his rancid breath breezing across her face in the warm air - so offensive it would have rotted the hide off a live buffalo.

"I hear 'talian broads got hairy legs 'n muffs," Scooter inquired almost graciously.

He threw Ben what he thought was a sly wink but he had problems closing just the one eye, so he blinked slowly using both his rheumy eyes.

"Only when we don't shave them."

Lisa's reply had been instant and playful, totally disarming Scooter and when he let his guard down she moved in for the verbal kill.

"You've never screwed an Italian woman before, have you Scooter?" She asked.

Scooter just lowered his head slowly, letting out a long breath while staring forlornly at his sacred bottle of hootch.

"No, ma'am." He replied despairingly, "I ain't never had no 'talian broad."

Poor Scooter probably never would either.

They bid the vagabond a good day and continued with their foot patrol, enjoying the sunshine and the quietness of an early morning. She'll do all right here, Ben thought this as they walked side by side through the neighborhood talking and laughing, their eyes constantly searching for something amiss or threatening. They had yet to get into a fight, something that could be the establishing factor as to whether a police recruit had picked the right career path or would change their mind and head for the nearest off ramp. Flinging each other around on padded mats in the thermostatically controlled environment of a gymnasium at the training depot could at times be fun. Fighting a criminal who had nothing to lose in a dark, wet ditch could supply your body with enough adrenalin and nightmares to last a lifetime as well the situation could become outright disastrous if you lost the fight and several did.

The fight that Ben hoped would never happen came two days later during their first night shift together. Ben had asked Lisa to stop a dark colored sedan filled with the dark silhouettes of many heads. She activated the overhead blue and red lights of the patrol car but the suspect vehicle continued moving, driving slowly for over a block before it pulled over. Once the vehicle had stopped Lisa flicked a toggle switch near the radio that engaged the take down lights. These were rectangular halogen bulbs with immense candlepower that were mounted above the roof on the light bar with the blue and reds as a factory package. The people in the violator vehicle couldn't possibly see beyond the hood ornament of the patrol car, which is just the way it should be.

"The Moxie's," Ben said quietly after radioing their location. "Street gang. They were busy hiding their dope, that's why it took so long for them to stop. Watch their hands at all times. This bunch won't hesitate to pull a weapon if they think they're going to the bucket."

Lisa placed the patrol car in the correct officer violator position directly behind the suspect vehicle so Ben would have full continuity on the passenger side should anything be tossed out the window. As she approached the violator vehicle she held her flashlight to her front and well away from her body, supplying a false image as to her actual position.

Anything thrown her way, or any desperate pot shots from a weapon would be aimed at the small bright disk of her flashlight beam. While this action might appear a trifle extreme, it had certainly saved lives in the past as a routine vehicle check was when a Police Officer was the most vulnerable. Lisa illuminated the interior of the vehicle with her flashlight and Ben could see at least six heads inside as he climbed from the passenger side of the patrol car. He stood behind the open door as he clutched the radio microphone, keeping it ready should there be a need to call for assistance.

Lisa approached the driver's window of the vehicle and Ben watched as she spoke to the driver, her flashlight still held high above her, its white beam impeding the drivers vision yet offering her another small edge to help equalize the odds. A short conversation ensued through the open window then Lisa stood clear as the driver got out of the car. She adopted the interview stance with her legs set apart to form a wide base under her body, her torso turned sideways with her sidearm away from the driver. This helped protect her weapon as well it made it more difficult to push her off balance. Another tiny advantage should she be abruptly attacked. Ben recognized the driver as a troublesome shit-rat named Spider Teed. A tall, broom stick of a man in his early twenties, he still had a pimply face and proudly displayed a large tattoo of a black widow spider across the back of his left hand. He had never amounted to much nor would he ever, having already achieved his lowly zenith as one of those types who wore his baseball cap backwards while he stalked the school yards selling drugs to the preteens. This he did when he wasn't committing break and enters on the small, corner drug stores downtown. Spider had become the boss of one of the local gangs but in the pecking order of street trash and in the limited esteem of the other gangs who roamed the area, he and his flunkies amounted to nothing more than dog dirt in the tread of an old sneaker. It was fully expected that during the next turf war, Spider "et al" would be run across the river without too much lip and even less of a fight. Nonetheless, the man and the people in the vehicle were dangerous and Ben watched carefully as Lisa spoke to Spider as he stood beside his car. Even though Ben couldn't hear the conversation, he could tell that Spider was agitated just by his body language. His hands were flapping around in the air, expressing the non-verbals faster than his brain could send a logical signal to his mouth. Watch it Ben thought, he's trying to distract you.

Spider couldn't have known that Ben was standing next to the patrol car, not with the take down lights flashing up the scene like a Monday night football field. This undoubtedly set a course for what happened next. Spider wrongly assumed that Lisa was alone and false courage could be an extremely dangerous bluster - it could turn a routine street check into something entirely different. Spider figured he could take Lisa. He would show this slut cop a thing of two as well as revere himself further within his own miserable group of losers. Spider would do to her what he did to that female Regional Police Officer who pulled him over about a month ago out in the complete darkness of the countryside. He'd left her lying at the roadside in the grass with her hands cuffed behind her back in her own bracelets. Spider had pulled her uniform slacks and panties down around her ankles before cutting her shirt off with his switchblade. She was easy, that one. Especially the way four of his boys had snuck off into the bush from the car and jumped her from behind when she returned to request more information on the car they were driving. Spider wanted to mount her from behind while she was all strung up, but his disciples would have nothing to do with raping a cop. They would have gotten away with it as Spider had used a fake license as well the car had been stolen just hours before and the cop didn't see much of their features because of the blackness of the night. Pussies, he thought as he spat onto the ground at Lisa's feet.

By now Spider had made his decision and he suddenly lunged, driving a bony fist into Lisa's sternum. He should have struck her directly on the nose but it wouldn't be right to hit her in the face. A lot of criminal's were like that for some strange reason; they couldn't punch a female cop in the face because it wasn't the gentlemanly thing to do. Yet they wouldn't hesitate to beat the hell out of them then shoot them with their own handgun. Many Police Officers - male and female - had died as a result of a bullet from their own weapon. Lisa had already sized this goon up and had seen the fist coming even as it became an active thought inside the vacuum that was Spider's brain. Instinctively she slid her rear foot further away from her front foot, which widened the base of her stance, and automatically hunched her body down low into a fighting stance. The kevlar soft body armor she wore under her blue uniform shirt absorbed a good deal of the kinetic energy from the vicious punch, but she would still be wearing a large purple bruise two weeks from now.

"Shit," Ben muttered, watching Spider make his strike. He threw the mike onto the front seat and jogged over to the passenger side of the gang's car, quickly drawing his nine-millimeter pistol from its basket weave holster. The time for formal niceties had come and gone and Ben's sudden concern would be to now keep the rest of Spider's gang from crawling out from under their rocks. If these toadies got out of the vehicle and gained the upper hand things might get a tad unsightly, which meant someone may not get to go home tonight.

Out of the corner of his eye, and just a second after she was punched, Ben saw Lisa bring her foot long metal flashlight down on top of Spider's head, the hard plastic lens shattering as it impacted with his skull.

"Punch a woman in the tits would you?" She yelled, then quickly shuffled in on top as the gang leader crumpled to the ground. She cranked on the handcuffs as blood gushed onto the pavement from the split skin on his forehead. Ben couldn't help but smile. She's going to do just fine, he thought as he ran to the other side of the gang's vehicle. He opened the single passenger door wide, and then pulled his own flashlight free from its ring holster, shining it into the vehicle at the rest of the turds as he instantly held them at gunpoint. The situation could go either way at this point. If it went the wrong way and Ben had to use lethal force then both the losers and the winners would be changed for life. Five sets of hands promptly shot above five heads as they sat still in the car, barely breathing. Thankfully it went the right way and Ben had the five remaining gang members get out one at a time and lay face down on the ground directly behind their car with their fingers laced together behind their heads.

Once a back up crew had arrived Ben and Lisa searched each gang member as well as their vehicle. Their efforts gave them a piece of hashish the size of a bullion cube that they'd found on Spider who was taken to the hospital in an ambulance to get his pumpkin stitched. The rest of his following were clean so they were sent on their merry way. After Spider received five stitches to his head he was escorted to the bucket where he was later released by a night court judge. Officer Carmaducci had charged him with assaulting a Police Officer and possession of a narcotic. This would be Lisa's first self generated criminal charge and much like her fellow graduates from the training depot she became a bit overwhelmed by the amount of paperwork involved in a simple court brief. Although, the paperwork, and the continuing education that made up Lisa's extensive field training had only just begun.

A large portion of the field training involved completing forms and writing mounds of paper. This meant that Ben and Lisa would be dedicating many hours on their days off if Lisa were to successfully achieve the program standards. Very little of it could be completed during their shift as their police duties would suffer and that kind of thing stops for nothing. The formal field-training course that had been formulated could literally fill up their days off, not leaving much time for any kind of play. Lisa would have to study case law and have a working knowledge of its application to law enforcement. Books as thick as five inches held local and State Statutes that needed to be researched as well as volumes of the Federal Laws and their applicable penalties. Then there were the addendums that required a constant peek as well as the District Orders that had to be read in their entirety and initialed. Ben would be there to guide Lisa through most of it, offering her assistance and knowledge and nudging her along if required.

As well he would administer her weekly exams. In the end Ben Trilby would have the strongest voice in whether Lisa Carmaducci had met the standards of the program or had failed them. Someone up the line would have the responsibility of job termination should there be a failure, something that occurred to the occasional recruit who couldn't succeed for one reason or another. All of Ben's past candidates had done well on the program, which reflected directly on his pride and dedication.

Usually all this book reading and scenario planning was done at the Headquarters or District offices but Ben preferred they remain conspicuously absent from these institutions.

Particularly on their days off. There was still an uncomfortable amount of fall out and bad feelings about the gorilla suit affair, so Ben loaded up the passenger side of his sports car with resource material and training video's then carted them over to his apartment. A harmless enough plan it would seem on the surface, however it would become the biggest contributor to a relationship that wouldn't be altogether appreciated by Ben's supervisors. Officer Trilby's innocent enough plans would become an ignition point that would quickly flare up some long laying, dormant fires. The majority of the work required Lisa to plow along on her own but there was enough of it that required Ben's attendance. Enough to draw the two together. During these hours alone with Lisa, Ben would conduct verbal quizzes and walk her through countless hypothetical situations, peppering her with questions regarding powers of arrest, possible charges laid, rules of evidence and the use of lethal force. At times they would open the books and review the video's in Ben's one bedroom apartment, taking breaks on the small balcony where the view of the river with its low banks and following rows of mature spruce trees helped break the tedium of their studies. These intermissions also helped to nourish their casual conversations in which they learned a great deal about each other.

Other times they would occupy the small kitchen table in Lisa's basement suite below the main floor of her family's large home. The Carmaducci clan owned two adjoining lots on the East side of the city, both with immense houses that had nearly identical exteriors finished in white Mediterranean stucco. The backyards of each house had been tilled under for vegetable gardens with nearly a quarter of the dark soil dedicated to growing grapes whose vines reached from the ground to follow the tall trellis's that had been made from painted pine slats. This annual, thin-skinned fruit grew plumper in warmer climates but some cultural traditions you just don't mess with. Ben especially like going to Lisa's suite for the training as this always accompanied a mandatory invitation to join her family upstairs for supper. They would offer Ben one of the two seats of honor at either end of the long oak table where he would sit down with almost twenty other people. It wasn't a meal they would have, it was a tradition that was filled with boisterous talk and laughter and none stop gestured conversation, which Ben found absolutely wonderful.

Even though the food would be magnificent, it was the atmosphere around the table that brought Ben the most joy. All the elderly family members spoke Italian and they spoke lots of it but there was no need to understand what was said as it became a pleasure to watch a family so full of love and spontaneous amusement. For the first time in Ben's life he became reflective of his own family upbringing, fully realizing all the happiness he had missed with his sullen father at the supper table - if and when he was there at all. Although he relished and was thankful for the Carmaducci's kindred embraces, the times in his life that he couldn't relive nor bring back or even fix was what truly saddened him. At times it would become a paining anguish that he would suddenly drift into, a state that would hold him for a few seconds until the ringing laughter returned him to the here and now of the Carmaducci's diner table. Just sitting there and watching the blissful interaction of Lisa's family reach out to embrace him made everything that had gone before him all seem worthwhile and then some.

The meals would always start with one of the Grandfathers saying grace and then the food would come and it wouldn't stop for almost three hours. They ate one course at a time, each portion delivered to the table by an endless flock of sisters or cousins, affably supervised by Lisa's mother. Each dish came with a small amount of food so there would be room for the next course and it was all consumed with a strong red wine that left a pleasantly musty taste on Ben's tongue. They never gave any hint as to how many courses were to be served at any particular meal, although Ben counted twenty-two during one memorable evening. It would start with small salads of lettuce or Belgian endives mixed with black olives glistening in a tangy, clear dressing. Other days they would start the celebrations with a bowl of soup, which could be either hot or well chilled and was regularly served with hot bread. After the appetizers the pastas would start to arrive at the table, putting to shame any noodles from a box that Ben had eaten in the past. All of these servings were homemade with a paste of whole wheat or white flour and of every shape and size you could dare to imagine. These delicate morsels were swimming in savory meat sauces or came as tender tubes stuffed with seafood in a pale glossy cream that spilled succulently from both ends. Then there were the fresh breads. Each loaf and slice held a delicious piece of history baked into it as the recipes they used had remained unchanged for a thousand years. The hand woven baskets would come to the table filled with coarse grain buns, long slender loaves or thick flat breads dusted with fresh green herbs.

Hard and crusty on the outside, the inner pieces were soft and yielding to the mouth and the amount of bread alone brought to the table would have fed a district office for a week. Ben of course just had to taste each kind as it was offered at the table, but, not before slathering each sample with a sheen of soft butter.

When one small, colorfully adorned empty plate had been removed, another would quickly appear. Each one held a treat for the eyes, the nose, and the thoroughly teased mouth. Ben saw vegetables mixed into each dish that looked so different he couldn't even identify most of them. The real enjoyment came when the food entered his mouth. Each bite held its own unique flavor and not for a few times did he think his taste buds were doing something rude they tingled and danced so much. Near the end of the meal and some two-and-a-half-hours later the desserts would be brought out to the table. Silver trays with paper lace doilies were laden with cakes, torts and puddings that contained enough sugar, chocolate, coffee and liqueurs to stimulate the population of a small town.

While difficult to comprehend to the diet conscious, Ben could easily say that the time spent at that long table was the most fascinating of his life. The Carmaducci family took the evening meal to new heights of wondrous emotions with its delectable satiation and animated conversations. Many times while he sat at that table Ben would feel Lisa gazing toward him while he spoke to one of her relatives and he in turn would look at her when her attention had been drawn away to someone else. This would be how it had all blossomed and it happened by pure fortune.

The simple plan of getting away together from the noise of the office while they waded through the field training manuals evolved into something neither of them could have predicted. Unintentional and certainly unforeseen in the beginning, within that short span of four weeks Ben had Lisa had become close friends and that's how all good relationships started. The chemistry was there, the feelings were there and only an emotionally deaf and dumb person would fail to see the energy in their faces when they would steal a look at each other.

All that aside, any guessing at what might still be an irrefutable affinity came to fruition one night long after the family meal. Mario Carmaducci was a proud, second generation Italian.

He had grown into an ox of a man with graying hair and a bald spot on the crown of his head that made him look monastic and lovable. He had seen the happiness in his daughter's eyes when she spoke to, or about Ben Trilby and this filled him with utter content. Finally he thought, at twenty-eight years old (almost a spinster by old country principles) Lisa might have found a suitable fellow. One who had his head screwed on right even if he wasn't Italian. Eh, he mused, we can't all be perfect. On this particular evening right after the meal, Mario invited Ben out to the large deck that overlooked the waking vegetable garden to sit and talk under the stars. This really pleased Ben because Lisa's father had given him more hugs in the past few weeks than his own father had in a whole lifetime.

They sat on thick cushions in plastic loungers and smoked long cigars and drank clear, syrupy Cointreau from short-stemmed liqueur classes while the big dipper slowly pivoted in the sky above their heads. Ben and Mario talked for hours while the elderly folk retired to their bedrooms and the younger family members worked in the kitchen on the stacks of dirty dishes. They sipped their liqueur and discussed everything from communism to aspirations most admirable, as well as touching on some of their own personal regrets.

To know a person's regrets is to find the center of their soul.

Midnight came and quickly passed; the dipper dropped low in the night sky and everything that needed to be toasted as well as verbally flogged received it due consideration by Ben and Mario. The brown, square bottle was dead when Lisa walked out onto the balcony and Ben thought she looked stunning, dressed as she was in a white tee shirt with a pair of nice fitting blue jeans.

The other thing that Ben noticed was that he was plastered to the point that he was afraid to even stand up. Truth be known, he was a real mess and he feared his new found kinship might consider him a liquor-pig of sorts even if did kind of sneak up on him. Nonetheless, the night was far from finished and the liqueur wouldn't be the only thing that would be sneaking up on Ben Trilby. Mario appeared to not even have a buzz on as he stood up, solid and satisfied with the way the evening had ended. He offered Ben a hand up and a place to sleep on the couch in the family room downstairs, which given Ben's pickled state was a much-appreciated option. Both Lisa and Mario steadied their friend by holding his arms as they slowly walked him through the house. Ben kept apologizing quietly for his condition but his hosts would have no part of it and kept shushing him. They guided him carefully down the carpeted stairs that angled around to the level entry basement.

The family room lay just beyond the double front doors and as Mario walked Ben over to one of the couches Lisa disappeared, returning moments later with a thick comforter and a pillow.

While Ben stood with his back to the couch, Mario's massive paw braced him as gentle hands undid his belt and jeans then slid them to the floor. Ben knew Lisa was undressing him front of her father, but this was an act of kindness and it mattered not in a decade where being publicly shy could be a social death warrant. Mario pulled Ben's sweatshirt over his head and he felt himself being eased onto the couch as Lisa spread the heavy comforter over his limp body.

The pillow beneath his head smelled fresh and clean as his head sunk slowly into it and that would be Ben's last cognizant thought before the sleep and the liquor rapidly overtook him.

It was dark when Ben awoke at what he guessed was three or four hours later and he could feel her presence seconds before he realized she was standing before him. White light fell upon her form, coming from the streetlight that seeped through the sheer curtains that hung along the wall behind the couch. Lisa wore a large bed shirt with a hem that reached to her knees and her dark hair tumbled down onto her shoulders. Ben had never seen her with her hair down and it made her face look full and soft as it bordered her ears and cheeks. She held a hand out to him and he reached for it as he searched for her eyes in the half darkness. Her hand was warm and reassuring and as Ben stood up he wondered what had become of his intoxication.

Without saying a word Lisa led him quietly into the main entryway near the front door and turned abruptly once they had left the family room. They followed a short hall and Ben could feel the warm carpet beneath his bare feet, and within seconds they passed through another door.

Lisa continued to hold his hand as he heard the door close behind them and he realized they were standing in the living room of her basement suite.

Ben had never been with another woman since that awkward night when he had graduated more than ten years ago. That had been a disaster when the seductive Margaret had dragged him into the bush during the alumni camping trip. Terribly shy around women he had gone out with a few after he had joined the Police Department but nothing became of these trysts and only one or two returned for a second night out. The bashfulness had become a disability of sorts but for some reason there appeared no sign of it as he stood with Lisa in the middle of her living room. Small amounts of light from the street fanned out from the dark edges of the curtains that covered the windows, offering them enough illumination to see the fleshy treats once they would become exposed. Ben could feel the awe well up inside him when Lisa pulled the tee shirt over her head and dropped it onto the carpet. She stood naked, her taut, right breast bruised from where Spider had punched her weeks ago. It would be the only flaw that could be seen in a body that reminded Ben of a painted and buffed, perfectly fired piece of porcelain. He kissed the bruise, feeling her shiver, using his lips on her buds before he slowly ventured down her body until he knelt on the floor. For a brief moment Ben wasn't sure if his actions came from within, or if someone was guiding him as his mouth fluttered lightly over Lisa's skin. He worked his lips in a manner he'd never given much thought to in the past and for reasons unknown it came to him naturally, even if there had never been much of a reason to think about it until now.

Human sexuality was as old as the earth and as natural as the wind and the rain and well it should be. Mankind was the only animal thus far in the universe that had sex for pleasure so therein lay centuries of ardent, dedicated practice. Lisa had somehow chased the timidity from Ben as well she awoke the instinctual nature that had slumbered for so long, held deep inside of him and this awakening only added to his new found pleasure. He

393

kissed Lisa's smooth waist, taking his time, moving down to her soft sanctuary, leaving behind a moist trail on her skin, which teased her and set her into a muted gasping. Ben nuzzled the flesh at her pubis, feeling both the soft tips as well the coarseness of her hair, breathing in and holding her female musk, feeling dizzy as its scent aroused him even further. He knelt even lower and when he moved his mouth across her thighs he knew exactly what to do with his tongue when he found and explored her moist, aching folds. Lisa's moaning was both intoxicating as well as encouraging and if they never left this room again it wouldn't have bothered Ben in the least bit. It seemed to him that everything needed to sustain him stood before him as he bathed in Lisa's sexual energy, taking it in like a dizzying tonic.

She soon kneeled to join him on the thick carpet, softly pushing him onto his back as she removed his underwear so she could reciprocate with her own lips and in her own unique way. The kissing, nuzzling and slow caressing went on for what could have been a part of eternity as they lay together, discovering and delighting in each others body's and the little secrets they gave up - one tender nibble at a time. Much like the desserts they had eaten with the evening meal, Ben and Lisa had saved the sweet stuff for the very last, as if there had been a menu to all this wonderment. As spent as any couple could be without reaching the spasms of a climax, Lisa straddled Ben and once again he became astonished with his own body, briefly marveling at the timed chemistry that exuded from their joyous coupling. They both cried out together and during the intense, draining sensations that flowed from their souls nothing else could possibly exist past the four walls that held them and gave them their privacy.

The sun had just broken the Eastern skyline when their energies were finally exhausted and both lay wrapped in a blissful security; a security that was born of the knowledge that the intimacy and all the happiness that came with what they had just shared was only beginning.

Lisa lay forward with her head on Ben's chest, her silky hair spreading over him, pleasantly tickling his ribs.

"I should return to the family room," he murmured.

"Why?" She asked.

"Lest big Mario Carmaducci catch me under his youngest daughter. He might have me neutered you know."

Lisa laughed quietly, snuggling into Ben's husky neck.

"Don't worry about that, Ben. My family has all the charm of the old world, as well as all the scruples of the new one. In fact my dad would probably shake your hand if he found out what we'd shared."

Ben however, hadn't heard much of what she had just said. He'd already fallen into a deep, contented sleep. Thinking how some things were so real that they made everyday life seem a fantasy was his final thought before nodding off.

*   *   *

Chapter Forty-one

Ben hated it when the afternoon shift of his first day back started on a Friday evening. He didn't like the five p.m. to one a.m. watch to begin with, and when it commenced on a Friday night this only compounded his disliking. Friday was the busiest night of the week and traditionally despised by all emergency personnel as this would be when a fair percentage of the population would turn stupid. The night could be even more of a grinder when it was your first shift following a couple of days off. Sometimes it could be like running a brutal marathon without warming up or doing proper stretching exercises. When the Friday night watch fell in the *middle* of Ben's shift it would be more comfortable because he was alert, having already set himself a pace, now readily able to adjust to the changing circumstances. He felt warmed up then, ready for just about anything a Friday night might send his way. Ben could never figure out how Firefighters jumped from a warm bed onto a fire truck where they would go instantly screaming through a cold night while still half asleep, to fight what could be a deadly blaze.

His own predicament would be one of the things Ben truly liked about police work; it placed him on duty already in his uniform, attentive and behind the wheel of his patrol car as he looked for trouble before it managed to find him first. But when your first day back started on a Friday night it could be like springing out of a warm blanket to leap cold and dopey into a swiftly moving and at times deadly bedlam. Eh well . . . we all have our own sacrifices to make for the common cause Ben thought as he sipped his coffee.

More than forty-eight hours had passed since he and Lisa had made love in her basement suite, but of course it hadn't stopped there. There were seven more incidents of joyous, physical rapture but who the hell was counting. They had coupled, kissed, and nuzzled anywhere they found some privacy, which wasn't hard even if it meant driving down to Ben's apartment on a simultaneous urge. It would be an honest statement to say that the pair had become smitten with each other. Regrettably, this beautiful development had presented a big enough problem that it had Ben pausing for a bit of serious thinking. The answer was simple and obvious - the problem lay in the manner in which he presented his solution without hurting any feelings, including his own. It would no longer be fair to Lisa or

397

even Ben himself for them to continue together on the field-training program. Ben would have to go and see the training Officer to request that a new trainer be assigned to Officer Carmaducci, but not until he had discussed these options with Lisa. He wanted to hang onto what had happened between them during these last days off, to allow the relationship to nurture slowly and completely. This could only happen without any outside interference such as the Police Department and their idiotic rules.

If Lisa were to fall short on any of the course standards of her field training - a doubtful occurrence at this point - Ben would be forced to make recommendations he didn't even want to think about. More important, he didn't wish to jeopardize a healthy relationship that was still in its infancy and had started to carry them along in all the right directions. Serving Lisa with a notice of shortcomings because she had missed making the mark on a weekly exam or was late with some assigned research project couldn't possibly do their budding emotions any good.

Ben didn't wish to chance any of those ugly formalities destroying the warm, all-encompassing feelings that mulled for him through much of his waking hours. Although he would now be compelled to see the Training Officer with a request that Lisa be reassigned to a new trainer and thinking about this caused the coffee in his stomach to sour. It went against his nature to ask that he and Lisa be separated, but doing so will oblige the rules of the Police Department and spare them from any possible grief in the future. Even though there existed no official rules about partners being intimate, it was frowned on as well as acted upon when it was discovered. Usually this meant a quiet transfer to another district for one of the culprits and it would be done for the obvious reasons. Ben had given thought to continuing on with Lisa and saying nothing, but word would eventually get out because you can't keep a secret from twenty-three hundred observant Police Officers.

Someone would see something somewhere, then the tale would snake its way up the line until someone decided this wasn't fitting behavior. There could be an unofficial penance meted out if they didn't step forward and volunteer the information, because in reality, continuing to work as partners wouldn't be right. If management wasn't advised and they happened to find out through coffee room conversation, action could come down from the top then Lisa might be posted to an opposite shift and down to the geographical South Pole of the city. If that took place, then they would rarely have time to see each other. Whatever time they'd have available would certainly be of a high quality, but Ben's biggest concern was that their present affections could be jeopardized because of the supervisory position he held with Lisa. He would hate to see their friendship fizzle out and die without the benefit of an honest chance.

They had to be separated.

The other problem lay in just exactly what Ben would say to the Inspector in charge of the Training Section. Ben couldn't walk in to see the Training Officer and request a transfer for Lisa without tabling a reasonable excuse, and one that wouldn't be an outright lie. Larkin was the Training Officer's name and a really good sort. However, Ben just couldn't wander into her office and politely advise her that he had become a bit enamored with Officer Carmaducci and vis a versa and that things had become deliciously physical and most wonderful - could she have a transfer please?

Nothing like strolling into an Inspector's office to casually announce that you were boinking your trainee but this was fine because you were rapidly falling for her and she was easily achieving the course standard and isn't life jolly? Ben had been in enough trouble as of late, and Larkin would be forced to advise his Watch Inspector; the same, self-serving Officer who had an earthworm for a backbone. This fellow now constantly scrutinized Ben from the sidelines, just waiting with a clipboard and a transfer form as well as a warm pen. They were short a person or two in the bucket with the recent suspension of Officer Ginty over the gorilla suit incident that put Ben at the top of the replacement list. A simple signature with a black pen on a form and the deed would be instantly executed. They would worry about who would police the Riverside District at a later date, for there was always someone else who needed to be jacked up. An hour working in that vile bucket would disable Ben. Six months would kill him.

Conversely, he certainly couldn't see Larkin spinning some kind of a yarn - such as he failed to get along with his recruit, or that Lisa consistently ignored his advice or refused to take direction. Larkin would soon see through that facade in a hurry and there could never be any turning back once a Police Officer had been caught telling lies. Even small ones. Ben had read somewhere that the footprint of all good relationships was maintaining equal and open communications with your partner. This would be one of the reasons they had stopped at the tiny café. He needed to discuss the matter with Lisa and listen to how she felt about the latest intimate developments as well as liabilities they posed. It had turned out to be a miserable Friday night with darkness coming early as the bloated rain clouds that covered the city loosed their chilling contents in a downpour. Their first shift back to work, it was the dreaded five p.m. to one a.m. watch, the one that Ben hated the most, the one where you took what came your way without the benefit of being fully alert. The café where they currently sat could best be described as a thin long room sandwiched between two other buildings. A place where the walls were glossed over with a layer of grease and you could smell the deep fryer as far away as two city blocks. But the coffee would always be hot, and the petite Chinese wife of the owner would show them a genuine smile as she waited on them like a devoted grandmother.

It bordered on the edge of their district and it was a perfect place to discuss their predicament. The café was empty at eight-forty p.m. and it got them away from the incessant rain that beat down upon the metal roof of their patrol car. Perfect, Ben thought, and the honest affection that danced across Lisa's brown eyes would hopefully make what he had to say that much easier. They sat in a booth near the door, nursing their coffees with only the walls for company when Ben reached across and risked stealing a touch on one of the fine fingers of Lisa's hand.

If not for the uniforms and the wide Sam Brown belts that securely held their sidearms and other equipment, they might have been mistaken for a pair of infatuated teenagers. Lisa smiled openly at him and Ben picked this as the appropriate moment to state his case. But then the microphone at his shoulder interrupted suddenly as it crackled out a potentially urgent message. This was when fate decided to strike, and it hit as it normally did - quickly and without any consideration for its compellable participant's.

"All units, ten and twelve districts, ten-sixty in progress, twelve-eleven Barkley Avenue, there is no answer from the key holder. Units' responding advise." The voice of the telecom operator was calm and clear, getting the important information out to the applicable Police Officers and he did so using only a couple of seconds of precious air time. It was a silent holdup alarm at a jewelry store two blocks up the road and a half block down a cross street in the downtown core. The telecom operator had already called to confirm that the alarm wasn't false as could be the case when it approached a business's closing hour; except there had been no answer. Ben looked at Lisa then nodded, and after she tossed a couple of dollars onto the table (it was her turn to buy) she followed him out the door of the café and into the drifting walls of rain. Lisa knew enough of Ben's methodical ways to know they wouldn't be using their patrol car to travel such a short distance which was just as well as they could see and hear more if they attended the complaint on foot. Other patrol cars would be racing to the scene so there would be enough of those to cause a traffic jam. They both ran past the front of their own car, heading up the wide, one-way street. The foul weather had left the road deserted and Ben took a brief moment to advise the telecom operator they were en route and on foot.

Forty-five seconds after leaving the café, Officer's Trilby and Carmaducci were nearing the end of the second block, quickly approaching Barkley Avenue as they ran side by side down the sidewalk. Their dark blue, short waist patrol jackets had soaked to a chalky black, their hair now plastered to their hatless heads. On the other side of the road Ben noticed a brown, unmarked sedan parked near the curb and he nodded to Detective Sergeant Andy Darby as he and his partner prepared to cross the street through the wet gloom. The two plain wrappers must have been in the area, deciding to drop whatever they were doing to assist in the call. Almost ten feet before they exposed themselves onto Barkley, Ben and Lisa broke their stride to a cautious walk, hugging in fairly close to the side of a red brick building that stood on the corner. Ben was about to put a hand out to stop Lisa so he could first peek down the street when they came jogging around the corner. There were two of them, and they were tall and skinny, dressed in dark clothing and each had a balaclava pulled down over their face. They stopped short when they saw the two Police Officer's blocking their intended escape route. The one standing near the curb held a pistol in his left hand, down close to his leg. Before Ben could stop her, Lisa instinctively reached down for her holstered handgun, barely touching the pistil grip when it all ended.

Within the space of a twinkling the armed suspect leveled his weapon and pulled the trigger. They would later ascertain that the devastating episode had developed over a period of only four seconds but it might just as well have been sixty. From where Ben stood the whole scene became surreal, moving very slowly and appearing extraordinarily terrifying. He heard a frightening bang then saw the blinding flash illuminate the scene for an abrupt instant, feeling the concussion wave from the bullet roll over him like a physical blow, a cruel confirmation as Lisa dropped forward onto her face. Ben never tried to reach for his handgun because it was futile. Drawing your service weapon on a criminal who held a semiautomatic pistol and had already found the range was not an entirely healthy thing to do. Neither he nor Lisa could have pulled their weapons out in time for it to be of any use, regardless of all that mindless shoot-ut crap they showed on television. The skinny suspect with the pistol panned his weapon over in Ben's direction in the period it took a snake to flicker its slender tongue. He dropped the barrel slightly as his pistol discharged a second time. Now the angle of exposure had changed slightly, just enough for Ben to see the tattoo of a black widow spider across the back of his left hand as the yellow flash belched from the barrel.

The concussion wave from this bullet was more acute this time, as well the deafening bang that followed it. For one vanishing pulse Ben thought the assailant had missed him, and that now would be a good time to be thinking about pulling his own handgun if he was to have any hope of survival. This was when he felt the pain in his right hip, as if someone had hammered a blunt rod of metal re bar clear through the ball joint. The pain really seared Ben when his leg buckled and he fell to the wet sidewalk. His face smacked into a puddle, dazing him momentarily and when he glanced back up the two assailants had vanished. Ben then heard two or three small caliber shots from behind him as the two Detectives engaged the assailants with their own pistols. The pain in Ben's hip made him gasp for breath it had become so fierce, causing him to pant like an overheated dog. He somehow knew that Lisa was dead but he forced himself to look one last time at her face. A circular shaped dark spot had pocked the center of her forehead and her eyes were half open but covered with a dark liquid where the blood had gushed from the bullet wound as she fell. The blood on her face was now pinking from the rain as it trickled to the ground and in another minute her stilled features would be clean again. Ben tried to crawl the three feet of open sidewalk that separated them but he couldn't even pivot in her direction the pain had become so overwhelming.

Lord, he thought, let the fat lady sing because it's all over.

Officer Trilby then passed out from the pain. This would be the only appreciable mercy to fall upon that desolate piece of soaking wet concrete. At least by Detective Darby's later reckoning.

*   *   *

Chapter Forty-two

Approximately two and one half hours after committing the fatal shooting on the corner of Barkley Avenue, Davie "Spider" Teed did the second most stupid thing in his life: the first was gunning down two Metropolitan Police Officer's who still had their sidearms strapped into their holsters. If he got caught and went to prison, that tiny bit of information wouldn't bode well with some of the boys on the inside. Like all groups of human beings, even serving prisoners formed societies. And like most societies, they had their pecking order and rules of conduct that at times could be quite brutally enforced. Cop killers and cops turned bad were one of the lowest life forms within the prison community; right down there with snitches, child sex slayers and rapists. The sex offenders were labeled Skinners and the cop-killers were called Poachers and those names followed them the moment they cleared the Penitentiary admissions area and walked into the loneliness of the protective custody unit. Should they be found anyplace outside of their segregated cells by the general population - especially where a guard failed to have direct observation on them - then the term "hang a licking" would take on a very realistic and painful fact. That's if they didn't have a shank stuck into their belly.

Spider had grown into an extremely naive and dangerous young man and he wouldn't have survived three days inside a Federal Penitentiary. He had become a Poacher; as well he had become so full of himself that he now failed to recognize his own reckless misdeeds. Whether by fate or by some obscene blessing, Spider Teed never made it to prison for the Murder of Police Officer Third Class Lisa Anna Carmaducci.

He never even got as far as the bucket.

This sad reality had created some anxiety for at least one law enforcement official who had a direct hand in the young man's luckless ruin. She honestly considered Spider's demise a tragedy within a tragedy and her gender had absolutely nothing to do with the way she felt.

But lets be clear on something - young Spider didn't go looking for the opportunity to commit this second big mistake . . . not by any stretch. He had been at home minding his own business like any good citizen when the occasion to enact his final error quite literally presented itself as a knock on the door.

After Lisa and Ben had fallen, Detectives Darby and Fenton had engaged the fleeing suspects with their handguns while crouched behind their unmarked car. The shorter barrels on their sidearms made for easy concealment under a sports coat but drastically diminished the effective range of the weapons. Matter of fact, they would have been better off spitting at the two suspects as they sprinted unscathed back across Barkley Avenue, quickly fading into the night as they scattered up a darkened alley. Fenton gave chase but he was in no shape to sprint the length of a bowling alley, never mind the ten blocks the suspects virtually flew over. These assailants were fueled for orbit as their adrenal glands pumped them with a fearful energy and there could be nothing faster than a pair of shit-scared criminals wearing sneakers. Darby crossed the street to do what he could which entailed calling for help on Ben's portable radio. He glanced over at Carmaducci, taking in her fatal wound before checking on Ben, whom he knew to be alive from his soft moaning.

When he slowly turned Ben over the wounded Police Officer surfaced momentarily from his unconscious state to murmur the words "Spider Teed." Darby found Ben's injury and applied direct pressure to the bleeding with both of his bare hands.

"Don't move pal, you're bleeding pretty bad." Darby whispered. "The ambulance is on the way. We'll get 'em. That's a promise."

Darby spoke this into Ben's ear as he kneeled over his prostrate body, attempting to shield his exposed face from the rain. The two simple words that Ben had muttered formed a name but more importantly, he had spoken them to the right person. It would be enough to obtain a search warrant and possibly effect a quick arrest. Andy Darby of the Serious Crimes Unit knew of Spider and knew enough about him to know he could reduce him to a blubbering mess minutes after he had sat him in the interview room. This highly anticipated scenario could soon develop into the signing of a murder confession at the bottom of a warned statement. That was if the lawyers didn't get to Spider first for he had the legal right to call one. Seconds ago everything appeared somewhat bleak for the Metropolitan Police Department, but as Detective Darby knelt beside the body of one colleague and controlled the bleeding of the another, he thought that the bad luck had unexpectedly taken a positive turn. They now had a suspect because of Trilby's sharp observations and Darby had knowledge of the place that Spider called home. If all went well he might have the skinny bastard in custody before midnight and if he resisted arrest, then there was always the elevator ride to the third floor bucket.

In the end however things moved along much smoother than even Darby himself could have expected plus they ended up saving the taxpayers thousands of dollars in trial fees.

The detective had flown through the preparation of the search documents, their subsequent signing before a Justice as well as the marshaling of equipment and people, and all within an astonishing time frame. There stood an urgent need to seize and secure all the evidence involved in the homicide before it was dumped somewhere very deep and cold. This alone motivated the two Detectives and the thought of extracting revenge had positively nothing to do with it.

And so at exactly eleven fifteen P.M., Detective's Darby and Fenton as well as eight members of the Emergency Response Team entered the back door of a shabby tenement building located on the far edge of the Riverside District. Darby was armed with a search warrant for an apartment on the second floor, and the eight Ninja's were all armed with wicked looking, short stock submachine guns. One of them clutched a round steel tube with metal handles welded to the sides while another held a full length body shield with a glassed viewing port near the top.

The steel tube was almost four feet long, capped at one end and with a diameter of seven inches it made for a marvelous battering ram. They were called Ninja's because of their black clothing, the black soft body armor they wore over their black tee shirts and the black helmets they wore strapped to their heads. Clear goggles covered their faces, completing their informal evening attire and they would all get quite snarly if they weren't fed on time. They could effectively kill another human being and would do so with the precision of a trained soldier. Although, each one carried the mindful code of all Police Officers, which was to preserve life if at all possible.

Rather quietly, the ten Police Officers made their way up the rear stairwell to the second floor of the apartment block. They gathered on the landing to make any final changes to their impending hard entry. Darby stood in front of them as he counted the apartments, using his finger as he mentally tallied the evenly spaced doors as they spread down the darkened hallway.

He tentatively identified the suite they were seeking and pointed out its location to the Ninja's team leader.

The whole building smelled musty and dirty and it had Darby thinking how it wouldn't even qualify for a stable when the door to the suite beside him suddenly opened up. A burst of adrenalin shot through a few of the more anxious Ninja's as they tensed and looked over to see an old woman standing in the doorway to her apartment. She was known to all the local tenants as Missus Gyorgi, and they avoided her like a fresh stool on a sidewalk. Missus Gyorgi was built like a metal mailbox - short and stocky as well as kind of squarish looking, she currently wore a dowdy smock with a greasy apron, and had a polka dotted kerchief tied over her head.

She stood with her hands on her hips, looking awfully pissed as she filled up the width of the doorway. In one hand she held a large wooden spoon and the rank smell of stewing cabbage and potatoes wafted out into the hallway. Why the hell she was cooking at this time of the night would be irrelevant. What did matter was the shroud of utter defiance she wore upon her wrinkled face, which looked even more imposing with a large hairy mole in the center of her ruddy chin.

Missus Gyorgi had fled a small European Country during one of the last century's archaic revolutions. She had left with her beloved Doody, eventually escaping to Austria with a few of their belongings on a donkey cart. As they crossed the open field of a patrolled border during the night, the Soviet tanks were rumbling down the main streets into the heart of their fallen Capital. Miserably enough, and as is the case with many refugees, Missus Gyorgi had left a bit of her mind back in her native country. Doody's death five years after they left Europe helped to finish off her failing faculties. Consequently, she was now a turnip or two short of a goulash and she considered anyone wearing a uniform a goddamned communist. This included the Police Officers presently standing on her doorstep but of course they couldn't have known that.

A clear river of spittle ran down her chin from her pursed lips, a distinct indicator to those who knew her that she was about to explode.

Darby could see the agitation in her eyes and he mistakenly assumed he could reassure her with some calming words. Putting on his best good cop voice, he promptly laid a simple and
generally comforting phrase upon her unenthusiastic ears.

"It's okay ma'am," Darby stated softly, "*we're* the police."

This obviously meant nothing to Missus Gyorgi because she instantly reached up and started to whack one of the Ninja's on the helmet with her wooden spoon, producing a loud slapping sound that carried the full length of the hallway. Stealth would be a vital key to this being a successful operation and now some old boot was sounding taps on a Ninja's head. This action could announce their arrival to the wrong parties and would do nothing to enhance their clandestine deployment.

Then it got worse.

Missus Gyorgi then launched herself into a scolding rebuttal, her voice sounding manly as it carried like a thunderclap across a treeless prairie.

"Vhat you do-ink here anyvays?" She yelled. "You God-dem fuck-ink comm-nist bas'turds. You dirtee khuntz . . . for to get out of meink hallvay. Fuck-oars . . . Eh?"

Christ, Darby thought, things were getting a little too tense here all of a sudden. He nodded to the team leader of the Ninja's, an Inspector named Haworth who used hand signals to instantly deploy his people down the hall. Darby and Fenton remained behind to keep the old lady from trumpeting too much louder but that didn't look like it was going to happen unless they gagged her. Missus Gyorgi continued with her spitting castigation of the plain-clothes officers, now thinking them to be members of the dreadful, secret police. She swung her dirty spoon menacingly through the air and both Darby and Fenton weren't sure if they should take cover or pull their chunks and wing the old bird. It would appear that hell itself couldn't possibly have any more fury than a communist-hating immigrant. The only good news was the Ninja team had now ghosted into their hard entry positions down the hallway. They crouched and stood to the side of the target door, all of them fit for bear as they awaited their Inspector's signal.

Directly on the other side of that particular door, Spider Teed had been laying in his pigsty apartment on a stolen love seat. He had been funking to his favorite rap-crap on his newly acquired, stolen stereo. Right now Spider wasn't operating at one hundred per cent of his full capacity. This was in part due to the sickening panic he felt over murdering that cop earlier on in the evening, but mostly because he had swilled the better part of a bottle of whisky. Spider had meant to kill the female cop but now he deeply regretted it. She was the one who had broken her flashlight over his noggin a few weeks back and he had fired the gun at her face impulsively.

The other cop he had only wounded because he was an all right kind of a guy. Still, the entire ordeal tormented him right down to his very marrow for if they caught him he would undoubtedly fry. The pistol he had used to murder Lisa Carmaducci lay cocked with a round up the spout on an old coffee table in front of the love seat. All he needed to do was point and shoot. The accomplice, with whom he'd robbed the jewelry store, had instructed Spider to throw the weapon into the river before they parted ways, but Teed had decided to keep it and why he did will never be known. Darby and Fenton would never be able to ask Spider's partner in crime because they never would find out his identity. That little secret went along with Spider to where ever it is that criminals go when they died.

Among other things, Spider had been festering in his own stupidity. This would be about the time he heard the old biddy from down the hall yelling at someone. She should be in a mental institute should that one, he thought. She had become a bona fide menace to the general public, constantly terrorizing everyone who lived in the building. It just wasn't right, at least to Spider's way of thinking. Then he realized that if Missus Gyorgi was screeching in the hallway that meant that someone had to be out there. Most abruptly, a very bad feeling fell over Spider as the color flushed from his face. Standing up, he took another pull on the plastic tumbler that held his watered down whisky, and then reached to pick-up the handgun from the table. He brought the weapon up in his outstretched arm, holding it firmly in his hand the way his stepfather had taught him to do years ago. It was now level with his face, and he aimed down the barrel at the door of his suite. He pretended someone was there, daring them to enter and challenge his liquored courage but heedful to keep his finger off the trigger should he accidentally discharge the weapon. This seemingly harmless action became the second most stupid thing that Spider had done during his short, miserable lifetime.

Out in the hallway, the men and woman of the Southeast District's Emergency Response Team had taken their positions, acting on hand signals from the team leader. Darby and Fenton had effectively stuffed Missus Gyorgi back into her apartment, closing the door behind them.

Albeit now she thought this pair of communist dogs were going take their pleasures with her so she took to yelling louder and who could blame her? Inspector Haworth gave two of his Ninja's a signal and they stood on either side of the doorway with the steel battering ram clasped between them. Haworth had already inspected the wooden door and had found a cheap bathroom type lock affixed to it. He could have huffed and puffed and blown the door open but you should never assume anything in police work. Spider, or whatever the hell is name was might have pushed a piano up against the door so they would be going in hard and fast.

408

Haworth held his right fist above his head then brought it down parallel in front of his body.

The two Ninja's holding the battering ram took one heaving swing, which splintered the door, wide open. There was none of this one-two-three crap you chanted when you threw your buddy into the lake at summer camp. No sir.

One swift bang and that door was no more. An instant after the door smashed open, the Ninja holding the square, twenty-six pound bulletproof body shield shuffled quickly through the opening. Crouching low on the shield man's left hand side and moving simultaneously, was an officer named Corporal Shelton, while another team member moved standing almost erect on the opposite side.

Both the escorts had their submachine guns up and they sighted down the barrels as they panned the room when they entered. Shelton would clear left while her partner would clear to the right then the rest of the team would tactically storm into the suite behind them. The first thing Shelton saw was a skinny kid with pimples on his face who held a handgun that was pointed directly at her. She squeezed briefly on the trigger of her weapon, sending two nine-millimeter bullets thudding into the young man's face just below his right eye. Because Shelton was crouched down low, both bullets angled directly up into Spider's brain, killing him immediately.

Dandy, she thought swiftly . . . just fucking dandy.

Spider Teed fell face first onto his stolen love seat just as the tinkle of the ejected cartridges from Shelton's weapon could be heard skipping and spinning across the wooden floor.

Now the rest of the team moved in and a moment later all three of the bare rooms had been cleared. The Ninja's all stood within sight of each other, holding a fist above their heads to indicate to Haworth that they were alright and the rooms had been secured.

Darby and Fenton then strolled into the apartment having left Missus Gyorgi behind in her own suite as she frantically dialed 911. Both plain wrappers walked purposefully over to Spider's body, looking down while they casually inspected him. Fenton pulled a formal looking piece of paper from his pocket and let it flutter onto the coffee table.

"Police . . . search warrant." He said quietly.

Darby was thinking what a shame it was now there would be no elevator ride to the third floor bucket. It was just as well. The two Police

Officers still had a long night of investigations ahead of them and now there would be two autopsies that they would have to attend in the morning.

Watching the Pathologist cut open this little turd would almost be a treat. Carmaducci on the other hand, would be a trifle painful.

* * *

Chapter Forty-three

Exactly six months, three days, and twenty-one hours after the fatal shooting of Lisa Anna Carmaducci, Ben Trilby sat on a high backed wooden bar stool inside his cottage behind the Country Junction Store. The store had been strategically located in the approximate geographical center of the island between the towns of Skinny's Reach and Balford.

This produced a brisk business that kept Ben hopping right from the day he had taken possession. Brisk was good though. Busy could be healthy and therapeutic, especially for a healing mind and soul that required a certain amount of daily distractions. Ben leaned against the rough surface of the large butchers block he used for a kitchen table, staring at the small styrofoam tray that held exactly fifty bullets. The bullets were packaged nose first in the tray, exposing their shiny brass bottoms and the small circular primers. Ben was dressed in blue overalls with a thick housecoat that was tied at his waist and wool socks on his feet.

He'd pinned a silver medal on the housecoat near his chest, allowing it to hang loosely and forgotten from its dark blue ribbon. Round and gleaming, it had the words "for meritorious duty" stamped across its back. It was about the size of a dollar coin and it kept tapping the butcher's block every time Ben reached over to count or play with one of the bullets. On the far side of the block, just out of his reach, lay a thirty-eight-caliber revolver.

Outside, a strong night wind blew in from the southeast with measured gusts that forced the rain to travel sideways. The drops constantly pecked at the pane glass windows, even causing the wooden frames of the sashes to rattle. It was warm and cozy inside the cottage's small kitchen, with logs of yellow spruce crackling as they burned inside the antique potbelly stove that sat in a corner. Inside of Ben though, it wasn't so warm and cozy.

He'd had a really bad day but Doctor Bonson had warned him there would be bad days along with the good days. Slowly, he was eventually recovering from the trauma of the shooting and the loss of Lisa, although the complete procedure might take years and he had been warned that he might never fully heal. How far he would get would be strictly up to him. Ben naturally carried the burden of survivor's guilt, willing to trade both his legs so that Lisa could have lived and this was a normal response. Nearly every evening after sleep finally came to him, his mind would ruthlessly take him back to the shooting on that wet corner at Barkley Avenue.

The flashbacks would come as terrorizing re enactments that always woke him in a disheveled bed. Ben would end this nightly custom with the mental haranguing he would give himself afterward as he lay in the darkness.

I should have pulled my sidearm earlier, he would taunt - or *I should have instructed Lisa to stay back.* He could be relentless at times, chiding himself as he lay soaking in his sticky sheets. Deirdre Bonson had counseled him countless times that no matter what action he might have taken at the shooting, Lisa probably would have died anyway and then he'd be scolding himself because he had worn the wrong color socks that evening. Deirdre had explained to Ben that his reactions to the trauma were quite normal but if he continued to search for needless faults

within - he would certainly find them. "Be kind to *you*," had been the reinforcing advice she had given him during their last visit in her downtown office. Although the Police Department had spent enough money on Ben's psychological treatment to cripple a west end bookie, he still wasn't completely restored the day he said good-bye to Doctor Bonson. The treatment was to continue long after his medical discharge from the Department and they of course would continue to pay the bills. This had been the plan but then Ben did something totally unexpected and out of character, and he had done so while still convalescing on the fourth floor of the hospital.

In fact, his actions had caused his life to turn in an entirely different direction and he'd coordinated it all from his hospital bed, requiring some help from his mother Bea and her new husband.

"It was if I'd heard a voice inside . . . urging me on," is what he had told Deirdre the day he announced his plans to move away. There could be no turning back as all the deeds and contracts had been duly signed. Doctor Bonson was both delighted and skeptical over this tremendous step. Her primary concern was that Ben might be attempting to run away from his past, even though a move to an island might prove very beneficial. Deirdre didn't think Ben ready to venture into such a dramatic change, but at the same time she decided to fully support him in his decision. She had to, for no one else outside of his immediate family seemed to care much what the ex police officer would be doing with his future. Ben's career was finished,

Deirdre had told him when they had first met. He would be given a monthly disability pension that would see him through his life but this did little to ease the stunning news.

Ben would have a bad limp for the rest of his days and would most probably have to move around with the aid of a cane. The sessions of reconstructive surgery to his ruined hip joint could only do so much. Ben of course came out fighting, vowing and praying that this would never happen. He would walk and run again and all without using a goddamned stick. The truth became obvious however when the painful, restorative process of rebuilding his hip quickly turned into a real piss cutter. Between the surgeries there would be merciless physiotherapy that at times left him breathless from the efforts. Ben realized that the walking he did with the assistance of the parallel bars and the ensuing hot baths were there to get him to the highest level possible - which would require the use of a cane. The days soon rolled over into months, and if Ben wasn't recovering from any recent surgery he would be down suffering in his physiotherapy or talking to Doctor Bonson. There were very few visitors, except for the kindly Padre but this had come about as a direct request from Ben himself. Those who had called on him hadn't really meant well, and it became obvious these anxieties he could have done without.

Four days after the shooting Detective Sergeant Darby came to his room, appearing uncomfortable, as if he had an icicle shoved somewhere sensitive. This made the dialogue sound wooden and insincere. Darby had brought a bouquet of flowers that he had left at the nursing station, as he was too embarrassed to give them to Ben himself. Apparently men didn't do that kind of thing. Darby stood at the foot of the bed and his words came out terse and brief.

But in all fairness, Ben didn't do anything to enhance the conversation much either.

"How are you doing there, pal?" asked the lumpy Detective.

"I'm alright," Ben lied.

"They had a nice funeral for Lisa yesterday. There were cops from all over the country. You would have liked it Trilby, you really would have."

"Yes I'm sure I would have. It's a pity I'm laying here with my balls nearly shot off, otherwise I might have gone."

"Oh . . . yeah. Too bad. Anyway pal, I guess you already heard, the Chief's putting you in for a bravery medal. It's in all the newspapers, and it looks like you're going to get it."

413

"Actually I hadn't heard," Ben replied calmly. "A medal. How very thoughtful. This bit of information changes everything. My mother used to tell me that for every wrong there will come a right. I guess this would be it, but what about Lisa?"

"Lisa's dead, pal."

"Really? I hadn't noticed. I meant what about a *goddamned* medal for Lisa - posthumously."

"Can't - she was still a recruit on field training. And you don't have to get so uppity there pal."

"Uppity? Hang on a second there, Darby - "

"*That's* Sergeant Darby."

"Yeah, whatever. Now you listen to me. You're the first police officer to visit me from the Department and I doubt you even came here willingly. I've experienced everything these past few days from terrible pain to a devastating remorse. Sarcasm would be the only thing I haven't explored - until now. But let me tell you, laying it on the likes of you beats the hell out of talking to the bed sheets. And I'm not your pal."

"Okay, be that way then," Darby said sullenly, as if his feelings were hurt. "Oh, and if it will make you feel any better, I dropped those insubordination charges I laid against you. That was the morning you gave me all that lip at the Twinkle homicide, remember?"

"I certainly do. *My* goodness but wasn't that an enchanting day? And all this time I had you figured for an asshole, and then you walk in here and put me straight by dropping your insubordination charges. That's very considerate of you. What's next Darby . . . honest thieves?"

"Hey now, I'd didn't have to come here you know."

"I see, so you *were* told to come and visit me. In that case, I wish you hadn't."

"Alright, I'll leave then."

"Please do. Can you find the door?"

Darby shook his head at Ben then left the room.

"Fuck you too," Ben muttered.

"I heard that," Darby called from down the hallway.

Two days after that dismal incident Lisa's father Mario came for a visit and that started out bad then degenerated from there. Mario Carmaducci had entered the anger stage of his grieving process and this agony caused him to spit out his thoughts at Ben. He called him everything but a decent human being. It promptly escalated to a one sided hollering match while Ben lay there staring at the ceiling. He let Mario vent, saying nothing because there was really nothing *to* say. A couple of nurses came to Ben's rescue, firmly asking Mario to leave then escorting him from the room; so much for sipping Cointreau on Mario's balcony and gazing up at the stars.

After that there would be no more people bearing ill feelings and from there on in only a chosen few were allowed past the nursing station. Ben would be left in relative seclusion to rehabilitate. Probably a good thing as this required him to utilize every fiber of his soul and spirit as well every portion of his physical stamina.

Two months later Ben's life took one of those unexplained twists that would drastically alter his world forever. He had been wheeled down to the x-ray department on a gurney so they could take a picture of his hip. The operations were finished and the Doctors wanted to have a look at how well the metal, nylon, cartilage, bone and muscle had knitted together within his joint.

Ben lay in the busy corridor when the now familiar x-ray technician came to speak to him.

"It would be a few minutes," the fellow had said, one of the x-ray machines had just broken down. They would get Ben into one of the other rooms as soon as they had cleared some of the backlog of emergency patients. "That would be fine," Ben had replied. He wouldn't be going anywhere and if he missed lunch in his room he wouldn't be too crushed. Ben put his head back down on the pillow and that's when he heard the child's voice.

"Want a magazine, mister?"

Ben glanced over to see a boy of about seven years, holding a magazine while looking expectantly into his eyes. Dressed in a hospital housecoat, the boy's head was bald, except where tufts of brown hair clung to his white skull. Chemotherapy Ben thought sadly. He took the proffered magazine then glanced at it. It was one of those colorful real-estate guides with pictures, prices and descriptions of listed property in the market area. Ben turned his head to thank the child but he was already gone. He sat up slowly and scanned both ends of the long hallway but the boy had vanished. Strange, he thought. Ben then opened up the thick real-estate guide and the page he had flicked to reveal a photograph of a rural property that nearly pulled him out of his pajamas.

Like many people, Ben opened magazines in the middle and that was where he started with this one. It would now be safe to say some happenstance had definitely fallen his way.

Someone had run a full-page advertisement with color photographs about a rural store and cottage located on one of the large gulf islands. The buildings stood amongst a stand of mature alder trees with an adjoining feed shop and a large open greenhouse. Everything about the place conjured up the words quaint, quiet, rural and friendly. All the buildings had character, including the small cottage located behind the store. This single story dwelling had been cedar sided like the rest of the buildings and the pictures of the inside were straight from a fairy tale, speaking the lines of a whimsical cabin in a deep forest. Built using the age-old post and beam method, the rough columns of redwood cheerfully accented the white, plastered walls. When the plaster ended near the entrance to the kitchen, intricate Dutch tiling had been applied and each blue and white square seemed to hold a story. The cooking area had an island made from oak, sturdy enough to support the white marble that had been laid across all the counter tops. Ben enjoyed cooking, so an efficient, attractive kitchen appealed to him.

He almost slobbered as he poured over the details of the property. Almost immediately, it became an enticement that would take his mind far and away from the hospital, as well the sorrow that accompanied it. A sad enough story itself, the place was a foreclosure and the bank had installed a manager to run the business until it sold. When Ben noticed the listed price, he instantly realized it was affordable. Such a purchase would clear out his long-standing savings account but then he had a pension coming in as well as a profit margin if he bought this store.

The ad contained all the facts and figures of the establishment and it set Ben to thinking, compelling him to formulate a plan. Something deep inside told him to research the property further. By the time they had x-rayed his hip he had decided to take another step toward this pleasing piece of country bliss. Ben spent the afternoon in his hospital room, sitting in the sunshine while he stared at the magazine, wondering if that kind of lifestyle couldn't awaken something inside of him while putting other matters to rest.

Whether it would awaken anything remained consigned to the future, but eight weeks later Ben and his bank held the deed to the property. He could have accomplished the feat alone, but his mother and her husband Will had made the transaction that much easier. They had flown out several times from the east coast to visit Ben while he recuperated and during their last visit he excitedly showed them the dog-eared page in the real-estate magazine. Bea saw a spark in her son's eyes she'd not seen since the shooting, so she sat next to him in his room, sharing and embracing these attainable dreams. When Bea and Will left the hospital at days end they returned to Ben's apartment and it was over a late dinner one evening that they decided to offer their assistance. Will had been a building contractor so one morning following a visit he and Bea drove out to the ferry landing and took the boat over to the island. Once they had met the real estate agent they had a complete look at the property. They took dozens of photographs as well they obtained stacks of informative brochures from the local chamber of commerce. Upon their return the next day Ben listened carefully to their reports, inspecting each picture and piece of paper that pertained to the business and the island it sat upon. He purchased the store and its cottage without ever making the trip there himself. Ben trusted Bea and Will but nonetheless the decision to buy had been his own, and only then after the surveys, business accounts, building inspections and licensing applications had all been scrutinized and cleared.

The manager that the bank had hired to run the store would be retained as part of the offer to purchase and he would resume his own island business once Ben assumed his new responsibilities.

Not soon after the deal closed, Ben was discharged from the hospital and sent home to limp around his apartment while his body continued to repair itself. The counseling with Doctor Bonson proceeded on a biweekly basis as well as the physiotherapy at the hospital. On all points Ben recovered remarkably well and the only debatable issue would be the gray area that surrounded his mental well-being. He knew he still had hurdles to get over as well did Deirdre but the time had arrived to move to the island and begin his life again. They both agreed to deal with any issues that could arise from his new ventures as they occurred. A forty-five minute ferry ride followed with a twenty minute drive would ensconce him safely back in Deirdre's office. Doctor Bonson carried a cell phone that she would answer night or day, so a back-up plan was already in place. On his last visit with Deirdre, Ben limped in carrying a dozen long stemmed roses to thank the woman who had helped him to manage his thoughts and feelings while at the same time cleansing his mind and soul. After the session Ben shook Deirdre's hand then left her office and she watched from her window far above the street as he shuffled to his car. What a courageous young man, she thought. Doctor Bonson hoped that he would at least call to let her know how his life was progressing but she would never hear from Ben Trilby again.

And so exactly two months, three days and twenty-one hours after moving to his new home on the island, Ben Trilby sat in his kitchen with his personal revolver gleaming against the dull wood of the butcher's block. It had been a horrible day, this one being much worse than the rest. Bad times were expected and Ben could sense them as he climbed from his bed in the mornings, knowing just when they were going to occur. A mood of intense sadness would fall over him minutes after his feet had touched the floor. Virtually any discouraging incident during this period could reduce him to tears despite the heavy dosing of antidepressant medication.

On many occasions he had to abruptly excuse himself from his young staff members in the store, returning to his cottage where he would weep alone until exhaustion overtook him. Ben would then wash his eyes with a hot face cloth to diminish the redness and go back to the store hoping no one would notice. Except they always did. These sorrowful days he had learned to manage, knowing good days would separate the bad days but this afternoon had been more acute because of the fight.

Ben had caught one of the local social failures attempting to steal a bottle from his liquor stock. This had been the second time he had found Martin Bandie stealing liquor and he had barred him after the first instance. Unfortunately, one of his employees had allowed him in, unaware of the prohibition. When Ben entered the store from the cottage he saw Bandie's truck in the parking lot then went to search the premises. He found him down by the produce section on his knees, out of view from the front counter as he slid a bottle of wine into the sleeve of his jacket.

Bandie was drunk and feeling brave, sniffing for a confrontation - which is precisely what he got. The discovered pilfering immediately turned into a loud discussion regarding Bandie's innocence and it fell apart from there. Ben hadn't been in the mood for an argument much less a fight, but when the younger man attempted to punch him in the face the gauntlet was down. Within seconds they were rolling across the wooden floor in the narrow aisle, upsetting over a table of apples and Ben realized that his damaged hip as well as the pain had become a serious physical handicap. Half a year earlier and Ben would have been powerful enough to turn this obnoxious turd inside out if he had a mind to. He attempted to apply some of his old police holds on Bandie but he found his opponent to be wiry and fast, displaying the energy of a cornered alley cat.

Ben quickly tired and it took every bit of his stamina to get the younger man out the door where he threw him down the stairs. The two girls behind the counter were still in high school and justifiably terrified while this little punch-up played out before their eyes. One of them called the police but they had been busy elsewhere on the island and when they did attend the only thing they found of Martin was a bad smell that hovered over the spilled apples. The incident had been humiliating for Ben, especially in front of his staff and the whole island would know about it before the sun had gone down. This pushed him further into the gloom that had shadowed him since the morning. Ben had nearly lost that fight, and to a drunken punk half his size.

I'm no longer the man I used to be, he thought sadly. This of course wasn't at all true but not even Deirdre Bonson would be able to chase the self destructive brooding away - at least not on the telephone. Ben had in fact called her later in the day once the store had closed but she was halfway around the world taking a much-deserved vacation.

The fight however, became the small push that he could have done without.

After playing with his food over a late supper, Ben made a quick trip down a hall that took him to his bedroom. He fetched the long barreled revolver from the safe in his closet then returned to the kitchen. Now he stared at the weapon, not really sure what he would do with it.

But there it lay.

A quick, final option.

Ben had investigated many sudden deaths during his years as a police officer and many of the suicides he'd attended could have gone either way. A simple nudge from the wrong direction could send a floundering person into a terminal abyss. Many who had chosen this route were usually unsure at first; simply making a cry for help until someone obligingly pushed them one last time.

Sometimes it was a devastating phone call from a lover ending a relationship. Other times it could be a painful debility for which they'd found no cure and at times it would be an employer who had made the persons life a rolling torment. Either way . . . Ben thought. This could go one way or the other and he suddenly understood what those people had endured prior to taking their own lives. He currently shared their loneliness and sadness; he now experienced the numbing resignation that must have pervaded their minds before they had died. Ben pulled a bullet from the middle of the stryofoam tray, examining the brass cartridge as he reached across for the revolver. Outdoors the wind blew and the rain persisted with its incessant tapping against the windows.

Tap, tap, tap.

Yes sir, this situation could go either way, Ben thought.

Tap, tap, tap.

A lead, hollow point slug, which would do the job. Leave a bloody, pulpy mess on the butcher's block if I didn't fall onto the floor.

Tap, tap, tap.

I'd best load only the one bullet into the cylinder. I don't want the local police thinking I was planning some sort of a psychopathic shooting spree.

Tap, tap, tap.

Christ - someone was tapping on the window near his back door. There had been a lot of that lately. People showing up on his doorstep after hours, asking to buy a loaf of bread or some milk, or rolling papers so they can smoke their cherished marijuana. A few even wanted to buy a jug of liquor, and oh, could they pay later?

Cheeky swine.

"Answer the door," the voice inside of him said.

Ben sighed irritably as he took a tea towel, spreading it over the revolver and the box of bullets before sliding from his stool. Leaning against his cane he limped over to the door thinking how he might have to put up a sign - 'Please call again, suicide being contemplated, have a nice day.' He opened the back door, feeling the wind in his hair as it gusted into the house, causing a calendar on the wall to flap noisily. She stood on the wooden balcony, dressed in a yellow raincoat with the hood pulled close into her face. Ben outright detested some of the people living on the island, but he treated them all with the same kind manners so he invited the woman in out of the weather. She stepped lightly inside and Ben closed the door behind her, looking at her attentively. They were nearly the same height and when she flipped her hood back Ben saw a clean, intelligent face, short blond hair and a smile that disarmed him completely.

When she spoke her voice came over as soft and easy but the way she stood told Ben plenty. The non-verbals alluded that somewhere inside of her there dwelled a solid independence.

"Hello, I'm Judith Noble," she said, holding out her hand.

Ben had heard all about this somewhat reclusive schoolteacher who held a gift for teaching the islands mentally challenged children. Everyone who spoke of her seemed to hold her in some kind of awe and that's just what Ben felt as he gazed into her eyes. He'd never had the chance to meet her even though she'd probably been in the store on several occasions. Ben's new responsibilities always had him busy in the back of the store working on the books or stocking shelves in the feed room. He shook her hand, finding it warm in spite of the chilly night.

"Hi, I'm Ben."

"The ex-cop, I've heard about you."

Ben could feel his face pinking when she said that, wondering what kind of rotten stories were circulating about him.

"I didn't know police officers received medals." She pointed a finger at the sparkling disc of silver hanging from his housecoat.

"Oh . . . yeah. We do at times, especially if we do something foolish."

"Well it's a splendid looking medal and I'm sure there's an exciting story behind it."

"Yes . . . as a matter of fact there was a considerable amount of excitement going on. A little too much in fact."

Ben said this jokingly, but as Judith smiled at his wit she could see a wounded trace waver across his face. She'd struck some buried sentiment and she hadn't meant to. Time to change the subject.

"I'm terribly sorry to bother you so late," she continued, "and I realize that you're closed. But one of my daughters has a dreadful cold and I wondered if you could sell me some cough medicine?"

"Why certainly. Just give me a second please."

Ben sat on the wooden bench by the door, trying not to grimace with pain as his hip protested when he slipped the black gumboots onto his feet. Ben had never even seen a pair of gumboots until he moved to the island but they were fashionable here and everyone wore them except for the animals, and that would undoubtedly happen, given enough time.

He's cute, Judith thought as she looked down at him. Not many people could dress the way he does, wearing a medal and a housecoat without coming across as some sort of a noodle.

Standing up, Ben pulled a raincoat from the wall hooks behind him and pulled it on.

He looked at Judith to indicate that he was ready and he found her looking directly at him.

"It's a nice place you have here." she smiled again.

"Thank-you," he said, "It kind of grows on you."

Ben led her out the door and she politely followed as he limped down the stairs and through the wet yard. Conversation was impossible as the wind plucked at their clothing and the rain stung their exposed skin. Once they entered the store Ben flicked on a set of lights, and then took Judith to the medicine aisle. Beneath their feet the wooden floors squeaked loudly, and they looked at each other and laughed. The shelves at the end of one aisle held an assortment of cough syrups and cold medications and Ben found himself watching Judith as she picked up one bottle at a time. She carefully read the contents that each one contained and Ben enjoyed the opportunity it presented. He could smell her delicate essence from where he stood, void of any perfume and he realized Judith Noble was the first woman he had paid any attention to since the night of the shooting.

"She's very nice," the voice inside him said, "and she's had her share of misery as well."

Ben became thankful that the previous owner had stocked the store with so much cough medicine, for he rather enjoyed the innocence of the moments he'd been given with her.

Judith suddenly looked over at him.

"I'm sorry about this, but they put so much garbage in their medications these days."

"Take your time," Ben smiled. "Believe me, I've got nothing going on back at the house."

In fact, you can take all night, Ben thought. Because that's how long I could stand here

admiring you. He had never believed in all that high school crap about love at first sight but his life had been changing so fast that he could only just hobble along to keep up. Something now stirred inside of him and he decided to do nothing to quell it. After a few delicious minutes, Judith picked out a bottle of cough syrup, holding it up so Ben could observe the price.

This was when she realized she'd forgotten her wallet at home and when she mentioned this

a smile spread the width of Ben's face and he started to chuckle.

"Don't worry about it. Drop by when you have a minute, the coffee is always on - or tea if you prefer."

"Thank-you. You're very kind Ben, I'm truly sorry - I can really be thoughtless at times."

"Not at all, I'm pleased that I finally got the chance to meet you. You have a considerable reputation on this island."

Now Judith blushed.

"Good," the voice in his head said, "she's humble as well."

They made their way back to the door, and Judith waited on the covered porch as Ben turned off the lights and locked the door to his store. The porch roof kept some of the wind and rain at bay, enough that they could converse.

"Thanks again, Ben. It was nice to finally meet you. I'll bring you the money tomorrow morning, if that's okay."

"That's fine, I'll be here."

Judith put the medicine in one of her deep pockets and walked back through the wind and rain to the mini van she had parked next to the cottage. Ben leaned against his cane, watching as she started her vehicle and backed onto the roadway. Within minutes the weather and the darkness had swallowed the red taillights of her vehicle as it moved away in the distance. Ben left the back of the store, returning purposely to his cottage. He moved as fast as his cane would allow. There was something he had to do and he had to do it before he had another weak spell - the voice inside him becoming nearly audible as it coaxed him on.

Ben entered the cottage and went directly over to the butcher's block, picking up the revolver and the tray of deadly bullets. He clutched them to his chest using his free hand, and then walked out on the porch and back into the night. Slowly, Ben worked his way to the other side of the house.

There, a field of deep grass covered the northern portion of his property and he walked straight into the weeds, placing his cane cautiously to his front before advancing his steps. By the time he had arrived at the abandoned well his pant legs were soaked through, the cold water seeping down into his gumboots. The wellhead sat in the middle of the field, capped more than three decades ago with a circular piece of fixed concrete. It had been left over from the original homestead when there existed no running water. In the middle of the cap they had fixed a round inspection port, also made from poured cement but not much bigger than a saucer. The port would allow the well to be recharged should the need ever arise. At the bottom, nearly one hundred feet below Ben's feet, the water was clear, sweet, and deep, filtered naturally through the layers of soil and gravel. Ben knelt on the cap, feeling for the metal handle, which he pulled on, freeing the inspection cover like a rubber plug from an old sink. Peering into the dark hole, all he could see was a black void and he wondered briefly if he should carry out this impulsive plan. It would be an irresponsible way for an ex police officer to deal with a firearm, even if it could never be retrieved.

"Do it." It was the voice inside of him again and Ben wasn't entirely sure if part of his conscious was talking to him, or if in fact it was some sort of spiritual instruction. He didn't care and it didn't matter, so he tossed the revolver and the bullets into the hole then slid the cover back into place. On the outside, Ben suddenly felt like an old man as he got back to his feet, his hip aching stubbornly. He reflected back on the afternoon and the stinging recollection of the fight he'd had with Martin Bandie seemed to help age his body further.

On the inside however, Ben felt entirely different as he plodded through the grass back to his warm cottage. Healing always came from the inside, Doctor Bonson had once informed him. Ben Trilby then understood that when he'd left the city he hadn't been running from his past.

He had in fact been moving toward his future. Now he couldn't wait until tomorrow morning, to see Judith's face once again when she came to pay her bill. Ben wasn't totally beguiled with this enchanting schoolteacher for he'd only just met her. Although he now knew he was certainly heading in that wonderful direction. The voice inside him told him this as he shambled through the tall grass. Ben was glad he had started to heed the things the voice would tell him and as long as he didn't answer back, he figured everything would be okay. And he was absolutely right.

*   *   *

Chapter Forty-four

A rhythmic thumping played against Ben's ears, seeming to bounce of his skull and the sound drew him back from his ruminations of Lisa and his sobering past.

He looked up into the darkness from where he sat, refocusing his eyes onto the walls of the waiting room before glancing through the double doors to where he had parked the ambulance. Outside the island's only hospital, the rain continued with its relentless deluge as the thumping noise got louder, vibrating the floor beneath Ben's feet. Just above the roof of the ambulance in the night sky, a winking red strobe red light appeared in the distance, rapidly approaching from the direction of Skinny's Reach. Helicopter, Ben thought. Inbound from the mainland.

The whoop, whoop sound, caused by the spinning rotor blades built to a sustained clamor as the aircraft neared the hospital. Ben watched curiously as the red and white machine flared, and then hovered momentarily in the air just above the parked ambulance, its wash plastering the vehicle and the hospital doors with rainwater. Seconds later the helicopter set down behind the ambulance on the grassed area that fronted the building. Ben could see the tips of the main rotor blades flickering on either end of the ambulance, the large body of the vehicle effectively eclipsing the aircrafts fuselage as it settled on the other side.

A minute later two men dressed in orange jump suits and wearing flying helmets entered the hospital, guiding a gurney that rolled beside them. They went straight into the emergency room and Ben suddenly thought this had to be a good sign. The aircraft was an air ambulance and they wouldn't dispatch one of those expensive units to pick-up a dead schoolteacher. Ben's answer came not two minutes later when the doors to the ER were abruptly flung open and the two air crew reappeared with Judith strapped securely to their gurney. She lay wrapped in blankets with wires leading to a small monitor placed near her feet. A clear plastic mask covered her mouth and nose, the pure oxygen fed to her from a thin cylinder tucked between her legs. One of the aircrew had an intravenous bag clamped between his teeth as he pushed the gurney while his partner pulled. Ben knew that Judith was at least breathing because he could see the condensation beading inside her oxygen mask. He felt a spark of absolute joy as the aircrew wheeled her out the door and he watched as they promptly disappeared behind the parked ambulance. A short time later the helicopter lifted from the ground, the pilot turning the aircraft skillfully under its main rotor before it thumped its way back into the night.

Again the doors to the ER flew open and the paramedics Fred and Barney wheeled their own gurney through the waiting room, clean blankets now folded neatly and secured across one end. "We brought her back there Buddy," Fred nodded to Ben. "She's still unconscious and it may be a couple of days before they know if she suffered any permanent brain damage. We've got another call to go to so you'll have to walk home - sorry. And thanks for your help."

Ben watched them, slightly stunned as Fred and Barney efficiently loaded up their gear then drove down the cement ramp, their ambulance wailing and flashing as it sped away to another call. Friday night, Ben thought, they'll be busy. He looked at his wristwatch as he limped out the door into the pouring rain.

Exactly twenty-one minutes had elapsed since he and Sergeant Cheryl Montague had started CPR on Judith as she lay in the wet grass at the accident scene. Ben prayed that she hadn't suffered any brain damage, wishing a full recovery more for her family and the children she taught than for himself. He was happy that she had survived, and he thought this as he walked away in the darkness. Why the accident had to happen in the first place he would never know. Ben had learned not to question these incidents after he had lost Lisa. Search as you may and as long as you like, you will never find the answer. Although Ben felt that somewhere within the realms of this earth, someone had to know why this accident happened. He was correct in his thinking, but in the end only Judith would know why a drunken Martin Bandie had driven into, and felled a power pole, that would electrocute her into a clinical death. The unsuspecting catalyst to all these events would be the young retarded boy, Brodie Bandie. An innocent child who ate worms, peed his pants at will, and dearly loved the schoolteacher he had very nearly lost.

*   *   *

426

Part Six
"Closure"

Chapter Forty-five

It was three in the morning and Corporal Dave Tuck, the Traffic Analyst, was drunk. He sat upright on the couch in the living room of Cheryl's cottage, asleep with a cigarette burning in a glass ashtray at his side, an unfinished drink on the coffee table. Dressed in a silk housecoat from Cheryl's bedroom closet, he was quite sight with the delicate, oriental embroidery that adorned the burgundy silk from collar to hem. Cheryl Montague sat opposite him in a love seat and couldn't help but wonder whatever happened to the fit, young police officer she had romped in bed with so many years ago. They had gone through training together, as members of the same police recruit troop, and had become study partners which led to a friendship, which opened the doors to things more intimate. Cheryl Montague had spotted a fellow renegade the very first day they had formed up as a troop at the police-training depot. Cheryl, a young black student newly graduated from University with a Sociology degree in her resume, and Tuck, a skinny white kid with dreams of becoming a cop. Their emotionally uncommitted affair started soon after they had met and continued long after they hit the streets as Police Officers, eventually coming to an end once Tuck had met his first wife..

Now, two grinding decades had passed for Dave Tuck - twenty years marked by three wives, one promotion to corporal and the consuming of countless bottles of scotch. Throughout this same time period Cheryl had remained an abstainer as well as single, focusing on her career and managing to obtain her sergeant's hooks despite her rebel tongue and attitude. She had taken numerous lovers along the way but found she could function quite nicely without sex, never really yearning for its lusty sweets like some people who treated the recreation as if it were an urgent commodity, like water or fresh air. Being the local Detachment Commander of the Regional Police meant modest behavior during your off duty hours and Cheryl's lifestyle fit that requisite well. Her quiet, cultured pastimes of listening to classical music, sipping Perrier with a lemon twist while loving her three-year-old German Shepherd kept her low key if not thoroughly satisfied. Cheryl spent most of her time off indoors or on a local beach if the weather was nice, far from the prying eyes of Harvey Bentley, the fat hippy who had the misfortune to be Cheryl's neighbor. Much like a large percentage of the Island's population, Harvey liked to wear farming coveralls and sandals, but unlike most he also preferred to wander through his backyard naked when the sun would shine.

This in itself wasn't a problem, for Cheryl couldn't have cared less what her neighbor did in his backyard until she caught him peeking through the thick, juniper hedge one day when she'd been sun bathing on her patio. Her Shepherd Roofus had sniffed out the cheeky bastard, snarling and baring his teeth while Harvey scurried back to his lawn chair, his pale, fleshy buttocks jiggling obscenely. Cheryl had seen him naked one other day as well, while doing her laundry. On that occasion Harvey lay in plain view through an opening in the hedge and she'd no doubt that he'd dragged his aluminum lounger out to that strategic location on his lawn to offer her an eyeful of his wormy manhood. She did in fact get a squint of his pathetic looking genitals and the only way to describe that scene would have been "a large, sun bleached turd pushing the structural envelope of an aluminum patio lounger." It had been hot that particular day and Harvey the hippy kept glancing over to see if Cheryl was stealing peeks at him through the opening. Once she'd hung her wet laundry on the line, she and Roofus had quietly disappeared back inside where the atmosphere was less noxious. Three hours later the laundry had dried and when Cheryl came back out to gather it in, Harvey had fallen asleep on his lounger and had sunburned to a painful calico red, including the bell end of his wee willy. "Just gotta hurt," Cheryl thought as she carried her laundry basket back inside.

She was also well aware that Harvey ran the local marijuana Coop and she'd gathered enough evidence for a search warrant but not enough time to go up to the farm with a battering ram and a few of her fellow officers. There would be ample time when things slowed down a bit, and she was reminded of that impending project when she caught Harvey peeking through his living room curtains when she and Tuck had entered her cottage just before midnight. Even from her front walk she could see his eyes - wide, red, and glassy looking from a transcendental evening smoking his treasured pot. Cheryl and Tuck had just returned from the fatal traffic accident that killed Martin Bandie and sent an unconscious Judith Noble over to a mainland hospital. Both police officers were soaked through from the rain and Tuck had missed the last ferry off the island so Cheryl offered him the bed in her spare room. She also provided him with a dry, if not somewhat feminine housecoat to put on but she knew Tuck would be appreciative of her offerings.

After the fifth drink, when the euphoria had taken hold and started to tingle inside Tuck's very pores, nothing bothered him and he couldn't have cared less if he sat on Cheryl's couch dressed in a Geisha's gown or a two-piece swim suit. The original plan had been to put one of those crappy frozen pizza's into the oven for a late dinner but once they'd gotten into dry clothes a liquor bottle suddenly appeared on the coffee table. After Cheryl fetched Tuck a tumbler and an ice cube tray, they soon fell into some deep, reminiscent conversation. Tuck always carried a bottle of twenty-year-old, single malt scotch in one of his briefcases for such occasions. His drinking problem had seeded itself and grown to the point that he'd learned to plan ahead when he would finish late or become stranded somewhere after an investigation and the bars had closed.

In the beginning, his scotch consumption had been strictly recreational, but the alcohol had eventually become a defense mechanism, it's delicious numbing an invisible wall to the brutal sights and realities of his thankless job. In the end, it's abuse would one day bite Tuck firmly on the ass, but like most veteran drinkers he didn't think too much about his distant future.

In all fairness, no one is totally immune to the harsh carnage of police work, not even the initial, attending police officers who could at least pass the torch to Dave Tuck once he'd shown up at one of these tragic accident scenes. They would quietly watch on as he worked his wizardry and cast his mathematical spells that in the end would explain how a vehicle came to be on its roof in a ditch, with its occupants dead. Including an infant who had been propelled dozens of feet from the smashed wreck. Dave Tuck despised these accidents, but he despised even more the inconsiderate mothers who coddled their toddlers on their laps while in moving vehicles. More than that, he particularly hated those rare occasions when his calculations failed to reveal the hidden facts behind the incident. A rarity to be sure, it could nonetheless be a strain when Tuck had to tell the surviving members of car crash victim's that their loved one's vehicle left the road then theatrically burst into flames on the other side of a ditch, and he had absolutely no idea why.

This evening had been one such tiring circumstance, another that ended with a pile of imminent paperwork and very few answers to Martin Bandie's motor vehicle accident. Once Martin's body had been carted off inside the Coroner's van and Judith Noble moved safely to the local hospital, the meticulous work of reconstructing just what really happened had begun. The heavy rain made the precise job all the more painstaking and while Tuck worked on his field sketch Cheryl drove once again up to the Bandie residence, following the familiar dirt road that led her through the neglected apple orchard. Cheryl didn't know what to expect from Martin's wife Nora when she notified her that her husband wouldn't be coming home drunk anymore to beat the hell out of her and her son Brodie.

Despite Martin's death being a blessing of sorts, Cheryl could taste her utter dread, her stomach feeling like it held lead shot as she mounted the wooden steps to the dilapidated trailer. Nora met her at the door before she could even knock and the look on Cheryl's face must have told the story. Nora started to laugh loudly when Cheryl spoke gently of Martin's death, standing defiantly at the entrance to her Joey shack with her arms crossed. Then she broke into racking sobs and Cheryl held her as she buried her face into the shoulder of her patrol jacket, soaking it further with tears and sticky mucus. Normally, Cheryl would have spent as much time as it would take to console a bereaving survivor but she had to return to the accident site. Whatever interpretive evidence lay back there might be flowing into the ditch with the rain. This evidence had to be recorded before it disappeared and Tuck would need Cheryl to hold the "dummy" end of his measuring tape so he could get reliable dimensions.

After comforting her for another ten minutes Cheryl took Nora out to the patrol car then drove her to a friend's house down the road. Leaving her in safe hands, she then returned to the accident, thinking once again how at times she hated her goddamned job. When she parked her patrol car back near the scene, a tow truck already had a hook on Martin's vehicle and the cable drum at the back of the wrecker whined as it hauled the pick-up across the wide ditch. The ex-cop, Ben Trilby, had limped back to the scene from the hospital and Cheryl rightly assumed the ambulance crew had abandoned him to race off to another urgent call, nothing out of the ordinary for the paramedics, not for a Friday night. Ben stood chatting with Tuck, making no attempt to get out of the rain and he nodded to Cheryl as she walked over to them. Cheryl thanked Ben for his help once he'd explained that Judith had been stabilized by the doctor after twenty-two agonizing minutes, and then taken in an air ambulance to the mainland. Ben then shuffled over to his sports car and drove away in the direction of his store. Good, Cheryl thought briefly, the schoolteacher was still alive. Now with any luck it would remain that way and there would be only one name to put on the sudden death report.

During Cheryl's absence Tuck had been busy, having used nearly all of the measuring instruments he carried around in his plastic cases. But still he had no clear answers. He'd pulled out everything from his sight clinometer to measure to angle of the slope in the road to a simple measuring tape, which he used among other things, to calculate the speed of Bandie's truck by examining the yaw marks left in the gravel. Tuck had used a rock to secure the dummy end of the tape, opting not to wait for Cheryl. Good fortune stood with them in that Martin's old beater of a vehicle didn't have anti lock brakes so it managed to leave a long, curving gouge in the gravel. When he'd climbed onto the brakes, the front passenger wheel bit hard into the roadway, arching toward the power pole while leaving a beautiful yaw mark in its wake. Measuring the gouge from tip to tip as well as the belly of the curve would give Tuck the proper figures to determine how fast Martin had been traveling before leaving the roadway.

They worked in the rain for a few hours, Tuck had set up his surveying scope, using Cheryl to pace over the scene while she held a telescoping pole with a reflective prism affixed to the top. Tuck's scope had a fixed lens that sent out a laser beam that would reflect off the prism, returning to the scope within a fraction of a second, digitally supplying him with measurements to a half-millimeter. Next, Tuck once again zeroed his sight clinometer to get a final reading on the slope of the road as well as the angle where it banked into the curve. He then took a compass bearing to ascertain true north, then lastly he set up his thirty-five-millimeter camera on its tripod. Slowly, Tuck encircled the entire scene, taking photographs from every conceivable angle of view. This in itself turned into a persnickety exercise as he had to constantly adjust the aperture and shutter speed to compensate for the falling darkness as well as the long shadows cast from the bright take down lights of Cheryl's patrol car. All this information would provide Tuck with the accurate dimensions he would require for the planned drawing he had to complete for all serious accidents. Juries at civil trials required a detailed, overhead drawing of any accident scene for their deliberations and subsequent rewarding of any punitive damages. What they could scan briefly in a warm courtroom ordinarily took hours of careful measurements in less than ideal conditions, followed by days hunched over a drafting table with clean white paper and India ink. Although the traffic analysts could cut their office time in half with the use of updated, computer soft wear, Tuck still preferred the fastidious, old school method of hand producing his planned drawings.

By the time Dave Tuck had worked his figures and measured every stain and piece of debris that had been left behind, there remained little time left in the day and even less that he knew for sure about the accident. He thought about this as he loaded his gear into the trunk of the patrol car while Cheryl collected the traffic cones that had blocked access to the road. Tuck knew for certain that Martin Bandie had driven his truck through an abrupt curve on a gravel road where the posted speed was twenty-miles-an-hour. He now knew that the vehicle had been traveling in excess of sixty-five-miles-an-hour and that no amount of skill would have kept the vehicle on the road. Not on that particular grade or in that particular curve. Tuck also knew by all accounts that Martin Bandie had been shit-faced drunk, and that he had most probably died on impact and the power lines he'd brought down had electrocuted an extremely popular school teacher, killing her clinically for the better part of a half-hour. He knew through simple mathematics that there existed a slight incline where the road banked into the curve, its highest point where Martin's pick-up truck had left the road to vault across a wide ditch before nosing into the base of a wooden power pole. Additionally, Tuck also knew that this incline defied all the laws of physics in that its grade was insufficient - at any speed - to cause Martin's vehicle to gain enough momentum and elevation to clear such a wide ditch. Another mystery, another traffic fatality void of any clear answers, and he told Cheryl this as he climbed into the patrol car beside her then lit a cigarette.

In the end, in the very end, a coroner's inquest would eventually exonerate Cheryl from her part in the high-speed chase that led to the death of Martin Bandie. They would conclude that the young man had died as result of excessive speed, a blood alcohol three times the legal limit and massive trauma to his head and body caused by a collision with a power pole. Of course, neither Cheryl Montague nor Dave Tuck could have known this at the time, nor could they have known that they would never solve all the uncertainty behind the incident. Nevertheless, as the pair of veteran police officers drove through the darkness and the pouring rain across the island to Cheryl's cottage, Tuck continued to work his figures on a clipboard he held on his lap. Cheryl drove the car slowly so Tuck could concentrate on his calculations, but mainly because her vision was impeded by the reflection in the windshield from the large dome light on the ceiling of the car. They said nothing for the next fifteen minutes as the vehicle moved over the gravel roads, the rain patting loudly on the roof, the world outside bleak and colorless. As the patrol car pulled into the driveway of Cheryl's cottage, Tuck pulled a thick, fluorescent yellow felt pen from one of his pockets then pulled the cap off using his teeth. He wrote some words across the bottom of the field sketch on his clipboard then returned the pen to his pocket, looking briefly at Cheryl while quietly shaking his head. The pair exited the patrol car and Tuck retrieved a leather briefcase from the trunk of the vehicle before they entered Cheryl's house through the front door.

As Cheryl turned some lights on, Tuck placed his briefcase beside the couch in the living room and put the clipboard on the coffee table as he flopped down on the sofa, concentrating on removing his wet uniform. Cheryl went down the hallway to her bedroom with Roofus padding dutifully behind her. When she returned she had on a housecoat, passing Tuck one of her clean, silky spares as he sat on the couch in his underwear. Nodding his thanks, he pulled the housecoat on over his bony shoulders. Seconds later the scotch bottle appeared on the coffee table and Cheryl knew her old friend well enough to wordlessly go into the kitchen to fetch him a glass tumbler and an ice cube tray. Tuck nodded his appreciation then cracked the seal on the tall green bottle, pouring the smoky, amber liquid over a couple of ice cubes, making them dance and crack over the bottom of his glass. Cheryl sat down in a love seat with her dog's black head on her lap and she and Tuck fell into some effortless dialogue, as free flowing as their breath - just the way friends who had shared a lot were meant too.

The conversation started the way all their private talks had over the years, the first verbal salvo always personal and tragic. Tuck's latest marriage had become a casualty once again.
"Marcie left me for a Highway Patrolman," Tuck shared. "Some guy half her age with a frontal lobotomy and an eight-inch dick."
"Really? Eight inches?" Cheryl stated quietly. "Not bad for a white boy."
"Who said he was a white boy, and you're not helping this any, Cheryl."
"Sorry Tuck . . . please go on."
"Yeah, eight inches. Of course she made damn sure I was aware of that little tidbit before she skipped out the front door. The asshole even drives a little sports car . . . candy apple red. Got lots of money too."

"I'm sorry to hear that Tuck, I really am."

"Honest to Jesus Cheryl, I really loved this one, I truly did."

He said "this one" like he'd lost his favorite dog or something and Cheryl wondered if Tuck indeed loved any of his wives. Like every human being Dave Tuck had his faults and like every human being he also had a lot of good in him. Cheryl knew just what it was that attracted women to his simple good looks for she had traveled that road herself. Tuck was a kindhearted, old-fashioned gentleman who could easily capture your attention with his sincere charms, and then your lust once he had bedded you. A true artist, any woman sleeping with Dave Tuck would be guaranteed at least one long orgasm as he lavished their bodies with his teasing touches.

But great sex alone does not a good relationship make, and in the end Tuck's drinking would be his failing and all his prior spouses had fled to sober pastures. Never obnoxious or belligerent when he got into the cups, he always become very relaxed and easy going, and if Tuck's partners had learned anything from living with him, it was to always wait until the fourth of fifth drink before you hit him up for a favor. All his former wives quickly clued to the fact that if they wanted an expensive ocean cruises or some new furniture, they simply waited until Tuck was really scotched before they asked him. The answer would always be a soft smile followed with an affirmative yes, but they soon tired of the permissiveness as well as his seemingly harmless drinking. They had all told him; as well Tuck knew he had a problem. He'd known for years, but he never really had a good enough reason to stop drinking and besides, he enjoyed it too much to quit. The Regional Police had check stops in place for such delicate issues, like counseling and dry out programs but Tuck had to make the first move for help. Unfortunately, the fact remained that the Force couldn't have cared less that he was embalming his liver so long as he showed up for work on time, and in a relatively sober state.

Throughout their long friendship, and whenever they fell into these quiet, revealing conversations, Cheryl would be polite enough to not ever mention Tuck's drinking for she saw no point.

As well, one should never scold an ear that is kind enough to listen to *your* problems.

The pair somehow managed an unplanned get together every so often and the last one had been nine months past when they had attended a course at the national Police College in the Capitol. These meetings were inevitable as well as healthy; for Cheryl could tell Tuck things she wouldn't ever tell another human being and vis a versa. It was always good to have someone you could trust with your soul secrets, someone who would just nod sympathetically, someone who knew quite well the paths you'd already walked and just where it was you were heading. As they always did, Tuck and Cheryl's heart to heart went well into the night and they invariably covered every personal topic that required their due consideration. And although the world outside the doors of Cheryl's cottage remained the same, the two people inside felt much better after being allowed to audibly vent their inner frustrations. The crappy, deluxe frozen pizza never did make it into the oven and Tuck fell asleep like he usually did after the required snoot full of scotch. Except this time he did it sitting upright on the couch with a cigarette burning in the ashtray.

Cheryl sighed heavily, studying her friend for a few moments before walking over to the front closet for a blanket and a pillow she kept folded on the top shelf. She placed the pillow at the end of the couch then gently lowered Tuck's head down. After she put his cigarette out, she pulled his feet up from the floor then covered him with the blanket. He didn't even stir from his liquor and melancholy induced stupor. Cheryl left a reading light on at the foot of the couch so Tuck could find his way to the bathroom should he awaken during the evening. Before she retired, she picked up his clipboard from the coffee table and read the three, bold words he'd written across the bottom of the page with the fluorescent yellow felt pen. Given Tuck's profession as a traffic analyst who took facts, road debris, skid marks, mathematics and measurements to unravel the most complex and baffling of traffic accidents, Cheryl became mildly surprised at the conclusion he'd drawn regarding the Bandie fatality.

She put the clipboard back on the table then walked down the hallway to her own bedroom, closing the door behind her. Roofus followed her in as he always did and jumped onto the down comforter that covered the huge bed. After removing her housecoat, Cheryl slipped naked beneath the cool sheets, laying very still, thinking and listening as her dog breathed deeply at her feet. She mulled over what Tuck had penned in yellow ink onto the field sketch attached to his clipboard, and wondered if that would be his final explanation.

*"**Act of God**,"* were the simple words he'd written across the bottom of the white page.

That just about summed up all of the events of the evening. Not the best way to start a weekend Cheryl thought, before drifting into a fitful sleep.

* * *

Chapter Forty-six

Exactly two days and three hours after being electrocuted into a well of unconsciousness, Judith Noble awoke in the intensive care unit of a mainland General Hospital. She pulled herself from the dark depths of a comatose oblivion to the sunshine that filled her room, at first stinging her sensitive eyes with its warm, blurring brightness. After a few moments the fuzzy images that surrounded her cleared and became focused, and the first thing she discovered was the even brighter smile on Uncle Walt's face. He stood at the foot of her bed, his deformed face beaming as he wrung his red ball cap restlessly in his leathered hands. It would be one of the nicest sights Judith had ever beheld for she recalled within an instant everything that had happened to her, including floating above the accident scene as well as her journey to the library. Seeing Uncle Walt's face confirmed that she *had* survived the terrible accident, although as she lay there she couldn't help but wonder if her experience in the library had been nothing more than an illusion.

Judith attempted to sit up in bed, but soon found any movement painful; as if every muscle in her body had been stretched to it's very limit then allowed to snap back in place. Her ribs throbbed continuously from the chest compressions where CPR had been applied to her just after her heart had stopped. She became aware of the catheter they had inserted to collect her urine as well as the intravenous needle taped to the back of one hand, its clear liquid nourishing her racked body.

A spreading, indigo colored bruise covered her hand where the needle entered her.

But her constant aching, which made her feel as if she'd been trampled by a small herd of something rather large, made the contusion the least of her worries. Judith was alive. And for whatever reasons, she had been allowed to survive a violent accident and go on with her life. She knew that many pieces of her existence had to be picked up off the floor, then put back together to become healthy and real. Instinct, and the quiet voice from the library had told her this.

Judith shook her head against the pillow as she thought about her journey there as well as the books she had read.

It had to have been a dream, she thought. I'm an educator. I've never been much on all that spirituality kind of stuff. Stuff though it may be to some people, Judith wasn't allowed to dwell any further on her journey and its implications. Uncle Walt spoke to her in his coarse language and her thoughts about the whole episode being a dream changed within the span of a few short sentences.

"By the powers of piss, girl," Walt began, "you scared the shit out of us."

"I'm sorry," Judith croaked, her throat dry and sore from its long slumber. "I didn't mean to scare anyone. How are the twins?"

"Oh, they're good, been scared to death about you though. Jody's been crying lots. That little bastard Martin Bandie drove his truck into that goddamned power pole we have out front of the property. Son-of-a-bitch tore it clear from the ground, bringing down live wires right where you was using the weed whacker."

Uncle Walt was telling Judith nothing that she didn't already know - something he couldn't possibly have known himself.

"Uncle Walt . . . you shot yourself," Judith stated suddenly and quietly.

The look of shock that fell over Walt Brem's disfigured face couldn't have been more intense if a bevy of dancing elves had just flitted naked through the hospital room.

"Jee-zus Christ girl," Walt breathed flatly, "ain't nobody else on this earth that knows that except me and my wife Grace . . . and she's been long dead."

"You shot yourself. And you did it with a semiautomatic, 9-millimeter Walther P-38," Judith continued, her voice still hushed, now filled with an uncanny confidence. The only thing she'd ever known about handguns was what she'd seen on television. Uncle Walt flopped down in one of the chairs at the foot of Judith's bed, looking and feeling completely stunned. "You took the pistol from the Commander of a Panzerkampfwagen V, a Panther Tank, then you shot him in the face with his own weapon." Judith's knowledge of a main battle tank was none existent, so the descriptive words that fell from her lips were just as astounding to her own ears. She continued with her highly accurate declaration of the event before Uncle Walt could utter a word "You and your section of paratroopers had just jumped from a C-47 Douglas Skytrain whose engine had caught on fire." All Judith had ever known about airplanes was that they were heavier than air and at times they crashed. "The aircraft had been off course over the

438

Ardennes Forest during a massive enemy break out," she resumed. "The plane crashed, setting a forest on fire while killing the three crew members. Within minutes you would be the only survivor."

"By the powers of piss," Walt whispered.

"You had parachuted onto an enemy armored column that was retreating from the front. After they killed your comrades, you sought refuge in a pine copse, but they came hunting for you, Uncle Walt. So you shot yourself before they had a chance too. They did find you, but with your face so badly mangled with a bullet by your own hand, they assumed you to be dead."

Tears streamed down the smooth, irregular patches of skin that had been grafted to Walt's face so very long ago. All he could do was listen. Slowly shaking his head as Judith exposed one revelation after another.

"The Army never did find out that you shot yourself Uncle Walt - an offence punishable upon Court Martial; especially after the surgeon dug an enemy slug from the back of your skull. You were then evacuated from the European Theater to an Army hospital near one of the Great Lakes, and it was there that you met your future wife Grace, an Army nurse. Off duty one day, she watched from a distance as you left the hospital in uniform during your first furlough. She followed you downtown, making it appear as if a chance meeting. Then you both went to a park with a small lake and fed some ducks. It was during the winter and cold, then you had your photograph taken together in front of a bronze statue of a mariner dressed in oilskins and a sou'wester. An African-American lady with a pair of tots took the picture using one of those ancient, Brownie cameras."

Walt Brem stood up from his chair then walked quietly over to the window, looking out to the busy world just beyond the glass pane. The bright sunshine lit up his face, the rays glinting and sparkling as they touched the rivulets of tears, highlighting the fine blue lines that formed the linear borders of his skin grafts. Walt stood for some time gazing out the window before turning to look at Judith who lay still in her bed, wordlessly watching the astounded old man. When he turned to face Judith, a look of complete contentment had replaced the tears and the shocked looks. Now, a slight smile lay across his face. It marked the appearance of a man who had just shucked a great burden. A terrible secret.

"They told me you was dead for twenty-two minutes, girl," Walt whispered. "Then they put them paddles to your chest at the local hospital to shock you back to life. That ex-policeman Ben Trilby came up to the house later that evening . . . told me so himself."

Judith only nodded at Uncle Walt's observations.

"Christ all mighty girl. Where the hell did you go for them twenty-two minutes?"

Judith studied the old man's concerned face for a few seconds before answering him.

"I think I know just exactly where it was, Uncle Walt," she sighed. "I'm just not so sure that I should talk about it."

*   *   *

Chapter Forty-seven

If you were to pick a day to visit the Island's only graveyard, then two weeks to the day following Judith's accident couldn't have been any better. From horizon to horizon the cloudless sky hung tinted the color of a blue, tropical surf and high above the arbutus trees that fringed the cemetery, seagulls cried out as they floated on the rising thermal's. Wearing a light cotton dress with fine leather sandals, the grass felt cool as it brushed against her feet as she walked. In her hand she held a single white rose surrounded in baby's breath then wrapped in crisp floral paper. She easily spotted the grave she had been looking for, as the rectangular piece of new sod lay just a shade greener than the rest of the lawn. She walked over to the gravesite then stood to one side of the fresh sod, reading the words chiseled into the flat, polished surface of the granite. "Martin Keith Bandie, beloved husband of Nora, loving father to Brodie." They also had the dates of his short existence etched into the stone, but she already knew one of those dates intimately. The last date designated the rainy afternoon when she had died for twenty-two long minutes. A day Judith would remember forever.

Martin Bandie had been buried five days after the accident, the same day that Judith had been discharged from the hospital. A rejoicing day to be sure, Uncle Walt had driven from the island in the mini van with the twins, Jody and Jenny. After collecting Judith from the hospital they decided to visit the zoo, enjoying the sights and sounds of the wild animals, smelling their heady musk as they wandered leisurely past the displays. They ate fish and chips at a picnic table in front of a kiosk where the aroma from the deep fryer wafted out over the aquarium, calling out to them as it touched their noses. They told riddles and jokes during the return trip on the ferry and in the end it turned into one of those spontaneous family outings that you lay recalling at days end as you gently drift off to sleep. That had been nine days ago, and a lot of good had happened in Judith's life since then, the most notable being the reconciliation with her mother Molly, and the never doubting Jeremy Salter. Judith had initiated the phone call, inviting her mother and Salter to the island, offering them the spare room downstairs. The voice in the library had told Judith that her mother had stopped drinking, and Molly's body had recuperated remarkably well from those dark days of inebriation. Her sobriety had suppressed the aging process that had been accelerated as her liquor intake became habitual. Molly's complexion was rosy and smooth once again and when they arrived at Judith's home there was none of the wooden uneasiness that she'd anticipated. From the outset everyone was cordial and warm, mainly due to Salter's affable character and Uncle Walt's simple ways.

The two men quickly became friends but best of all, Judith's twins had inherited another grandfather and for the first time were allowed the opportunity to meet, as well as get to know their maternal grandmother. The days became long and fulfilling, the house brimming with constant laughter and it wouldn't be until the cool evenings on the back patio that Judith and Molly could talk long into the night. During these precious times the twins would be in bed while Uncle Walt and Salter sat inside watching the television. On one occasion the sun had started to pink the eastern spires of the coastal range before Judith and Molly realized they had quietly talked a whole evening away. It was worth it though, for a good amount of misgivings were finally put on the table and the decisive denominator that would emerge would be their mutual forgiveness. At the end of the visit a mother and daughter would share their lives again and blessings didn't get any better than that.

Molly Noble would be the only human being that Judith would ever confide in about her journey to the library. She was told everything about the experience from start to finish. Molly had absolutely no problems with the story, especially when Judith revealed some family secrets she couldn't possibly have known. Molly would sit on the patio, completely stunned under the glow of a billion stars, sipping licorice tea as Judith softly made one disclosure after another. Calmly, and with exacting detail, Judith told Molly how she knew that her sister Meryl had been fathered by another man, and that she now knew that Meryl has been pregnant when she perished along with her father in the helicopter crash. Judith said nothing to her mother about what she'd read about Uncle Walt, for they were his secrets and would remain that way. During these nightly talks, the mother and daughter covered a vast amount of distance, making great progress toward recovering their lost time as well they finally understood one another, bringing about a togetherness. The togetherness however, had only just started for Judith.

Although the sun's descent into the western sky above the cemetery signaled the late afternoon, Judith's day was far from over. She had plans

In the Lord's Library

for the evening, heeding more of the advice from the voice in the library. A few days ago she had gone into the Country Junction store to thank Ben Trilby for his part in keeping her alive. As he stood behind the counter, he blushed noticeably when Judith shook his hand, voicing her gratitude. He smiled when on the heels of the thank-you came an acceptance to his standing offer to join him Friday evening at the concert in Balford. Ben had asked Judith out nearly two weeks ago, the day she had entered the store with the twins. The afternoon of Martin's deadly accident. He had made the hopeful pitch to her, only to receive her routine but polite no. Ben had forgotten all about the concert and joy welled up inside of him when she revisited his proposal. Judith thought once again about Ben's delight over a simple date, at the same time appreciating her peaceful moment at the cemetery. She really shouldn't have been outdoors. She should have been at home resting her recovering body, and the doctor would have had several conniptions had he received word of his patient's wanderings.

But she'd fobbed off his prescription for bed rest, her basic recovery already being viewed by her practitioner as something of a miracle.

Besides which, life must go on, and concerts on the island were a rarity so Judith seized the opportunity before it became a memory and Ben gave up asking. "He needs you as much as you need him," the voice in the library had said. And so Judith would be going out with a man for the first time in over a decade. Another occasion added to an already busy week. There were however, two more important functions she needed to perform before the concert that evening; one was of her own choosing, something she felt she needed to do. This is what brought her to the graveyard on such a fine, Friday afternoon. She glanced down to the gray-flecked headstone at her feet, reading its inscription one more time.

"Martin Keith Bandie," she said aloud, "I forgive you, I truly do."

Despite his tragic young life, Judith Noble had decided to forgive him for what he had done to her. As she knelt down to place the single rose onto the fresh sod, Judith wondered why there had been no book in the library telling Martin's story.

Maybe there had been no need for her to know.

Maybe, just maybe, he had gone somewhere else.

Judith stood, turning to leave, noticing the silhouettes of two people as they approached her down the grassy hill, the dazzling sun at their backs. One of them was a woman, the other a child who walked beside her, fiercely clutching her hand. An instant later she recognized the small form of Brodie

Bandie, clumping over the grass in his orthopedic shoes. Judith smiled as one of the little treasures that made up her tiny class of mentally challenged students walked toward her. His mother Nora Bandie walked with him, but she was hardly recognizable, the changes she'd made were both astonishing as well as refreshing. She wore plain, but clean clothes and her short brown hair shone in the afternoon sun, dancing as she moved her head. A hint of lip-gloss was the only make-up applied to her face, but it complimented her smooth complexion. The metamorphic change of just two weeks without Martin around to brutalize and subdue her had finally allowed the sleeping butterfly to emerge.

They stopped when they got to the gravesite, and Judith felt her heart squeeze at the sight of the wild flowers young Brodie grasped in his hands. Despite the horrific home life that Martin Bandie had exposed this pair too, the mother and son had nonetheless come to lay fresh flowers upon his resting place. Brodie looked up into his teachers face, his eyes blinking with excitement at this chance meeting. Judith returned the boy's smile, hardly noticing the cruel features of the Down's syndrome as his face beamed with impulsive pleasure.

"Hello Miss No-bull," Brodie chirped.

"Hello Brodie, how are you today?" Judith asked.

"I'm fine. 'N' you Miss No-bull?"

"I'm fine, thank-you Brodie."

"My papa's dead, Miss No-bull."

"Yes, Brodie. I know that and I'm very sorry."

The two women watched on as the boy lumbered over to the carved granite marker, then laid the flowers near the edge of his father's headstone. Brodie then stood up straight, closed his eyes and bowed his head as he mustered a prayer, his lips moving silently as he mouthed his secret petition. Nora looked over at Judith, forcing a smile that appeared almost pained as it emerged through the shame that covered her face.

"How are you feeling, Judith?" Nora asked. Her voice remained quiet, but there now lay a barely discernible determination fixed to the edge of her enunciations.

"I'm fine, Nora. How are you doing?"

"Well, as you can see, social services have given Brodie back to me. I think we'll eventually get over all of this. I'm terribly sorry for what Martin has done to you."

In the Lord's Library

Judith shook her head as she gazed into Nora's eyes. "You have nothing to be sorry for. What Martin did, he did of his own free will and in the end nobody would have been able to stop him. More importantly though Nora, something good has come from this tragedy and we must gather that up and run with it. Many good things have come back into my life because of this accident. Things I would have gone on pushing aside, but not anymore."

Nora nodded her head when Judith had finished speaking, for the same could be said about her own, as of late miserable life. Martin's death had unshackled the young woman and mother from a tyrannical man who thought nothing about beating those he was supposed to have loved. Nora Bandie was now in a position to get her and her son away from the tumbledown trailer they called home, and move him into a very real house elsewhere on the island.

"What will you do now, Nora?"

They both stood watching young Brodie, his feet towed in as his head remained bent in worship, his lips moving as he continued his silent and very private benediction to his father.

The boy symbolized a living statue to the innocence of childhood and their determined ability to forgive. Nora took her thoughts and her eyes away from her son to give Judith her full attention.

"A man from the winery on the other side of the island has bought our property. He's going to remove the old trailer then build a warehouse in its place. He also figures he can rejuvenate the apple orchard to make candied fruit and bottled cider. I had no idea what property on the island was worth until he came by with a blank check.

"Will you stay here?" Judith asked.

"Oh yes. We've bought a nice, clean cottage not far from the school so I can walk Brodie there until he gets older. He thinks you're the beginning of the universe, Judith, and it would break what little remained of his confidence to take him away from his favorite teacher. This place is his home, and mine. The island is where we both belong and now there is enough money to allow us to stay here in comfort."

Judith nodded quietly and smiled, recalling the voice from the library and what it had said about Brodie Bandie, requesting she be his mentor. "Like all children he is important and must be cherished . . . although his importance will be realized with the son he will sire twenty years from now." Nora's decision to stay on the island would make binding the voice's request for Judith to carry out her tutorial obligations with Brodie. It could now follow a natural path, evolving as the child grew and became wise, learning from Judith in the coming years. Nora approached Brodie and stood beside him as he remained with his head bent. Judith moved up to Nora, gently squeezing her arm. "Call if there is anything I can do," she whispered.

Nora smiled and nodded her head. Judith turned and walked away from Nora and Brodie, glancing at her watch as she slowly made her way up to the parking lot.

She had one last assignment to carry out before she met Ben Trilby for their evening out; one of the final requests that the voice in the library had made of her, a final tribute to her sister Meryl. When she arrived at the parking lot, she turned one last time to look down upon the mother and her small son as they stood beside the gravesite. A dark, wet patch had spread around the bum of Brodie's cotton shorts and Judith laughed despite the poignancy of the moment. That was how all this had started, only fourteen days ago. A simple, harmless act that had set into motion a chain of events that would forever change the lives of two unrelated families. It had all started with a little boy seated on his lunch box, playing with the worms he'd found in the moist dirt of a schoolyard.

An inoffensive little boy . . . who had peed in his pants.

*   *   *

Chapter Forty-eight

The rocky bluff had to be one of the most aesthetic places on the island, which would have been the main reason Judith had chosen it. It rose well above the frothing water, crowned with a patch of fir trees that provided both privacy and a break from the wind when it blew out of the southeast. The waves that broke at its base had fetched far from the beginning of the strait, gathering momentum with the wind on their backs, gaining height and becoming ground swells as the sea bottom shallowed to just a couple of hundred feet. On a calm day without wind and on a high flood the waters were so clear you could see an oyster fart, straight down to a depth of almost forty feet.

Both isolated and serene, it was the perfect place for Judith to carry out her final task, but more important, she felt that Meryl would have liked it. As she carefully picked her way under the stout fir boughs she cradled in the nook of her arm the copper urn that held her sister's remains. She had parked her vehicle on the roadway above the bluff then followed the goat trail down to the small forest. Standing near the edge, she watched the waves turn to foam as they smashed onto the rock face, then the creamy froth would bob up and down as if confused, on the endless crests that would follow them in. Here the water was deep, yet all the turbulence occurred just a few meters below Judith's feet, its incessant pounding making conversation futile. She stood alone with only her thoughts, but she could hear those well enough as she clutched the urn firmly in her arm, unscrewing the cap from its wide mouth with her free hand.

The gray powder inside was fine, like talcum and spilled easily from the container as she tipped it, watching it flutter on the light breeze like corn silk. The ashes blew out into the middle of a swell and floated momentarily on the rising back of a wave before flickering and shimmering through the shafts of sunlight as they melted into the dark depths. Judith then tossed the urn into the ocean, watching it tumble end over end as it went straight for the bottom. She knew that polished copper and the sea went together, much like the mountains and the glaciers that carved their way across them. She sighed heavily as she thought of her sister Meryl, and of the voice from the library that had asked her to cast her ashes into the sea. "That is how she

447

remembers you Judith," the voice had intoned, "as two sisters playing hopscotch in the sand, next to the ocean."

She puzzled once again over whom the voice in the library might have been, and if she would ever know. "Someone who loves you," it had said. Judith glanced once more to the breaking waves below her feet and thought once again of her sister Meryl before turning to leave. As she made her way back up the goat trail she held a picture in her mind of the two little girls who had thrown clamshells onto a simple hopscotch game. A game that had been carved into the sand with a stick, not far from a house where they'd been growing up. The picture stayed with Judith as she climbed back into her mini van, started the engine then drove up the road. Only this time, she never looked back.

*   *   *

Chapter Forty-nine

There wasn't much in the way of buildings that made up the town of Balford.

Never has been - probably never will be. If you looked the place up on a map you'll find that the Cartographer's had designated the community with one of those insignificant little dots that told you the population stood below a constant two-hundred-and-fifty souls. Located at the North end of the island, its structural allotment consisted of a Gas station, Riley's Pub and Marina, a small organic food store located next to an old, white clapboard sided church with a louvered bell tower - and of course the communities only theater. A single story building, it was long and narrow with a split-level roof raised higher than the main, where the stage was housed. The building paralleled the roadway with a worn, covered boardwalk that extended along its entire length. The roof that covered the boardwalk had been added on as an afterthought, a token effort to keep the theater patrons sheltered from the winter rains. Token, because the rain usually blew sideways in Balford during the winter months. Cedar sided with long wide boards, the building had never held a lick of stain, which allowed the wood to sweat itself to a natural gray where the oils had wept. No one could quite remember who had built the theater or when. The importance being that it had been built, and thankfully so for nights such as this.

A concert band from a mainland university had booked the hall months ago, which caused some mild excitement for they were accompanied with a five-piece string section. Far from a sell out crowd, the combination of music and the subsequent gathering of seventy to eighty of the islanders, nonetheless promised a night out with few distractions. Most of the theatergoers had already gathered along the boardwalk, talking while enjoying a sunset that dyed the stratosphere a burnt, orange buff. Ben Trilby stopped his green sports car across the road in a convenient gap he'd found in the long line of parked vehicles. Dressed in tan cargo pants with a matching open neck shirt and dock shoes, Ben had already caught the attention of the gathering people as he limped with his cane around to the passenger side of his vehicle. Not a whole lot of excitement ever happened on the island, and seeing the reclusive, good-looking schoolteacher out on a date with the withdrawn ex-cop who owned the country junction store was definitely fuel for the local gossip.

In fact, a kind of fairy tale was playing out before their very eyes, an extreme oddity on an island known for its stereotypes. It brought joy to the gathering theatergoers, the little drama more than making up for the price they'd paid for admission. They watched and talked quietly from the boardwalk as Ben stood with the passenger's door open, offering Judith Noble a hand as she stepped up lightly from the low-slung sports car. She too was a delightful site in her cotton dress and fine sandals, and the ripple that went through the line-up of people was unmistakable when she reached over to hold Ben's hand. Together they crossed the road, hand in hand, walking slowly to compensate for Ben's limp. Most of the people standing there had heard bits and pieces of the misery that Judith and Ben had endured during their young, separate lives. Seeing the two of them as a couple was reassuring, that good, did at times, overcome the bad.

Judith and Ben joined the line-up holding hands, talking softly and smiling at each other, their obvious pleasure appearing natural and unrehearsed. As they stood on the boardwalk interacting in their own quiet way, an invisible energy, almost a tingling sensation coursed through their warm palms. They had both endured some very emotional turbulence during their short lives, but they had survived and moved on to start over again. They were not naive enough to think that the road ahead would not be difficult. They seemed to share the same thoughts, at the same time. Thoughts that told them the worst was now behind them. These were mutual, hopeful thoughts they both held for their future. As they stood holding hands on a boardwalk, in a small town on an island in the Pacific Northwest, neither one of them could have known this.

No one knew, except the voice from the Lord's Library.

*   *   *